Joan Collins is one of the most
planet – a versatile actress, a
accomplished producer, a succes
devoted mother. Born in London, she studied at RADA before making several films with the Rank Organisation. She was then signed by 20th Century Fox and went to Hollywood where she made, amongst others, *Land of the Pharaohs*, *Sea Wife* with Richard Burton, *Rally Round the Flag Boys* with Paul Newman, *The Virgin Queen* with Bette Davis and *The Girl in the Red Velvet Swing*. Winner of the Golden Globe and People's Choice Award and countless others, Joan has appeared in more than 55 feature films, 25 TV programmes, such as *Star Trek* and *Mission Impossible*, and many theatrical plays. She is internationally renowned for her TV role of Alexis Carrington Colby in *Dynasty*, has published 3 novels and 6 lifestyle books, is a tireless worker for charities worldwide and in 1997 was honoured by the Queen with the OBE.

BY THE SAME AUTHOR
ALL PUBLISHED BY HOUSE OF STRATUS

Love & Desire & Hate
Prime Time
Second Act
Star Quality

JOAN COLLINS

Too Damn Famous

This edition published in 2001 by House of Stratus, an imprint of Stratus Holdings plc, 24c Old Burlington Street, London, W1X 1RL, UK.
Also at: Suite 210, 1270 Avenue of the Americas, New York, NY 10020, USA.

www.houseofstratus.com

Typeset, printed and bound by House of Stratus.

A catalogue record for this book is available from the British Library and the Library of Congress.

ISBN 0-7551-0180-4

I should like to thank Rossie Cheetham for her belief in me, her caring, her encouragement, and her dedication to this book.

And thanks also to Joan Maddern for always being there when I needed her.

LOS ANGELES 1988

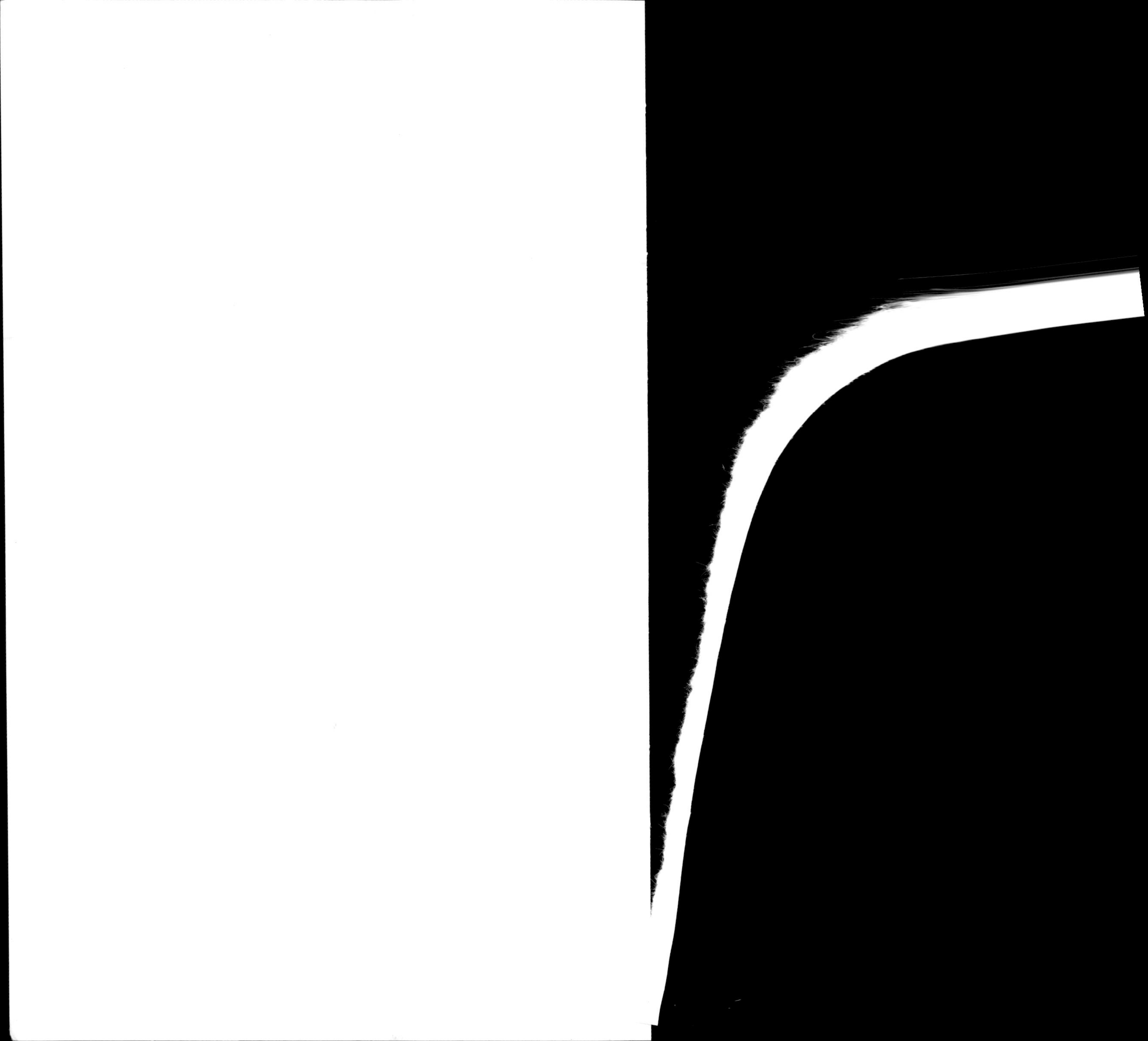

CHAPTER ONE

'I don't need a husband, I need a wife,' Katherine Bennet declared, just loudly enough for the covey of reporters snapping at her heels to hear. She was hurrying through the winding corridors of Santa Monica Superior Court, with her expensive and expansive divorce lawyer Barry Lefcovitz in tow, who was parrying the journalists' intrusive questions in his usual humorous way.

Katherine's smile was cold and tight-lipped, in no way reaching her pale green eyes, but nevertheless it would look [illegible] enough splashed across every tabloid front page and television newscast.

She didn't want to appear too happy after an [illegible] divorce.

And splashed her face would certainly be, as it had been for the past three years, on every front page, magazine cover, and across every gossip column from New York to New Delhi. Katherine Bennet was that rarest and most ephemeral of creatures, a television superstar, so famous that everyone wanted to know everything about her – many even wanted to *be* her.

The swarm of news hounds seethed around their prey like flies on a carcass – the carcass she'd almost become in that courtroom: practically picked clean of all her hard-earned money and possessions by a pontificating male chauvinist of a judge, whose main interest had been in posturing for the benefit of the television news cameras which he had allowed into the courtroom with such a show of reluctance.

Thank God for Barry, thought Katherine glancing towards him. The attorney's thick silvery hair and amused black eyes seemed to take on an added lustre as he fended off the paparazzi, who snapped her relentlessly while they inched their way down the steps to the courtroom entrance, and to the cool sanctuary of the waiting limousine. Katherine smiled to herself.

How Barry Lefcovitz *loved* publicity. Column inches were food and drink to him. He was never happier than when appearing on the panel of an Oprah Winfrey or Phil Donahue show discussing abused wives, equal rights for minorities, or pro choice for women. But if he hadn't agreed to take on Katherine's divorce for a modest fifty thousand dollars, naturally plus expenses, and plus all the coverage a publicity-hungry divorce lawyer could attract for defending one of the most famous women in America, Katherine could well have been in the hole for north of a quarter of a million. That, including what she had had to settle on Johnny, would have cleared out her savings, which, by mega-star standards, were still meagre. Although she'd been a star for three years, it hadn't been quite long enough to have yet reaped the financial rewards.

'What are your plans now, Katherine?' enquired the midget in the mac, the one to whom Katherine had directed her comment about needing a wife, not a husband.

'Back to work,' she answered as pleasantly as was humanly possible with twenty flashes exploding inches from her face. 'It's time to put all this behind me.'

The flashes were blinding her, so Kitty slipped on her dark glasses.

'Aah, no – Katherine – please, don't, honey. We wanna see those beautiful eyes.'

'You've seen these eyes for the past five days. Now they need a rest, gentlemen – and so do I, if you don't mind.' She struggled hard to give a show of good humour she didn't feel.

'Let the lady through, gentlemen, *please.*' Her bodyguard Burt had three or four burly back-ups in close attendance. Huge, beefy, men, they were all over six-feet-four and seemingly just as wide. Their task was to move the press out of the way without using force. However much Katherine was jostled, they weren't allowed to use hand-on-body contact, because of the possibility of being sued for criminal assault. Their job was to guard and protect their charges, without rough-housing which some paparazzi with a grudge often resorted to.

The world had no idea how tough it really was. The toes of Katherine's shoes had been trampled on half a dozen times and twice a camera had narrowly missed smashing into her face as an over-zealous snapper had swung around for a better angle. She had ink stains on her silk jacket where one of the journalists had carelessly allowed his pen to brush against her sleeve, and all in all she felt a complete mess. This was Hollywood's latest, most dramatic divorce, so the press were desperate for a sensational quote from Katherine and if they couldn't get one, they would make it up. The fabrications she had read about herself in the newspapers over the past week had been mind-boggling.

'*Katherine Bennet, 43, has appeared in court in a different designer outfit every day during the week of her divorce case*' screamed one tabloid. '*With each over-the-top, high-priced outfit, she flaunted an equally flamboyant hair style, and she was wearing enough make-up to stock a medium sized drug store.*'

That was a complete distortion for a start. Katherine had always been well-dressed and groomed. Even as a child, her hair ribbon had to be tied at the right angle and her white socks pulled up just so. All she had actually worn in the courtroom were three or four classically cut jackets in subtle shades of taupe, grey, or beige, a couple of simple skirts, and high heels. Katherine always wore heels, even with trousers. She liked making her five-feet-five inches into five-feet-eight, and if some would describe her as a throwback to the sixties, why should she care?

Katherine prided herself on being her own person. She didn't particularly mind what people thought of her, and she always spoke her mind. She wore what she wanted, what suited her, and she never, ever suffered fools in any way gladly. Sometimes Katherine's stubbornness and self-sufficiency made her seem cold or aloof, and to those who thought of her as their enemy, she could appear alarmingly like the venomous shrew she was currently playing so successfully on television.

'So, are you off all men for ever then, Kitty...?' smirked the stringer for the New York tabloid which her mother devoured every day.

'Never say never, my friend,' smiled Katherine, Raybans masking the flatness in her eyes. 'Who knows, maybe I'll turn Sapphic!'

'What – wha' she say?' The reporter's eyes swivelled round to look at his cronies, who had completely misinterpreted Katherine's quip, and were scribbling 'You know I'll still stop traffic' on to their stenopads.

'For Christ's sake, Katherine,' said Barry *sotto voce*. 'Start tellin' these guys you're a goddam lesbo, and the shit'll *really* hit the fan.'

That gave Katherine the first real laugh she'd had for days.

'It's a *joke*, Barry – a feeble one I guess, but I'm not up to Robin Williams' standard today.'

It had been hell in that courtroom. For five days, seven hours a day, on a hard wooden seat in full view of the court and the two dozen assorted hacks behind her, she had sat as motionless and expressionless as was possible with a breaking heart and a lump in her throat the size of a melon. At one point during her husband's testimony she had scribbled to Barry on her yellow legal pad the words 'He's lying! *Lies. Lies. Lies*!!' and that appeared as the third most important item on the six o'clock news all over America that night.

Now, with the covey still yapping questions and snapping their hateful cameras, the open door of the black limo seemed like a haven. She eased herself carefully into the rear seat, the way any woman in a shortish skirt learns to do. Bottom on seat first, legs firmly together, then swing them in swiftly before the pack could grab a leg shot.

But not swiftly enough today. One of the sleazier snappers had set the timer on his camera and placed it strategically on the pavement so that as Katherine swung her legs into the car, the camera flashed twice, getting a full view up her skirt.

'Son of a goddam bitch!' Burt heaved a kick at the offending camera, which clattered into the gutter.

'Fuck you, buddy,' screamed the red-faced paparazzo, scrabbling to retrieve it. 'I'll get you for grievous assault to personal property, you prick.'

Burt didn't answer. He signalled to his cohorts to slam the doors on Katherine's side, and jumping into the front seat beside the chauffeur, barked, 'Move it.'

'Oh God, let's get out of here.' Katherine leaned back on the upholstery, and, secure in the dark-tinted windows of the limousine, took off her glasses and gave a huge sigh.

'Well *done*, honey.' Barry patted her shoulder. 'We won!! You won! You're a free woman at last, Kitty. When I think of what that son-of-a-bitch was trying to grab from you, and what we finally settled on, you're one lucky lady.'

She nodded wearily. Yes she was free. Free of Johnny and his drinking and his lying and his drugging – free of the ghastly courtroom fiasco and the gawping mobs. But really *free*? With her life? No way.

As a married woman, and the television bad girl whom America loved to loathe, she had some degree of immunity from the semi-slanderous gossip that always circulated around unmarried female celebrities. Now that she'd finally cut the cord which had bound her to Johnny, would she be allowed to live a normal life again?

The limousine dropped Barry off at his Beverly Hills office, then Katherine closed her eyes as Sam drove up the winding Benedict Canyon to her house. This was a vast white concrete edifice, like a big ugly chunk of cement that Johnny had persuaded her to buy two years ago, when she'd first hit the jackpot on *The Skeffingtons*. Built in the 1930s by some long forgotten movie mogul, it had been christened Hitler's Bunker by one of Katherine's wittier friends.

She had told the gardeners to cover the bleakness of the exterior with trailing English ivy, but the plant didn't want to attach itself to those stark white walls, and now only a few greenish brown patches testified to their efforts. Sam pressed the clicker and the gates creaked open. They were rusty, in spite of having been given a new coat of paint only last year. Katherine sighed again. The upkeep of this mansion was never-ending, what with the pool man, the pond man, the tree man, the indoor plant girl, the outdoor gardeners, plus the cook, the butler, the housekeeper, her secretary, the twice-weekly laundress, and the thrice-weekly trainer – not to mention the chauffeur, Warwick Kingsley her adorable but expensive publicist, and Brett Goodman her business manager whom she was convinced was ripping her off. It was a miracle she managed to hang on to a dime. Last but by no means least, was Brenda Corlew, her dependable friend and secretary, and housemother to her son, Tommy.

How could she cope without Brenda? Come to think of it how would Tommy cope without Brenda? The self-styled tough old dame with a marshmallow heart had become a second mother to him. Since most of Katherine's days were spent at the studio, often until well past midnight, Brenda spent several hours a day at work with Katherine but always insisted on being home when Tommy returned from school. She herself knew the trials and tribulations of being a television star, for she had been one herself in a sit-com back in the fifties as second banana to the much-loved Kookie Cazanova. They were close only to Lucille Ball and Vivien Vance in the ratings then. Almost as funny, almost as popular, but not as durable, and when Kookie finally retired to a mansion in Kentucky, she did so not only on the basis of her own considerable residuals, but on those of the whole cast, whom she had bought out for a paltry five thousand dollars each.

Katherine and Brenda had met at an off-Broadway audition a dozen years ago. Kitty was surprised to see an actress so famous at a 'cattle call', but as Brenda said: 'Three Emmies, one People's Choice, and a couple of Tony nominations; for ten years I've bin fightin' like everyone else for a job. Show-biz – huh! Don't it suck? – But don't we love it?'

Brenda's career was never going anywhere now, so when Katherine got the part of Georgia Skeffington, she asked her to come to Hollywood to help out. Kitty sometimes thought it was the best move she had ever made. Brenda became a constant source of support to her, and a comfort to Tommy, who was always less insecure and angry when she was around. Brenda's tart tongue and salty language hid a wisdom and warmth which they had both come to value immensely.

The car stopped outside the main entrance and Sam jumped out and opened the doors.

'I won't need you tonight any more, Sam, thank you.' Katherine was so tired that even getting out of the car seemed too much of an effort. Even though she had hardly eaten for days, her body felt heavy and leaden.

'Fine, Ms Bennet. Have a good evening now. I'm sure glad everything went well for you today.'

'Thanks Sam. We were lucky.'

Pedro opened the shiny black front door from which Katherine noticed the paint was beginning to peel. When they had moved in two years ago it had been lacquered so thickly it looked as though it would last forever. So much for LA weather.

'Tommy?' she walked across the wide chequered marble foyer into the whiteness of her living room.

'Tommy are you home, honey?'

'Tommy's gone to the Lakers game with Brenda, Miss Bennet.' Not the least of Brenda's attributes was that she loved basketball.

Faithful Maria, the housekeeper, appeared, wiping work-worn hands on her apron.

'They said they'd grab a bite after the game – so don't bother to wait up for them.'

Katherine nodded; she looked around the room. The ice-cream whiteness of the thick pile carpet, the silk damask walls, and the velvet upholstered sofas and chairs almost hurt her eyes. It was not at all comfortable; it was a sterile show palace, created to be a setting for Katherine in her designer clothes; a backdrop for those endless photographic layouts of her in the glossies.

The setting sun reflected off her new gold and diamond watch. It was just six o'clock.

'What time would you like dinner, *señora*?' Maria asked.

'Oh I'm not really hungry tonight –just fix me a boiled egg and some toast around seven, please.'

Maria disappeared into the kitchen from where Katherine could hear sounds of laughter. The TV news was on, and that part of the house echoed to the chatter of family life. Katherine wished she could go in and join them around the scrubbed pine table – Pedro, Maria, and Suzy, her pretty teenage daughter who helped Katherine with her clothes and packing. A couple of the gardeners would be chewing the fat with them, and Sam would be drinking Budweiser from the can as he reported on the events of the day. Yes, normal life was taking place in Katherine's house, but her own existence was a big island of emptiness.

She walked up the white-carpeted stairs to the master suite. It had not been easy to divorce Johnny. Even though he'd changed because of alcohol and drugs, she hadn't liked the way they portrayed him as a blustering liar in court, a pathetic wreck. She'd had to end the marriage for her own self-preservation. Johnny had become a major embarrassment – falling down drunk at restaurants or industry parties, making up ludicrous stories about her which he leaked to the press. But worse than anything was the pain on Tommy's face as he watched his father turning into a drunken buffoon. Johnny had been a reasonably well-balanced jobbing actor who had become a neurotic mess, and all the AA meetings, counselling, and clinics hadn't helped one iota.

It was Johnny who suddenly decided to make theirs an acrimonious divorce. His shyster of a lawyer, best known for defending and getting off rapists and other no-hopers, had put Katherine through the wringer in court, while Johnny barely looked at her. Only the unsteadiness of his legs as they took breaks each day, betrayed the fact that he was still heavily on the sauce – and the speed too.

Well it was over now. Finished. A twenty-year marriage and a twenty-five-year relationship destroyed first by drugs and drinking, then by a week of hatred in a public courtroom. Now Katherine had to pull herself together for work tomorrow, even though she was still raw from the ordeal.

'I want to sleep,' she whispered. 'If only I could get some proper sleep.'

She opened the door to her bedroom and thought once again that this house summed up everything she disliked about Hollywood. It was overpowering, nouveau-riche, pretentious. Her bedroom could easily have housed a small jet, with space for a couple of helicopters too. Like the rest of the rooms, its decor was white. Etched glass and mirrored panels alternated on creamy taffeta walls, and there were thick bearskin rugs on either side of the enormous round bed, which was covered in a white satin spread, embroidered with their initials: J & K. That'll have to go, thought Katherine, grimacing at the mirrored ceiling above the bed.

She had fought Johnny and their interior designer over that mirrored ceiling. He insisted on leering up at it during their infrequent bouts of lovemaking, and it was that which finally drove her over the edge. She didn't know whether it was the dope or the booze that had done it, all she knew was that her sensitive, intelligent husband had turned into an insensitive lecher, who got his sexual kicks from cheap voyeurism. Like many women, kinky sex left her cold. She supposed that some went along with it because their men enjoyed it – and maybe even she could have pretended, if Johnny hadn't been so spaced out all the time. She'd begged, pleaded, and entreated Johnny to stop drinking and taking drugs but he wouldn't, or he couldn't.

As moderately successful actors in New York, they had both been in the same career boat, managing to exist reasonably well, doing off-Broadway plays, voiceovers for radio advertisements, and occasionally minor roles on TV. Then, when Katherine – out of the blue – landed the role of Georgia in *The Skeffingtons*, their lives turned upside down.

The Skeffingtons was the ABN's network's prime time soap opera drama. It was the story of a rich, dysfunctional Los Angeles family who owned half the vineyards and wine distilleries in Southern California. The three main protagonists were Charles Skeffington, the flinty much-married patriarch and father of numerous gorgeous children, Candice Skeffington, Charles's third wife, and the saintliest female on the television screen since Donna Reed, and Georgia, Charles's unscrupulous second wife, the arch-villainess of the piece.

Georgia was a supporting role to Charles Skeffington, played by Albert Amory, and Candice, played by Eleonor Norman, but in the three and a half years since she had played the part, Katherine had become one of the most popular and beloved stars on TV; dubbed the woman they loved to hate. Within a year Katherine had become a household name and Johnny a drunk, and there wasn't a damn thing she could do about it, except feel guilty. That was show-biz. The classic case of a star is born for her, and the end of shelf-life for him.

To compensate she'd let him buy this vast pile of marble and malachite, which they really couldn't afford, and Johnny had spent his time lovingly re-organising and decorating with the help of their interior designer Tracey, a daily bottle of Scotch, and God knows how much white powder up his nose. Soon that daily bottle increased to a couple of bottles, and as the house neared completion, so did the marriage.

Katherine threw off her jacket and shoes and paced the floor of the huge bedroom, smoking furiously. Gone now. Gone forever.

They had been good together until then. Ups and downs of course, who doesn't have those? But affection and their love for Tommy had bound them with strong ties. Katherine shivered despite the heat of the room. She wished Johnny were still with her. The old Johnny, not the block of wood he'd become.

She also wished Tommy were here. In spite of his adolescent problems, he was the apple of her eye. She knew he had been upset by the divorce, and lately he'd become surly to the point of rudeness with her. But even though he turned now to Brenda when he needed affection, and seemed to dislike being in the same room as his mother, Katherine loved him wholeheartedly.

She stubbed out her cigarette, went into her dressing room, and pushed the message button on the answering machine. There were only two. One was from her mother in New York: Vera Cribbens had come to the States as an English GI bride, been widowed young, and now her main activities were eating chocolate and watching television. No one was more thrilled with Katherine's success than Vera, but none more critical either, and Katherine had learned to tolerate the well-meaning, but often hurtful remarks her mother couldn't help dishing out. She had been particularly scathing when she read about her daughter's impending divorce in *The Star*.

'How can you divorce him, Kit-Kat?' She had always called her only child after her favourite snack. 'He was such a *mensch*.' Since becoming friendly with the Goldsteins, who owned the delicatessen-cum-general store next to her apartment, Vera had picked up a smattering of Jewish expressions.

Katherine wearily explained Johnny's substance abuse, but since Vera had not read about them, her daughter's words meant nothing. Now she said:

'That skirt was too long. You've got great legs, Kitty; you should show 'em off. And I hated that lipstick colour, dear. It looked like something Cher would wear. Call me, Kit-Kat.'

The second message was from Steven Leigh, a writer on *The Skeffingtons*, who had become one of Katherine's closest confidants. Steven had been immensely supportive during the last weeks. He understood Katherine's problems, and had the knack of coming up with sensible solutions.

'Hi Kitty. Saw the news. Told you you'd win, and we're thrilled for you. Let's celebrate. Can you do Mortons Monday night? Time you showed this town your gorgeous face, and I'll make you two promises. I'll give you a steak which is medium rare, and the truth which is very rare –' Katherine smiled. Trust Steve. He had an endless fund of movie quotes, and could be relied on to come up with one for every occasion.

'Bet you don't know what that's from. Call me back if you guessed.'

Katherine looked wistful. It wasn't possible to know for sure what went on behind the closed doors of other people's marriages, but from the outside Steven and Mandy Leighs' looked about as solid as it could get. No one knew much about Mandy, who stayed at home doing the good mother bit, while Steven slogged fifteen hours a day at the studio, but it seemed as though she was perfectly fulfilled cooking and cleaning, and taking care of their two daughters.

Katherine was disappointed that there were only two messages. She eschewed the kind of effusive acquaintanceships which passed for friendship in Hollywood, and her genuine old friends still lived in New York. But even some of *them* appeared uncomfortable around Katherine now. When she telephoned they sounded different, defensive, as though they thought that now Katherine was a star she wouldn't want anything to do with them any more. Of course that wasn't true, but it was hard for Kitty to pretend she was just an ordinary person, when the simplest outing – even to the corner drugstore – resulted in being mobbed by autograph hunters.

Although many actors worked towards exactly this – the instant recognition and the constant applause, it would have been a lie for Kitty to pretend that she didn't appreciate certain things about stardom. It meant an instant entree into the world of the rich and successful; it meant being offered the best of everything, from trips on private jets, to gifts from the great couture houses. It was just that she missed some of the more ordinary things in life which she had once taken for granted.

Katherine was also shrewd enough to realize that only those born in Hollywood could count on having real friends there. It was a company town, and those who lived in it only sought out their own social level. She did have a clique of friends – the Johnsons, the Hawns and the Laskers – with whom she mixed, but Katherine sensed that they were not altogether sorry when her marriage crashed. Not that they actively wished her ill, but there was such a thing as being too lucky. When it came down to it, Steven and Brenda were probably the only two friends she could trust completely.

Katherine's business manager and press agent would have received dozens of calls. Requests for interviews, invitations to charity galas, which were usually about as gala as a night alone on a desert island, messages from fans offering sympathy. They would all be dealt with efficiently, so as not to bother Katherine. But tonight she wanted to be bothered.

She stared at the claustrophobic, mirrored and silk-hung walls, seeing her reflection from every angle: seeing every flaw on her forty-three-year-old face and body – flaws the viewing public never saw. She wanted to scream. The room was hot, so she clicked on the air conditioner, then realized that, as usual, it wasn't working. She buzzed Maria.

'Maria, why hasn't this air-conditioner been fixed?'

'I'm very sorry, *señora*, the man he come today. He say it's a very old system and it needs much work. He come back Monday.'

'Monday?' Katherine's voice rose. 'It's Thursday now, must we go through the weekend stifling in this heat box?'

'I'm very sorry, *señora*,' Maria said apologetically. 'Would you like Pedro to bring you up a portable fan?'

'Yes please,' said Katherine through gritted teeth. 'Bring up two.' She slapped the phone down.

She was suddenly dying for some fresh air. She threw on shorts and a T-shirt and went into the garden. She loved gardening; few people knew – and her public would never have guessed – that at weekends Kitty spent hours weeding and watering her plants. She started to breathe freely for the first time in days, deep lungfuls of what passed for air in Los Angeles but was actually a brownish yellow soup. Kitty could see the smog on the horizon, and above it the pale greyish blue of sky, where the haze and exhaust fumes from millions of LA cars had not yet obscured it.

The lawn was covered with huge patches of barren brown earth, and weeds were pushing up in the flowerbeds. As she bent to inspect her rhododendron bush, she saw that three-quarters of the blossoms were brown, and had not been dead-headed by the gardener. The gardener! A thousand dollars a month, and all he and his team ever seemed to do was sweep up dead leaves with a machine so loud that all conversation had to stop in the house. Kitty sometimes thought that it blew out even more noxious fumes than the LA traffic. She loved the garden, but she had to admit that it was a mess. Like me, she thought. A mess into which she had poured thousands of dollars, plus her time, energy, and organization. Most of the trees, bushes, plants and flowers were drooping in the last heat of this smoggy day. She turned on the sprinklers, but two of them weren't working.

'Pedro,' she called irritably.

Pedro came running from the kitchen.

'*Si, señora.*'

'What's happened to these sprinklers?'

'Sorry, *señora*,' he said apologetically. 'They haven't been working properly for nearly two weeks. I called the gardener and he say he do something about it soon, but…' Pedro shrugged, '…he hasn't done anything yet. I'm very sorry.'

'It's all right, Pedro, it's not your fault.'

She stared sadly at the withered remains of her favourite camellia bush, and bent down to pull a weed out of the flowerbed, when a sixth sense made her look up. On the hill opposite, she glimpsed the glint of a camera. She stood up, hands on hips, and stared at the horizon. There was no question about it. Two paparazzi were trying to hide behind a tree about five hundred yards away.

Paparozzo was the Italian word for an irritating gnat. Kitty thought it exceedingly apt. She could almost hear the click of their shutters, see their bulging anoraks stuffed with lenses, film, and flasks of drinks to sustain them through the long stakeouts. And I'm the prey today – oh they're going to love this picture – Kitty thought. Wasn't it enough that they had thousands of photos of her in court, dressed in designer suits? This one – complete with baggy shorts, crumpled T-shirt and tear-stained face – would be the picture to make the cover of the *National Enquirer*.

'God damn it to hell,' she shouted, closing the glass sliding doors with a bang as she went back into the house. 'Why can't they all leave me alone?'

She walked into the enormous breakfast area, a cool eggshell of a room, with hard steel chairs, and a round marble table laid for one. Pedro appeared again, smiling.

'Would *señora* like a drink before dinner?'

'Yes, please, Pedro, I'll have a double vodka on the rocks.' To hell with the diet, to hell with the bloated face, to hell with the bags under her eyes. To hell with everything. She was Katherine Bennet, television superstar, but she was alone, divorced, unloved, and she felt like getting very, very drunk.

Her boiled egg tasted as if it had been in the fridge for a month, the toast was cold, and the bits of parsley with which Maria had decorated the white and silver Wedgwood plate looked as limp as Katherine felt. Irritably she pushed the plate away, drained the vodka, and lit a cigarette.

'Pedro,' she called. 'Bring me another vodka, please.'

'*Si, señora.*' He appeared with the decanter almost immediately, still smiling.

Katherine wondered why he and Maria were always smiling. Maybe if you made three thousand dollars a month, had all your living expenses paid for, including colour cable television, steak five nights a week, and alternate weekends off, those were good enough reasons for a middle-aged couple from Tijuana to smile a lot. Sometimes they did more than smile. Many was the time when Katherine had wandered into the kitchen and found Pedro, Maria, Suzy, and other members of her extensive staff all giggling away, as they stuffed themselves with cheeses, pâtés and exotic fruits regularly ordered from Gelson's, the most expensive market in LA. They all ate a great deal, but only drank diet cokes, ordered by the crate from the liquor store.

Whenever Katherine wanted something like apple juice, Evian water or white wine, they had always just run out of it. Profuse apologies of course. It would never happen again – but it always did. On one of their days off, Katherine had studied the contents of her refrigerator. It was a dieter's nightmare: stuffed with guacamole dip, cream sauces, ice cream in every possible flavour, tubs of butter, creamy salad dressings. The freezer was full of meat: veal, chicken, kosher hotdogs, fillet steaks, hamburger patties, and endless varieties of frozen pies. Katherine always asked for diet and vegetarian dishes, but there were precious few of those. She had taped a list of essential foods to the kitchen wall, but somehow they had usually just run out of whatever she particularly wanted.

Katherine had tried discussing the problem with Brenda, but at almost two hundred pounds, Brenda loved her food too much, and could never resist loading her shopping cart with cakes, pizzas and Haagen-Daz.

Not that Pedro and Maria were a bad couple by any means. Certainly not. Friends often congratulated Katherine on their loyalty, good humour and honesty, and she supposed they must be honest. She didn't have enough time to check the Gelson's grocery bill which Pedro politely handed her on every last Friday in the month. Often the amounts were ludicrous. Five thousand dollars a month for groceries was certainly high by normal standards, but she wasn't normal, was she? She was a star. A television superstar. And stars didn't stint their staff, or nickel and dime their grocery bills.

Wearily Katherine drained the second vodka and went into the den. There was a Steuben dish of cashew nuts in the centre of the enormous malachite table, and she stuffed several handfuls into her mouth, heedless of what her dresser would say tomorrow.

'To hell with it,' she muttered. 'I'm starving hungry.'

The phone rang, and she picked it up on the first ring. 'Hello, gorgeous. How are you feeling?' It was Steven.

'Oh, Steve. Hi darling. Thanks for your message.'

'I wish I could have been there.'

'It was insanity.' She leaned back and poured herself another vodka. 'Actually it was so mad you'd probably have loved it.'

'Yeah, I could have used it for next week's courtroom scenes. So – did you guess the quote?'

'No, you're too good for me, Steve.'

'*Seven Days in May*. Everyone knows that.'

'Not this dumbbell,' said Katherine.

'Not so dumb. Are you sure you're OK to work tomorrow?'

'Sure, sure, I'm fine.' She took another sip of vodka. 'Just fine. Work'll be good for me.' She felt her words becoming slightly slurred, and giggled.

'How've the gang been getting along without me?'

'Oh, the usual screaming and yelling and tantrums. The full shchmear – Everything except fistfights. Albert and Eleonor have been ruling the roost for the past week. There's no love lost between you and those two, honey. Because of all this publicity you've been getting, they hate your guts even more.'

'You don't have to tell me that. But it'll be interesting tomorrow to see how they behave. They'll be thrilled to see that I look like a hundred miles of unpaved road.'

'Bullshit, you're always too hard on yourself. You look like a shiny new highway to me.'

'Oh God, Steve, I wish I hadn't let this divorce thing affect me so much.'

'Hey, c'mon. You've been married to the guy for twenty years, for Chrissake. You're only human.'

'Yeah, I guess so.' She stuffed another fist of cashew nuts into her mouth without a pang.

'How's Tommy taking it?'

'Not well. He's angry with me. He's not here now. He went to the Lakers game with Brenda.'

'Well, he's young. He'll get over it. Look, Kitty, don't worry, take a couple of valium, try to get some sleep.'

'Sleep!' She looked at her watch. 'It's only seven thirty and I've been crunching valium like cashew nuts – and those too – oh God!' She stifled a sob.

'None of that, sugar – no guy is worth it.'

Katherine smiled. '*Some Like It Hot* – right?'

'Right. You want to come over and hang out with us?'

'No, thanks, darling. I've just eaten one boiled egg and two pounds of cashews. So I'd better do the nightly ritual. I don't want to look like a total fat slob tomorrow.'

'You'll never be that. You're lovely, and you're loved – don't ever forget it. See you on the set, kid.'

'Thanks Steve.' She put down the phone, picked up her glass, and wandered around the den, examining long ago photographs of herself with Johnny and Tommy. Happy Families in silver frames. God they looked happy: moments frozen in time. She was lost in the sadness of her thoughts, when a loud and familiar laugh interrupted her reverie. Brenda was back. Katherine walked through the living room and pushed open the swing doors to the kitchen.

Brenda was there, with the usual suspects sitting round the table. Pedro, Maria, Sam, and Suzy the maid.

'Surprise, surprise, I thought you were with Tommy.' Katherine had never been so glad to see Brenda's plump, comfortable face.

'He went out with a friend after the game,' said Brenda. 'I just got back, so Pedro and Maria were giving me a little snack.'

There was a mountain of pasta and salad on the table. It smelled so delicious that Katherine wished she could sit with them and devour a whole bowl. She was always hungry, but she and Eleonor had to remain seven pounds under their normal weight to look good in Maximilian's tight, flamboyant creations. That was because the camera added ten pounds to a woman's figure.

'Who did he go out with?'

'That boy who lives in Westwood. The one whose mother is that game-show creature.' Brenda spoke disdainfully.

'He went out with Todd?'

'Yes. Todd was with us at the game. He was flirting with a couple of bimbos sitting beside him. All teeth, hair and giggles.'

'I guess Tommy's old enough to get interested in girls now.'

'Right, he's a big boy. Sixteen in two months' time. What sort of a party shall we have? How about Playboy style – hot and cold running bunnies?'

'We'll do whatever Tommy wants.' Katherine smiled, finding it hard to come to terms with the fact that her son was almost a young man. 'Are you going to wait up for him?'

'Of course. You worry too much, Kitty. You've got enough on your plate. Do you want me to run lines for tomorrow's scenes?'

Katherine shook her head. 'No thanks. I'll study them in the car on the way to work. It's just another scene with Eleonor. It's not difficult, just the same one we've done a thousand times, only the outfits are different.' She kissed Brenda's cheek and said goodnight to the staff. She took a bottle of vodka to the bedroom with her. Tonight this would be her sole companion.

Todd Evans and Tommy Bennett drove down Van Nuys Boulevard. Tommy was at the wheel of the sleek black BMW, driving much too fast.

'Slow down, man,' Todd yelled. 'The cops are gonna nail us for sure.'

'Chicken.' Tommy swerved to avoid a helmeted motorcyclist, who shook his fist and cursed. Tommy laughed, tipping the Budweiser to his lips. The beer trickled down his chin on to the faint beginnings of his beard.

Todd looked anxiously in the rear view mirror again. 'I think you should let me drive,' he pleaded. 'If Dad finds out I've let you drive his car, he'll give me hell.'

'Yeah but I won the bet; you promised me I could take the wheel.' Tommy gulped the last of his beer, crunched the can in his left hand, and threw it out of the window. It hit a newsstand and bounced twice, before nearly hitting an angry pedestrian. Tommy put his foot down on the accelerator. 'How about picking up a couple of chicks that'll put out for us tonight?'

'Where do you think we're gonna find put-outs on Van Nuys Boulevard on a school night?'

'How about there?' Tommy jerked his head to a neon-lit bar, where a few adolescents lounged outside. 'There's bound to be some prime pussy struttin' their stuff in there. Maybe even some of the mattresses from twelfth grade.'

'Yeah, OK, let's hit it,' said Todd hastily. Anything to get his friend out from behind the wheel.

Tommy turned into the parking lot with a screeching of tyres. Todd shuddered. His father was going to know for sure that somebody had been messing with his BMW. Todd was sixteen and had just gotten his licence, but Tommy was still two months away from his sixteenth birthday. If the police found him driving, they'd both be in the deepest of shit.

The crowded, dark Edelweiss bar smelled of beer, cigarettes, and the cheap drugstore perfume of high-school girls. The boys swaggered up to the bar and ordered a couple of Buds; then they lit up and surveyed the assembled talent with what they imagined were super-cool expressions. Both boys were tall and good-looking; some of the girls looked back at them and giggled to each other. Tommy had his mother's black curly hair and light green eyes. He was wearing the usual teenager's uniform: dirty blue jeans, T-shirt and a black leather jacket. Todd had light brown hair that flopped over his forehead. With his glasses and tweed jacket, he fancied himself like a much younger and sexier Woody Allen.

The boys stood at the bar for ten minutes, when one particular brunette caught Tommy's eye.

'Get a load of those knockers,' he whispered.

'Hot,' Todd whispered back. 'Real hot.'

'I think I'll make a move.' Tommy spoke with a confidence brought on by six Budweisers.

Todd looked worried. 'She's taken,' he said, watching the two guys who were lounging protectively near the girl.

'So what?' said Tommy. 'I'm taller than them.'

And quite a bit younger, thought Todd. One of those guy's at least eighteen.

Tommy drained his beer quickly, paid for two more, and then sauntered over to the girl. She was a beautiful brunette of about seventeen, with tumbling auburn curls and pale eyes that reminded him of his mother.

His mother. The workaholic. She hadn't given a damn about him recently. All she seemed to care about was her career, and her clothes, and her publicity. She never had time for the things they had shared when they lived so happily in New York. Sometimes Tommy believed that it was she who had turned his warm, kind father – a far better actor than she was actress – into a drug addict. He didn't like to think about his parents' divorce. It made him too angry. It made him so angry that he wanted to hurt somebody.

'You got some sorta problem, man?' The lanky nineteen-year old stepped in front of Tommy as he approached the table where the two girls sat.

Tommy looked the bigger guy over arrogantly. 'I think I know this young lady. It's Jennie isn't it,' he yelled over the din of the juke box.

The girl raised dismissive, limpid eyes. 'Yeah. So what?'

'I'm Tommy Bennet. We go to the same high school. I'm in twelfth grade.'

The tall boy jabbed a giant fist into Tommy's chest. 'I told you to get lost,' he snarled. 'So piss off, dickhead.'

'Take your fuckin' paws off me.' Tommy tried to make his voice sound menacing. 'Right now, buddy, or you'll get hurt.'

'Oh yeah, who's gonna hurt me? You, you little punk? You couldn't hurt a pustule on a pimple.'

Tommy swung his fist at the other boy's face and eagerly the others turned to watch. A fight on a dull Thursday night. Great. Something to break the monotony. Within seconds the two boys were pommelling each other while the girls ran squealing in fake fear to another corner.

'You fucking little creep, you're dead,' yelled Tommy's opponent, and from behind the bar, the proprietor raised his eyes to the ceiling. Picking up the telephone, he dialled the police.

Katherine sat at her dressing table brushing her hair the way her mother had taught her when she was three. One hundred strokes every night. She stared blankly at the face in the mirror, and was not pleased by what she saw. Her skin was sallow and blotchy. Lines of fatigue were etched under her eyes, which were puffy from all the tears she'd shed over the past months. She looked every one of her forty-three years. She knew that the magic of Jasper's lighting could erase most of the damage, but her weariness was like a veil over her face. There was no sparkle, no light in her blank eyes.

Still, she had to finish the nightly ritual. She massaged sixty dollar performance cream vigorously into her face, paying particular attention to the area under her chin, which she was convinced had become flabby. Then she got on to the floor, and with gritted teeth, did one hundred sit-ups. She was supposed to do these every day, but had missed some in the past week. She could feel the strain as she tried to regain the lost tone in her stomach muscles – muscles that would soon turn to fat if she didn't work out regularly. Despite feeling so tired that she could barely stand, she picked up her weights, and watched herself grimly in the many-mirrored reflections as she did fifty arm curls on each arm.

At last she staggered to the bed, crawled in among the nest of lace and silk pillows and sheets, closed her eyes and waited for sleep to come. But exhausted as she was, the vivid images of her courtroom experience kept coming back to her. She couldn't sleep without help. She opened the drawer of the bedside table and took out a sleeping pill. With a sigh of resignation she swallowed it, drained the vodka, then lay back and waited for oblivion.

* * *

The jangling of the telephone woke Katherine from a deep, drugged slumber. Pedro was on the intercom.

'Sorry to disturb you, *señora*, but it's the police. They say they must talk to you personally.'

'The police?' Katherine shook her head and pushed herself into a sitting position. 'What do they want?'

'They didn't say, *señora*.' Pedro's voice was thick with sleep. 'But they need to speak to you. They're on extension one.'

'Thank you.' She pressed the other telephone button and, full of dread, said, 'Hello?'

'Katherine Bennet?'

'Yes?'

'We have Thomas John Bennet here in the police station. He says he's your son.'

'What's happened to him?' Her voice was fearful. 'He's in custody, Mrs Bennet. He's under arrest, and you should get down to the Van Nuys Police Precinct right away. 7789 Van Nuys Boulevard.'

'I'll be right there.' Katherine was suddenly horribly clearheaded. 'Is he OK? Is he hurt?' but the line was dead.

CHAPTER TWO

Four-thirty was the time Katherine usually got up to prepare for the day's filming. Now the alarm clock shrilled as if to goad her into action, and she switched it off, standing in the centre of the room, dazed and uncertain. If she went to Van Nuys Boulevard and bailed Tommy out for whatever offence he was supposed to have committed (and she shuddered to think what that might be) she would be late for work. The precinct was in exactly the opposite direction from the studio.

She knew there was much at stake. Her bosses were not concerned about the personal lives of their stars; indeed they were already annoyed at having to give her four precious days off for her court case. That meant shooting around Katherine's scenes, which in turn meant serious re-scheduling problems. One episode of *The Skeffingtons* took six days to shoot. Katherine knew that the producer had scheduled all her scenes for today and tomorrow. She had to be there for them. But she felt she had to be there for Tommy too. Her son meant the world to her – especially since the divorce. She bit her cuticles, agonizing about what to do. She looked at the clock again. Blood was thicker than water. She had to be with her son. Fuck the studio.

There was a tap on the back door of her dressing room, and Maria appeared with a tray of espresso coffee, mangoes and grapefruit juice.

'Will the *señora* be ready for the car at five o'clock?'

'Yes, yes, I will be taking the car, Maria, but tell Sam that I'll be going to Van Nuys Boulevard instead of the studio. Ask him if he knows where the police precinct is.'

'*Si, señora.*'

Katherine pulled on jeans and T-shirt and downed the scalding coffee in one gulp. Then she punched the sixth autodial button on her telephone.

'Hello,' a deep voice slurred.

'Ben?'

'Yup, what's up, Katherine?' The production manager's tone was gruffer than usual.

'Ben, I have a major personal problem.' Katherine hesitated. He had to report everything to the producers, and she suspected that one of them had a direct line to America's leading scandal sheet, *The National Sun*.

She stumbled, then burst out – 'Ben, I can't come in for a couple of hours, I've got to go on a really urgent errand. It's terribly important, Ben. It's family business.'

'What family business? Hey, there ain't nothin' more important, Katherine, than you bein' in make-up in forty-five minutes, and on the set at seven. We've already shot around you for four days. We're location shooting at the airport, and with this fuckin' weather we've been having, we can't take *any* chances. We need you pronto.'

'But I'm only in three scenes. Just three scenes that's all, out of five. Can't you spare me for an hour? Please, it's really urgent.'

Ben was unmoved. 'Listen, Katherine,' he snapped, 'you've been gone for four days on your goddamn divorce. We've got the network yapping at our heels to finish these two episodes, so we've held your scenes back. But we're down to the *wire* now. If we don't get today's scenes in the can, and five other scenes of yours that the editor is screaming for, we're up shit creek without a fuckin' paddle. So tell me what's more important than that, will ya?'

'Nothing,' said Katherine bitterly. 'It doesn't matter, Ben. I'll be there on time, I promise.'

'You better be,' he snapped, and hung up.

Katherine pressed the buzzer for Brenda.

'Who is it?'

'Brenda, sorry to wake you, but something awful's happened to Tommy.'

'Tommy, what do you mean? What's happened?'

'Don't get upset. I know this sounds terrible, but the police just called. Tommy's in custody, they need somebody to bail him out, and the goddamned studio won't let me go.'

'You don't need to say any more, honey. I'll go. What's he been arrested for?'

'They wouldn't say. They refused to tell me, Brenda. I just pray it isn't something really serious. I'll keep my mobile on me all the time, so you can ring me as soon as you know anything. Have you got the household cheque book?'

'Yes,' said Brenda. 'And I'm on my way. Don't worry about anything. I'll see you later.'

Immobilised, Katherine stared at the time, now edging towards five fifteen. She had to leave for work. Now.

Eleonor Norman watched Katherine arrive in the make-up room late, dishevelled, and looking as if her mind was in another place. Eleonor was already reclining in a leather chair, with her eyes closed, blonde hair carelessly pulled back into an untidy pony tail, black roots showing.

'Morning Eleonor,' said Katherine coolly.

'Morning Katherine,' said Eleonor even more coolly, and gave a secret smile.

Ever since six-year-old Eleonor Norman had stepped off the boat from England in the 1950s and soon after started playing leads in major motion pictures, gossip had swirled around her like summer mist. There was a huge amount of conjecture as to exactly *how* and why an unknown British brat had snared the lead in the all-American production of *Heidi*, when every moppet from NY to LA had been angling for the part for months.

Ugly rumours said that her mother, a vivacious spike-tongued widow, had sold the kid sexually to the production head of Palladium Pictures to get the part. Although no one had ever proved this sordid fact, it was no secret that the widow Norman and her pretty daughter were often spotted weekending at Fritz Pallenberg's top security walled estate in Bel Air. Usually they would be the only visitors there.

Although that was thirty years ago, and Eleonor's mother was dead, along with Fritz Pallenberg, and most of his cronies, the faint aroma of scandal still lingered around Eleonor. She had never confided to anyone what had really happened between her and the notorious old paedophile on those long ago Los Angeles nights. Only sometimes was she woken by nightmares. Then she would lie sweating and shaking with fear, as she confronted her ogres again. Mostly, though, she'd learned to deal with them, and Dirk, her live-in lover, did his best to keep the dragons at bay.

Now, with her make-up finished, Eleonor went next door into hairdressing, poured decaff into a styrofoam cup and picking up today's edition of *Variety*, flicked through it, then studied Army Archard's daily news and gossip column.

'*Rumours rumbling from the set of ABN's hit serial,* The Skeffingtons, *are that Katherine Bennet is giving a performance this season to make Emmy voters sit up and take note. According to our informant on Gabe Heller's lot, Ms Bennet pulls out all the stops in her sensational interpretation of the frisky Southern Belle who is in this, the third season of the show, out-Scarletting Miss O'Hara herself. Watch this space for more news on Ms Bennet. She's one to watch for the Emmys.'*

Eleonor crushed her styrofoam cup and threw it angrily into the bin. Upstart bitch! How did that story appear? Eleonor Norman was the heroine and main female star of *The Skeffingtons. She* and Albert carried the show. Katherine Bennet was supposed to play a supporting role. But didn't it seem that all the scripts had been more slanted towards Katherine lately? Didn't she get more juicy dialogue with each show? More dramatic scenes? More focus on her character? Eleonor threw down *Variety* and, plucking next week's script from her tote bag, quickly scanned it. Her lips moved as she counted. By the time she had finished she was enraged.

Katherine had at *least* thirty or forty more lines in this script than she or Albert. How dared the producers do that to her! Had she slaved in the movies all her life to play second banana to some washed up Broadway actress? Had those endless days, weeks, months and years of slogging away as a child star been for nothing?

Eleonor shuddered. She remembered the routine, the deadly boredom of being a child actress. She had to try so hard to please everyone, especially her mother. They had had no family and few friends. Although it occasionally crossed Jemima Norman's mind that her daughter was missing out on the more normal things of a girl's life, like parties, ice skating and friends of her own age, ambition overcame maternal instinct.

By the time Eleonor was twenty-one she had the exterior of a peaches and cream English rose, but inside she was as tough and hard as an army boot. Just as well, because although Eleonor was still considered a star by the public, as far as Hollywood was concerned she was no longer on the A list. In her adolescence, movie roles were few and far between. The money she had made in childhood had been squandered since Jemima the profligate hadn't realized a child star's life is brief and she was reduced to starring in television mini-series and movies-of-the-week. Eleanor didn't like to remember now that sometimes she had even had to take jobs as a waitress or service escort – a disguised form of prostitution.

But with the role of Candice Skeffington, her luck changed. She was hot again, and if she had one ambition it was never to play second fiddle to anyone, especially a previously unknown New York actress with a phoney *theatah* accent.

'Good morning sweet lady.' The portly and imposing figure of Albert Amory entered the hairdressing department. His auburn wig was flecked with silver, and a heavy coat of orange pancake disguised the network of wrinkles on his face. His eyes were shrewd and deep-set, his lips sardonic. He looked rather like a massive oak tree, strong, brown, and invincible.

'How are you this fine morning, Eleonor, my dear?'

'I'm very well thank you, Albert. Or at least I *was*. Have you seen this?'

Albert put on his glasses and read the piece slowly, his craggy face creasing into a frown as he did so.

'And,' hissed Eleonor, 'she's got at least *forty* more lines than me in next week's episode, and a lot more than you! What are we going to *do*, Al?'

'*Don't* call me Al,' he snapped.

'Sorry dahling, I forgot.' She stroked his hand, trying not to remove the pancake which almost, but didn't quite, erase the liver-spots. 'Albert dahling, what can we do?'

'We'll think of something. After all, we are the stars of this show, Ellie dear. We *are* the Skeffingtons. You are the wife and I am the patriarch. *She* has only married into the family.'

Albert talked about the Skeffington family as though it were his own. Forty years in the English theatre, playing every kind of character from butlers to kings, had given him the stature to play Mr Skeffington Senior perfectly. Stardom had come to Albert Amory late in life and he was determined not to let it ever get away.

'We shall remain the stars of this show,' said Albert, 'Whatever it takes, my dear.'

Katherine studied her lines, while Blackie, the make-up man, did his best with her tired face.

George Black had worked at the studio for as long as anyone could remember. A car accident, in which he had lost one eye, had ended a promising career as a stunt double in the forties, and after paying him compensation, the studio had let him work as a junior in the make-up department.

They nicknamed him Blackie for with his dark hair and eyes, swarthy complexion and black eye-patch, he looked like a character straight out of a fifties pirate movie. In fact he was gentle and avuncular, and always had a sympathetic ear for the actresses whose faces he transformed daily. He had his favourites, of course, and this year it was Katherine, who had more than once confided her woes to his sympathetic ear.

Today's script called for Georgia Skeffington to take a business trip to Alaska, and the first scene would be Georgia arriving at LAX in her private jet. Katherine had told Maximilian, the costume designer, to use his own discretion for this episode. She usually put a lot of her own input into Georgia's wardrobe because Maximilian had a tendency to go over the top – but recently the divorce had occupied all her time.

Make-up and hair finished, the studio driver took Katherine to a small private airport on the outskirts of LAX. She clutched her mobile phone, checking every few minutes that it was working, but there was no word from Brenda and she was getting more and more nervous.

It was cool in the early California morning. The July sky was pale blue frosted with zig-zag clouds, but already there was a hint of the blistering heat to come.

'They say it's gonna to be a scorcher today,' said Blackie. 'A total scorcher. Eddie and Marcia told me it was so hot in the valley yesterday, the water in their pool started to evaporate.'

'Let's hope Maximilian took that into consideration when he was designing my outfit,' said Katherine, as the car entered the airport.

Maximilian – no one knew his second name – had for years been one of the most influential and popular costume designers in Hollywood, and *The Skeffingtons* had only increased his fame. A middle-aged Spaniard, he always dressed in the height of continental fashion. His thick, sleek hair was jet black and combed into a pompadour. His skin was always deeply tanned, but with scarcely a wrinkle, because Maximilian treated his face as if it were rare porcelain. Everything about him gleamed – from his polished chestnut brown shoes to the sparkling white chambray handkerchief which graced the breast pocket of his olive green, creaseless linen suit. He was sartorial perfection, and expected the same from his leading ladies.

'Hi Katherine, have a good vacation?' Various crew members called out cheerily to her.

'It wasn't a vacation,' Katherine repeated a dozen times, 'it was a divorce.' She went into the wardrobe truck. Maximilian was waiting with a proud smile.

'*Corazon*, so sorry. This might be slightly too warm for today's scene,' he apologized. 'But she is coming back from Alaska, after all. Do you like it?'

Katherine stared at the costume which Becky, the wardrobe girl, was holding. A bright red, double-ply cashmere maxidress, with a polo neck and long sleeves edged with black fur, was covered by a heavy, red wool cape, edged with black astrakhan. A black astrakhan cossack hat went with the outfit, which was finished off with knee-high red boots, red leather gauntlet gloves and an astrakhan muff.

'A muff?' Katherine raised her eyebrows. 'I thought they went out with the nineteenth century?'

'They're coming back!' said Maximilian excitedly. 'And who, other than Georgia Skeffington, could give them a seal of approval?'

'This seems so – so – heavy,' Katherine plucked the outfit from Becky's hand. 'My God, it weighs a ton!'

'*Corazon*, you'll only be in it today. The rest of the episode I've got you in little floaty chiffon numbers.'

'Great,' muttered Katherine. 'On air-conditioned stages I'm in floaty chiffons, in one hundred degrees heat I'm in double-ply cashmere. Good thinking, Maximilian.'

Maximilian and Becky exchanged significant, raised eyebrow glances, intercepted by Katherine. She smiled to break the tension. 'OK, OK, OK, just kidding folks. Of course I'll wear it. Everyone knows you must suffer for your art. C'mon Becky, let's get dressed; they're ready to rehearse and we don't want to keep the great British Thespian waiting.'

Everyone burst out laughing. '*Corazon*, shall we take bets on the old fart remembering his lines today?' said Maximilian

Katherine's mobile rang as she was adjusting her astrakhan hat to exactly the right angle.

The voice was muffled, the line crackled, but she could hear Brenda saying, 'Kitty? I'm down at the precinct. I've been here for three hours now, but the sons of bitches won't let Tommy out.'

'Why?' Katherine's voice rose. 'Surely they have to release him if we post bail money. Won't they take bail?'

'No – and they won't tell me why,' Brenda said despairingly.

There was a knock on the thin plywood door.

'Ready for you on set, Katherine. Director says we've got to chop-chop today.'

'Be right there. Brenda, listen to me. What the hell has Tommy done?'

'He got in a fight with a boy in a bar. It doesn't seem to be any big deal, except the cops say he'd been drinking.'

'Is the other boy filing charges?'

'Nobody will tell me anything,' Brenda sounded angry. 'I've seen him, he's OK, but they won't let him out without a lawyer and an official word from you.'

'Oh, God, what are we going to do?'

There was another louder rap at the door, and the voice barked:

'For Chrissake, Katherine, you've got an entire crew out here waiting for you, it's one hundred fucking degrees! Are you going to take all day long?' It was Ben, the production manager, on the rampage.

'Just a *minute*,' Katherine yelled, 'I'm trying to put my damned costume on.' She lowered her voice. 'Listen, Brenda, I tried to call my lawyer this morning, but he's in New York. It's only eight o'clock here, so nobody's in the New York office yet, and I don't know his partner's number. There's just a machine at his office. Shit. I'm going to ask Steven. He's the only person I can think of who can help. It's a bloody madhouse here.'

'It ain't a million laffs here. Tommy's real upset, Kitty. I've never seen him like this. He's been crying his eyes out, but he's belligerent too. He wants out of there. You can't *believe* the kind of people he's spent the night with in his cell. Drug pushers, pimps, tramps. We're gonna have to delouse him before we get him back home.'

There was a loud bang on the door, then it flew open and Buzz Smith, a moustachioed has-been from the days of *Starsky and Hutch* and *Policewoman* stood hands on hips. He was to direct this week's episode of *The Skeffingtons*. He entered the wardrobe truck bellowing, 'For God's sake, Katherine, who the hell do you think you are, holding us up like this? It's shit hot out there, it's already eight o'clock, and we've been waiting for you for fifteen minutes. We've got five scenes to finish. Now get your ass out there, lady, otherwise I'm going to be on the telephone to the network.'

'I've got to go, Bren,' Katherine tried to suppress the lump in her throat and the panicky stress in her voice. 'I'm going to try to find Steven and ask him to go down to the precinct. I'm sure he'll take care of things, Bren. But please don't leave there.'

'I wouldn't dream of leaving. Tom's been dumb, but he doesn't deserve this sort of treatment.'

'Call me any time you hear anything, Brenda. I'll keep the mobile switched on all the time.'

Katherine sat slumped in the cabin of the Lear Jet, waiting for the magic word 'Action' which would release her from this roasting prison. Sweat ran down her back onto the thick cashmere dress, collecting in a puddle around her tightly belted waist. It was so hot she could even feel her mascara melting.

The interior of the plane was tiny and the two bit-part actors playing pilot and co-pilot were doubled over from the waist at the door, waiting to be galvanized into action at the sound of the director's voice. Sweat from their foreheads dripped on to their shoes. A trapped bluebottle, attracted by Katherine's scent, was attacking her face. 'Make-up' had left a small mirror and powder puff for repairs, but every time

Katherine patted her face dry, it was damp again within five minutes.

Then she heard the magic word.

'Aaaaction!' shouted Buzz from the melting tarmac and like automatons the two actors leaped to life, and opened the door of the plane for Katherine with a flourish.

She stood on the top step, breathing the smoggy ninety-five-degree air gratefully, surveying her surroundings with Georgia's haughty stare. Then with great assurance she sashayed down the steps on four-inch stilettos to greet Albert Amory, who was also not without his share of troubles on this sauna morning. His toupee, fixed to his bald head by a special paste, kept loosening in the heat, and his fine black military moustache, usually groomed and upturned, was drooping in a curiously lop-sided manner. The heat and discomfort, not to mention the embarrassment of his loose-fitting wig, were causing Albert to go up on his lines and, to Katherine's chagrin, he had fluffed the last four takes. On this, take five, he didn't disappoint.

'How are you Georgia, my dear. You look very well as usual,' was supposed to be his opening line. Once he had said it, Buzz could dispense with the long shot, and go into cutaways, thus releasing Katherine from the roasting prison of the plane.

But Albert couldn't get his one line right.

'Georgia, what are you doing here?' he boomed, out of character for someone who had come to the airport expressly to see her.

'Cut–cut–*cut*, for Christ's sake Albert – get it *right*, man!'

Buzz was as fed up as the rest of the crew. This hiccup was costing them valuable time, not to mention the rental of the private jet, a supposed bargain at three hundred and fifty dollars an hour.

'What the hell's the matter with you?' Buzz snapped. 'It's only one line, for fuck's sake – can't you get one line right?'

'Sorry old chap. Very sorry.' Albert flashed what he considered an endearing smile while 'Hair', 'Make-up', and 'Wardrobe' primped, patted, and painted him back to perfection. Katherine stood on the steps stoically. She wasn't about to add her own two cents to Albert's discomfort. Although she was embarrassed for him, she needed to save her breath for the interior of the plane, and she was still nervous about Tommy.

Albert huffed and puffed apologies, whilst the wrecking crew attacked his recalcitrant hairpiece with vigour.

'For God's sake, we *can't see* whether he's wearin' a wig or a fuckin' fez, we're so far away!' Buzz exploded, but the crimper ignored him and continued fussing with the toupee.

'Git *outta* his face you guys. If we don't get this mother-fucker in the can, we'll have the goddamn studio down here, kickin' all our asses to hell'n back.'

Katherine quietly climbed back into her sauna-like tomb as Albert's eyes flickered venomously towards her. 'Get it right,' she breathed. 'Get it *right*, you silly old fart.'

Albert screwed up his lines on the next take, and the next, but Katherine couldn't allow her fear, or her exasperation to show. She had to play her role – the cool Georgia, and not let her own turmoil show.

Eventually Buzz had enough in the can to yell, 'Cut – that's a print. Fuckin' hell. Three goddamn hours on this shit. Next set-up, guys.'

Between set-ups Katherine sat in the relatively peaceful cool of the tiny departure lounge, fanning herself, and sipping iced water. It was far too hot to talk, especially the banal chitchat that passed for conversation on the set, and anyway, she was on tenterhooks waiting for the phone to ring.

Steven had promised he would sort things out, but it was hours since she'd spoken to him.

'Ready for you, Katherine. Next set-up.'

Charlie, the second assistant director, flashed his cute lopsided smile, and with a good-humoured groan, Katherine wrapped her suffocating cape round her again, and walked on to the melting tarmac into the ring of lights.

By lunchtime Katherine was on the brink of hysteria. She had tried to call her lawyer, but he was stuck in Chicago, and when she rang home Maria told her that Brenda and Tommy had still not returned.

The unit moved their main location from the airport to a house nearby, and lunch was called at midday. Katherine ripped off the thick costume and hat, and put on a light cotton kimono. She tied a scarf around her hair, and went to stand in line with the rest of the cast and crew at the buffet on the trestle tables which were set out in a clearing.

Some curious onlookers gathered around to watch the strangers in their midst. A couple of them pointed at Katherine.

'There's the Georgia Poison Peach.' A fat woman, wearing stretch pants patterned with sunflowers, and earrings to match, giggled loudly. 'She don't look too good today, do she?' The other two, who were even fatter, cackled, and made some unflattering comments about Katherine's kimono.

Katherine knew better than to pay any attention. She was accustomed to people discussing her within earshot, as though she didn't exist, as if she were still a figure on their television set. Today, in any case, her only thoughts were of Tommy. Why the hell hadn't Steven called? Or Brenda? What was happening?

For the fiftieth time she checked the battery on her mobile phone, then arrived at the top of the line and surveyed the assorted salads, pastas and cold meats. In spite of everything she was starving, so she loaded her plate. Then she heard her name called.

'Katherine Bennet? Hey Kitty, Kitty, Kitty.' She tensed and clutched her tray. The two men approaching were obviously journalists, and the look in their eyes said 'Scoop'. Katherine looked around for protection, but there was none. Even though *The Skeffingtons* was a number one show in the ratings, there was no security to prevent the stars from being mobbed or mauled in public. Locations were chosen for their suitability, but no consideration was ever given to the privacy of the actors. Katherine and the rest of the cast had grown used to it. To the men in dark suits who sat in the fifth storey black-windowed building on Franklyn Boulevard, controlling the network's finances, actors were completely replaceable commodities.

'Hey Kitty, Kitty.' They were on her now, stenopads and microphone at the ready.

'We just heard that your son's been arrested; he's at the Van Nuys precinct now. Do you have a comment for us about that, Kitty?'

'Yeah, what do you have to say?' said the other one. 'He assaulted another boy in a bar, big fight, we've heard. Give us a quote.'

'I have nothing to say,' she said stiffly. 'Please leave me alone.' She looked around for the unit publicist, who as usual was not there.

Katherine seethed, thinking of all the salaries she paid to so many people. Why hadn't she insisted that Kingsley, her personal publicist, accompanied her to the location? Katherine gritted her teeth and moved out of the queue, putting down her tray of uneaten food, although her stomach was grumbling.

The sob sister from the number two network put on her most beguiling face, 'Come on Kitty, you're not the only mother whose kid has been arrested. Tell us, how does it feel to have your boy in jail?'

Katherine took a deep breath, conscious that she was looking far from her best. She had to say something. There were four cameras stuck in her face.

'Like any mother in America, I'm extremely distressed about Tommy's arrest. I don't know the complete facts yet, because the studio didn't allow me to go to him in person.' She heard anger creep into her voice, and tried to sound calmer.

'However, I'm convinced that whatever happened, Tommy is *not* guilty, and I hope that he will be cleared of this charge. Whatever happens, I shall stand by my son in this terrible situation.'

She walked quickly away, but the journalists ran after her, gabbling questions. Pleadingly she signalled to Charlie, who at last slouched over, cute grin in place.

'Come on now guys and gals, time to move on. Miss Kitty here has gotta have her lunch, and we gotta get back to work, so please, that's all folks. Time to split now.'

Grumbling, the journalists left, and Kitty entered her tiny dressing room. She sank on to the sofa and started crying.

'God damn it, why can't I stop blubbing?' she stared angrily at the black rivulets running down her cheeks. 'Steven, please, please *call* me and please God let Tommy be all right.'

Just as Blackie was putting the finishing touches to her make-up, the mobile phone rang.

'Kitty,' Steven said breathlessly. 'It's done. Tommy's been released, I got him out, and he's just fine, so don't worry any more.'

'What was he doing?'

'Just a couple of kids having a fight up in a bar. It was nothing really. Cops needed a bust for their quota, I guess. I've taken care of it, so don't you worry. Get back to work. And make my hack dialogue sound as good you always do.'

Katherine smiled, while the trailer shook with Ben yelling: 'On set Kitty – *now*.'

'What would I do without you, Steve? God knows what happened to my lawyer, and all my hangers-on today. They seem to have done a disappearing act.'

'Happens all the time. More people you employ – less help you get. Anyway Tommy's home now, all in one piece, and he'll be waiting for you like one grateful kid.'

'I can't thank you enough, Steve.'

'That's what friends are for, Kitty. Time you got on that set now, gorgeous.'

'I'm on my way,' she said. 'To magic time.'

At the end of the day Brenda greeted Katherine at the door.

'Where is he?'

'Sleeping,' Brenda grinned. 'Poor kid didn't get any rest in that filthy cell. He was awake all night with pimps and pushers and God knows what scum – Jeez, Kitty, don't ever get slung in jail – it's a Hammer Horror story there.'

'What time did he go to sleep?' Katherine was disappointed not to see Tommy.

'About an hour ago. He wanted to wait up for you, but he was exhausted. The bail was a couple of grand, but Steven took care of it. He's a real good friend of yours, Kitty.'

'Don't I know it. Believe me, a friend is somebody I need in my life these days.' Katherine looked at her watch. Eight o'clock. 'You want to have a bite with me, Brenda?'

'Oh, I'm sorry, hon. I ate in the kitchen with Tommy and the rest of the gang, but I'll sit with you and gab while you have your tasty sole and spinach rice cakes.' She shuddered. 'I don't know how you can stomach that boring food.'

Katherine smiled. 'You know a TV tart's got to be ten pounds lighter than a normal human.'

'Sure, I know; it's tough at the top. Oh, by the way, this arrived for you.'

She handed Katherine a flat gold cardboard box.

'Looks interesting; what is it?'

'Don't know. A surprise I guess.'

'Hope it's not a bomb,' said Katherine, opening it.

She held up a gilt-framed, gold-painted record, nestled in crimson velvet. 'How sweet – what an original idea. Don't you think it's adorable?'

'Mmm – I'd rather have a gold bracelet,' said Brenda. 'What's the record of? Somethin' you recorded?'

'No.' Katherine examined it. 'It's an old seventy-eight, probably from the thirties. It's called *I Found a Million Dollar Baby in a five and ten Cent Store*. Look, the brass plaque at the bottom has a message engraved on it. "For Katherine Bennet, a great star and a great actress. You deserve much more than a million dollars."

'Mmm. Cute.' Brenda was not impressed. 'I got one of those once from Tom Jones. Said he was a fan of mine, so he sent me his platinum disc. I didn't know where to put the damn thing. Who's this one from?'

'Well, let's see. There's no signature anywhere, just a card that says "To the most beautiful woman in the world, with love." '

'That's original,' Brenda said sarcastically. 'Must be either a real Einstein, or a real nutcase.'

'Well I like it.' Katherine propped the framed disc on her mantelpiece. 'It's practically the only thing in this house that isn't white or silver, and I never had a gold record before.'

'Well, I'm off to bed,' Brenda hugged Katherine affectionately. 'I need a full night's sleep. No doubt number one son will be up with the larks, and ready for some electronic fun 'n' games.'

'Please wake me when he gets up, Bren. I really want to see him before I go to work. My call's not until eight, thank goodness.' Katherine sighed. 'If only I could spend more time with him.'

'You do the best you can, and that's all anyone can do. Goodnight, Kitty.'

Alone in the huge white room, Katherine looked at the gold record again.

'To the most beautiful woman in the world', she whispered.

Was this from a genuine fan? Or, from one of the many deranged people who had become obsessed with her in the past few years? As she walked up the wide stairs to her lonely bedroom, she wondered who her admirer was – probably some nutcase. Anonymous admirers were not always good news for stars like Katherine Bennett.

CHAPTER THREE

Tommy opened his sore eyes slowly. His palate felt thick and dirty and there was a dull, pounding ache in his head. Daylight filtered through the blackout curtains, faintly illuminating what his mother's fashionable decorator had designed as the ideal room for an adolescent boy. In no way was the expensive Swedish furniture, and overstuffed red, white and blue zig-zag patterned sofa and armchair to Tommy's taste, but he had more or less managed to obliterate them with the avalanche of dirty clothes, which Brenda was forbidden to move. The wallpaper was patterned with replicas of famous racing cars, and Tommy had tried to erase them by smothering the walls with posters of his pop idols.

He squinted at his digital clock – 10.30. Jeez, he'd been flat out for fourteen hours. He pressed his remote and MTV sprang to life. The frenzied figures of the latest anti-social rap group were on screen, gyrating to their new hit. He pressed the volume until the sound enveloped him, then started lip-synching with the group, strumming an imaginary guitar.

He hardly heard the knock on the door. 'Can I come in?' asked Brenda.

'Sure, come on in.'

Brenda could barely carry the enormous tray, heaped with every possible breakfast delicacy.

'I thought you'd be starving.' She pulled a table up next to his bed, 'So I brought you a bit of everything.'

'Gee, thanks, Bren.' He looked at it appreciatively. 'Mmm, looks good enough to eat.' They laughed compatibly.

Throwing down the orange juice and papaya and strawberry starter in one gulp, Tommy asked, 'Where's Mom?'

'Gone to the studio.' Brenda plumped Tommy's pillows. 'She was real upset she couldn't see you but I refused to wake you.'

'Yeah, well I'm sorry too.' He speedily shovelled three fried eggs and half a pound of bacon into his mouth, eyes never leaving the screen.

'You want to tell me what happened?' Brenda sat on his bed, watching him warily.

'Not now Bren. It was nothin'. I just got stupid that's all. You know I get stupid when I'm fried. I'm real sorry.'

'How many times have I told you not to drink?' she chided. 'First of all you're under age, and second of all it brings out your rotten side.'

'I know, I know. But I can't be the only one of my gang who doesn't drink. Face it Bren, what else is there to do at night, other than watch TV?'

'If you were smart, you'd get some hobbies – do something with your spare time, like we all did when we were kids, instead of frittering it away.'

'Oh sure,' he said dismissively. 'Drawing and fret-work. That was in the Dark Ages wasn't it? Before MTV?'

'None of your lip. You're getting too much of a mouth on you, Tommy Bennet, it's about time you zipped it up.'

Tommy dunked a chocolate doughnut in his coffee, studying the short-skirted TV presenter. 'Jeez, I'd sure like to give her one,' he said appreciatively, then, seeing Brenda's disapproving look, winked and said, 'Just kidding.'

'Well your mother's *very* upset with you. She's hardly slept all night worrying.'

'It's me that should be upset with her.' He wiped up the remains of his fried eggs with another doughnut. 'She doesn't give a fuck about me, Bren. You know she doesn't. All she's interested in is her stupid career, and her stupid publicity, and her fancy clothes. That's what drove Dad to drink, because Mom only cares about Mom.'

'How dare you say that, Tommy. You know that's not true. Your mother adores you – but she's got a hard, demanding job and nobody knows better than me how difficult it is.'

'Yeah, yeah, yeah,' Tommy yawned dismissively. 'We all know you were the flavour of the year in nineteen fifty somethin'. Well, I don't see what's so demanding about prancin' about in front of a camera, covered in make-up, wearing stupid outfits and saying idiotic lines. It's stupid, the whole thing's stupid and it's just because of her and that gross show that Dad did what he did.'

'No, Tommy, *you're* the one who's stupid,' said Brenda firmly. 'You're irresponsible and you don't think about anyone except yourself.'

Tommy glared at her sullenly.

'And what was it, pray, that your poor father did, that your mother drove him to?'

'You know what I'm talking about. Now I'm tired, and I wanna go back to sleep.' He pressed the sound up to maximum, lay back and closed his eyes.

Picking up the empty tray, Brenda yelled above the din: 'Okay. Go back to sleep now. I guess you need to sleep off that drunken spree. But I'll tell you one thing, Tommy Bennet. Your father took to the bottle long before your mother became successful, and I'm telling you this because it's about time you knew the truth, and stopped blaming her for everything.'

Tommy pulled the sheet over his head. 'I don't wanna hear it. I won't listen, Brenda – I'm tired. Leave me alone.'

Brenda turned at the door to look at the gawky boy hunched beneath his covers.

'One day you'll understand things, Tommy,' her voice was soft but angry. 'And maybe one day you'll realize how much your Mother really cares for you.'

'Mandy, where's my blue denim shirt?' Steven Leigh came out of the bathroom, towelling his sandy hair. As usual he was in a rush.

'Where it always is,' Mandy answered, her eyes never leaving the TV set where she was copying the movements of the exercise instructor exactly. 'Second drawer from the left, underneath your yellow shirt.'

Mandy was a prettyish, thirty-something blonde, still with the round baby face and innocuous blue eyes that had intrigued Steve at an audition ten years ago. He had been an aspiring writer, and she a secretary. They had quickly fallen for each other, and within one year she had presented him with twins.

Now Mandy said, 'Would you go downstairs and see what's going on with the twins? It's been suspiciously quiet for much too long.'

'Sure.' He took the stairs two at a time, buttoning his shirt on the way. The house was small and untidy, with evidence of small children everywhere. The girls were sitting at the breakfast table, riveted by a cartoon show, their cornflakes untouched in front of them.

'Morning me beautifuls – Fee Fi Fo Fum Firls – I smell the blood of delicious young girls,' Steve growled, in a convincing imitation of a bloodthirsty giant.

'Daddy, Daddy, Daddy!' The twins squealed with happy terror, and attached themselves, limpet-like, one to each leg. Steve attempted to pour himself some coffee.

'Hey, c'mon, let go of Daddy now. Daddy's got to go to work – make a buck to keep little girls in pretty clothes.' He tweaked their blonde ponytails and they shrieked with glee.

'C'mon, eat up those cornflakes, otherwise you won't get to be beeyootiful ladies.'

The cartoons finished and the news came on. Steve sat watching, sipping coffee, a twin on each knee. After the main headlines, the anchor announced that Katherine Bennet's son had been arrested, which was followed by a clip of Katherine leaving the divorce court the previous day.

'An unidentified family friend came to the precinct to make bail for the youngster, who was released without formal charges being pressed,' said the announcer.

'Daddy, Daddy, look, it's *you*,' screamed the twins, excitedly rushing up to the screen for a closer look.

Steven groaned. Yes, it certainly was him. There he was, holding a morose Tommy by the hand, wearing creased jeans and a shirt he'd thrown on, hair even more dishevelled than usual, as he hurried out of the precinct, with a flustered Brenda behind him.

Mandy came in, glancing at the set, sweating from her workout. 'Why you're a real TV star,' she said ironically. 'You've missed your calling.'

'Well, I'm missing my call right now.' Steven glanced at his watch. 'We've got a big rewrite today. Gabe Heller feels we've been concentrating too much on Katherine's character. I've got to come up with some plot situations to make her part less important.'

'Why?' Mandy buttered some toast with low-fat margarine. 'She's the best thing in the show.'

'I know,' said Steven. 'That's half the problem.'

As he drove to the studio, Steven started thinking about Katherine. Recently she had begun to confide in him: he enjoyed talking to her and felt flattered by her trust. God knows, it wasn't easy for a star to have a friend she could rely on. But what worried him was that she didn't seem to realize how much her problems were mounting at the studio. Admittedly, she had been preoccupied with her marriage during the last two miserable years with Johnny, and maybe she didn't kow-tow enough to the right power group.

Steve was on his way to becoming the top writer on *The Skeffingtons*, and sometimes now he felt a conflict of interest between pleasing his paymasters and protecting Katherine. If he was honest he was also a little troubled by his feelings for her. Now that his workload was so heavy, he found himself irritated when Mandy complained about finding the children and housework too much to cope with. He knew that basically they had a good marriage, and a lifestyle which was the envy of most friends – including Katherine. It was just that every now and again he found himself having erotic dreams about Kitty. Katherine in a swimming pool, Katherine laughing, looking over her shoulder seductively, Katherine in a bubble bath, in a scene he himself had written for her. He managed to keep these images at bay during the daytime, but at night, before drifting off to sleep, or in the drowsy early morning, they would come into his mind, then linger there subconsciously. And his day was always improved when he saw her.

Katherine finished work early, and rushed home to find Tommy playing basketball outside the garage. She hugged him tightly.

'Darling, I've been so worried about you. How are you feeling?'

Tommy squirmed; his green eyes that matched hers wary and guarded.

'Okay, Mom, I'm fine. For pete's sake don't fuss.' He aimed the ball into the basket, made a perfect pitch, and grinned.

'Well done,' said Katherine. 'Listen, Darling, I'm not going to discuss what happened that night, because I feel that whatever it was, you needed to get it out of your system, right?'

He didn't answer.

Katherine made her voice sterner. 'Tommy, I know things have been tough recently, and I know that what happened with your Dad and me has been hard for you, but you know the reasons why, don't you?'

'Yep,' he nonchalantly flipped the ball into the net again. 'I know 'em all, Mom.'

She tried to put an arm around his shoulder, but he shrugged her off, and began throwing the ball at the garage door.

'I was thinking about what we should do for your sixteenth birthday. The show's going to be in hiatus then so I thought maybe we could go somewhere for fun – just the two of us. Where would you like to go?'

'I don't know.' He bashed the ball on the ground several times, then threw it expertly into the net again. 'Wherever you want.'

'School will be out. How about taking in Paris? Or London? Or the South of France? You haven't seen any of those places. I love them, and I think you'd enjoy them too.'

'I really want to go to Fire Island with Todd.' His voice was peevish. 'His folks have taken a house there for August. That's what I'd like to do.'

'OK, but your birthday's July sixteenth,' she firmly took his arm and steered him into the house, 'So let's have dinner tonight together and talk about it. I *really* want to spend more time with you, Tommy, do lots of things together.'

His eyes were still wary, 'Do you?'

'You know I do.'

'Okay. How about Paris. I've always wanted to see those girls at the Crazy Horse Saloon.' he grinned mock-lecherously.

'We'll go on a gastronomic tour,' she said delightedly. 'Then maybe we'll stay in the South of France for a few days. I know you'll love it.'

'But what about Fire Island, can I go there after?'

'Yes, I promise you. We'll take two weeks in France, and then you can stay with Todd.' If he doesn't get you in any more trouble, she thought.

That night Tommy and Katherine ate together in the breakfast room, watching the lights of the city, and chatting away like any mother and son. But he refused to be drawn on either his night in jail, or his feelings about his alcoholic father.

Let sleeping dogs lie, thought Katherine, as she brushed her hair the requisite hundred strokes before falling exhausted into bed. At least we've made a step in the right direction. We're beginning to get close.

Vera called Katherine on her mobile, just as she was rushing out of her dressing room.

'I knew that something terrible would happen to Tommy if you divorced his father. It's all over the tabloids, Kit-Kat.'

Katherine sighed.

'Mom, it's nothing to do with my divorce and you know it. He's just a teenager, that's all.'

'I love that boy like he's my own son – the ones I lost.'

Vera never lost an opportunity to remind her daughter about her various miscarriages.

'I think he should come and stay with me on his vacation,' Vera went on. 'He loves New York, and I bet he misses it too.'

'Hey Katherine – what the hell's goin' on – we're ready for you.' The assistant director rapped exasperatedly at Katherine's door. 'Old Albie's blowin' his top.'

Makes a change from blowing his lines, thought Katherine; then said: 'OK – I'll be there, I'm talking to my mother.'

'Yeah, yeah – always the personal,' the assistant grumbled.

'Why don't you come and visit Tommy out here, Mom? He'd love that; so would I.'

'Oh no, honey, I can't travel on planes. You know it's bad for my asthma.'

'Well, maybe Tom can spend a long weekend with you after France.' There was another bang at the door. 'Look Mama, I've *got* to go.'

'Of course,' Vera said frostily. 'Never enough time to talk to your poor old Mum.'

She was only half serious but Katherine could hear the loneliness in her voice. TV, chocolate and gossip magazines weren't enough to fill anyone's life.

'OK Mama, I *will* call you tomorrow, I promise, and we'll have a long chat. Bye now,' Katherine said firmly and hung up.

Later she called Steve to invite him and Mandy to dinner, but Steve said Mandy was visiting her mother in San Diego for a week.

'Come and have lunch with me tomorrow, instead,' he suggested. 'In my office. I'll have a surprise for you.'

When Katherine saw what was laid out on Steve's coffee table she was delighted.

A twelve-ounce pot of Sevruga caviar, sour cream in a delicate white china bowl, finely chopped onions, eggs and parsley. Two baked potatoes steamed on a silver dish, and there was a bottle of ninety-per-cent proof Russian vodka, in a chilled silver container.

'What about my waistline? Maximilian'll kill me!'

'What the eye doesn't see the heart doesn't grieve over.' He pulled out a chair for her. 'He'll never know.'

'What's that from?' she asked.

'Oh – I made that up.'

'What a delicious feast!' Katherine laughed. 'Oh my God – booze! It's against studio rules. We'll both get fired now.'

'No way,' he said. 'Vodka?'

'Oh why not? What the hell. I'm fed up with their damn rules anyway, aren't you?'

'Well some of 'em work, and some of 'em are just to intimidate the poverty-stricken workers.' Steven scooped a heaped spoonful of caviar on to his potato, and squeezed lemon juice liberally over it.

'How did you manage to cook this potato?'

'Haven't you heard of the microwave? I'm not in the same league as Mandy when it comes to cooking, but I know what I like to eat after a hard morning in Gabe Heller's salt mines. Since I know you adore caviar too – why not?'

'Why not, indeed. Makes a change from tuna on rye.'

Katherine had a hearty appetite when she allowed herself to eat, and they both tucked in with gusto. At first they ate in silence, secure as only friends can be who know each other really well. Then he asked at last.

'How's Tommy doing?'

Her face clouded. 'I just called him. He sounded – well, okay, I guess. I didn't see him this morning because he was still sleeping. He's been sleeping a lot recently. I've kept him out of school for a few days too, because I guess he's been so knocked out by this thing.'

'At least Gabe's been keeping the press off the lot,' said Steve.

'I know,' she shuddered. 'They're like a bunch of cockroaches. You never know when they're going to come out and terrify you. I'd like to stamp on the lot of them. You know what's so terrible, Steve? – I just don't trust anyone around here any more.'

'Don't get paranoid, hon. Not everyone's your enemy. What about that story in Army's column? That was flattering.'

'Yes, I'm actually getting a bit of good publicity – makes a change.'

She took a sip of vodka, her eyes sparkling.

'You deserve it,' he said. 'I bet those two English bitches, male and female, were tearing their toupees out when they read it.'

Kitty laughed. She was eating with relish. It was the first time for days she'd been able to eat properly, and she was beginning to feel that life was worth living after all. 'And my scenes in this show and the next are *great*! My cup is beginning to run over.'

Steven avoided Katherine's eyes. He simply couldn't tell her that Gabe Heller had ordered him to change her scenes in the next show, and replace them with juicier ones for Eleonor and Albert. He'd fought Kitty's corner hard – possibly too hard for safety – but he couldn't afford to lose his job, even for her sake. Now he found that he couldn't bear to burst her bubble; to erase the first hint of real happiness he'd seen on her face for months.

'I think Tommy's going to be OK,' she said. 'I know he's still suffering from the divorce, but I'm going to make it up to him. I'm going to try to be the best darn mother any kid could have.'

Steve raised his tumbler of vodka. 'I'll drink to that. It's about time you stopped getting the fuzzy end of the lollipop.'

'*Some Like It Hot?*' she asked.

'Right on. Hey, you're getter better.'

A week later the *National Sun*, sleaziest of all the supermarket rags, ran their cover story.

'I'm so miserable I want to kill myself. I hate my mother. She's a stuck-up bitch. She's just like the character she plays in that stupid soap. My father is a great guy but she's turned him into a drunk. I wish I were dead.'

Steven brought it apologetically to her dressing room in the morning. Katherine read the piece with horror. It consisted of two pages, detailing the alleged misery of Tommy's life with her, and quoting extensively from a diary he had supposedly written. Katherine could not believe the vileness of it.

'I can't finish this,' she said to Steven. 'Oh my God, what can I do about it? Tommy'll go crazy when he reads it; but Johnny and my mother will shit bricks. He'll blame me for it, I know he will.'

'Where the hell did they get that story?' Steven asked. '*Did* Tommy write a diary?'

'I guess he must have done, but I should think it was several years ago,' said Katherine wearily, 'I just don't know how that rag got hold of it, or why someone at the studio couldn't have killed it. Could you get me Brenda on the telephone, please?'

The runner rapped on the door, popped his head around, and handed in a large manila envelope. 'Rewrites,' he barked, before disappearing along the corridor to the other cells.

'More rewrites?' Katherine asked. 'Why so many? They're going crazy this week.'

Steven shrugged uneasily. 'Sorry, sweets. We're just trying to make your part better.'

If Katherine had been less preoccupied, she would probably have noticed the evasion, but instead she picked up her phone and dialled. It rang for a long time before Brenda came puffing to answer it.

'Hello.'

'Brenda, have you seen the stuff in that rag?'

'I certainly have. Maria brought it back from the market this morning – And *that's* when she discovered her missing husband.'

'Her missing husband? What the hell's going on?'

'What's going on? Ha! *Everything* has hit the fan here, honey. Everything. Pedro's gone. Scarpered without a word, and not only has *he* pissed off, but he's taken Suzy with him! Maria's going mad.'

'But she's Maria's *daughter*! For God's sake, she's only seventeen. What a nightmare.'

'Obviously Pedro and Suzy had been...well, you know, schtupping.'

'Yes, I guess they were,' Katherine said grimly. 'But I also reckon that Suzy's not the only thing Pedro's been interfering with.'

Charlie rapped on the door and called, 'Ready for you, Katherine. Pronto.'

'Okay,' she shouted. 'Have Pedro and Suzy really gone?'

'Definitely. They've done a bunk – clothes, car and all. They've fucked off – gone bye-bye. Exit left, no applause. Oh shit, I can hear Maria in screaming hysterics from here. It's pandemonium.'

'I bet.'

'We think Pedro had something to do with that disgusting story.'

'Of course he did,' sighed Katherine, as Charlie banged on the door for the second time. 'He obviously stole Tommy's diary and flogged it to the paper. What an unspeakable thing to do. Look – I can't talk now, I'll talk to you later Brenda – but *please* – don't say anything to anyone, and for God's sake, keep Tommy away from that toerag that calls itself a newspaper.'

Katherine put down the phone. Steven went to her and wrapped his arms tightly round her.

'Just remember, Kitty, I'm always here if you need me,' he said gruffly.

'I know,' she whispered. 'And I can't tell you how much that means to me, Steve.'

Katherine kept her mobile switched off all day, determined to call Vera before her mother called her, and hoping to find her in a better mood.

At eight thirty she rang, and a sleepy voice answered.

'Mama I'm so sorry – did I wake you?'

'It's OK, Kitty; I'm in bed, but I'm awake. I've been trying you all day – what's all *this* stuff with the papers now?'

'It's a bunch of cheap baloney, Mama. A diary he wrote years ago – I'm dealing with it.'

'Yes – well – poor boy... – that won't happen when he's staying with me – '

Katherine could hear the sound of Johnny Carson's opening monologue in the background. Vera adored Johnny Carson.

'I'll have Tommy call you tomorrow, Mama – he's OK I promise you – he's going to be just fine.'

John Bennet woke up from a fitful sleep. His head was throbbing badly, but then his head was always throbbing these days. When you knocked back a couple of bottles of vodka a day, intermixed with as many joints as you could inhale without keeling over, your head was rarely together. He leaned over the bed to pick up a bottle from the floor, tipping it to parched lips.

'Shit,' he mumbled, 'It's fuckin' empty.'

He fumbled under the bed, then got up and went through to the living room. He grappled under the sofa and then ransacked the kitchen, but could only find a couple of half-filled cans of stale beer.

'Shit.' He went back to the bedroom and pulled on a pair of unwashed tracksuit bottoms, sticking his feet into a pair of tatty moccasins. Checking that his pockets contained enough cash, he staggered down to the Seven Eleven store, which was located conveniently on the corner of his West Hollywood block.

As he handed over twenty dollars for two bottles of the cheapest vodka, his eye was caught by the headlines in the *National Sun*.

'Shit,' he expostulated yet again, grabbing the paper and throwing another dollar to the counter-manager. 'That's my fucking son, fer Chrissake.'

Back at the apartment, Johnny sat on his unmade bed, swigging vodka from the bottle and reading the article. He smiled grimly when he read the references to himself. They were glowing – as flattering towards Johnny as they were harsh and vituperative towards Katherine. But that didn't make him feel any better. His alcohol-fuddled brain still felt fatherly love for his son. But he no longer had the energy or the wherewithal to show his affection.

He lit a Camel, one of the thirty or forty strong cigarettes he would smoke that day, and inhaled deeply. The colour of the walls gave testament to the amount of cigarettes he had smoked. No one could distinguish any more between stains from cigarette smoke, and traces of the original yellow flower-patterned wallpaper. Johnny had lived here since he and Katherine had gone their separate ways. She was paying the rent, which wasn't a lot by Hollywood standards, but it had a decent enough address to give to potential employers.

He finished the article and lit another cigarette. It was time to do something about that bitch. Time to make her as miserable as he was.

Katherine picked up her private hotline on the second ring. It was the lunch hour, Brenda was holding the fort at the house.

Katherine was glad to be alone. Munching a tuna salad and sipping iced tea, she read again the foul article about her son. All day the telephone had rung at her publicists, and all day reporters had been trying to get to her, even bribing some of the crew to let them on the set.

'Hullo,' she answered quietly.

'You bitch. Your fuckin' ego is ruining our son's life. You cow. How dare you do these things to him? Who the hell do you think you are?'

Her heart started beating faster, but she tried to remain calm.

'I'm not going to listen to you, Johnny. It's all a bunch of damn lies, and you know it. You *can't* believe what you read in those rags, you simply *can't*.'

'That diary extract isn't lies,' he snapped. 'That sounds exactly like the way Tommy was a coupla years ago.'

'Exactly,' she said crisply. 'The way he *was*. Look – I'm working and I'm not going to have this conversation any longer. Just for your information, Johnny, those quotes were taken from a diary that was stolen *from* Tommy's room. It was something that he wrote about three years ago, when he was just a kid.'

'Oh yeah,' he sneered. 'Who gave 'em the diary then?'

She sighed. 'I'm very sorry to have to admit it, because I'll have to hold myself responsible for being stupid enough to employ him in the first place, but it appears that it was Pedro, my houseman.'

'That lousy spic,' he sneered. 'Don't you vet your fuckin' staff? You've always had terrible taste in people, Katherine.'

'That's probably why I married you,' she snapped.

'Funny. Yeah, you think you're real funny, Miss Big TV Star. Well let me tell you something, Ms Katherine Bennet. When I get on my feet again, and I *will* – you better not doubt that – I'm going to have Tommy come *live* with me.'

'I've always told you,' she said quietly, 'that you could see and be with Tommy whenever you wanted, but it seems to me that you never want to see him.'

'That's because I've been sick.' His voice was self-pitying, 'but I'm getting better now, and I've got this job coming up.'

'That's great,' Katherine feigned enthusiasm. 'What job, Johnny?'

'Never you mind. None of your damn business. You're not the only one with contacts in this town, you know, Katherine. I've got friends too. Important friends. And they haven't forgotten that I'm a good actor, a really good actor, not some TV twerp. I mean, were *you* nominated for any awards when we were living in New York?'

'No, Johnny. I wasn't.'

'Well I was. I was nominated for my Hamlet – remember? Best newcomer of the year.'

She certainly did remember the year. It was 1970, over fifteen years ago. What had he done since then, other than some off-Broadway revivals and a double handful of voice-overs? She banished that thought. It was churlish. She really did wish good things for her ex, even though he was his own worst enemy.

'So, what are you trying to say to me, Johnny? This is my lunch hour, and I'm trying to learn lines.'

'Naturally the great diva is busy, as usual. Just like a little worker bee, aren't you, sweetheart?'

'Look I've got to go. Do you want to see Tommy this weekend?'

'Why? You wanna get rid of him?'

'No, I do *not* want to get rid of him.' She was exasperated now, unable to eat the salad half congealing on her plate. 'I thought you might like to exercise your fatherly rights for a change.'

'I'll let you know.' His voice was becoming slurred, 'I'll let you know in a couple of days.' He sounded sleepy. She knew that he must have been on some vodka and dope.

'Well, I'm taking him to France for a couple of weeks in my hiatus. That OK by you?'

'Yeah – yeah – s'fine.'

'Okay, Johnny,' she said brightly. 'Well give me a call when you want to see him. Any time.'

She hung up and stared at her reflection in the mirror. A gaunt, haggard face looked back: red painted lips, black painted eyes, pale and frightened. She looked haunted.

As if on cue there was a knock on the door. 'Ten minutes, Katherine.'

'I'll be right there.' Quickly she swallowed a few more bites of tuna. They're not going to be able to blame me for any delays today, she thought. Not this time.

Maria greeted Katherine at the door when she came home. Her plump body was shaking with sobs.

'*Señora*, oh *señora*, I'm so so sorry, *señora*. I don't know what happened to Pedro. Please, please, forgive. I've asked the Blessed Virgin Mary to forgive him. I know that Pedro was not always a good man. He had his faults like all men. But I thought I had changed him.' She started to sob again. 'Now he's gone off, and with my baby too.'

'Maria, please, you mustn't torture yourself.' Katherine felt completely helpless. She wanted to go and see Tommy. She wanted to lie down, she was exhausted from the day's work and stress, but Maria insisted on clinging on to her, shaking hysterically. Brenda walked in from the office, clutching a pile of faxes.

'You want the good news, or the bad?'

Maria, with a final sob, went into the kitchen, mumbling, 'I'll get dinner ready, *señora*.'

Katherine walked into the stark drawing room, took off her raincoat, and sat down on the sofa with a sigh. 'I can't take any more bad news, Bren, not until I've had a drink.'

'Coming up,' Brenda handed her a frosty Martini. 'I made it as soon as I heard the tyres on the gravel.'

'Where's Tommy?' asked Katherine. 'How is he? Has he seen that dreadful piece?'

'Well, he – we don't exactly know,' Brenda said slowly. 'Maybe somebody told him about it at school. But he's gone to the movies with Todd. He'll be back about nine.'

'Right. So why don't you give me the good news first.'

'Well, the good news is that *The Skeffingtons* went up one point in the Neilsons last week.'

'That isn't such wonderful news for me, but it's great for Gabe and Luther. Is that the best good news you've got?'

'Well, the cleaners got the stain out of your green chiffon.'

'Oh great, that's *really* made my day.' Katherine threw back the icy vodka, feeling it glide down her throat and give her a burst of much needed energy. She stared at Brenda. 'I want the bad now.'

Brenda handed her a fax. 'This just arrived from Gabe's secretary. Royal command performance I'm afraid.'

Katherine took it from her and read: '*Dear Katherine, please be at my office at one o'clock tomorrow for an important meeting. Regards Gabe.*'

'Sweet,' she said. 'Terse, and rather threatening, wouldn't you think?'

'Don't think the worst. They could just want you to – um – change your hair style,' Brenda said brightly, 'or maybe get a nose-job so you can complete with Miss No-Nose Norman?'

They giggled, then Katherine sighed.

'No, I feel it's bad vibes time. They're going to do something drastic for the show, I sensed it from Steve. He could hardly look at me today. Oh well, as my dear old mother says, when rape is inevitable, relax and enjoy it.' Katherine took a handful of stale peanuts from a bowl, then glanced at the pile of mail which Brenda was carrying. 'What's in that parcel?'

'Oh another of those gold records. You wanna see it?'

'Of course.' Katherine pulled the box towards her, opened it, and stared at a gold disc identical to the one already on the mantelpiece.

'What's that one called?' asked Brenda.

'*You are my Lucky Star*,' Katherine smiled. 'And the card says "How I wish you were." '

'Well, maybe it's a good omen. You're certainly one star that could do with a bit of luck right now. But this guy sounds like a crank, Kitty.'

'Well, if he gets to be a nuisance like that last one who kept sending the candy, we'll have to call the cops in.'

'Oh, that was a heap of laughs. That guy was psycho-city.' Katherine looked at the disc again. 'I have a feeling that this one's OK.'

Katherine and Brenda hurried across the lot to Gabe Heller's office.

'So I wonder what he does want,' Katherine said.

'Probably wants to fuck you, or give you your own spin-off!'

'Oh sure, dream on. Either of those would be a miracle. I'm Gabe and Luther's pet piranha at the moment.'

'Don't take any flak from 'em,' Brenda replied, heading towards the commissary. 'And at least get some lunch! Good luck.'

Katherine was ushered promptly into Gabe's inner sanctum, an impressive suite of interconnecting offices, buzzing with activity.

The enormously tall, fat producer sat behind a giant glass desk which he almost dwarfed. A tiny baseball cap perched on his huge bald head. A riot of clashing green and blue chintz sofas, over stuffed chairs, and fake Regency commodes were placed around the room in orderly profusion. Sitting on a multi-coloured sofa, was the other pivotal partner of *The Skeffingtons* production team: Luther Immerman.

Luther was small, dark and Jewish: a man who had struggled for years in the pitiless hills of Hollywood, and finally pulled himself up the ladder by a lot more than just talent. At fifty-five he had become the number one producer-writer in television with three hot shows on prime time, of which *The Skeffingtons* was the hottest. Luther was actually the brains of the team and the hard one. Although most people were afraid of Gabe, he was really just a big pussy cat underneath the superficial toughness.

Today Gabe was ominously stern-faced. Katherine smiled coolly, and plonked herself in one of the plump armchairs. Enormous pairs of ivory tusks and deer heads were attached to the wall behind Gabe's desk, sandwiched in between about a thousand plaques and awards from his lengthy and illustrious television career. On a bookshelf stuffed with leather-bound copies of every script he had ever produced, was a jeroboam of vintage champagne, with a label covered in signature squiggles. These represented the entire cast of *Serial Killer II*, Gabe's blockbusting success of last summer's movie season. There was so much TV and movie memorabilia scattered throughout his office, that Katherine found it hard to concentrate. Photographs of Gabe mugging with Stallone, Schwarzenegger and Nicholson were intermingled with glossy black and white forties glamour stills of Greer Garson, Claudette Colbert and Lana Turner.

At sixteen Gabe Heller had started out in the MGM Mail Room. He was an avid movie maniac even then, and slowly but surely graduated up the ranks until he was a top film producer. Having made a dozen box office hits in the sixties and seventies, he decided to dip his toes into the potentially lucrative waters of TV production, and soon became even more successful.

He loved Hollywood, and he loved the stars who made it what it was, but he also agreed wholeheartedly with the old studio bosses' maxim: don't ever let the inmates take over the asylum. This was why Katherine had been called on to his Aubusson carpet today. Since he hadn't remained at the top of the TV heap by being Mr Sweetness and Light, Gabe got straight to the point.

'Have you seen this, Katherine?' he handed her a faxed clipping from the New York tabloid which her mother read avidly.

'The Diva tore off her endangered species fur cape, and throwing it into frail 69-year-old Albert Amory's face, screamed, 'I've had enough of this old f—. If he can't remember his f—g lines, get another actor who can. I'm not standing around in one hundred degree heat to work with a washed up old b— like him.' The Georgia Poison-Peach, as she has been aptly named, then stormed off the set into the air-conditioned airport lounge, where she insisted on drinking an entire bottle of white wine, refusing to return to the scene unless it was filmed only on her close up, with Amory's stand-in saying his lines.'

'How *can* you believe this nonsense?' said Katherine. 'It's complete crap.'

'Enough crew members have already corroborated the story.' Luther sniffed.

'Oh, really! Who may I ask? Albert Amory's cronies? His publicist, his make-up man, and his wigsticker? They'd say the Pope was Jewish if Albert told them to. Oh God, it's absolute bullshit. A *complete* fabrication. Ask anyone what happened on the set that day. It was boiling hot. Albert was going up on his lines – the director was furious. Why am I the fall guy in this? It's utter lies – you *must* realize that?'

'Apparently this story has broken worldwide,' Luther said coldly. 'This is very, very bad for you, Kitty.'

'Just because it's in the newspapers doesn't mean it's true. I mean, have you seen that horrible story about my son? No one believes such nonsense, surely? Do you *really* think I could do those things, Gabe – do you?'

'It's not just the newspapers,' Gabe said wearily; he was fond of Katherine, admired her pluck and drive, but he had to keep her in line. He couldn't play favourites, especially not with her.

He had had enormous problems in the past two seasons with Albert Amory. To say that Albert was jealous of his co-star was an understatement. Priding himself on being an affable British gentleman actor of the old school, Albert was exceedingly intolerant of those who did not share his illustrious (and some said imaginary) theatrical past. If the cast heard one more time that Richard Burton and Albert had both started their careers at the same time by carrying spears at the Old Vic they would scream.

His close friendship with Gabe Heller dated back to World War II, when they had become drinking and whoring buddies over one long hedonistic week in bomb-blitzed London. Both had been very young, and Gabe newly married. Now, more than forty years later, Hollywood insiders believed that, somewhere in the events of that long ago week lay, the clue to Albert Amory's excessive influence over Gabe Heller.

Gabe knew Katherine infuriated Albert because she wouldn't acknowledge that there was a pecking order among the actors in the show. In most TV shows, cast and crew acknowledged one particular actor as their leader. On *The Skeffingtons* it was supposed to be Albert Amory.

There was a clause in Amory's contract precluding any other performer from making more money than he did.

Another clause gave him approval of his leading ladies, particularly those he had to kiss, and yet another said that he must have more dialogue than anyone else in one out of three episodes. The final stipulation was for publicity to send out as much copy on him as they did on anyone else. Albert had already arranged for three publicists from ABN to be fired, because of what he considered to be excessive coverage on Katherine Bennet.

For the past two seasons Gabe had been bombarded with complaints from Albert. One particular incident had caused such a furore that Gabe would never forget it. It was Steven Leigh's famous bubble bath scene. As usual, when anything faintly sexual was being shot, the ABN photographer turned up. As soon as the film was developed, the photographer realized that in one frame some of the soap bubbles had burst – clearly revealing one of Katherine's nipples.

This negative soon found its way, via a disloyal photo-lab assistant, to the cover of a pornographic magazine, and thence to the international newspapers. Far from damaging her in the eyes of viewers, the picture had vastly enhanced her popularity.

But not with Amory. He had stormed into Gabe's office in a towering rage, carrying the offending rag as if it were a dog turd.

'She has low moral standards,' he barked. 'We're a family show, Gabe, and this – this creature is contributing to the breakdown, not only of our series, but of our society as a whole. You *must* get rid of her.' Then with a sly look at the oil portrait of Selma, Gabe's enormous wife of forty-five years, whispered:

'Heard anything from you-know-who in London recently?' Gabe stammered, 'No – but don't worry Alb, I'll take care of Kitty.'

Ever since then, one particular ex-tabloid hack, now working for ABN, was employed to portray Albert and

Eleonor, the two 'good' leads, favourably, and make Katherine and Tony Bertolini look bad in the media. Katherine played the part of Georgia so convincingly that it was a piece of cake for the publicity department to portray her as the Poison Peach in real life.

But no amount of bad publicity could prevent the television public from loving Georgia Skeffington, because – although the character was manipulative, sexually predatory and devious – Katherine also played her with charm and a wicked sense of humour. It was no coincidence that, for the past three years, Georgia had shot to the top of the league for favourite girls' names. For the producers and Katherine's jealous co-stars this only added salt to the wound.

'We cannot – I repeat we *cannot* have our actors behave in such an outrageous and unprofessional fashion. It's against every principle,' Gabe said now.

'But I *didn't* do it – I *didn't* – don't you *understand* – ?' Katherine was almost weeping with frustration. 'It was boiling hot... I just took off my cape... I didn't throw it at Albert...oh shit.' She couldn't be bothered to argue.

'Now, we understand that you've also been late into make-up practically every morning this season,' Luther intoned, consulting a thick sheaf of papers.

'No, I'm not. It takes me less time than the others to get made up. I've *told* the assistant director to put on the call sheet that I only need half an hour, instead of an hour, but they don't list...'

They weren't listening, either, as Luther continued relentlessly. 'Last season not only did you refuse to wear at least fourteen different outfits which Maximilian designed *especially* for you, but on at least five or six occasions, you threw a tantrum in the fitting room and stalked out, leaving the fitters in tears.'

'I did not! The *newspapers* said I did. I just insisted that a couple of outfits weren't right for my character, and it only happened once or twice. How can you believe the newspapers – how can you?' Katherine blew her nose.

'We have people in Wardrobe who say you scream and shout, you insult and attack the fitters, that you throw garments on to the floor and grind them in with your heel.'

'I – do not –' Katherine wanted to burst into tears but she was not going to give them the satisfaction.

'It's all here, Katherine. Everything. Here, look.' Gabe held up a huge handful of clippings. 'Dozens of stories. All pointing to you as far worse behaved than Georgia could ever hope to be.

'Katherine walks offset' – 'Katherine insults Albert Amory' – 'Katherine refuses to work with Eleonor Norman' – 'Katherine pretends to be ill and holds up shooting for days'.

On and on. You know the old saying – there's no smoke without fire.'

'This is unbelievable,' Katherine's throat was dry and swollen. 'You're condemning me for things I never did. You're accusing me on the basis of newspaper clippings!'

'Well, you'd better start behaving yourself from today, Katherine, or we'll start writing you *out*,' Luther said belligerently. 'You may have noticed that you have fewer scenes in the next episode. It wouldn't take much for Georgia to have a bad accident. We could put her in a coma for a few weeks – then decide whether she lives or dies. We made you and we can break you. Don't you forget it.'

'I won't,' Katherine said quietly. 'And I've already been in a coma – OK, OK – I get the picture. I'll behave, I always have done, but I'm going to say this one more time. None of these stories is true, Gabe, not one of them, I swear it.'

She stood up and stared at them.

'I need this job,' she said simply, breaking one of Hollywood's cardinal rules, which was never to let them know you needed *anything*. She was making forty thousand dollars a week, and she couldn't afford to lose it.

'So, play the game, then, Katherine dear,' Gabe said pleasantly. 'Play by our rules. Do everything everyone tells you to. *Don't* make any more waves. None at all, and we'll all get along just fine, I know we will.'

Katherine nodded bitterly.

'Well, we'll see you at the TV Favourites Awards next week,' Luther said brightly. 'No hard feelings, Katherine dear – OK?'

Katherine had planned on giving the TV Favourites Awards a miss this year. But there was no way she could do that now.

'You can go now, dear.' Gabe stuck out an enormous paw. 'And let's be friends, Kitty, like always – OK dear?' She shook the hand and muttered goodbye. Then, stumbling across the two-inch pile carpet, made her way back to the relative sanity of the sound stage.

'They're ready for you in five, hon,' announced Brenda, the minute she arrived in her dressing room. 'How was lunch?'

'Lunch – ha! – *I* was lunch,' hissed Katherine, taking a bite from an over-ripe banana. 'And if I get through the next few weeks in one piece, Bren, it'll be a bloody miracle, I swear it.'

CHAPTER FOUR

Katherine knew Tommy was home, because the heavy padlock on his door knob was unlocked.

'What do you want?' said a surly voice, when she knocked.

'I need to talk to you, Tommy, it's important.'

'I've got nothing to say to you, Mom.' The 'Mom' was bitterly sarcastic. 'Did you see that lousy fuckin' newspaper?'

'Yes Tommy, I saw it, and I know how upset you must be. It's total trash, darling – garbage. Please don't take any notice of it. Let me come in, Tommy, we need to talk.'

'Aw, shit, Mom – OK, wait a minute.'

Footsteps shuffled to the door, and there he stood, dishevelled and gypsy-eyed, half-man, half-boy: her son, with a face filled with pain.

The room was a junkyard of opened videos, comic books and piles of dirty clothes. The stale smell of fast food hung in the air, but she wasn't about to give him a hard time about any of that. Not now. She attempted to hug him but he shrugged her away, and went to slouch on the bed, where MTV was blasting away.

'When did you read it?' she asked resignedly.

'This morning – every crappy word.' His voice was jeering and tough, but his tightly hunched shoulders and tense, angry lips betrayed his misery. 'Not only me, but the whole fuckin' school must've read it, Mom. I just don't know how I can face any of them any more. I feel like a total asshole.'

'Tommy, I know this is hard for you to understand.' Katherine sat tentatively on the bed, thankful he didn't attempt to move away. 'But I'm almost as hurt by this as you. I feel responsible. It's the most horrible, cruel thing that anyone could possibly do, particularly to a child.'

'Yeah, you better believe the cruel part. But I'm not a kid any more, Mom.' He pulled away from her to look at the bald black rapper intoning, *'Bitches are only around to ball – Make 'em scream, git 'em to fall'*.

Katherine wondered how many of the kids and teenagers who watched their rap idols, actually listened to the lyrics. Did they understand that these Gangsta-Rappers were actually preaching hatred of women, and admiration for drugs, gang warfare, and violence?

Tommy shook his shoulders, strumming his fingers in time to the music. What kind of influence did these songs have on him? Katherine wondered.

'Just because these things happen to *you*, Mom, doesn't mean that I should have them happen to me. Just 'cause you're some stupid TV star, doesn't mean that my life has to be ruined, does it?' His green eyes were teary, in spite of his anger.

'No, darling, you're absolutely right. It's an outrage, and they're nothing but scum. I've already got my lawyers on it, and I promise we're going to sue their pants off.'

'Mom, they used my diary from when I was a little kid. It was years ago. They *stole* it.'

'Yes I know, I know – it's unspeakable.'

'But did they say that it was when I was a kid?' he asked. 'Did they say they were written by a twelve-year old who didn't know nuthin' from shit then?' He stared at her accusingly. 'Nah, they say "Tommy Bennet, aged sixteen". I'm not even sixteen until next month. It makes me sound like the pits, it makes me sound like the Nerd of the Western World.'

'Tommy, there's absolutely nothing I can do about this now,' she said. 'I've got Barry Lefkovitz on it, and he is going to stop it being published anywhere else.'

'Fat lot of good that'll do me,' he snapped. 'Do you think I care if it's published in fuckin' Australia or fuckin' Europe, or wherever?'

Katherine ignored the outburst of bad language and temper. She longed to cradle her son, rock him in her arms as she had done when he was a baby, soothe his pain. But of course she couldn't.

'I wanna go to sleep now, Mom. Shit – I'm glad I don't have to go to school tomorrow.'

'That's a good idea. Sleep, and don't worry about what the kids say – they'll forget it in a couple of days. Honestly Tom, believe me, yesterday's newsprint is tomorrow's garbage.'

'OK – I'll try.' He attempted a smile.

'Well, thank God there's only another week before the hiatus starts,' she said brightly. 'Brenda got the plane tickets today; we're off on our grand tour, darling.'

He brightened perceptibly. 'Yeah? Where do we start from?'

'First we fly to London. We'll stay at the Connaught for three or four days, see all the sights. There's a ton of stuff to do in London. Theatres – museums – palaces – it's great, you'll love it. I haven't been there for years. Then we'll hit Paris.'

'Can we go to the Crazy Horse?'

'You bet, and we'll go to the Moulin Rouge, and up to the top of the Eiffel Tower. It's so tall we'll probably get nosebleeds. Then we'll do the Left Bank, and the Right Bank, and Pigalle and Montmartre, and Montparnasse, and we'll stuff ourselves with croissants, and drink *café au lait* in sidewalk cafés all day long.'

'And watch the world go by?' he said.

'Yes.' She smiled. 'Then we'll fly down to the South of France, to the little house I've rented near St Tropez. We'll spend a week or two there together, then, when you go to Fire Island, I'll stay on for a bit.'

'Great. Sounds cool. Hey listen, Mom, I'll try not to take this too hard. It's not me it bothers so much, it's the other kids, y'know?'

The sadness on Katherine's face made Tommy blurt out, 'I guess things have been tough for you too, huh Mom?'

'A bit.' She nodded. 'But you know what they say – when the going gets tough, the tough get going – or go shopping. Whatever. We'll do both. I'm going to be in the mood for some *serious* French shopping.' She leaned over and risked a hug. 'I've got to get up at the usual witching hour tomorrow, darling, five o'clock, and you should get some rest now.'

'Okay.' She turned at the door to smile at him.

He felt a surge of affection, and wanted to say, 'I love you Mom', but he couldn't. Instead he gave a cheery wave, a 'G'night Mom', and took a huge bite of pizza, before turning back to the television.

'Surprise, surprise.' Brenda threw the purple-bound final script of the season on to the sofa. 'Just look at this piece of absolute crap.'

'What's the matter with it?'

Katherine was having a pink satin and lace gown fitted by Maximilian. She had been standing for half an hour, and had had at least eight pins stuck into her.

'Read it and weep.' Brenda gave a meaningful nod towards Maximilian, who was known to be the eyes and ears of the lot.

Maximilian exchanged glances with Becky. They had already read the script, so they knew what Brenda was talking about, and neither of them wanted to be around when Katherine found out what was in store for her. Not that they weren't fond of her, but show business was show business. Maximilian quickly finished the fitting, and they both left the room.

Katherine went to her dressing-table chair and started repairing her makeup. 'Right, Bren, shall I read it, or do you want to tell me all the gory details?'

Brenda sighed. 'I'd better tell you. This episode ends with Naughty Georgia, Saintly Eleonor, and Wicked Tony trapped on a yacht, in an explosion.'

'Really, that's never been done before,' said Katherine sarcastically. 'I suppose somebody dies?'

'You bet somebody dies,' Brenda said grimly. 'The only thing is, the audience ain't gonna to know who the corpse is, until the beginning of next season. There's a dead body, or bodies, and the last line in the script is: "My God, they're dead". They *don't* say whether the corpse is male or female, and they don't say who it is, or how many have snuffed it.'

Katherine stared at the purple script.

'Then I guess that little number holds my fate.'

'Well, I wouldn't go so far as to say that. But let's face it honeychile – Popular Petula you haven't been recently, so if those piranhas in suits are looking to get rid of you –' she shrugged, 'They'll just do it their way – a nice clean explosion at sea. Not even an eyelash left. D'you think they give a shit?'

'No, I don't think they'd give a tiny tosslet.' Katherine winced as the inevitable knock came: 'On set in five minutes Katherine. Mush-mush.'

'What d'ya think she is – a huskie?' said Brenda indignantly. 'Well, my vacation in France should give me nice peaceful time to think – Jeez, what a bummer.'

'Don't think about it now.' Brenda helped her into a black satin dress embroidered with jet flowers. 'You're still worth a dozen of any of the rest of those chumps that call themselves actors. Christ, Albert *still* can't remember his goddamned lines, not even when he's got them written on cards all over the set.'

'Unlike Richard Burton, I guess he didn't learn enough at Laurence Olivier's knee.'

'Richard Burton wouldn't ever have considered this shit.' Brenda snorted.

'Well, screw it.' Katherine carefully placed an enormous lavender organza and straw hat, covered in black roses, on her head. 'And screw all the suits too. I don't give a damn if I have to go back to earning a crust off Broadway. At least the piranhas there tell you the truth. Hey, do you think this outfit is just a touch over the top?' She looked wryly in the mirror.

'Just a smidgeon.' Brenda smiled. 'I wouldn't dare wear it at Safeways. But why change the habits of a TV lifetime?'

Kitty's mother called on Sunday afternoon to report on her latest love, as identified by *The Star*.

'Last week it was Clint Eastwood; this week it's Don Johnson. What the hell's going on, Kitty?'

'Oh Mom, it's just a bunch of lies. Ignore it.'

'Yes, well, you must be careful, Kit-Kat. You're not as young as you were, and you're getting yourself a bit of a reputation as a good-time gal. That's not nice for a lady.'

'Mama, for goodness sake, I'm almost forty-four years old. I'm not a kid any more. Do you really believe I'm dating every eligible male from Johnny Carson to Arsenio Hall? It's *ridiculous*.'

'Well, the tabloids say you are, and they're not always wrong. You know the old saying, dear; where there's smoke there's...'

'Yeah, Mama, I know. Look, I've got to take a shower now. It's the TV Favourites Awards tonight, and the wrecking crew'll be on my doorstep any minute.'

'But it's only one thirty there. How long is it going to take you?'

'Hours, Mama, absolutely hours. It starts at five thirty. As you pointed out, I'm not as young as I was, and I need a lot of help to face these paparazzi.'

'Well, I'll be watching you,' said Vera. 'Who's your date for this year?'

'Tony – my schtupp of the month on *The Skeffingtons*. And he's gay, so don't worry.'

'Gay? Be careful, Kit-Kat – especially when you do those kissing scenes. They're so realistic, dear.'

'*Mama*! For God's sake!' Katherine heard the bell. 'That's Blackie at the door now. I've got to run. 'Bye now; enjoy the Awards.'

'Good luck, dear.'

'Dates!' said Katherine grimly. She couldn't even remember the last time she'd been on a proper date. Her career left no time for romance. The portals of her heart were firmly locked against intruders, and that was the way she expected it to stay.

Katherine started her elaborate toilette for the Television Favourites Awards at two o'clock on Sunday afternoon. This gave her three and a half hours before the white stretch limousine came to fetch her.

First Maximilian bustled in carrying the dress. He and Kitty had spent hours thumbing through the latest issues of *L'Officiel*, and French and Italian *Vogue*, and had put together, from the top designers, a confection of pure fantasy.

Sheer nude-coloured chiffon souffle, the exact colour of Katherine's skin, was overlaid with cobweb like black lace, embroidered in places with jet bugle beads. Long-sleeved, high-necked and very, very tight, the dress was so constricting that Maximilian warned her not to eat – let alone move suddenly in it.

'*Bella*,' he exclaimed breathily. 'You did what I told you? You 'ave eaten very, very little the past week. No?'

'You bet your butt. Just like you ordered. Half a mug of whatever. Mostly fish.' She shuddered. 'Ugh, how I hate damned fish. Now get me out of this thing, it's killing me, and it's time to put the warpaint on.'

Mona had done Katherine's hair for the last three years, now she washed and conditioned it in the professional backwash installed in her bathroom-cum-beauty room, blow-dried it, applied a ton of stiff setting lotion, and put in several dozen hot rollers. While she cooked, Blackie began his transformation process.

It took an hour to paint, pluck and powder her, during which time Katherine planned all the things she would do with Tommy in Europe. It was exciting. The first time they would be taking a foreign trip together. She prayed they wouldn't have rows.

'*Voilà*,' Blackie pushed the leather chair back up to sitting height and admired his handiwork, 'Picture perfect, honey. You look Dreamboat time.'

Katherine turned her head this way and that, eyes half-closed. 'Not bad. A bit Barbie-dollish, though, and I think I need more eyeliner on the right eye.'

'No,' said Blackie, 'I think the shadow over the left eye is a little too heavy.' With a Q-tip he skilfully blended it, and they both stared critically at the perfect oval face, subtly shaded and enhanced, with more than a dozen different powders and paints.

'Yup. Eat your heart out, Eleonor Norman.' Blackie was smug. 'You look good enough to eat, sweetie, and I sure hope you're gonna win tonight.'

'Thanks, Blackie, but I'm not holding out much hope for that. Tonight's a popularity contest, and Eleonor's been winning that hands down recently. Also, you know the other two girls in our show are new and hot.' She shrugged. 'I know I'm *not* new girl in town any more. In fact I might even be getting past my sell-by date.'

'Never,' he said packing away his paraphernalia. 'You're the best actress on the show, and one of the best on all of the prime time crap. Don't let the bastards get you down, sweetie.'

'Oh I won't,' she said. 'Now scoot, Blackie. It's hairpiece time.' She glanced at the clock. 'Oh God, Tony and Kingsley will be here in forty minutes and tonight we simply *can't* be late.'

Half a mile away Eleonor Norman was committing herself to a similarly tortuous process of preparation. The make-up man had finished her face, but now she was insisting on a third set of false eyelashes. He thought she was absurd, but why should he give a damn? He got well paid for taking ten or fifteen years off these dames' faces, and now that it was Sunday, he was into golden hours.

Craig, Eleonor's favourite hairdresser, brought a huge blonde fluffball of a wig for her to inspect.

'Do you think it's big enough?' Eleonor enquired anxiously.

'Big enough?' Craig looked at the candyfloss confection, and raised his painted eyebrows. 'Honey-*bun*, if it was any bigger, Dolly Parton would claw your effing eyes out.' He tossed his fake auburn ponytail. He wore it clipped to the inside of a straw stetson, to conceal his bald patch.

'And now for the Hollywood lift.' He smiled.

'Oh no, not that.' She pretended to giggle helplessly.

'We want to look twenty-three, don't we, when the big harsh movie cameras are on us?' he said. 'We've gotta think *beauty*, babe, beauty – and we gotta pull those jaws *up*, up, *up*, girl.' Taking a piece of hair from the edge of Eleonor's forehead, he pulled it back as tightly as possible, and started making a tiny braid.

'Ouch,' she yelled, 'Ouch, ouch, ouch, *enough* already!'

'Shut up.' Craig was enjoying his moment of sadism. 'You're gonna get nine more of these little mothers on your scalp before I've finished with you, honey-bunny. So relax and enjoy the pain, and Craig will tell you a few juicy stories.'

Eleonor closed her eyes against the agony, and listened as he regaled her with all the most titillating gossip from Hollywood and Beverly Hills. Craig knew everyone and everything that was going on; it was one of the reasons the ladies liked him – and allowed him to charge a thousand dollars a visit.

Maximilian had arrived with Eleonor's gown and was sitting in the den, admiring the hundreds of photographs of her that decked the walls. There was no doubt that Eleonor had been a beautiful child, and a gorgeous young girl. Unfortunately, age, and her obsession with sunbathing, had cruelly coarsened that early beauty. Her delicate Anglo-Saxon skin was covered in fine lines, and it took twice as long to get her camera-ready as it did Katherine.

Eleonor was no fool, and she allowed her wrecking crew maximum time. She indulged them with presents, took them with her on exotic trips, and rewarded them generously for their loyalty.

Craig, the hairdresser, was a special-occasion treat which Eleonor allowed herself for events as important as the TV Favourites Awards. Her usual hairdresser was Kris, a quietly unassuming young man, who was a wizard with wigs. Tonight Kris stood quietly by, watching Craig, as he teased, twisted and combed, and gossiped. It was Kris, however, who was entrusted with Eleanor's magic black box of tricks, and who would keep a sharp eye on his mistress's coiffure and maquillage all evening long. Eleanor was admired by many a Beverly Hills matron for never glancing in a mirror, or retouching her hair or make-up during the evening. They did not realise that Kris lurked nearby the whole time, ready to step in and make repairs.

Lurking in the doorway, watching the proceedings, was Eleonor's live-in lover Dirk. Dirk was a secretive Scandinavian, with ice-white hair and a florid complexion, who serviced Eleonor in many different ways. He was attractive, in a sinister yet compelling way, but taciturn to the point of mono-syllability. Women drew lots at dinner parties in order not to sit next to him. Rumour was that Eleonor had found Dirk through a lonely hearts ad. Others hinted that he had a penchant for slim black boys, and mustachioed leather queens. But since Dirk confided in no one except Eleonor, the Hollywood set was none the wiser about his very private life.

On the all-too frequent occasions when Eleonor blew her cool on set, Dirk could be relied upon to calm her, and it was clear that whatever went on between the pink satin sheets of her bed, satisfied her completely. Dirk, Kris, and Nina, who doubled as lady's maid and make-up girl, formed the secretive triumvirate that made Eleonor's world turn.

Craig and Nina finished their fussing around Eleonor's face and hair, and Nina carefully slid Eleonor's slim but voluptuous body into the white low-cut sequin sheath which Maximilian had brought.

Tanned twin peaks, a tribute to the expertise of Dr Sylvester Brown, spilled fetchingly out of a deep decolletage which almost touched her chin. Her slender silk-stockinged legs peeped coyly out from the tight skirt, split almost to the crotch.

Eleonor was as expert at dressing for effect, as she was at crying. They wrote special scenes in *The Skeffingtons*, just so that Eleonor could turn on her famous taps. She was the most brilliant weeper the TV screen had ever seen. On the word 'Action', her lips would tremble, her nose twitch, her eyes blink fast and her mouth open. Then her eyes would fill with tears, and a look of mournfulness so profound would wash over her face, that the onlooker would feel like crying too. As soon as the director yelled 'Cut', off went the waterworks, and Eleonor would return to normal, as though nothing had happened.

'Well?' Eleonor turned to Dirk. 'What do you think? How do I look?' She turned this way and that in front of the three-way mirror, fascinated by her reflection.

'Gorgeous.' Dirk walked slowly into the room, his eyes flashing lust. 'Simply gorgeous.'

'Well, that's a lot of words darling from you – thanks. Shit, I'm so nervous I could chew my nails to the quick.' She patted the piled profusion of hair and bit her collagen-enhanced lower lip.

'Why should you be nervous, my angel? Do you want me to calm you down?' he asked softly.

'Well...yes,' she breathed through thickly glossed, cyclamen lips. 'But Dirk – please. Be careful – you mustn't...disturb anything.'

'I shan't,' he whispered, standing assertively in front of her.

Carefully, as though taking precious eggs from their nest, he removed first one breast, and then the other. His hand cupped one, while his skilful lips caressed the other. Throwing back her head, but careful not to dislodge the massive blonde wig, she began to let out little moans. Dirk's hand moved to the slit in her skirt. He found her panty-less and moist, her bronzed thighs bare except for lacy white garters and stocking tops. His fingers worked swiftly. He'd done this many times, and knew exactly how to bring her to fulfilment.

This time, it was something of a record – even for her. It was less than a minute, before her back arched, and she gave the high-pitched little scream which meant that she had reached a climax. Dirk carefully put her manufactured breasts back in place, and handed her a wad of Kleenex.

'Feeling better?' he asked, noting how her face fell, as she searched in vain for a swelling in his trousers.

'No time, sweetheart.' He playfully took her exploring hand and kissed the palm. 'Later, after you've won. Ready?'

'For anything,' smiled Eleonor.

It promised to be the most glittering of all the major Hollywood Awards: wall-to-wall starlets, with dresses cut to their navels; agents wearing insincere smiles; Beverly Hills wives, in twenty-thousand dollar beaded gowns and two million dollars' worth of real jewellery; dozens of paparazzi, and TV cameras galore.

When Katherine stepped out of her stretch white limousine, her figure a sensation, in what looked like sheer jet cobwebs over her nude body, a vast cheer went up from the crowd in the Bleachers.

'I love you Georgia, you peach,' screamed Darren, her most ardent fan, who never missed a public appearance if it was within a seventy-five mile radius of LA.

He rushed forward, in spite of the straining police, to present her with a perfect yellow rose. Once Katherine had told an interviewer that she was quite fond of yellow roses; ever since then, a steady stream had arrived at her house and the studios – most of them from Darren. Katherine was sick of the sight of yellow roses by now, but she sniffed it appreciatively, and then, with a flamboyant gesture, threw it into the centre of the whooping crowd.

A phalanx of policemen sweated behind a red silken rope, in order to keep the baying mob from their prey. Microphones, like snakes' heads in a pit, were pushed forcibly into Katherine's face as she stopped to answer questions.

'Are you excited about being nominated?'

'What does this event really mean to you?'

Kingsley Warwick, Katherine's PR agent, his face flushed and pink, was by her side – dismissing queries, and quickly moving her on. After the unofficial paparazzi and amateur cameramen outside the theatre, then the blocks of fans, and then the electronic media, pushing cameras into her face, it was time to face the great banked mass of professional photographers.

Over two hundred and fifty men and women were there, representing practically every publication in the world. It was necessary for Katherine to adopt various different poses, whilst moving slowly down the line, until each lensman got his quota of snaps. Some of the less professional photographers started pushing and shoving and screaming at one another, and tempers became heated as they vied to get the best picture of Katherine and Tony.

She would be linked to him in the gossip columns tomorrow – as sure as eggs make omelettes. But what did it matter? He was good looking and he was nice. He was also gay, which was no good for his image as a TV sex symbol. It was useful for him to be seen dating one of the town's most fabulous women. It also suited Katherine, now that she had no one in her life. Tony was safe; there would be no need for an undignified scramble in the car at the end of the evening, no hard dick pressing into her thigh, nor wheedling voice begging to be asked in for just one nightcap.

As soon as she thought they'd finished with her pictures, Katherine heard an even bigger cheer. Kingsley quickly tugged her away.

'Eleonor's arrived, and the media want pics,' he hissed.

'Oh God, must we?' she whispered.

' 'Fraid so – otherwise there'll be nasty tales in the tattle press tomorrow.'

'OK, boss, where is the gorgeous diva?'

'Here she blows,' Kingsley said sarcastically, and, as if on cue, Eleonor stepped forward.

'Dahling Kitty!' she drawled, in the fake English accent which she still managed to retain, in spite of thirty-five years in America.

'You look *deevine*, dahling.'

'So do you, sweetie. Pretty as a picture for sure.'

The two women air-kissed, ten inches from each other's pancaked cheeks, taking in every detail of their respective outfits as they did so. The photographers went into feeding frenzy. It was rare to get a photo of the two favourite divas of prime time TV together, and these photographs could appear on at least eight magazine covers in Europe.

The two actresses made a fascinating contrast – they were like night and day, darkness and light, black and white. Katherine raven-haired, carmine-lipped, sheathed in jet lace and beads, with her pale skin glowing, and Eleonor, golden-tanned and ash-blonde, shimmering in white iridescent sequins and trailing an enormous creamy fox stole.

An animal rights activist in the crowd hissed at her, while the actresses beamed and pouted into the flash of a thousand bulbs. Then, to groans of dismay from the photographers, Kingsley and Eleonor's press agent pried their clients loose.

'God what a nightmare!' Katherine muttered to Tony, sinking into her chair, at the round table in the Beverly Hilton Ballroom, where the rest of the cast were already assembled.

Albert glanced at his watch.

'You're late,' he snapped. 'The show's due to start in three minutes.'

'So sue me, Albie. Eleonor's even later.' Katherine lit a cigarette, ignoring Albert's disapproving stare.

She smiled at him sweetly, and blew a perfect smoke ring in his direction. He snorted, and almost literally turned up his nose.

'It's about time smoking was banned,' he humped.

'Oh c'mon Albie, I know you love a cigarette. I've seen all those old stills of you from the forties. You always had a cigarette going.'

Tony grinned, and lit up too.

'Don't you just *love* our happy family?' Katherine whispered into his ear. 'We all adore each other, don't we?'

At the next table Mandy and Steven were chatting but, as soon as Steve saw Katherine, he got up to kiss her.

'If you got any more gorgeous, kid, they'd have to ban you.'

'What's *that* from?' Katherine's eyes were dancing. She was having a good time tonight, and her adrenalin was flowing. Film industry affairs were all too often long-drawn-out and dull, but Katherine's love of a party stood her in good stead, and she knew how to make the most tedious function fun for herself.

'*That*, my lady, is from the lips of Steven Leigh himself. An original *bon-mot*, writ specially for you.'

Katherine smiled. Why couldn't she meet someone like Steven? A regular down-to-earth nice guy, funny, good-looking, self-deprecating. She glanced at Mandy, who was deep in conversation with Maximilian, and apparently so secure in her husband's love that she never worried about any of his working relationships with women.

Steven and Katherine became engrossed in their badinage; four tables away, a man called Jean-Claude Valmer was watching the mischievous expression on Katherine's beautiful gypsy-face.

'That woman has the most beautiful mouth I've ever seen,' he said to his companion – a tiny man with a face like a kind-hearted frog.

'Who? Kitty Bennet? Why don't you tell her then? Or are you too shy?'

'Shy – *moi*?'

Black eyebrows, curved like new moons, rose above eyes so green that they almost made Katherine's look dull by comparison.

'I've already told her she's beautiful – but she doesn't know who I am.'

Jean-Claude pulled a black alligator notecase rimmed in gold, from the pocket of his dinner jacket, and, in black ink from his gold Cartier fountain pen, wrote:

'Miss Bennet, you have the most beautiful mouth in the world.'

While Billy Crystal was doing his warm up, a waiter brought Katherine the note. She asked who sent it, and the waiter gestured towards the corner table, where Jean-Claude was still watching her.

Katherine looked over, and her heart beat faster. Even from here, she could see that the gorgeous-looking man had astonishing eyes. As she stared at him, he raised his glass of champagne in a silent toast. She toasted him back. Why not? she thought. Where has he been all my life? Glorious hunks like him don't grow on trees in this neck of the Hollywoods. Then, her view became blocked by a phalanx of Mexican waiters, clattering the first course down in front of everyone, and when she looked up she could no longer see him. She felt a frisson of disappointment.

'You have the most beautiful mouth in the world.' She smiled as she read it again, and placed the note carefully in her jewelled Judith Lieber *minaudière*.

'Well, Mr Gorgeous,' she thought, 'You sure ain't too bad yourself.'

The Skeffingtons cast already knew they were winners. Gabe had told them that Albert Amory would accept the coveted golden statuette on their behalf. This was fine by the cast, especially Katherine, who disliked making speeches.

One by one the nominees for other awards were announced, and the winners flounced, sauntered or tripped up to the stage, many in varying degrees of intoxication from drink or drugs. *The Skeffingtons* was a popular winner of the best dramatic series award, and the whole audience cheered, as Amory led the ten cast members up on to the stage.

It was at this moment that things began to go awry. The blonde starlet who was holding the golden statuette, walked past Albert Amory and Eleonor Norman, who were right in the front, and placed the precious award in Katherine's hands, with a breathy 'Congratulations Miss Bennet – you deserve it'. For a second Katherine was stunned by the girl's mistake, but quickly her stage presence took over, and bending towards the mike, she said sincerely, 'On behalf of all our cast I want to thank you for this great honour. And now, I should like to hand this over to our fearless leader.'

She held out the gold figurine to Albert, but he shook his head and refused to take it from her. Then, without any of his usual *savoir faire*, snarled at the audience, 'I've got nothing to say – she's said it all.'

'Here, Albert, *please* take this. You were *supposed* to have it.' Katherine hurried to catch up with the irascible old man, who had stalked off the stage, and was now walking stiffly down the corridor. Without looking at her, he hissed out of the corner of his mouth:

'No way. You want the damn thing so much, you keep it.'

'I saw you *grab* it!' Eleonor said. 'You're so bloody pushy, Katherine.'

Tony Bertolini squeezed her hand, and whispered:

'Don't let 'em get to you, kiddo. I saw it. You're lookin' upset... Don't... Cool it. Stay calm, *calma*.'

'How can I be calm, Tony? You saw what happened? That idiot bimbo plonked the award right *at* me. What was I supposed to do, drop the damned thing?'

'You did OK kiddo – you did OK,' he soothed. 'Now straighten up and forget it. We gotta meet the press, so tits out, and let those beads shimmer; it's magic time, babe.'

The steaming anteroom contained hundreds of photographers, and an equal number of journalists. Katherine thrust the award into the PR girl's hands, who managed to get Amory to hold it, while the smiling cast posed and preened.

'Flash – over here please.'

'Bang! Hey guys, look over here. Smile, Kitty – smile, Albert. Thank *you* ladies and gentlemen, thank you very much. Thank you and *wallop*.'

It was done, finished, over – and Katherine couldn't wait to escape from the frenzy.

But she couldn't, not yet. Even though she truly believed she hadn't a prayer, the public's favourite TV actress had yet to be announced, and she had to be smiling and in her seat when it was.

The word was out that whoever won this award would be front runner to play Emma Hamilton, in a new mini-series which ABN network was planning. Katherine's agent believed she had a fighting chance, and that the network was interested. However, everyone was awaiting the outcome of this award, before the final casting decision was made.

At last the time came, and Don Johnson, resplendently tanned and tuxedoed, announced the five Best Actress nominees.

Eleonor took out her compact, licked lipstick off her teeth, then quickly applied another layer of gloss to her mouth, and took a deep breath. The youngest actress there, Patty O'Rourke took a drag of spliff and giggled at her boyfriend, one of the 'brat-pack', who hadn't bothered to throw on anything more formal tonight than a ravelled black T-shirt, a leather jacket, and a red bandana over long greasy locks. Patty's hair was done in tiny braids all over her head. She wore no make-up, a white satin slip dress that clearly showed the outline of each nipple, and clumpy black Doc Marten boots.

Donna Mills was pleased. She knew she wouldn't win, because she'd taken the prize last year, but it was nice to be nominated, particularly alongside these illustrious actresses. The celebrated New York actress, Jessica Brandon, took a tiny sip of wine and smiled at Harold Brandon, her husband of fifty years.

'Good luck,' he mouthed.

'I don't stand a chance,' she whispered. 'But isn't it fun, darling?'

Katherine caught the eye of Jean-Claude Valmer, now only three tables away. Again he lifted his glass in a toast and she felt herself blush like a schoolgirl.

'And the winner is...' Katherine held her breath. 'Eleonor Norman.' She let it out in a silent hiss.

'Oh well, you can't win 'em all,' said Tony comfortingly, after Eleonor had tottered up to the podium and given a seven-minute speech.

'It doesn't matter. There'll be other times.'

It would have been a fantastic career break to win this award. There was no way now she would play Emma Hamilton. In spite of the warm night, she felt a chill. The winds of change were blowing, and it did not feel as though they were bringing her good fortune.

After the final award for best actor, no one waited for the soggy chocolate souffle, the warm coffee, or stale mints. Carrying off their table centrepieces of carnations, dyed turquoise daisies and limp red roses, the rich and famous of Hollywood made a beeline for the door while Billy Crystal was in the middle of his closing remarks. The rush was like the escape from Alcatraz. Katherine was jostled by the crowds and mauled by roving fans, as she searched the throng for the gorgeous blond man with green eyes. But he was nowhere to be seen.

'Just my luck,' she said ruefully to Tony, as they sank thankfully into the back of the limo. 'Mr Gorgeous just disappeared into thin air.'

'He was probably gay, anyway,' said Tony cheerfully. 'In this town most good-looking blond guys are, you know. Either that or he's a waiter, or an *actor*.'

Katherine wrinkled her nose.

'I don't want another involvement with one of *those*, thanks a lot. Most actors aren't capable of giving love, because they're so desperate to receive it from their audiences, or fans, or anyone at all.'

'Yeah, I agree most of 'em are egomaniacs who can't return it. But how about actresses, then?'

'We're all flawed, darling. Every one of us gets our kicks from the applause, even if we don't admit it. It's a stupid profession really. Marion's right.'

'Brando's certainly made enough from it, whatever he says. Anyway two more weeks of this crap, Kitty, and you're on your way to Gay Paree. I bet you'll have the time of your life, honey.'

'I hope so, darling – I really do hope so.'

CHAPTER FIVE

At the studio the following morning, the first voice Katherine heard was her mother's on the mobile, commiserating with her on losing to 'That trumped up English Cockney bitch', and the first thing she saw was a huge display of balloons, suspended over a cake in the shape of the award, with two golden hands clasped together as if in mid-applause. It was hard not to feel jealous.

Then there were the photographs. First Eleonor with the whole cast, to celebrate the success of the show. Then with Eleonor clearly centre stage, to record her personal triumph. From being the woman whom workers on the set went out of their way to avoid, and had nicknamed the British Open, she was suddenly the Queen Mother of sweetness and light, and wanted to be everyone's friend.

She was on a roll, and she knew it. At lunchtime her agent called, crowing: 'We've done it, sweet-stuff, you've got it. You're gonna be Emma Hamilton sweetheart. Congratulations *again*!'

Katherine, however, was the recipient of upsetting lunchtime news. She was munching rice cakes and turkey breast in her spartan dressing-room, learning dialogue with Brenda, when the red hotline rang.

'Mom – is that you, Mom?'

It was Tommy's distraught voice.

'What is it darling? What's the matter?'

Through a burst of uncontrollable sobbing, she heard her son trying to speak.

'Mom, it's Dad. I've just talked to him on the phone and he's...he's...'

'Tommy, Tommy, please honey, stop crying and tell me what all this is about.'

'It's Dad...he told me...he's got...they've told him...'

'What?' Katherine asked anxiously, glancing at the clock. 'Tommy *please* tell me.'

It was five to two. Oh God, whatever was going on in her family, in her life, why did it always happen at the end of lunch, when that dreaded rap on the door would come at any second?

'Tommy, you've *got* to tell me why you're so upset.'

'Dad's got cancer,' he sobbed.

The receiver in Katherine's hand started shaking.

'Cancer? Oh God, darling, are you sure? Is *Dad* really sure?'

'Sure I'm sure.' His sobs were lessening now, as if sharing the burden made it more bearable. 'So is he.'

Brenda looked up from a pile of correspondence, and saw Katherine's white face.

'Tell me about it, darling, please.'

'I was getting ready for school this morning when Dad called. He said he had to see me. He said it was real important. I said I was late for school but he said this was more important than school. I called you, Mom,' his tone was accusing, 'But you weren't there.'

'I was probably on the set, darling.' Dammit, why couldn't she ever be available for her child when he needed her?

'Well, I went over to Dad's apartment. Jeez, what a dump. Have you seen it?'

'Yes darling, I have. I know this is hard for you, but please go on.'

'Dad was sitting in a chair, I guess he was kinda drunk. His eyes were, you know, glassy.'

'Yes,' she nodded grimly. 'I know.'

'Well, he sat me down, gave me a coke, and said he'd been to this doc yesterday, and the guy had told him he'd got cancer.'

'Where? Where does he have it?'

'I dunno,' Tommy said in his blank, adolescent way. 'He didn't tell me. He was drunk, Mom, I think he'd been smoking dope too. What are we gonna do? He's got no money, he says he hasn't got enough cash for the treatment he needs. He says he's gotta have an operation. He says it's gonna cost – shit, I can't remember, but it's like thousands and thousands of dollars.'

'Does he have health insurance?' Katherine already knew that answer, then the knock on the door came, and the voice yelled, 'Five minutes on set, Kitty.'

'OK,' she yelled back.

'Now listen, Tommy, listen to me. I don't want you to be upset by this. First of all, cancer is curable today, you know that.'

'Is it, Mom? Are you sure?'

'Of course I'm sure.' She put an optimism into her voice which she didn't feel. If Johnny had cancer, the chances were that it was lung cancer. With the amount of cigarettes that he'd smoked over the past twenty years, that wasn't surprising. When she had started doing the show, he'd increased his consumption to an unbelievable three packs a day. She'd given up nagging him. It was his life, wasn't it? It wasn't going to be much of a life now, not with cancer, but she had to try and help him, for the sake of their son.

'Tommy, you're not to worry about anything. It's two o'clock now. Isn't this your baseball afternoon?'

'Yep.'

'Well, I want you to just go and play baseball. It doesn't matter if you missed school this morning. Tell the teachers the truth. Tell them that your father was sick. Now I'm going to call him myself, and do what I can.'

'Hey, Mom, will you?'

'Of course. You know I'm going to do everything I can.'

'Listen, Mom,' anxiety was in his voice again. 'Is Dad gonna die?'

'No he's not.'

'Well, if he does die, you better not let anything happen to you,' he said accusingly. 'Promise?'

'Don't worry, darling.' There was another knock on the door. 'I'm fit as a fiddle.'

'Get your keister on the set right *now*, Kitty,' yelled the production manager. 'ASAP. We're waiting.'

'Oh, fuck off.' Suddenly Katherine's temper took control. 'I've got a family emergency here, Ben.'

'What else is new?' Ben said sarcastically. 'You have more emergencies than I have hot dinners. Tell that to Gabe Heller. We've got eight minutes of screen time to get in the can by tonight, and we're all waiting for you.'

'OK, OK,' she yelled. Then quietly to Tommy: 'Nothing's going to happen to me, Tommy, I promise you.'

'Great, Mom, will you be home for dinner tonight?'

With the resilience of youth, Tommy was suddenly in a better mood.

'I wouldn't miss dinner with you for the world.'

Johnny stared blankly at the yellow-stained wallpaper; it was peeling off from the top, where some badly painted moulding housed a family of cockroaches. He watched dispassionately as first one, then another, slithered down the wall. He knew where they were heading – to the leaking pipe underneath the broken washbasin in the corner, where another whole army of them lived below the rotting floorboards.

'There's absolutely no fucking reason for me to go on living,' he muttered, loudly enough so that one cockroach decided to scamper back to its hiding place until later.

He stared at the bureau which housed several cheaply framed photographs. The silver ones that he and Kitty had painstakingly divvied up between them had long since gone to the pawn shop, but he'd kept a few that still meant something to him. Their wedding photo. He couldn't bear to get rid of that one, they looked like children sitting in the back of the convertible car, so young, so happy, so in love.

'So pregnant,' he said cynically, and picked it up. Then, sliding the photograph out of its frame, he tore it into strips, into quarters, and finally into eighths which he scattered like confetti on to the floor.

Yes, she'd certainly been pregnant all right, that beautiful, joyous, raven-haired gypsy he had married. It would have been difficult for her not to be, with all that lovemaking. They were as poor as the proverbial church mice, and they had lived in a dump a lot worse than this, with a lot more cockroaches too. Kitty spent lots of time with the bug-killer, but it never seemed to make much difference.

They were actors, but he was the only one in work then, whilst she was content to play house and revel in her pregnancy. Johnny was an up-and-coming juvenile lead, rehearsing for a new off-Broadway play. Great things were promised by his agent, and even some of the critics had given him favourable reviews.

How old would that kid have been now? He glanced at a day-old copy of the *Los Angeles Times* – June 10th, 1988. Kitty had been pregnant in February 1968. Twenty years. Their kid would have been twenty years old now. That kid she destroyed.

Johnny lit the first cigarette of the day, and tipped the whiskey bottle to his lips. Oh sure, she *said* she hadn't destroyed the kid. She *said* it was just an accident when she fell on stage. He'd argued with her about accepting a role when she was three months pregnant; he'd tried to assert his rights, but she had tossed her black curls and laughed in his face.

'Darling, darling Johnny,' she'd said, throwing her arms around him. 'It's only going to be a six-week run. The play's crap, but let's face it we need the money, darling, for Junior.' She patted her flat stomach and grinned. 'I want this baby, Johnny, I really do.'

He'd shrugged; he hadn't had much of a choice. When Kitty made up her mind to do anything, not too many people were able to stop her – in fact no one ever had. So, she'd decided to be in this shitty play, a thriller by some hack author, and on the night of the dress rehearsal she'd tripped backstage, and broken her arm. The stupid producer couldn't afford an understudy, so she'd gone on opening night with her arm in plaster. She'd run around the stage, hiding behind cupboards, jumping in trunks, playing a woman terrorised by a gang who had burst into her house. The whole thing was ludicrous, and he'd shuddered at the awfulness of the play, while grudgingly admiring her pluck. And naturally it had happened. Three nights after the opening, she'd lost her balance on the stage, clambering one-armed out of a trunk, fallen down in front of three hundred people, and later that evening, started haemorrhaging. Next day their baby was gone.

He inhaled deeply and stared at another photograph. Johnny and Kitty and baby Tommy. This time they'd finally produced the kid they both craved, and he was making almost enough money for her to stop working and stay at home. But no. No, no, no. Miss Katherine Bennet was not about to stop trying to be a serious stage actress.

'There are too many good parts out there, darling. And I want to play most of them. I don't give a damn about being a star. I know I'm never going to be a star, I'm not the type, but while I can find work, and while Tommy is young enough to come along with me, what's the problem with that?'

What indeed? he'd thought. He was on the upswing then, getting incredible reviews, and huge applause at the curtain call. Important agents started to make moves towards him after he played Hamlet. He stared at that photograph now, mesmerised by his thirty-year-old brooding, handsome, actor's face.

Then, raising his eyes to the mirror, he saw the reality. His complexion was mottled and rough, his once-thick black hair was thin, greying, and far too long for a man of his age. But he couldn't afford a decent haircut. Not on what the bitch gave him for support. Although he hardly ever ate, he was bloated, his jowls were puffy, and even his chest hair was grey and patchy. Those parts of his body which had been small and firm, had become saggy and large; those which had been large and firm, had become saggy and small. He cupped his hand around his genitals. They, too, seemed a shadow of their former selves. Had he really managed to get it up practically every morning for Kitty? And when Kitty wasn't around, there were plenty of pretty young actresses ready to oblige. Well it was over now. Or was it?

The doctors had been kind, but not optimistic. The cancer was in his lungs, but it had not yet spread. They had said that they could operate. For money of course. Now all he needed to cough up was ten thousand dollars for the operation. He stubbed out his cigarette, then immediately lit another. He knew that Tommy would tell his mother about the money, and that the goose that laid the golden eggs would most likely come through. He didn't like asking Katherine for the cash himself; he wanted her to offer it willingly.

As if on cue, the telephone rang. 'Johnny.' Her voice was warm, concerned. 'Tommy told me the news. Tell me it isn't true.'

'Yup.' His voice, by contrast, was laconic, hard. 'It's true, hon. I've got the big C. John Wayne couldn't lick it and I guess I don't have much of a chance. The doc said if I'd been in a traffic accident, they would have known I was a three-pack-a-day man, just by looking at my lungs during the autopsy.' He started to laugh, but it turned into a coughing fit, and then he lit up again.

'Is there *anything* they can do? Is there anything I can do?'

'Sure,' he said. 'Sure I can have the op, but it's gonna cost.'

'How much?'

'Ten grand, just for the operation. Jesus, Kitty, I feel like shit.'

'Listen Johnny, when the chips are down, you're Tommy's father. You know he's the only thing that matters to me.'

Oh sure, he thought. After your illustrious TV career. But he said meekly, 'Oh, I know that, Kitty, I know.'

'Would you like me to come and see you? I'm in my car, on the way home. I could drop by for a minute, if you like.'

'No, I don't want you to see me. It might be too much of a shock.' He cackled, and coughed again.

'Look, I insist you have this surgery, Johnny, and I'm going to pay for it, for Tommy's sake if not your own, so don't argue. Just send all the doctor's bills to me. Better still, send them to Brett, my business manager. You know the address. Look I'm nearly home now, and I want to spend some time with Tommy. So I'll speak to you tomorrow. Goodbye Johnny, and I'm really sorry.'

'I'll bet you are,' he murmured, draining the last of the gin. 'I'll just bet you are.'

When Katherine told her business manager to take care of Johnny's hospital and medical bills, he laughed mockingly. 'Ten grand, Kitty? Where the hell do you think that money's going to come from?'

'Well, for God's sake, Brett, I'm making almost forty grand a week, aren't I?'

'Yeh, and Uncle Sam's taking forty per cent of it. Your agent's taking ten, and I'm taking five, that leaves you less than eighteen grand a week. Between your lawyers and butlers and maids, and your cook and your housekeeper, and your chauffeur, and your hairdresser, and your exercise guru and your psychiatrist and Tommy's school fees and – '

'OK, Brett, cool it. I know things are tight right now, but I'm hoping for a raise next season.'

Fat chance of that, thought Brett, glancing at the latest issue of *The National Tattler*, where the cover story was yet another hatchet job on Kitty.

'Just take care of Johnny, Brett. Do it, OK?' Her voice was cold.

'Well, I guess we'll just have to take another mortgage on the house,' he said sarcastically. 'When you decided to invest in Tiffany lamps, art deco armchairs, and elephant tusk coffee tables, you didn't seem to realise the money wasn't going to last forever.'

'I earn it, don't I, I earn every damn cent of it, and I should be able to do what I goddamned like with it.'

'That's all very well, Kitty, but you *cannot* go on with this profligate spending. You are not Cher or Madonna, who make millions a year, you're just on a salary, and frankly, you've been overstretching it.'

'Well, that's why I'm paying you. Get another mortgage, Brett, I don't care. Mortgage the damned house to the hilt. I want to finish the next two weeks shooting, then take a vacation. And don't you dare tell me I don't have enough money for that.'

He sighed. 'OK, OK – I'll do it – you're the boss. So – what news on Emma Hamilton?'

'Oh, haven't you heard? Her Serene Gorgeousness, our very own English Rose, has plucked that plum.' Katherine laughed hollowly. 'But *c'est la vie*, there'll be other parts.'

Katherine was aware that other parts, and good scripts hadn't exactly rocketed her way recently. When tough, meaty parts came along, casting directors thought Katherine was too obvious a choice, yet they considered her too hard for other softer roles. It was a no-win situation, which often made Katherine bitter, even though she realized how lucky she was, compared with most other actors.

'Oh, and by the way,' she said flatly, 'I want you to fire my agent.'

'Fire your agent? You've only been with the poor schmuck three months.'

'Yes, I know. And in three months he hasn't come up with a single offer for my hiatus. So, do as I say, Brett – fire him.'

'And just where are you going next? You've already been through William Morris, CAA, and ICM. There aren't that many top agencies left in town.'

'That's *your* job, darling,' Katherine said sweetly. 'You take five per cent of my salary, you find me a new agent. I've got to get on with my life, and with my son's life, and try to keep my head above water. And with all this shit I'm getting hit with, it ain't getting easier.'

Tommy was so excited by the thought of the European trip, that he quite forgot to be awkward and antagonistic towards his mother. Most evenings they stuffed themselves with Maria's delicious cooking, and afterwards played games. One night Tommy suggested Scrabble.

'I've been working at my game; I think I finally figured out how to beat you.'

Katherine laughed. 'You know I'm the champ, and I warn you, I won't give an inch.'

Tommy had inherited Katherine's competitiveness, and as the game wore on, they were neck and neck. They both had around two hundred and fifty points when Tommy got the Q and the U and put 'Quids' on a triple letter score, thus securing him the game.

'That's the first time I ever beat you, Mom!' he said exultantly.

'And I'm sure it won't be the last.' She smiled. 'Oh my God, it's nine thirty, it's time to hit the sack.' She checked her watch. 'I've got lines to learn. And you, number one son, have got school tomorrow.'

'Yes, sir, ma'am.' He gave her a joky salute, and the most affectionate hug she'd had from him since he was a child. They could almost be brother and sister, thought Maria, as she cleared the dishes.

'Thanks, Mom,' he whispered, 'for what you're doing for Dad.'

She nuzzled his neck. 'Off to bed, kid, we'll play again tomorrow and *I'm* going to beat you!'

Thanks to several nights of unbroken sleep, Kitty's skin was beginning to glow with new vitality, and she found her desire for exercise returning. Early the following morning she went jogging. Halfway around Benedict Canyon, she was greeted by a man running in the opposite direction.

He grinned. 'Hi, I'm Jake Moffatt. I just moved into the house two blocks down from you.'

'Hi, I'm Katherine Bennet.'

'Yeah, I know who you are.'

Jake Moffatt was a familiar name; he was a British rock star, famous in England, but practically unknown in America. He was also one of Tommy's recording favourites. 'He's a bit old, Mom, but he's real *bad*!'

'Bad?'

'Yeah, you know, bad, bad, like *fantastic*.'

'Oh, yes, bad. Got it.'

Jake had small sharp white teeth in a pointed, ferret-like face; he had receding brown hair and a compact but wiry body. He didn't attract Kitty in the slightest, but he did seem interested in her, and for the next three days, she bumped into him several times. On Friday he handed her an envelope.

'It's for a party I'm throwing tomorrow night,' he said. 'I hope you'll come. It'll be a good gig. Lots of your friends will be there, 'cos it's a celebration.'

'Of what?' smiled Katherine. Celebrations always appealed to her and she could do with a bit of relaxation.

'I've just signed with *Face Records*. It's a fab deal, so I'm breaking out the shampoo and the dead bits on toast.'

'I'm going to the Lakers game with my son, but maybe I'll make it after the game.'

In fact, after the basketball game, Tommy announced that he wanted to go to a party at Todd's.

'You're not going to drink, are you?' asked Katherine, motherly instincts sweeping over her.

'Of course not. Hey, I put all that stuff behind me. Todd's having some of the gang over and it's Saturday night, Mom, party time. Why don't you go to Jake's? Have some fun for a change.'

When Kitty arrived, the party was in full rave. Several dozen girls, some actresses, some obvious hookers in various stages of decolletage, and with mini-skirts so short that they barely covered their pudenda, were circulating through the crowd of Hollywood socialites. In the Spanish-style forecourt, a Margarita fountain was flowing. Jake greeted her with a too-familiar hug. She tried to free herself from his encircling arm, but he turned to the photographer who was snapping away at all the guests and said, 'Show 'im your teeth, Kitty.'

Katherine smiled faintly, trying to disguise her irritation, then pulled herself free and prepared to plunge into the throng. As she did so, she caught sight of a tableau which made her heart miss a beat. It was the blond man with the green eyes, her mystery admirer, with – of all people – Eleonor Norman. She studied them anxiously. It looked as though he were being polite, but not much more, even though Eleonor was clearly interested in him. Perhaps she was fooling herself.

There was no doubt that Eleonor had dressed to kill. Not so much gilding the lily, as embellishing it, to a point where she was almost a parody of herself. A black spandex dress was cut down to her navel, and split to her thigh, revealing black lace stockings and red garters. Her white-blonde hair was a bouffant halo around her head, and her rhinestone earrings were so long that they grazed her mahogany-coloured shoulders. She was gazing up into the stranger's eyes, and every now and again, would pause to play finger games with the lapel of his beautifully cut jacket.

Kitty stared, transfixed, and suddenly, as though aware of being watched, he turned to meet her gaze. For the second time Katherine felt that earth-shattering whoomp, as though her stomach had swallowed itself. She would like to talk to him, but how could she, if he was talking to Eleonor? He raised his glass, smiled, and for a second she thought he was going to walk across to her. But then someone tapped her on the shoulder, she turned to see who it was, and when she looked for him again, he had been swallowed by the crowd.

Now Steven was at her side, asking affectionately how she was, telling her how beautiful she looked – wondering privately what had got into her. She looked bemused, distracted, as though someone had just given her disturbing news.

'Where's Mandy?' she said, making a visible effort to concentrate.

'She's been practising for the LA marathon all day with her new trainer, and she's exhausted.'

There was a certain bitterness to his tone which caused Kitty to look at him searchingly, but his expression told her this was not the moment to press it.

'Hungry?' he indicated a table groaning with food.

'Starving,' she said, her eyes focussing again. 'All I've had is a hot dog, and bucket of popcorn all day.'

There were sausages and fried onions, bangers and mash, baked beans and kippers, a strange assortment which some people in Beverly Hills thought was a typically English dinner, but was more like an English country breakfast. Steven sat down with her, and soon they were joined by Jake and others. Their table was in the middle of the tented tennis court, and Katherine kept glancing at the entrance to see if the blond stranger would come in. But he didn't.

Steven was entertaining the table with a funny story, but Katherine couldn't concentrate. Steven noticed that once again she seemed distracted, as though looking for someone, and as soon as he saw a flash of excitement cross her face, he knew what she had been looking for. A tall, blond guy, undeniably handsome. Steven felt a flicker of jealousy.

Katherine had drunk several Margaritas, and now she wanted to dance. It was a long time since she had felt so free of inhibition, and, with a mischievous smile, she held out her hand across the table to Steven:

'Listen, it's a flamenco,' she said. 'Shall we?'

And so, to the intoxicating music of Los Paraguayas, Katherine and Steven launched into a wild fandango. Katherine felt light-headed as Steven took her in his arms, and whirled her around the floor. Her head was thrown back, her black hair was flying, and she was laughing.

She didn't think about anything else except the beating throb of the music and the wild pulse of the dance. She didn't think about the gossip columnists who were already writing her professional obituary, or the Hollywood talk that said her career was declining. She didn't think about being forty-three years old, and that she was one of the oldest women in the room. Tonight she was young, wild and alive. As the music ended, the crowd burst into applause, and Steven bent Kitty back in the classic tango pose. Still playing to the gallery, she arched her back playfully, and as she did so she saw – out of the corner of her eye – the tall blond stranger.

He was standing in the doorway, staring at her. She knew that her make-up must be smudged, her hair was awry, and that sweat beaded her brow, but she didn't care. She couldn't let him disappear again. Asking Steve to get them both a glass of champagne, she set off across the dance floor – only to see Eleonor appear at his side, take his arm and lead him out of the room.

Steve had come back with the champagne. 'You must be dying of thirst.'

'You bet.' Katherine took a sip, then drained the glass. It tasted like nectar. Champagne was usually top of the list of forbidden fruits, because of its bloating qualities.

'I never knew you were such a John Travolta.'

Kitty's eyes gleamed, her face was flushed, and Steve thought she looked exceptionally gorgeous.

'You want to try again?'

'Sure,' she said. 'I love this band. Oh, by the way. Who was that guy with Eleonor tonight?'

'What guy?' said Steve. 'I didn't see a guy with her. Wasn't she was with that Scandinavian number she hangs out with?'

'No, she was with some tall blond. You didn't see him?'

Steve shook his head.

'Ah well,' thought Kitty, as they started to dance again, 'I guess we're destined never to meet.'

It was the last day of shooting; they were filming the scene before the boat explosion. Tony, Eleonor and Kitty were doing their close-ups, but a lot of special effects were involved, including blazing firesticks, often held too uncomfortably near to their faces, and walls which exploded into flames behind them. Eleonor, with Emma Hamilton in her pocket, was being particularly friendly to Katherine as they sat in make-up between takes, having repairs done.

'You really did a great dance at Saturday's party,' she gushed. 'I didn't know you had it in you, dahling – *loved* the frock.'

'Thanks. I didn't know it either. Oh, by the way – you looked great too.'

'Thanks, Kitty.' They smiled insincerely at each other.

'Who were you with?' Kitty stared fixedly in the mirror while she applied mascara.

'Dirk.'

'Oh, I thought I saw you with somebody else, a blond guy?'

'No.' Eleonor outlined her lips in fuschia gloss. 'You know me, ever faithful to my Scandinavian stud.'

The make-up men almost choked on their chewing-gum. It was widely suspected that Eleonor screwed the world when she had the chance.

Albert had not exchanged more than cursory greetings with Katherine since the awards fiasco. Now they had to shoot a scene in which Georgia was chased up the stairs by Charles Skeffington. Kitty was nervous. Even though Albert was sixty-nine, he was still quite strong, and a pair of hands around an actress's throat in the heat of passion could be dangerous. Katherine decided to make up with him.

'What are you doing in the hiatus, Albert?' She smiled endearingly.

'What? Are you speaking to me?' The old actor looked confused. To prepare for his scenes with Katherine, he needed to feel antagonistic. This wasn't usually difficult, because he sincerely disliked her, but her sudden rush of bonhomie threw him.

'I'm going to England,' he huffed.

'How lovely. To see your parents?'

The make-up men raised their eyebrows once again. Sometimes Kitty put her foot in it right up to her neck. Albert Amory's parents were long gone, and, from the doddery way he was behaving recently, it looked as though he wouldn't be around much longer either.

'As a matter of fact,' he said frostily, 'I am going to visit my daughter. She is about to have a baby.'

'Oh, you're going to be a granddaddy, how lovely!' Katherine was genuinely pleased for him, unaware that this was probably not what he wanted to hear. Getting married was one thing in Hollywood, having a baby was another, but becoming a grandparent was a no-no. There were no grandchildren in *The Skeffingtons*.

Aware she had offended, Kitty went over to him. 'Listen Albert, I'm really sorry we've had our differences this past season.'

The old man looked around for help, but he was stuck in his make-up chair, with Blackie applying thick greasepaint to his liver spots, so there was no escape.

'Well, er, thank you, Katherine. I, er, have always believed in forgiving and forgetting, actually.'

'I absolutely agree. I'm glad you feel that way, because it's been upsetting me, and you too I expect. Since we're not going to see each other for six weeks, I think we should all leave with good memories, don't you?' She put her hand out. 'Friends?'

He shook it distastefully.

'Yes, my dear. Friends.' God, he hated this woman, but she was putting him in an impossible position.

Whether it was her gesture or not that did the trick, Kitty never knew, but the scene ended without mishap, and no bruises anywhere. Gabe Heller's assistant brought in a large cooler filled with non-vintage champagne, beer and soft drinks. Fifty boxes of pizzas were delivered, and the crew set to with a vengeance.

They were packing up her dressing-room, when Brenda handed Katherine a message from Johnny's doctor. 'Operation accomplished. Patient recuperating well; however, will not know full rate of success for several months.'

'Well, *that's* certainly good news,' said Brenda. 'Now Tommy's going to feel a lot happier on his trip.'

'Thank God,' said Katherine.

She surveyed the bare, shabby room with its ancient sofa, now without its Paisley shawl, and showing both its stuffing and its age. The walls were stained and blotched, and without her Spanish rugs, the carpet was threadbare.

'I wonder if I'll return next season?' she mused.

'Of course you will, kid. They couldn't do this piece of shit without you.'

'Oh yes they could. They *damn* well could. And with the ratings slipping, if they can save fifty thousand dollars a week next season, you can bet your ass they will. If anyone's going to get bumped off, it will be the Georgia Poison Peach. And we won't get the new script, to see who does snuff it, until a week before we start shooting next season. Jeez, Bren – I could be out on my ass.'

'Don't think like that, hon, just enjoy Gay Paree, keep Tommy out of trouble, and keep yourself out of trouble. I've heard about those Riviera fleshpots.'

CHAPTER SIX

Extract from Suzy's Column, *New York Daily News,* June 28, 1988.

That ultimate TV star, Miss Katherine Bennet, packed her several dozen Louis Vuittons, and jetted off with her darling son to all the European hotspots, and then to her summer hideaway in St Tropez. Kitty darling, or as you prefer to know her, the Georgia Poison-Peach in ABN's hit series, The Skeffingtons, *is taking some well-earned R and R. She's just finished the third season of the super-successful soap and is due back in LA-LA land in mid-July to start the fourth. Bravo Kitty! And don't be sad that the plum part of Emma Hamilton went to that other glorious TV bitch, Eleonor Norman. We hear that Gabe Heller is seriously considering you for the lead in a new spin-off of* The Skeffingtons. *We hope you give 'em as much hell in the show next season as you have in the previous ones. We all love ya, Kitty!*

The villa was tucked away high in the hills behind St Tropez, near enough for Tommy to be able to bicycle into the bustling port with its trendy boutiques and cafés, and to water-ski, windsurf and sail on the nearby Pampelonne beaches, but far enough away from the eyes of the paparazzi and the curious. Katherine felt protected here, although by the standards of the Riviera super-rich, the house was modest. The large, comfortable living room was furnished with several inviting sofas, and old but beautiful Provencal wooden furniture. There was a small dining room, five bedrooms of varying sizes, and a cosy television room where she and Tommy watched videos, and where she sometimes persuaded him to play Scrabble or cards with her.

A French couple shopped, cooked and cleaned at the villa, leaving Katherine with time to relax in a garden filled with the scent of lavender and jasmine, and vivid with purple bougainvillaea and pale blue plumbago. Sometimes she lay by the pool, with its spectacular view of the yacht-filled harbour, happy to do nothing, or to spend time with Tommy in those moments when he was not with his teenage friends on the beach. She knew he had enjoyed the two weeks they had spent together in London and Paris. She had loved showing her son her two favourite cities, but now he needed friends of his own age. He also needed distracting from his anxiety about Johnny. Tommy had been in regular communication with him, and he was worried that his father's stomach pains had returned.

On one of these lazy days, Katherine was half-dozing in a chaise-longue after a late lunch, lulled by the tinkling, crystal sounds of the tiny fountain in the garden, when Steven called from LA.

'Kitty, I just came from a meeting with Gabe. They've made a decision – Georgia's not going to die after all!'

Kitty felt a mixture of relief and disappointment. She knew she would have been devastated if her character had been axed, on the other hand the sybaritic life she was living in the South of France agreed with her. She felt lazy, totally happy, but with a little growing sadness that it was all too soon coming to an end. Much had been made in the press of her failure to snare the role of Emma Hamilton, but secretly Kitty knew that it was a good thing. She realised now that she had been completely exhausted, and that it was just as well her precious hiatus hadn't been spent working.

Now she said: 'That's great news, Steven.'

'I know – and all because of the public. All the polls and the questionnaires that Gabe and Co have been doing for the past month have come in now, and it's overwhelming, kid. They like you – they like you!' His imitation of Sally Field made Katherine laugh.

'Well I couldn't be happier – I'm really thrilled.'

'Yeah – well I figured they couldn't snuff the Peach. If they did, the network would have had a riot on its hands. That Emma Hamilton crap is all history now. I'm off to write some killer scenes for you, kid – stay tuned.'

He rang off; Katherine got up and walked back into the house. Suddenly, unaccountably, she felt assailed by pangs of loneliness. Without a job to go to every day, she had time to think, and she was beginning to see how much she wanted someone to share her life – a man who would love her unconditionally for what and who she really was. Kitty Cribbens from Queens.

'Just a family gal at heart,' she mocked, catching sight of her melancholy face in the mirror. Not the glamorous Katherine Bennet from Beverly Hills, so famous she couldn't go out of her own front door, without heads swivelling.

Is this how an eighties woman should think? she reprimanded herself. Eighties women are supposed to be self-sufficient, self-supporting, oozing self-esteem and chutzpah; able to take or leave men! God, I'm a throwback to the fifties, Katherine scolded her reflection. She'd been a child in the fifties, and had often watched her mother and friends groom themselves to perfection, for even the humblest outing. She had loved to see them adjust their veils and little pill-box hats, or smoothing out wrinkles in their gloves. Discussions would centre around the merits of a Toni versus a Clairol perm, or on whether it was acceptable to wear white shoes after Labour Day. But whether it was that, or deciding which kind of dessert to serve, there was only one real point to it all: to please your man and make him love you forever.

Vera's advice to her daughter was uncompromising.

'Men only want one thing, Kit-Kat, and if you let 'em have it before you've got the gold ring, you're a fool.'

Vera loved to boast about how she'd kept her virginity, when most of her girlfriends were giving it freely to good-looking GIs with candy bars and nylons to spare. And Vera had succeeded where many had failed. She snagged Barney Cribbens, the cutest of the batch, and lived happily ever after until his death. All – so she said – because she'd *not* played her trump card during the Blitz.

Katherine sighed. Those days were long gone now. But why did she identify so much more with that era than with the 'No men, thanks, we're doing fine' outlook of the eighties? 'You're a throwback,' she muttered again.

In spite of her protestations to the contrary, Katherine wanted to be married eventually. Much of her twenty years with Johnny had been happy. She wanted that again. She wanted to belong to someone, and they to her. She wanted to go to sleep in the arms of the man she loved, and wake up the same way. She wanted to come home every evening to see him there, and talk over the events of the day. Would she ever manage it? Many men were intimidated by her fame, and were afraid that they, too, might be caught in its glare. Katherine knew she was a challenge.

Katherine had had plenty of invitations from neighbours and acquaintances, but she refused them all. All, that is, except one. She decided to accept a lunch party invitation from Betty and Stan Chalmers, a Texan couple from California. They were extremely rich, extremely social, and spent two months each summer, at the height of the season, in their villa overlooking St Tropez. Because the Chalmers had a son Tommy's age, Katherine decided it might be fun to go.

It was a boiling hot day, and the Riviera sun was blazing down when Katherine and Tommy arrived at the Chalmers' magnificent villa. The black iron gates creaked open as soon as she pressed the button. She drove her rented Renault up a grey, gravelled driveway, lined with parasol pines and olive trees, to the white stone and marble house. Beneath them they saw the glittering bay of St Tropez. The sea was completely calm, and sprinkled here and there with the white sails of boats. Once they neared the house, a uniformed butler guided them across a cool black and white marquetry marble floor, down to a smooth emerald lawn, which overlooked the bay.

'Hi, Kitty, *darling*! I'm *sooo* happy you could make it.' Betty Chalmers, an authentic Southern Belle, with the charm to match, rushed forward to hug Katherine. To protect her milky-white complexion from the sun, Betty wore a large straw hat, festooned with miniature American flags.

'Ah wore it for my July fourth party, honey, and Ah had such a success Ah thought Ah'd give it another whirl!'

Betty's superbly toned body was clad in a tight red Spandex bathing suit; she had a Stars and Stripes pareo slung around her minuscule hips, gold, sapphire and ruby chains around her wrists and neck, and in her ears she wore enormous ruby and diamond hearts. Her wide, generous mouth was a slash of crimson in her handsome face.

'You look wildly patriotic.' Katherine had always admired Betty's flair with the dressing-up box.

'Oh, Ah *am*, Kitty, you *know* Ah'm the original All-American gal!'

Her husband Stan was famous for being a barracuda in the boardroom, and a pussy-cat in the drawing room. Now he sauntered over to Katherine with his courtier's smile.

'Sure are happy to see you heah today, Miz Georgia,' he raised his red, white and blue stetson.

'Stan! *Don't* call her Georgia, that's just her TV name. Sorry, honey, sometimes Ah just don't *know* what comes over him.'

Betty scowled at her beefy husband, then taking Katherine's arm, led her around to the rest of the group. It was an eclectic mix of Eurotrash, middle European bluebloods, without a dime to their names, an ageing playboy or two, a couple of minor English aristocrats, and a grand dowager cosmetic queen from New York, who, although in her mid-eighties, looked as fresh as a daisy, in a pink sunbonnet and Schiaparelli chiffon ruffles.

Then her heart started to pound in slow, painful thuds, her hands felt clammy, her mouth dry. Standing on the far side of the swimming pool, was her handsome, blond mystery man. He seemed to be shimmering in the sunlight like some mirage or vision; she wondered if she could be hallucinating. But when she saw who he was talking to, she began to feel better, more normal.

Quentin Rogers was a man she knew well; a famous old playboy and *bon viveur* from Hollywood's glory days, He had been a fixture at every A list Hollywood party since the 1940s.

'Kitty, honey, this is my deah, *deah*, oldest friend from Hollywood, Quentin Rogers, whom Ah'm *sure* you've met before?'

'Of course. Quentin, it's great to see you again.' Katherine extended her hand; the tiny man took it in his own perfectly manicured, miniature one.

'Likewise, my dear Kitty. You're looking wonderful as usual.'

He wore a cream panama hat at a jaunty angle, a light-weight black and white striped cotton shirt, and immaculately pressed linen trousers. On his feet were black and white co-respondent's shoes, the kind made popular by the Duke of Windsor in the 1930s, and he exuded a dapper aura of old world chivalry and bonhomie.

'May I introduce Jean-Claude Valmer?'

'*Enchanté, mademoiselle.*' He stood up, with a dazzling smile, to greet Katherine.

She took his firm, brown hand. His handshake was exactly right. Not too hard, as if he wanted to prove his masculinity, but not like a damp fish either. Katherine surveyed him. Close up he was certainly gorgeous, there was no other word for it. He was much better looking than she remembered. In fact, with his black eyebrows and fair hair, he was definitely one of the handsomest men she had ever seen.

In spite of what the experts said about sun worship, you couldn't get away from the fact that a tan accentuated a man's best features. Jean-Claude was deeply tanned, almost mahogany-coloured. His thick, windblown hair, streaked by the sun, had a few strands of silver at the temples. It was a little too long, so he kept pushing it off his forehead boyishly. He removed his sunglasses, and Kitty was immediately struck by the luminous intensity of his pale green eyes. His pupils had contracted in the strong sunlight, so that his irises looked translucent.

He was, she guessed, around forty, but in his light blue cotton polo shirt, and white shorts, he looked young and casual.

'Please, Kitty dear, won't you join us?' Quentin, indicated the chair next to his. 'It's been such a long time, and it's a great treat to see you again.'

Katherine sat down, conscious that Jean-Claude's eyes were fixed on her, his mouth smiling slightly.

She was glad she had made a special effort today. Normally she wore shorts and a T-shirt in St Tropez, but this time she had pulled out a few stops. An off-the-shoulder white silk shirt accentuated her tanned cleavage, and a full mid-calf blue and white Provencal print skirt, cinched with a wide silver belt, made her waist look tiny. Espadrilles, silver hoop earrings, and a wide-brimmed straw hat on her gypsy hair, completed a look which was a far cry from her television designer show-pieces.

As she sipped vintage champagne and peach juice, and enjoyed the sun on her shoulders, Katherine was conscious that Jean-Claude's gaze was on her all the time, but he had put his opaque sunglasses back on so that it was impossible to read his eyes.

'So – what do you do?'

'I build hotels,' he answered. 'Quentin and I have just finished one in Avignon; pity it's so far away. I'd love to show it to you.'

'Well Avignon's not too far from St Tropez, where I'm staying,' said Katherine, not caring if he thought she was being too pushy.

'It would be wonderful to see you, but we must leave for Paris tomorrow.'

She started to feel a tightening in her stomach, a frisson of excitement. Stop it, she told herself, taking a sip of Bellini and flicking her eyes away from him. Stop it you idiot; he must be involved with someone, maybe even with Eleonor.

She asked where he was staying.

'With Stan and Betty. We've been here now for a week.'

'Oh, how nice,' she said. Ah, so that was it! This golden god was obviously Quentin's latest toy boy. She should have known.

'Oh, it's not what you think!' Jean-Claude smiled. He had noticed the flickering look of apprehension on Kitty's face. 'Quentin and I have been friends since I was a boy. He's like a father-figure to me. Neither of us had taken a vacation in years, so when Betty invited us, we jumped.'

'Betty's good at making people jump,' said Katherine.

'She's a strong woman.' He glanced over to where Betty was telling a bawdy story. 'Strong, and beautiful too,' he said, 'but not nearly as beautiful as you.'

Katherine felt a blush rise from her neck.

'Thanks...' she murmured. 'It was you, wasn't it, who sent me that message at the TV Favourites Awards?'

'Guilty,' he said. 'I'm not usually in the fan mail business, but I had just seen you for the first time on television, then I saw you there, in the flesh and I thought: earth has not anything to show more fair.'

'And you're a Shakespeare scholar, too?' She couldn't tear her eyes away from him.

'Wordsworth. I just had an uncontrollable impulse – I hope you don't mind?'

'Of course not.'

He took off his sunglasses and stared at her. 'I can't believe you're real.'

'Actresses aren't supposed to be real. According to some people, we're just around to be on display like peacocks – or to be stared at.' She glanced over to where several of the guests were giving them stealthy looks.

'You were made to be stared at.' His words seemed to caress her.

'I don't know how to answer that.' She felt dizzily light-headed, incredibly happy. 'I'm at a loss for words.'

'With those eyes, you don't need to say anything,' he whispered, smiling at her with that devastating charm. She felt herself glowing with warmth, and with the kind of anticipation she had forgotten existed. What a face, what a body, what a smile. How could someone that handsome possibly be that interesting, that warm, that nice?

Jean-Claude leaned towards her, about to say something, when Betty clapped her hands loudly, announcing: 'OK, everyone, lunch is served. It's good old dyed-in-the-wool American chow from Texas. Hot dogs, hamburgers, prime ribs, black eyed peas and mah *favourite*, southern fried chicken, flown in from Dallas, by the jet last night!'

'No expense spared at this *petite maison*.' Quentin had woken up to the smell of food, and was arranging his Panama at a jaunty angle.

'May I get you something, Katherine?' asked Jean-Claude.

'Oh, please, call me Kitty. That's really kind of you, Jean-Claude, but I promised I'd eat with my son.'

'Well, perhaps we could all sit together. D'you think he would mind?'

Katherine looked over to where Tommy was cavorting in the pool, with two bikini-clad girls, and grinned:

'I don't think he'd mind one bit.'

Jean-Claude took her arm, and with his face close to hers, gave a dazzling secret smile, then he led her across the grass to the buffet. Katherine felt herself blushing.

Lunch was so delicious that Katherine ate and drank twice as much as she usually did. After lunch the children went to play inside the house, while the adults lounged around the pool, in the shade. Katherine lay in a chaise, on the point of dozing, straw hat tipped over her eyes, listening to the hum of voices. Some guests had left, and it was a hot, langorous, Riviera afternoon. She could hear the ceaseless buzzing of bees in the lavender, and in the trees the music of the cicadas was almost deafening.

'Jean-Claude, honey, why don't you give us all a song?' Betty came over, full of crackling vivacity.

'Oh, no thank you, *chérie*. It's very kind of you, but my singing days are over long ago.'

Jean-Claude suddenly looked slightly vulnerable. Katherine was fascinated. Sing? Play the guitar? Was he some kind of star in France? As well as an hotelier? He must be, because the French guests were all looking enthusiastic.

She took off her sunglasses, cajoling him with her famous eyes. 'I'd love to hear you sing, Jean-Claude.'

'Yeah, yeah! C'mon, c'mon Jean-Claude. Let's hear it. Quentin says you were the greatest at Olympia.' Betty signalled to her formally dressed butler. 'Let's *go* for it, honey. Alphonse, get on over here. Bring my son's guitar for Monsieur Valmer, *s'il vous plait*.'

Jean-Claude shrugged his shoulders, while Quentin dragged a chair into the middle of the lawn, and pushed him into it. Everyone clustered around expectantly, and when the guitar arrived, Jean-Claude reluctantly began. First he sang an old French folk song about a rabbit and a fox which he performed in two voices. A high-pitched, almost soprano-like cadence as the rabbit, a deep growling tenor for the fox.

It was a whimsical, yet astonishingly polished performance, quite unlike anything Katherine had expected, and she whispered to Quentin, 'Is this what he does for a living?'

'Oh no, my dear, not at all. He used to, of course, but you should feel quite honoured. He is really doing it for you.'

Jean-Claude inclined his head, golden hair tumbling over his forehead, a faint smile on his lips.

Quentin continued: 'Jean-Claude was quite a famous folk singer in France, when he was a teenager. He performed for a few years, made a couple of hit records, and actually became extremely popular. But he found it such an empty, stressful life that, in his early twenties, he gave it up and went into business instead.'

'Smart cookie,' said Katherine admiringly. 'Maybe I should have done the same thing.'

'What a loss that would have been to our TV screens!' purred Quentin.

Jean-Claude's sparkling green eyes seemed amused by the success of his concert. Everyone begged for more, and even the children abandoned their video games to watch.

By the time Jean-Claude Valmer had finished, Katherine was more than a little in love.

* * *

By the kind of coincidence which spells destiny, Jean-Claude, Quentin, and Katherine were all booked on the same flight to London ten days later.

Katherine's six week vacation was almost over. She had packed Tommy off to the Hamptons, and had decided to go to London for the opening night of Zev Carter's new play. He had been one of her off-Broadway producers, and a supportive friend. Afterwards she intended to take the Saturday morning flight to LA, ready for work on Monday morning.

Her London stopover promised to be fun, except for one important drawback. Katherine wasn't comfortable attending public functions on her own, and had not yet fixed an escort for the play. Now, as she stood in the Riviera Club lounge at Nice airport, and saw Quentin walk in with Jean-Claude, she felt a familiar shiver of excitement; she knew what she wanted to do. Waiting until Jean-Claude was engrossed in getting himself some coffee, she walked up to Quentin.

'How was Paris?' she asked.

'Hot. Much too hot. So we finished our business there, then we had to come to Monaco, for a day, on our way to London.'

'Does your friend bring a dinner jacket with him on his travels?' she asked.

'Of course he does – he's a Frenchman. Why do you ask?'

'Do you think he would like to take me to the opening of *Tomorrow is Now* on Thursday night?'

'I'm sure he would!' The little man beamed. 'He told me he finds you extremely *simpatico*, not to mention *very* attractive. As do I, of course.'

She blushed again. What the hell was it about Jean-Claude that made her behave like a teenager?

'Oh that's terrific. I like him too. But Quentin, would you mind asking him for me? I'm not used to asking men out on dates!'

It was true. Katherine had two or three walkers in LA, mostly gay men who could be relied on not to arouse comment among the gossips, or to make sexual advances, but she never pursued men she fancied. Frankly, she had never had to.

'I shall ask him for you myself,' Quentin said smoothly.

Katherine smiled, and the die was cast.

The play was enthralling. Grittily modern, engagingly frank, its harsh, slangy dialogue had originality and freshness. Katherine loved it, and so – very much to her relief – did Jean-Claude.

She wore a slender column of grey silk jersey, with an empire bodice and jewelled gun-metal shoulder straps. Her black hair was pulled back in a simple chignon, and she looked classically elegant. Betty, who had flown with Stan in their jet for the opening, was Texan spitfire personified, in a red ruffled taffeta and lace mini dress, which accentuated her tiny waist. To match it, she wore red lace stockings, and *all* her rubies.

'Ah *declare* Ah've *nevah heard* such language in mah life!' she murmured, as she and Katherine made their way backstage after the performance.

'Well that's what you get when there's no censorship,' said Katherine. 'I enjoyed it though, didn't you?'

'Ah'd rather see an Andrew Lloyd Webber musical any day. Give me *Cats*, or *Phantom of the Opera* – those are what Ah call shows. This was jest plain filth!'

The party afterwards was at the Savoy, and the paparazzi went mad when they saw Katherine walk in escorted by Jean-Claude Valmer. The entrance to the River Room was at the back of the Savoy. It faced the Thames, and the narrow pavement there was jammed with reporters and photographers.

'Is this your new boyfriend, Kitty?' shouted one, shoving a tape recorder under her nose, and blocking her entrance. 'What's his name?'

'We're just friends.' Katherine felt the proprietary touch of Jean-Claude's hand on her elbow, and smiled through gritted teeth, edging away from the intrusive hack as she did so.

'Hey, matey! You and the Poison-Peach. What's happenin' chum? You two look hot together – what's goin' on?'

Jean-Claude shook his head, gripped Katherine's arm tighter, and ignored them all. He managed to get them inside the plush hallway without damage.

'Well done!' Katherine was impressed. 'You handled those bastards really well.'

'I hate the bloody press,' he said, with a vehemence that surprised her. 'They're all scum.'

As if on cue, one reporter called Frank Tamlin, who had managed to follow them inside, hissed a clearly audible obscenity. Jean-Claude whirled around, grabbed the man by his garish bow tie, and pulled his face close to his own.

'I heard that,' his voice was deadly quiet, but his eyes blazed. 'And if I ever hear you say anything like that again about this lady, you will regret it. Deeply.' He smiled, and released his grip on the man's tie, so abruptly that the hack almost lost his balance.

'Shall we join the party?' Jean-Claude smiled, as though nothing had happened.

'Let's.' Katherine smiled back. She had to admit that having a battle fought on her behalf, even such a minor one as this, was a refreshing change. Johnny had never wanted to fight any battle for her.

Although Jean-Claude looked totally cool as he guided her down to the ballroom, Katherine could sense anger simmering in him. He must have had a bellyful of the press when he was famous, she mused. I wonder what they did to him?

They danced, and flirted, and laughed over a passable dinner, although Katherine was so intoxicated she could barely eat. Later, as she was on her way back from the powder-room with Betty, they passed a table of press cronies. Katherine had to walk behind Frank Tamlin's chair, and as she did so, she heard him say quite clearly, 'Katherine Bennet is an ageing tart, with about as much talent as my Aunt Fanny.'

Katherine's face flamed.

'That rat-turd,' she hissed to Betty. 'How could he say such a thing?'

'Bastard!' said Betty.

'Who's a bastard?' asked Jean-Claude.

'Oh, it's no one you know,' said Katherine quickly, not wanting another scene

'Oh, but no gentleman would evah speak like that about a lady where *Ah* come from, and Ah think that columnist needs to be taken down a peg or two,' said Betty.

'Oh, cool it Betty, please. Honestly, Jean–Claude, it's nothing to worry about.'

But Betty was not to be stopped now, and she regaled the table with what she had heard. An indefinable expression crossed the Frenchman's face; there was a flash of something in his eyes, then he smiled at Betty, and bending his head towards Kitty, asked 'Would you like some more wine, *chérie*?'

'I'd rather dance with you,' she whispered. Instantly he was on his feet.

They stayed on the floor for several dances, with half theatrical London rubber-necking around them. Then Jean-Claude escorted Kitty back to their table.

'Excuse me, *chérie*,' he said, and walked slowly over to where a grinning Frank Tamlin had been watching them. With one swift movement, Jean-Claude pulled Frank's chair from under him, then bent over the fallen journalist.

'I told you not to mess with Miss Bennet again,' he hissed, the smile never leaving his face. 'That's the second time you did so this evening. It had better be the last, my friend.'

'What a guy,' Betty sighed admiringly. 'A real man. They don't make 'em like that any more, Kitty.'

'They certainly don't,' Katherine said, quietly observing how cool Jean-Claude appeared as he strolled back to the table.

He sat down and whispered: 'I'm sorry, *chérie*. Someone had to teach that pig a lesson. I hope I wasn't out of line.'

'Never.' Katherine felt like a teenager. 'You were right on your mark, Jean-Claude.'

At the end of the party, Betty and Stan insisted they go on to Annabels for a nightcap. The exclusive night club in Berkeley Square catered only for the richest, most famous, and aristocratic people in the world, and membership was strictly limited. Chris de Burgh was singing *Lady in Red* as they arrived. The lights were low, the atmosphere smooth and romantic, and Katherine melted into Jean-Claude's arms again, almost as if she belonged there. He was a good dancer, moving sensuously to the music on the small floor. He seemed to Kitty to be a man who knew his own mind, where he was headed, what he wanted. Yet if he didn't get exactly what he wanted, Katherine believed he'd accept that too. She found the combination of his intense personality and perfect manners extraordinarily attractive.

When he talked to her, she felt as if she were the only person in the world who existed for him. He also had an endearing line in self-deprecating humour. She wondered what it would be like to make love to him; the anticipation made her feel light-headed. She *wanted* to go to bed with him. She hadn't slept with anyone since her husband, and if Jean-Claude wanted to, she knew she would.

After several bottles of Krug, they left Annabels at four a.m., and dropped Katherine at the Ritz. The Chalmers waited in the car while Jean-Claude escorted her to the entrance. He took her hand and kissed the palm of it.

'*Au revoir*, Katherine,' he said softly. 'It has been the most wonderful evening. I cannot thank you enough, *chérie*.'

He looked into her eyes, and Katherine panicked. He couldn't go. Not yet. She wanted him to stay, and she wanted to see him again. She *had* to see him again, but she knew as well as he did, that if he spent the night with her at the Ritz, tomorrow's papers would carry the story as cheap gossip.

He visited LA several times a year, he'd said, but when? When would he be coming again?

'Will you be coming to LA soon?' Her throat was dry; it made her voice thick. She knew she sounded too eager.

'I may have to visit the States in the next month. There's been some interest from Las Vegas in my hotel company. I must follow it up.'

'Well, if you do come, promise to look me up.' Katherine pressed a slip of paper into his pocket. She had scribbled her telephone number on it. 'I'd really like to see you again.'

'*Moi aussi*,' he whispered, bending his head to her ear. 'If I believed in souls, Kitty, I would say that yours and mine have known each other for a very long time.'

Then, brushing her hand with his lips, he walked slowly back to the car.

CHAPTER SEVEN

Extract from The National Enquirer, *August 20th, 1988*

Talk about stuck up stars!! Toffee-nosed Katherine Bennet is trying to pretend that she wasn't a failed Broadway actress. Whenever anyone on the set of The Skeffingtons *tries to talk about her stage career, the Georgia Poison-Peach walks away in a huff. The whole cast and crew are outraged by her hoity-toity attitude, which seems to be mirroring her Skeffington character exactly. Watch out Kitty, better be nice to the people on your way up, otherwise you'll meet them coming down and find you've failed again, like you did after your last off-Broadway play!*

Extract from The Globe, *September 20th, 1988*

Ha Ha Ha Department! Diners at posh Spago eatery were pleased as punch when super-diva Georgia 'Poison-Peach' Skeffington, also known as ex-New York thesp Katherine Bennet, slipped on a lettuce leaf and fell flat on her derriere! The hilarious incident happened whilst Katherine was exiting the trendy restaurant on the arm of yet another of her boyfriends, hairdresser Carlos di Souza, 27, eighteen years her junior.

'That's shown her,' chortled ex-fan Belinda Nash, 16. 'She's become much too big for her breeches recently. She

won't even sign autographs any more. It's us, the fans, who made her, and we can break her, too.' Hear hear, Belinda, we say. Better watch it Miss Georgia P.P. Once your fans desert you, the TV public can't be far behind.

Extract from the New York Daily Post, *September 29th, 1988*

GEORGIA POISON PEACH TO BE KILLED OFF PERMANENTLY?

Skeffington Star, Katherine Bennet, is to be a potential murder statistic as her character Georgia Skeffington gets killed by a hitman. Producer Gabe Heller is reported to be edgy at reports of more tantrums and bad behaviour on the set, and is considering replacing Bennet with a new star, possibly Donna Mills.

Sources, close to the set, report that there is little love lost between Bennet and co-star Eleonor Norman, who has just played the eponymous lead in the ten million dollar mini-series, The Loves of Emma Hamilton, *and has been gaining in popularity in the last season. An insider was quoted as saying: 'Mr Heller doesn't like his stars behaving like spoiled children. He feels he gave them this break and that they should be more loyal to him. (Bennet was a Broadway unknown until four years ago). Besides, Georgia Skeffington's murder could become one of the most watched episodes in TV history.' Skeffingtons' ratings have been on the slide for over a year and are now at an all time low. Georgia's murder could make the show sizzle again.*

'Honey, you're gotta stop acting so swelled head. Who d'ya think you are – Liz Taylor?'

Katherine gritted her teeth. 'No, Mama, I don't think I'm anyone except me, and I'm sick to death of you believing all this crap!'

'Last week you stood Clint Eastwood up on a date. This week you're biting the hand that feeds you. You gotta stop it, Kitty, or they're going to can your keister – the papers say so.'

Katherine rolled her eyes heavenward. Why did her mother, a sane Englishwoman in every other respect, believe the claptrap in the gossip rags?

'OK, Mama – I've got to go now – I'll catch you later.'

She hung up before another tirade started, and turned to Brenda.

'I've had enough. It's a bunch of *absolute* lies, all of it.'

'I know, honey, I know. It's really a bummer.'

'We've been back on the show for a month, and it's worse than ever. But why?' said Katherine. 'Why is it always me they pick on? Why not Eleonor, or Suzanna? It's unbelievable. Who feeds them this trash?'

'I don't know,' said Brenda.

'It's a constant stream of lies,' Katherine flipped through some of the latest press clippings piled on her desk.

'*None* of it's true. Look at this one! Me, jealous of Eleonor! I mean peleeze!! She can't act, she's meaner than a skunk, and her hair's falling out, so why should *I* be jealous?'

'You're never jealous of anyone, let alone that bag of silicone.'

'Obviously I don't like her – she's got the brains of a pea,' Katherine said fiercely, 'But since she doesn't like me either, it's a stand off. And that *ridiculous* story about me slipping on the lettuce leaf! That happened to Suzanna last week, at Hamburger Hamlet.'

'Well, you know what the tabloids are. Today's crap for the eyes; tomorrow no one remembers.'

'They're getting even more dishonest than ever. Oh God. Do you think people will really believe this latest thing?'

'Nah! Ignore 'em. And get a move on with your hair. It's almost magic time.'

'Well it sure is magic, the way this shit gets in the columns every week.' Katherine tugged a comb through her hair. 'It's as though it's being deliberately planted to discredit me.'

'Who'd do that? No one could be that destructive. They certainly weren't in my day.'

But somebody *was* that destructive. Eleonor wanted Katherine out of the show, and she thought she had found a foolproof way to do it. In exchange for two or three scandalous titbits about Katherine every now and again, *The National Tattler* would print favourable pieces on Eleonor. The only trouble was that the ratings for the show had slipped since last season, and now the producers – and Eleonor – faced the possibility that it would have to close altogether. A sacrifice needed to be made, and the obvious choice, in the wake of the bad publicity, was Katherine – except, as everyone knew, the public loved her, and had reacted vehemently against the notion of Georgia Skeffington's death. It was a dilemma. Katherine asked Steven what he thought would happen.

'I can't tell you what's happening in future scripts, Kitty. But you don't have anything to worry about. You're the cherry on top of our cake. The show can't make it without you.'

'God, I wish I had your confidence. I can't help feeling that there's something ominous in the air.'

'You mean we're back to something like the shooting of JR?'

'Well look what it did to *their* ratings,' said Katherine. '*Dallas* zoomed up the charts, and stayed there for three seasons.'

'I guess so. But Kitty, don't fret. I promise I'll tell you if they're going to dump you.'

'Oh gee, thanks...' Katherine hesitated. She wanted to ask him if what she'd heard around the studio was true: if his marriage to Mandy was on the rocks. She had to know; there was no point in beating about the bush.

'By the way, they say you and Mandy are splitting up. I'm so sorry...' Her voice trailed away; she felt embarrassed, but to her relief, he smiled.

' 'Fraid so; I was no match for that trainer of hers, the Schwarzenegger-lookalike. She was a good kid, and we had a good run. Listen, I hear there's a new man in your life.'

Kitty shrugged. 'Wish there was, Steve. I met someone in France but he hasn't picked up the phone since. I guess he's forgotten me.'

'Then he must be a fool,' said Steven, suppressing a spasm of jealousy. 'By the way, how's Johnny responding to the treatment?'

'He's doing really well, and Tommy's much more relaxed about the situation, thank God.'

Jean-Claude Valmer read the gossip item on the Paris plane to New York, and felt angry for Katherine. Even though they had only met twice, he felt an incredible empathy with her, and he did not believe what he read in the press. He knew only too well how the media loved to smash idols of the day to the ground. He'd kept the scrap of paper with her telephone numbers in his wallet, and as soon as he arrived at the Carlyle, he dialled her dressing room.

An unfriendly woman's voice answered.

'Yeah?'

'May I speak to Miss Bennet, please?'

'I'll see if I can get her. Who's calling?'

'It's Jean-Claude Valmer. Tell her we met in France.'

'Jean-Claude! How wonderful to hear you. How are you?' In a flash the voice had changed from vinegar to honey.

'Was that you, Kitty? It sounded like an old dragon.'

'That's to keep my frantic fans at bay.' She laughed. 'You'd be amazed how many people get hold of this number, even though it's private. Where are you?'

'I have some business here, in New York, then in Nevada. But after that I could take a trip to LA. How long are you there for?'

'Oh, I'm always here. I never get away, except at hiatus time, and that sure does seem ages ago.'

'Must be hard for you.' His voice was sympathetic.

'Sometimes.' Suddenly she wanted to confide in Jean-Claude. He touched a nerve in her, she felt warm and safe just hearing his voice.

'I saw that piece of trash about you, I couldn't believe it.' His voice crackled across the three thousand miles of fibre optics which separated them.

'That's show biz!' She laughed weakly. 'I seem to be on trial by media these days.'

'You don't deserve it,' he said softly. 'You're too good to have all this sort of garbage written about you.'

Feelings that she had put on the back burner for the past few weeks came roaring back. The sound of his voice made her melt. She wanted to see him; she needed to see him.

'Where are you staying in LA?'

'The Beverly Hills Hotel. That's where I usually go. Or I might stay with Quentin.'

'Or you might stay with me.' Before she could stop herself, it had popped out. She was shocked at her own audacity. What had come over her? Lust? Infatuation? Neediness? Her face went hot, and there was a long, long pause.

'I don't think that would be quite right, do you?' he said gently. 'After all, we hardly know each other.'

'You're right.' God, why was she blushing?

'But I would like to see you again, Kitty, very much indeed. I feel we have many things we still have not said to each other.'

'Ditto.'

'I will telephone you as soon as I arrive, and we shall make plans.'

'When do you think that'll be?' She bit her lip. Miss Over-Eager again.

'In about a week I hope. Can we play?' His voice was filled with promise.

'If we don't, I shall sulk for days.' Katherine smiled.

When she got home from work the following day Brenda handed her another gold record.

'What's it say?' demanded Brenda. 'No fun in keeping secrets.'

'It's *You'll Never Know*,' said Katherine. 'Oh, that was one of Vera's favourite songs. And the note says: "Ah but I hope you soon will".'

On their first Los Angeles date Katherine took Jean-Claude to a dinner party at Ma Maison. This extremely popular restaurant was the closest thing in LA to a French bistro, and in the balmy September night, the patio would be packed with celebrities, wannabees and never-gonnabees.

Katherine had been in an agony of indecision about what to wear. She usually knew exactly how she wanted to look, but this time she had discarded at least six outfits, and still was unsure that she'd made the right choice. Jean-Claude had admired her shoulders in St Tropez, so she decided she would give him the shoulders again tonight. She wore a short white lace dress with a neckline low enough to accentuate her tan, and give the merest hint of a cleavage, then she brushed her hair until it shone, removed her heavy television make-up, and applied minimum eye shadow, blusher and lipstick. She stood before a full-length mirror, indecisively putting on and removing a variety of earrings.

'To hell with it,' she said, suddenly chucking them all down, and pinning a fresh gardenia behind her left ear.

Katherine wasn't quite sure about the language of flowers. Did a flower behind the left ear mean availability? She shrugged. Who cared? She knew how she wanted this evening to end, and if he thought she was wanton, so damn what? It was a long, cold time since a man had shared her bed, and even though she had an early call on the set the next day, the excitement at seeing him again, of being close to him, overrode her professional discipline.

He arrived at seven o'clock and when she saw him standing in her white living room, studying the three gold records on the mantelpiece, she thought that he looked even better than she remembered. His tan was more golden, his blond hair more endearingly unruly, and his transparent eyes greener than the sea.

'I see they amused you,' he said.

'They're adorable. I wish I knew who sent them.'

'You do know who.'

Katherine looked hard at him.

'Yes, of course it was me. I wanted to meet you.'

He had suggested dinner at L'Orangerie, but was not the slightest bit fazed when she proposed going to the party instead.

Kitty knew she was testing him. Many of her friends, and half the entertainment industry would be there tonight, and they would be only too willing to air their views on Katherine's latest guy. The party, given by Beverley and Hal Hawn, honouring Gabe Heller's birthday, was in a private room upstairs in Ma Maison. As they walked in, Katherine felt all eyes on them. She was perfectly well aware that they made an arresting couple, and that Jean-Claude's charm and sex appeal would make him a target for many women.

'My God where did you find that gorgeous piece of man-flesh,' gasped Donna Mills, as they tweaked and powdered in the ladies room.

'I imported him,' Katherine smiled.

'Let's face it, honey, guys like that *don't* grow on trees around here. Are you sure he's not an actor?'

'Positive.' Katherine looked at her face objectively. She certainly didn't need any more blusher. She was flushed, sparkling-eyed, and positively fizzy with anticipation. 'He's definitely *not* in the biz, Donna darling. He's a civilian, thank God.'

'Well you look like the cat that swallowed the canary.' Donna grinned, fluffing her long blonde hair.

'Not yet, but the night is still young.'

When she returned to the main room, Jean-Claude was charming Sharon Lasker, the young wife of an ancient Hollywood mogul. Sharon Lasker was known to be a man-eater, and now she was positively oozing sexual availability. Her heavily-powdered face was inches from Jean-Claude's, and her eyes, with their turquoise contact-lenses, were fastened on his face. She licked her collagen-enhanced, glossy lips as if she would like to devour him, and, with one deft movement, slid her calling-card into his breast pocket. But Jean-Claude gave not one flicker of acknowledgement. Instead he moved slightly backwards, turned towards Carolyn Lupino, the wife of Paradigm Pictures' president, and adroitly brought her into the conversation. Then he greeted Katherine with a dazzling smile, and offered her a cigarette from an elegant gold case. There was some handwriting engraved on the inside. Katherine peeked surreptitiously.

'Mad about you', it said. She felt a hard sharp pang of pure jealousy, but knew that she mustn't let anyone see.

'I would just *love* you both to come to Lew's birthday party on Saturday night. It's his *sixtieth*!' Carolyn Lupino was gushing at Jean-Claude. 'Don't tell anyone – he's sooo sensitive about it!'

Katherine was about to reply, when Jean-Claude said smoothly: 'That's terribly sweet of you, Carolyn, but Kitty and I have made other plans. We're going to Palm Springs for the weekend.'

Katherine's eyebrows rose. Was this a ploy to get out of a party gracefully, or was he becoming proprietorial? Either way she didn't really mind – she was far too happy in his company. Palm Springs? Why not? She wanted to spend time with him. A lot of time.

'Oh well, let's all do another evening.' Then, in a whisper loud enough for Jean-Claude to hear:

'He's *gorgeous* Kitty. And so *nice*. I always did like Frenchmen, ever since we had that Yves Montand to dinner.'

After that the party passed in a whirl of gossip, laughter, and – for Kitty – happy anticipation of what she was now sure was to come. Even the sight of Eleonor Norman, obviously flirting with Jean-Claude, did not spoil her contentment, and she was wise enough neither to comment on it, nor to press him for details of his friendship with her. Some other time.

And she knew there were going to be other times, when he encircled her waist with one arm, bent his head, and said: 'You are the most beautiful woman here tonight – by far – Kitty.'

While Jean-Claude drove her home, they laughingly discussed the party. Katherine did a wickedly hilarious imitation of Mrs Lupino, and of Eleonor's fake upper class English accent. By the time they stopped laughing, they had reached the gates of Katherine's house.

Her heart was thumping so loudly that she felt sure Jean-Claude could hear it. The iron gates clicked open, and she noted that Tommy's bedroom lights were still on. This would certainly stop Jean-Claude coming in for anything other than a nightcap. Tommy being up at this hour usually meant problems. He had been on his best behaviour recently, a model son. Maybe too good to be true?

Whilst Katherine rummaged for her keys, Jean-Claude stood at the front door. Taking her hand, he pressed it softly.

'So – we meet on Friday then – Do you like Palm Springs, Kitty?'

'I love Palm Springs,' she whispered.

'Good.'

Then he kissed her softly on the mouth and with a whispered, 'Still the most beautiful,' got into his rented car and drove off.

Katherine stared after him, slightly disappointed, but after all, Friday was only the day after tomorrow. She could wait, and first there was her son to be dealt with.

Kitty sensed trouble, even before she went into Tommy's room. The sound of rap music from inside was deafening. She knocked hard, but he obviously couldn't hear her. She pushed open the door, and saw him, lying fully dressed, on the bed. His eyes were closed, but there were tearstains on his cheeks. Empty beer bottles lay on the floor next to his bed, as well as dozens of candy wrappers, and a whole uneaten pizza was overturned on a pile of dirty socks. The room looked as though a wild animal had been rampaging through it.

'Tommy, what the hell's going on here?'

He didn't answer, his eyes remained tightly closed, while the anarchic music continued to shake the room. She crossed to the TV set and turned it off. This galvanized Tommy into action.

'Why'd you do that, Mom?' His eyes snapped open, accusing and angry.

'Tommy, it's past midnight. You've got school tomorrow. Why are you still up – what's wrong?'

He gave a bleary, drunken grin and a little hiccup.

'It's nuthin', Mom. Nuthin' at all. I'm fine.' His words were slurred. Katherine's eyes narrowed as she crossed over to his bed. He tried to avert his head, but she took his face in her hands and turned it towards her. The pupils of his eyes had contracted to pinpricks, and he had a strange, soft expression on his face.

'Tommy,' she said, keeping the flood of panic out of her voice. 'Where have you been? What have you been doing?'

'I've been with Dad.' Petulantly he moved away from her.

'Oh really. How is he?'

'He's OK, I guess. But that's like a pigsty he lives in, Mom.' He stared at her accusingly. 'How'd' you expect him to live on that pittance you give him?'

'Pittance? Do you know what you are talking about, Tommy? Your father and I are divorced. We settled everything in the courts. It was a perfectly fair deal.'

'Yeah, well maybe for you, but not for him.' Tommy took a slug of beer, and looked at his mother with challenging eyes. 'Women – can't live with 'em – can't kill 'em,' he giggled.

'You're stoned, aren't you, Tommy?'

His face set in a sulky expression. She shook his shoulders hard.

'Lay off me, Mom,' he whined.

'I won't. Not until you tell me the truth. Did your father give you any drugs?'

His wary, startled eyes showed that she'd hit the mark.

'Yeah, he did – so what? It's only a joint that's all.'

'Only a joint? That's all? Your father's recuperating from a serious illness, and he's taking dope, and giving *you* dope, and you say, so what? What the *hell* has gotten into you, Tommy.'

'You're too old-fashioned, Mom. Get with it, why don't you? Smoking grass is no different from those stupid Marlboros you're always puffing on.' He turned up the MTV volume again.

'Get real, Mom. All kids today smoke – *all* of us, and nuthin' you say or do is gonna make me, or any of us, stop doin' it.'

She knew better than to argue with someone drunk or stoned, even if he was her son.

'OK, Tommy, I guess I can't stop you from doing what all the kids do,' she murmured. 'I'll tell you one thing. I've never met a person who takes dope or smokes grass, spliff, or whatever you call it, whose brain functions properly. It destroys your brain Tommy; it fries your mind.'

Her words didn't seem to bother him. He took a bite of pizza, a swig of beer, and mumbled 'Night Mom – see you in the ayem,' but his eyes never left the screen.

With a heavy tread, Katherine went up to her bedroom, and as she did so, her thoughts turned to Jean-Claude and Palm Springs. She would deal with Tommy after the weekend. She would put all her problems out of her mind for those two days.

'Ain't nothin' gonna stop me,' she sang softly to herself as she brushed her hair. 'Nothin' can stop me now.'

Quentin's white bungalow in Palm Springs was on one of the streets off Bob Hope Drive. It had a perfect view of the thick green grass of the golf course, and a breathtaking vista of the purple-tinged Jacinto mountains. Jean-Claude and Kitty arrived just after lunch, in the boiling heat, and he immediately suggested a swim.

'There are no staff here,' he told her. 'It's just a tiny house, but Quentin likes his privacy, and so do I.'

'So do *I*,' Katherine thought, undressing, in a quaint 1950s-style bedroom. It had charming Indian prints on the walls, and faded Aztec rugs on the polished wooden floors.

There were only two bedrooms in the bungalow and Jean-Claude had given Katherine the bigger one. He put his own black suitcase down, then carried in several sacks of groceries, which had been stacked outside the back door.

Katherine pulled up her sleek black bathing suit, grimacing as she looked at herself in the full-length mirror.

'Too fat,' she muttered. 'Better diet, kid, otherwise Gabe's gonna have you on the carpet yet again.'

She threw the latest script on to the bed. It was bound in yellow, with *The Skeffingtons Number 106. Who Dunnit?* printed on the front.

She should really read it this weekend, but her mind was too full of Jean-Claude. She knew she wouldn't be able to concentrate. She felt the tiny hairs on her arms rise in anticipation, and in spite of the humidity she shivered.

She could hear him humming in the kitchen while he put the groceries away. 'He's certainly organized,' thought Katherine. 'Just like a wife. Just what I need.'

Katherine had never been much of a domestic animal, and because nowadays a visit to a supermarket all too often started a mini–riot, she seldom went, or – for that matter – cooked in her own kitchen.

In the blisteringly hot Palm Springs noon, the pool glittered invitingly, the shallow end partially shaded from the sun by tall palm trees. The small back yard was well tended, with cacti growing in regimental spires; the patio furniture was old but clean, and the mattresses, on the two chaise longues, were covered by crisp white towels.

Jean-Claude came out of the back door, carrying a tray of drinks. He was wearing blue swimming trunks, which showed off his elegantly muscled physique.

'*Voilà*,' he set the tray down on the table, and handed her a plastic glass, embossed with cherries.

'Madame's favourite. Champagne and peach juice.'

Did he never forget anything? She had casually mentioned at Betty's that she adored Bellinis, and here they were, made with Vintage Krug and freshly squeezed juice. How had he managed all *that* in ten minutes?

'There's a local woman who comes in and does what's needed.' He grinned. 'She's very obedient.'

'Is that how you like your women?'

'No, I like my women rather feisty, extremely intelligent, and very beautiful. Like you.' He was close to her, towering above her, now that she wore no shoes. He bent his head and nuzzled her cloud of hair.

'You smell of rainbows,' he breathed. 'Rainbows and lilac.'

'Two of my favourite things,' she said, sipping the drink, and thinking that rainbows didn't smell – as far as she knew. 'This is the most delicious Bellini I've ever tasted – do you do everything well?'

'Almost everything.' He raised his glass. 'It's up to you to find out.'

She looked over at the small tennis court. 'I suppose you're a whizz at tennis too?'

'Try me,' he smiled. 'I'm very competitive, I'm afraid.'

'That makes two of us.'

Katherine felt deliciously light-headed from the Bellinis and Jean-Claude: she moved away to find a cigarette but he offered her one from his gold case, and again she noticed the inscription, 'Mad about you'.

'Would you like to know who it's from?' he asked. She smiled, shook her head and said, 'I'd rather not.' Katherine was wise enough never to ask men precise details about their past loves. She didn't need to know names, dates and relationships. Jealousy was a useless emotion; the only important thing was now. She couldn't stop her hand coming up gently to cup his chin as he lit it for her. She could smell him, husky, male, potent, but pure. His freshly shaved face was smooth to her touch, and his clear green eyes were looking into hers now. Gently he took her glass, and put it on the table. Then even more gently, he drew her into his arms.

Sounds of distant laughter from neighbours, and the Mozart clarinet concerto which Jean-Claude had put on the stereo, faded into the background. All Katherine could hear was the beating of her heart. His lips met hers. She had kissed a hundred times on the screen, but this was different. It was the first, sweet exploration of a lover. Soft, yielding, tender, but so filled with passion and sensuality, that Katherine knew without reservation she wanted to be his. She was made to be his. She would be his now.

He took her on the soft grass by the swimming pool, where the palm trees shaded them from the scorching sun.

Katherine had often thought of herself as sexually square. Unlike some of her girlfriends, she was not into erotic acrobatics or any form of sado-masochism. She believed in that old fashioned and corny thing – true, faithful love. As Jean-Claude explored her body with his own, teased and titillated her with his lips and tongue, she felt an explosion of such intensity that it made her body shake. She also felt an enormous outpouring of love. She had pretended for years that she didn't need it, or didn't want it. But now, on a langorous Palm Springs afternoon, she found that she did. And so it began.

Over the long, sybaritic weekend they became consumed by each other.

For Katherine this roaring passion was an entirely novel experience. She found that he was spectacularly well endowed, and that he loved making love. He didn't have to learn how to please Kitty; it came to him as naturally as breathing. Over and over again, he took Katherine with him on an unforgettably sensual journey, telling her that, like the psychologist William Reich, he believed man's highest achievement of passion to be based on the orgasm.

'That's certainly a theory you never seem to get tired of testing,' said Katherine, who was starting to believe it herself.

'For me, making love with you is a marvellous emotional experience, and that is because I am beginning to care for you so much.'

'So soon?' She never wanted to leave his arms.

'We were meant to be together,' he whispered. 'It's destiny, Kitty.'

Throughout the magical weekend, Katherine felt a harmony with Jean-Claude that she had never experienced with any man before. He was everything she had ever dreamed of in a lover. Tender, romantic, sexy, intelligent, loving, sensitive, passionate and totally in charge, the epitome of all masculine virtues. For his part, he admitted that although he had been involved many times, he had seldom been in love before.

For four years Katherine had been alone at the helm. Making the decisions, running her career, the household, Tommy's life, and being responsible for everything. But despite the power of her position, she was vulnerable. Her excessive fame made her so, and she knew it. In some extraordinary way she felt that Jean-Claude had been sent to save her; she knew without a doubt that she was falling in love with him.

On the second night, as they lay half asleep, entwined, watching *Rebecca* on American Movie Classics, Katherine heard a noise from outside. It sounded as though the screen doors were being pushed open. She had noticed earlier that Quentin's bungalow was quite vulnerable to intruders, but, preoccupied by the first stages of her new love-affair, she had decided not to worry about it. Now she quickly pressed the remote control volume button down, and listened. She could definitely hear footsteps in the living room. Jean-Claude had heard them too. Sliding silently out of bed, he went to the door and listened.

'Shall I call the police?' she mouthed, but he shook his head.

He wrapped a towel around his waist, stealthily opened the bedroom door, and walked softly down the short corridor to the living room. Throwing on a robe, Katherine tiptoed to the bedroom door, to see where Jean-Claude was.

The living room area was dark, but by the moonlight from the open window, Katherine could clearly see the outline of two men. She held her breath. This was insanity. Why didn't he come back to the bedroom, lock the door and call the police? Jean-Claude beamed the light of a strong flashlight onto the faces of the two intruders. They were teenagers, scarcely older than Tommy, and now they froze, like rabbits in the beam of car headlights. Jean-Claude's voice cut through the silence like a whip.

'Get the fuck out of here, right now! Otherwise you'll both get a bullet in your kneecaps.'

Jean-Claude held a Luger in his right hand. A big, black, deadly-looking gun. Where had that appeared from, Katherine wondered?

'Stand up. Put your hands above your head and by the time I count to three, you better be out of here.' Jean-Claude's voice was as hard as a drill sergeant's.

They turned around. One of them had a knife in his hand, which he dropped; it clattered across the stone tiles. The other suddenly saw Katherine, standing framed in the doorway.

'Jesus Christ, it's the Poison Peach,' he hissed.

'Kerist!' said the other boy. 'The witch! Let's get outta here!'

With a yelp of fear, the thieves belted out through the open window, leaving their haul lying on the floor.

'Oh my God,' Katherine collapsed onto the sofa, 'You could have been killed.'

'Don't be ridiculous,' he said briskly, frowning, as he examined the broken window. 'Not many people, burglars or otherwise, are going to mess with this.' He put the gun on a table.

'Oh God, I hate those things,' said Katherine, staring at it.

'They're a necessary evil, *chérie*.' He closed the window, checked the latch, and picked up the garbage bag full of cameras and nick-nacks, which the boys had been about to cart away.

'Don't worry *chérie* – they're only druggies.' He put his arms around her comfortingly. 'They're just kids high on junk, and needing some quick cash.'

'But they could have been dangerous.'

'Not if you know how to handle them. Most people respond to command. They react to authority, especially if it has this to back it up.' He gestured towards his gun.

'I think it's time to go back to bed, don't you?'

'Yes, I most certainly do,' she whispered back.

Jean-Claude moved into Katherine's guest room the following week, with two suitcases, a laptop computer and a locked briefcase. There was no question in Kitty's mind that this was what she wanted, and there was no question in Jean-Claude's mind that this was also right for him, but Tommy was not at all happy about it.

'Mom, why do we have to have this guy in the house?'

'Because I like him.' Katherine was in her dressing room, late for work, while Tommy was kicking his heels, instead of preparing for school.

'I told Dad,' he said sulkily.

'Told him what?' She was trying to run a comb through hair, matted from last night's lovemaking. They made love three or four times a night, with endless variations. Her face was flushed, her eyes were sparkling, and she looked like a woman in love. This would have been obvious to most women, but not to her son. 'What did Dad say?'

'He says you're a slut.'

'Charming!'

She thought about the numerous cheques she had signed recently for her ex-husband. Johnny was still having chemotherapy several times a week, and he needed a variety of expensive, legitimate drugs for his illness. Money seemed to be running away from her like a torrent, and the last thing she needed was Tommy telling her how to live her life.

'You're sixteen, Tommy,' she said firmly. 'It's about time you realized that your mother needs a life too.'

'You've got a life; it's at the studio. That's all you really care about.'

'Just because Jean-Claude has come to live here doesn't mean that I don't love you as much as I always have!' She tried to hug him, but he moved away and started fiddling with her perfume bottles. He seemed more on edge than usual, and she noticed that his eyes were very bright.

It was eight o'clock, and she had to be at the studio by nine.

'Look, I've got to fly, and you've got to get to school. Let's talk about this tonight.'

'OK, fine, Mom,' he said sullenly, and walked out of the room.

Katherine stared sadly out at the smoggy Beverly Hills skyline.

'*Pauvre petit chou.*' The warm voice made her turn. Jean-Claude stood in the doorway. 'You really do have your problems, don't you, *chérie*?'

'I guess so.'

He held out his arms with a smile, and she went to him. When he held her she felt invincible, as though nothing could harm her.

'Is there anything I can do to help, *chérie*?' He stroked her hair, which was so unruly this morning that it almost seemed alive.

'No thank you, darling,' she murmured. 'This is one battle I'm going to have to fight alone.'

What with all the excitement of her new love affair, Kitty hadn't had time to study the script for the following week. It wasn't until now, when she went into her dressing room, sparkling with happiness, and saw Brenda's miserable face, that she found out what was in store.

'You're a goner,' said Brenda dolefully.

'A goner? What do you mean?'

'Just what I say. You snuff it. They're killing you off. You die kiddo – it's right here. Read it and weep.' Brenda jabbed a finger at the last page of the script, and read out: 'Georgia says… "*I will never forgive you. Never – you'll rot in hell for this." Stage direction – Georgia dies. The intruder, whose face we do not see, laughs softly and closes the door. Freeze frame on Georgia's lifeless face. End.*'

'I can't believe this,' said Katherine.

'Believe it. I read it last night but I didn't want to call, and spoil your weekend.'

'Have you talked to Steve?'

'Yeah I called him, asked him if it was true, or just one of their usual red herrings.'

'What did he say?'

'He said they're killing you off. They're all the same, these soap operas. Every season they have a cliffhanger, and someone's got to die. Keeps the actors from getting greedy when contract re-negotiations come up.'

Kitty sat down heavily on the sagging sofa.

'I don't believe it. I thought the public really wanted me. Look, call Gabe. Tell him I've got to see him now.'

The inevitable knock came at the door. 'On set, Kitty. They want you in hair now – on the double.'

'The show must go on.' Katherine gritted her teeth. 'Whoever said there's no show biz like showbiz, was right. It sucks.'

Later Brenda told her that both producers were out of town.

'Great,' said Katherine. 'Have you talked to my agent?'

'He's getting back to me. He had a breakfast meeting.'

'For God's sake,' exploded Katherine, 'What the *hell* is going on around here? I'm being killed off, I can't reach my agent, or the producers, my life is falling apart, and nobody seems to give a damn.'

Her mobile rang, and picking it up she barked 'Yes?'

'*Chérie*, are you all right?'

'Oh, Jean-Claude. Oh God, the shit is *really* hitting the fan here today, darling. I'll tell you all about it tonight. Can't talk now.'

Charlie knocked again. 'You've got three minutes to get into hair and on to the set, Kitty,' he yelled.

'OK! *OK!*' She jammed a ridiculous hat on her head, and dashed out of the door, into hairdressing.

Eleonor sat in the next chair, with a pleased smirk on her puffy face.

'Morning, Kitty dahling, did you have a nice weekend?' she asked sweetly.

Kitty glowered at her, while the team fidgeted with her hat and hair, and Becky tugged at the collar of her itchy purple suit.

'Lovely,' she said curtly. 'I had a great time.'

'I'm *sooo* glad, dahling. I'm *désolée* you're leaving us, *chérie*.' Her bad French accent reminded Kitty that Eleonor had been with Jean-Claude at Jake's party all those months ago. She must remember to ask him about it. 'But it's great news that Donna Mills is coming in as your long-lost sister.'

'Oh well, you can't win 'em all,' Katherine quipped, with a lightness she did not feel.

'Oh, I always think you can,' Eleonor said, her over-mascaraed eyes glittering.

Katherine stood up, tugging at her too-tight, too-short skirt, and walked downstairs to the set, where the magic circle of arc lights awaited her.

'Well, at least I've got Jean-Claude,' she thought.

Charlie came over in one of the breaks.

'Phone for you, Kitty – your Mom.'

Kitty sighed and picked up the phone, which was on a light portable table, next to the craft-service running buffet.

'Hi, Mama – how are you?'

'Well I'm fine, Kit-Kat, just fine – except for my asthma. But I'm on a new pill now, so I don't have my turns any more.'

'Good, Mama; I'm glad.'

Charlie tapped her on the shoulder, mouthing: 'Ready for you now, Kitty.'

She nodded, knowing perfectly well that it was impossible to stop her mother once she was in full flow.

'So who is this Jean-Claude Valmer, or whatever he's called?' she asked now. 'Is it serious this time, Kit-Kat?'

Katherine took a deep breath and broke out a smile. 'Yes, Mama, it's serious – I think – and he's the best thing that's happened to me for years.'

'Well, I'll keep my fingers crossed for you, then, dear. You be careful now. You know you're not very good with men. If he's so great, try not to let him get away.'

'I won't,' said Katherine fervently.

That night Katherine poured out her heart to Jean-Claude. She told him about her financial and tax problems, about her business manager who, she was convinced, was ripping her off, about Pedro's replacement, Won, the enigmatic young

Chinese, whom Tommy called 'Soup' behind his back, about how Tommy's sulks made her feel guilty, and about her sick ex-husband, whose constant need for money was draining her resources to the last dollar.

By the time she had finished, she was almost in tears. She clung to Jean-Claude, as he held her in his arms, and soothed her. 'Don't worry about a thing, *chérie*, I'm going to help you, my darling. I'm going to solve all your problems, I promise you.'

CHAPTER EIGHT

The following day Katherine saw Gabe and Luther. As usual, they made her feel like a naughty schoolgirl. 'Are you seriously killing me off?' she asked.

Gabe fiddled with an ivory and malachite letter opener.

'You know the show's ratings are plummeting. We've got to do something to raise 'em.'

'Yes, everyone knows that.' Katherine was only too well aware of the vagaries of the TV ratrace. It was a constant war between the networks, and a running battle between the top prime-rated shows. A show could be top of the Neilson ratings one week, but slip to number nine or ten the next. Some shows shot up and down like yo yos.

'We were against the Superbowl last week, and for three weeks before that we had that blockbuster mini-series up against us,' said Katherine.

'I know, I know. But some of those weeks we haven't even come *second*.' Gabe's voice was irritable.

'But why must I be sacrificed?' Katherine lit a cigarette with trembling hands.

'It's all for the good of the show, Katherine dear,' Luther snapped. 'That's the only thing that matters at the end of the day.'

'But I've been loyal to you all. I've been loyal to the show, in spite of all that crap that's been in the papers. I just can't *believe* that you guys pay attention to what those scummy rags write.' She stared at them, but they averted their eyes. 'Do you *really* believe all that shit?'

'That's not the point here,' said Luther. 'The point is we've got to raise the ratings. You know what JR's attempted murder did to Dallas? This is what we want to do with *The Skeffingtons*.'

'But what if the ratings don't rise?' Katherine asked. 'With all the bad things written about me, don't forget there've been some good things too. Like for example that this show would be nothing without me.'

She saw a flash of anger in Gabe's eyes and hastily corrected herself. 'No, of course I don't mean it would be *nothing*. I mean it would still be great – but – different – oh well, what can I say? I'm supposed to be the spice in this pie, right?'

They both nodded then Gabe said, 'To put you out of your misery, Kitty, I'll tell you that we *are* going to shoot an alternative ending to your death. But – ' he lowered his voice dramatically, 'We're gonna shoot it on a closed set, with a confidentiality agreement, involving everyone.'

Katherine, who had already begun to suspect that some of the bad stuff in the papers came from Eleonor, said, 'Do the rest of the cast need to know this?'

Gabe also suspected the same thing, but he had made no attempt to put a stop to it, because until now the alleged feud between Eleonor and Katherine appeared to improve the ratings. 'The only actor who will know about it, Kitty, is you.' He pushed a couple of sheets of paper across the table at her.

'Here, read this, honey. I think you'll like it.'

Katherine skimmed the pages, then smiled.

'This is the other ending?'

He nodded. 'Uh-huh – '

'And what exactly does the outcome depend on?'

'We're gonna do a poll. It all depends on them, on the viewers. If they want Georgia Poison Peach to die, she goes. If they don't – '

'She stays?' Katherine asked.

'Yep.' Gabe looked at his watch, 'But we won't know the result until two weeks after the show's aired.'

'So what happens to me in those weeks?'

Luther grinned slyly. 'You take a nice little vacation, dear. With pay, of course.'

'And what happens if the viewers decide they want Georgia to die?'

'I think, sweetheart, that's something we're going to have to discuss with your agent,' said Gabe.

Katherine swallowed. God, whoever said that hearts were hard in Hollywood certainly wasn't kidding. These two had hearts of flint. And eyes to match. Cold, granite eyes without a shred of warmth or kindness in them. They didn't give a damn about her. It didn't matter to them that, because of her popularity, the show had zoomed to the top of the ratings, and stayed there for nearly two years. It didn't matter to them that if she lost this part, she would be back on the actor's equivalent of Skid Row. The show was all that mattered.

'OK Kitty, time to get back to work, sweetheart,' Gabe said.

'Have a nice day, dear.' Luther's yellow teeth looked like fangs as he smiled.

'Yes, thanks Luther, I'll certainly try.'

Katherine smiled back through gritted teeth, and returned to work.

'And like my dear old mama always says, the show must go on.'

When she relayed the information to her agent, Hal, he was not particularly sympathetic.

'We just gotta wait and see, I guess, sweetheart.'

'That's *all* you're going to do? Just wait and see?'

'What else can we do?'

Hal's agency represented not only Katherine, but also Albert Amory, Gabe Heller and Luther Immerman. Actors and actresses were disposable. Big producers were not. Katherine had certainly been popular, but her shelf life was undoubtedly coming to an end, and there were plenty of younger, tougher actresses pushing to get on to that shelf. Hal was not in the pity business. In fact, like many in Hollywood, he secretly despised all actors. If Katherine left the show and left the agency, so what? There were plenty more where she came from. Plenty.

But when Katherine told Jean-Claude everything, he was furious.

'Those mother-fucking bastards. How *dare* they do this to you? You're one of the most famous women in the world. In France – Europe – Africa – *everywhere* this show is played, you're incredibly well known, and they treat you like this?'

'When you get right down to it, darling, I'm just a tiny cog in a very big wheel, and quite unimportant. They can get rid of me whenever they want, like tossing out an old pair of shoes. If the network wants the ratings to zoom, and they think my death on screen will do it, then that's what'll happen.'

They were lying close together, the light of the television flickering as they watched an old Spencer Tracy movie.

'Kitty, would you trust me to get involved in this?' he asked, stroking her hair.

'What could you do?'

'Ah, I think I've got the beginning of a plan. I only had three years in show business, but I've got a pretty good business sense, and I believe in your talent, even if they don't.'

'So what do you want to do?'

'Ah, that would be telling.' He kissed her forehead and stroked her bare shoulders. 'It's time for you to get some rest, diva-darling. You need your beauty sleep. You've got a five o'clock call *n'est-ce pas?*'

'Yes.' She smiled, closing her eyes. It was hard to imagine how Jean-Claude could get her out of this mess, but she loved the idea that he was in her corner. 'Goodnight, darling,' she whispered.

During the ensuing weeks, Katherine and Jean-Claude thought of little else but each other. He was everything she'd ever wanted, and she spent each moment that she was not working with him. His sexual appetite and prowess were infinite, and his obvious commitment and dedication to her made the bond between them grow all the time. They did all the things together that new lovers do: went for long walks in the wild hills behind Benedict Canyon, took in movies at the Universal Cineplex, munching popcorn, eating hotdogs, and going from one movie house to the other, until they were satiated with the cinema. For these expeditions Katherine would disguise herself in jeans, T–shirt, trainers, dark glasses, and wear her hair scraped back in a baseball cap. It didn't always work perfectly, but it usually allowed her the privacy that she wanted with Jean-Claude.

'That disguise is not good enough,' he whispered one night, as they were followed into the parking lot at the Universal City by a crowd, flashing bits of paper and pens, begging for Georgia's autograph. 'You'll have to do better than that if you really want to hide yourself, *chérie*.'

Katherine grinned good-humouredly through the sea of hands.

Sometimes they drove in his black BMW convertible to the Malibu or Santa Monica beaches. Katherine loved to feel the wind in her hair, and to watch it ruffle his, as they zoomed down the Pacific Coast Highway with the sun high in the sky, and Sarah Vaughn or Ella Fitzgerald blasting out from the stereo.

Several times he asked her to come with him to Las Vegas on business, but she always begged off.

'Darling, you know I can't stand those crowds. I went there two years ago, and was practically mobbed at the blackjack table.' She stroked his hair, conscious of his disappointment.

'Why can't you wear your baseball cap disguise?'

'Darling, that doesn't really work; you know it. And I'd much rather be recognised looking like me, Katherine Bennet, than like some scruffy geek.'

He sighed theatrically. 'OK, but don't think I like it.'

Georgia Skeffington was shot on Friday night, just after seven o'clock. Then, after everyone else had gone for the weekend, Katherine, a dozen technicians and the director went back to the set, signed a confidentiality agreement in front of Gabe and Luther, and proceeded to shoot a scene in which Katherine, swathed in bandages in a hospital bed, recovered from her injuries. Now all she had to do was wait.

Six weeks after he had moved into her house, Jean-Claude asked Katherine to marry him.

'But I just got divorced,' Katherine replied weakly. 'Don't you think it's a little soon?'

'If two people love each other as much as we do, I believe they should be married. Why not? I want to spend the rest of my life with you, Kitty. I think I knew that the first time I saw you. I told you that if I believed in souls, then yours and mine would have known each other for a long time. That was the truth. We are meant for each other, Kitty, and you know it too.'

Katherine didn't answer, twisting a piece of her hair round one finger, and staring at him. 'I do love you, Jean-Claude. But I just can't make that commitment yet.'

'Why not?' he said, coming over to her, and holding one hand tightly while he stroked her ring finger. 'I want you to be Madame Jean-Claude Valmer.'

'Yes – maybe one day – but we've known each other for such a short time, and what about my career? Such as it is.'

She had pushed the forthcoming *Who Dunnit?* episode to the back of her mind. Her professional fate would be sealed soon enough. Instead of giving her the promised two-week vacation, the studio was sending her off on a national tour to promote *The Skeffingtons*, and to test the public opinion of Georgia Poison Peach.

'I guess they want to see if I can still cut it with Joe-Public,' she'd told Brenda.

'I'm going to keep asking you to be my wife until you agree,' Jean-Claude said. 'I shan't stop, because I cannot see any reason for us not to be married.'

'Children,' she said. 'You know I probably can't have any more; the doctors told me that after Tommy was born, and I think I'm too old anyway.'

'I don't care about children. I don't particularly like them, and we already have Tommy. It's you I want, Kitty.'

She didn't answer, staring pensively out of the window instead.

'*Chérie*, I understand you, and I want you to be mine forever. I'm never happier than when I'm with you, and I know you're happy with me. Just the two of us, watching television, going for drives, or making love.'

'It's all going so fast, too fast, Jean-Claude. I need time to think. After all, I've only *just* gotten divorced.'

His face clouded. 'I have to go to Vegas this weekend, to check on the new hotel. I want to show it to you. Will you come with me?'

She shook her head. 'Darling, I'm really sorry. I can't. Tommy's playing in a basketball game and he wants me to be there.'

'Very well. Then I will just have to be a lonely bachelor in Las Vegas.'

'Don't make me feel guilty, Jean-Claude, please. It's hard to be fair to everyone.'

She sat on his knee, and looked into his clear green eyes. 'Please don't ever forget that I do love you, darling, will you?'

He shook his head, smiling, but she sensed sadness in him. 'Well, if you won't be my wife, then you'll just have to be my main squeeze, as you say out here.'

'But I already *am* that.' Although the idea of marriage appealed to Kitty she knew she couldn't commit herself to another one so soon, not after twenty years with Johnny. The last four had been pure hell, and the thought of marrying again made her break out in a rash.

While Jean-Claude was in Las Vegas, Katherine's agent called. 'Kitty, I've got some really good news for you,' Hal reported excitedly. 'We have definite interest from ABA network for you to do another series, if you're bumped off in *The Skeffingtons*.'

'You're kidding. Are things finally looking up? How did this happen?'

'You can thank your boyfriend for it, sweetheart.'

'Jean-Claude? What did he do?'

'Apparently he had lunch with Carolyn Lupino, who, as you know, is the brains, the brawn and the bread behind Lew's empire. Don't ask me how it happened, but Jean-Claude talked to Carolyn, and Carolyn talked to Lew, and Lew talked to the network, and they want to develop a new show round you, Kitty baby. Hey, that's some great guy you've got there, hang on to him.'

'Oh I intend to. This is unbelievable, Hal. Jean-Claude is certainly persuasive.'

'You can say that again, kiddo – I hate to admit it, but what the agency couldn't do for you, he has.'

'I'll call him right now to tell him that.' She smiled to herself. But when she called Jean-Claude in Las Vegas, the hotel said he'd checked out for Reno. He was going on to look at a site, but hadn't said where he was staying.

He returned the next day, full of good news about his hotel.

'It's going to be a beauty, *chérie*,' he enthused. 'It will be just like a Provençal hotel, but right in the heart of the desert.'

'It sounds divine,' she said, and they celebrated with a bottle of Krug, then made love for so long into the night that Katherine never got around to discussing Hal's news.

The following night Kitty returned just in time for the opening credits of the *Who Dunnit?* episode. Jean-Claude and Tommy had already eaten pizza, and were glued to the set. Maria brought Katherine some grilled fish and broccoli; she was back on her boring diet again. The episode finished with the words, 'Oh my God, they've killed Georgia Skeffington'. As the end titles came up, Kitty turned to Jean-Claude.

'You really are an operator, aren't you, darling?'

'I guess Hal told you.' He grinned.

'You bet. But how – how on earth did you manage to talk the other network into having me? After all this crappy publicity I've had, and everyone in Hollywood badmouthing me behind my back, I thought I was history.'

He put a finger to her lips, smiling enigmatically. 'Never ask how, *chérie*. All that ever matters is the end result. So, now we must wait to see how this show has been received, I suppose?'

'Yep, and Sunday I go off on the grand tour. Oh God, darling, it's going to be a *nightmare*. Eleven cities in two weeks, with everyone asking the same stupid questions, over and over again, and cameras popping into my face, wherever I go.' She shuddered. 'I wish I could give it all up.'

He came and sat beside her. 'Give it up, Kitty,' he whispered. 'Please give it all up, and marry me.'

She looked deeply into his wide green eyes and slowly shook her head. 'Oh darling, no. I do love you – I adore you, but...I can't, not yet. I don't know you well enough. Please wait, darling, just a few more months until we're sure of each other. When I get married again, I want it to be forever.'

CHAPTER NINE

Katherine returned from her two-week national publicity tour, exhausted, but excited at the thought of seeing Jean-Claude again. Absence certainly does make the heart grow fonder, she thought, admiring the tall, powerful figure standing in the entrance hall to greet her. Expecting to be swept into his embrace, she was surprised to find a coldness in his attitude, a subtle edge of hardness which she hadn't seen during their two months together.

'How are you, darling?' she said anxiously. 'Have you missed me?' She tried to snuggle close to him, but he held her at arm's length, looking at her with dispassionate eyes.

'Mmm. A bit.'

'A bit?' A claw of doubt assailed her, but attempting a laugh, she threw off her coat, took his hand and led him into the living room.

The setting sun was particularly strong this late afternoon, reflecting in a dazzling blaze off the white sofas, the chrome mirrors, and the dozens of glass and silver rococo objects. Instead of sitting beside her on the overstuffed sofa, as he usually did, he chose to lounge on a hard silver gilt *bergère*. Its stark, sparse lines seemed to reflect his mood. He placed his hands on the sharp armrests, and clicked his fingers restlessly. When she looked at him, his transparent green eyes seemed to gaze through her, as if she were not really there at all.

'You look tired.' His voice was unsympathetic.

'I *am* tired. I'm utterly whacked.' She attempted another laugh, but it sounded tinny and fake, so she picked up a cigarette, which he made no attempt to light.

'I don't know why you drive yourself so hard, Katherine.' He examined a fingernail, pushing at an imaginary cuticle with great intensity.

'Oh darling, don't be so silly.' This time the attempt at an insouciant giggle stuck in her throat. 'You know I had to do this. It's a PR exercise. With any luck it worked, and they won't want to axe my part. I hope so.'

He shrugged, almost contemptuously, and lighting his own cigarette, turned to stare out at the view, blurring now with late afternoon Los Angeles smog.

Katherine stubbed out her cigarette. It tasted like ashes. This was not the man she loved. What had happened whilst she was gone? Their telephone calls had been brief, because her schedule was so rough she was almost too tired to talk at night. Certainly now she seemed to recall that he, too, had seemed colder, harder, more distant on the phone. She'd put it down to long distance loss and thought nothing more of it.

'Drink, darling?' She gave him her most seductive look, flashing sheer black-gartered legs through a swirl of skirt, as she glided to the mirrored and silver bar. He usually adored a garter belt, but tonight he didn't even look at her.

Instead he snapped irritably, 'I don't want a drink. Why don't you let the houseman get it for you?'

'But darling, we must celebrate. We haven't seen each other for over two weeks. We've got a lot to catch up on.'

'You drink too much,' he said shortly, watching his cigarette smoke spiral lazily up to the ceiling.

Katherine poured herself a stiff Chivas Regal, and felt her face start to colour. Hearing the chink of ice, the new Chinese houseman came in.

'Welcome home, ma'am,' he said, 'I hope you had a good trip.'

'Yes I did thank you, Won.' She swallowed half her drink.

'Maria has prepared your favourite supper. What time would you like to eat?'

'Oh, I don't know, Won.' She glanced at her watch. 'What do you think, darling?' she asked the back of Jean-Claude's head. 'What time would you like dinner?'

'Whenever you want,' he said in the emotionless voice she'd heard for the first time today. 'Do whatever you want, Katherine. You always do whatever you want, anyway.'

She gulped down the rest of her whisky, and signalled to the waiting Won to fix another.

'We'll eat at seven.' She tried to sound normal, although her heart felt as if it were being crushed in her chest. 'In the – no, in the breakfast room.'

Jean-Claude slowly inhaled his cigarette, and blew out three perfect smoke rings.

'Well, I guess I'll go and get changed.' She smiled brightly, even though she felt a sense that something horrible was about to happen. 'I'll put on something more comfortable, then we'll eat – and talk. I've got a lot to tell you about, darling.'

Her seven Vuitton cases were being noisily unpacked in the bedroom by Maria and the new housemaid. Maria chattered excitedly to Katherine about how happy she was to see her back.

'We missed you, *señora*. It's not the same here without you.'

'Thank you, Maria.' The kind words brought a rush of tears to Katherine's eyes, and she quickly went into the bathroom. She stared at her weary, baggy-eyed face, every flaw exaggerated by the harsh lights and the magnifying mirror. Jean-Claude was right. Not only did she look exhausted, she felt burned out, like a crumpled dead leaf.

The bathroom walls were floor-to-ceiling mirrors, and as she removed her clothes, she couldn't avoid seeing herself reflected a hundred times from all angles. The mirror never lies. This one showed all too clearly the effects of those lonely night in hotels. Two weeks of seeking solace from the mini-bar in her room; goodness knows how many miniatures of scotch and vodka – it was all written there on her body. To most women she would still seem very slender, but to herself she seemed overweight and full of cellulite. She pinched the excess flesh around her waist. Maximilian will kill me, she said to herself. He had always told her that she could even make a sack look chic.

'Not any more,' she muttered, slipping into the comforting, scented bubbles with which she had filled her marble tub. 'Tomorrow it'll be fat girl sings the blues – all over town.'

After a dinner in which Caesar salad, steamed sole and mango sorbet stuck in her throat, while she and Jean-Claude tried to make polite conversation, Katherine's eyelids were so heavy she could hardly keep them open. But exhausted as she was, she had to get to the bottom of his obvious displeasure.

'What's wrong, darling? Please tell me. Why are you so upset?'

'Upset? Me?' He sounded amused and dismissive at the same time. 'There's nothing wrong with me, Kitty, I assure you. Nothing at all.'

'Good – I'm glad – you seemed – well, out of sorts... different. I hope it's nothing to do with me?'

'Nothing at all.' He gazed out of the window again and lit another cigarette.

'Well, I'm not sure I believe you, but I hope that whatever it is that's eating you, can wait until tomorrow. I'm too tired to discuss it, and obviously you don't want to either. I've been up for nearly twenty hours. I can't keep my eyes open.'

'Fine.' He smiled that new cold smile again, which made Katherine's mouth go dry. 'You go to bed. You're always tired, Kitty. You need your sleep, from the look of you. I've got a few calls to make, so don't wait up. I won't disturb your beauty sleep.'

His sarcasm made her grit her teeth, but she refused to let it show, and swallowing the last of her wine, stood up and tried to hug him, but his body was ramrod-stiff and unyielding.

'Goodnight, darling. I'll see you in the morning,' she whispered, and with as much dignity as she could muster, walked over to the marble staircase.

'What time tomorrow, ma'am?' Won was padding up the stairs behind her in his soft Chinese slippers.

'Five forty-five,' she said. 'Tell Sam to have the car ready.'

But exhausted as she was, sleep wouldn't come, and two hours later she was still awake, listening to the sounds of Jean-Claude undressing in the 'Master's' bathroom, an impressively masculine mahogany chamber, designed for a previous owner. She snuggled down into the cool white linen sheets.

'God, these sheets feel wonderful after all those hellhole hotels,' she remarked, as Jean-Claude came in, wearing the bottom half of a pair of pyjamas. Pyjamas? He *never* wore anything in bed. What in hell was going on?

'Still awake?' he commented, then turned on the TV, flicking the remote control restlessly from channel to channel at one second intervals. It was a habit that had always irritated Katherine, and now it almost drove her mad.

'Why don't we watch Larry King?' she suggested, after five teeth-grating minutes of seeing two-second flashes of everything, from hockey to rap music. 'All this channel-changing is keeping me awake.'

He sighed, flicked the 'off' button, extinguished his bedside light and turning his back to her, said coldly, 'Goodnight, Katherine'.

The room was dark, dusted faintly with misty moonlight. Katherine wanted Jean-Claude to hold her, she felt empty, cold and sad. She didn't want anything else except his familiar arms around her, their bodies entwined in loving intimacy.

Not sex. She certainly didn't want to have sex. She was far too tired for that. But suddenly Jean-Claude did. Ferociously, silently, he pulled her to him, pulling up her nightgown and touching her roughly. Was this what he'd been sulking about? Well, she'd try to be enthusiastic; maybe he'd felt starved. Jean-Claude pushed her head roughly under the sheets, wanting her to jump-start his motor. It was the last thing she wanted to do, but she was determined to please him if she could. After ten minutes her jaws ached, and her mouth felt dry and useless. She had failed to awake any significant response in him. Usually her lightest touch made him rock-hard; but not tonight. He tugged at Katherine's hair.

'Damn it, woman, you do that like you're milking a cow,' he snapped.

Startled, shocked, Katherine stared at Jean-Claude's angry face, which was illuminated by soft, filtered light from the window slats.

'Not tonight, Josephine.' He pulled up his pyjamas. 'Let's call it a day. The thrill is gone. I want to get some sleep.'

Moving as far away as possible, he folded his body into a foetal position, and closed his eyes.

Humiliated and furious, Katherine pulled down her nightgown, and moving far into her corner of the bed, said frostily, 'Goodnight. Sorry I'm so tired.'

'Don't be.' His voice was weary, almost bored. 'It's not important. It really doesn't matter, Katherine.'

But she knew it did. It mattered a lot.

In the cold, morning darkness, a bleary-eyed Katherine awoke to the bleep of her bedside alarm, and tiptoed into her dressing room. Her mail, along with various faxes and papers lay piled on the desk opposite her dressing table, and as she drank the strong espresso Maria had left, a headline, in yesterday's *Daily Post*, caught her eye. It had been faxed by her mother, who had scribbled, 'Tell me it isn't true', on the border.

Extract from The American Tattler, *September 8th, 1988*

There is no love lost at all between the two leading ladies in ABN's fading soap The Skeffingtons. *Katherine Bennet, 43, who plays Georgia 'Poison-Peach' Skeffington is said to be furiously jealous of all the attention paid to gorgeous Eleonor Norman, 38. Kitty recently lost the coveted role of Emma Hamilton to the British Beauty, so is she fuming!!! However Kitty is fighting back.*

'She may be 9 years younger than I am, but I chew her up and spit her out in little pieces when we act together,' the Poison-Peach crowed.

Katherine, miffed at being ignored by Hollywood for years and worried about ageing, is said to be so difficult and demanding on the set that even good-tempered Albert Amory, 69, is supposed to be furious at her diva-like behaviour. It's well-known in Hollywood that none of the other networks would even work with Katherine Bennet.

'God damn it, why the hell do they always write this shit.'

'What's going on?' Jean-Claude appeared at the door. 'What's the matter now? God, what a fuss you make about everything, Katherine.'

'Look.' She showed him the paper. 'Look at this – how would you like this written about you? Oh God!'

'What difference does it make? You know it isn't true.'

'What difference...? What difference? God Almighty, it makes a lot of damn difference, Jean-Claude – a helluva *lot*.' Her voice rose an octave. '*Everyone* in this damned *town* will see this. They'll think it's true. It's like career suicide...I'll be a pariah in no time at all. Washed up – unemployable – out of...'

'Oh shut up,' he interrupted. 'Shut the fuck up, Katherine, and stop yelling at me.'

'I'm not yelling *at* you.' She dropped her voice, even though she was shaking with rage. 'I'm just yelling, *period*. Can't a person yell once in a while?'

'I think you do it just a bit too much recently. Just a touch, Katherine. It's been driving a lot of people mad – including me. You remember the straw that broke the camel's back, *chérie*?' Turning, he strode into his bathroom and closed the door.

'Oh Christ, Jean-Claude, *don't* get mad. For God's sake. Please don't be ridiculous. Look, I'm sorry, I don't mean to overreact but it's my career, for God's sake, and I've worked bloody hard for it; you know that. God – what's wrong with you?' she yelled. 'You're like some sort of zombie, Jean-Claude – I – I don't even know you.'

'As for your illustrious career,' he called, turning on his shower. 'That's all you ever think about. You don't give a damn about us, Katherine – you and me – and you never have.'

'I do, I do, *I swear I do*.'

She was getting shrill, and seeing the clock, Katherine realized she had to leave immediately. She could not afford to be late. Not today. Today was decision time. Today she'd know whether Georgia would live or die. If she died, the only scene left to shoot was a flashback with Tony. If she lived, on the other hand, she would have to go into top gear right away; be a winner, look a winner. Right now she felt like a loser all round.

'Oh God, Jean-Claude, I've got to go now. If I'm late today, they'll have even more reason to kill me off.'

He didn't answer, and all she could hear was the sound of running water. There was no time for her to shower; throwing on jeans, trainers, T-shirt and baseball cap, she realized she hadn't even cleaned her teeth. She rushed to the basin to brush them. As she dashed through the bedroom, Jean-Claude was lacing up his highly polished shoes with a look on his face that filled her with dread.

'What are you doing?' she asked.

'Going,' he said coldly.

'Jean-Claude don't leave like this. Let's talk about it tonight – please.'

'Oh no, Katherine.' His voice was even icier than before. 'Not tonight, not tomorrow night, not ever again. I've had it up to here with you. You are nothing but a self-obsessed, selfish *actress*, who doesn't give a damn about anyone or anything – least of all our relationship.'

'But I thought our relationship was great. It's been fantastic from the beginning in every way, you know it has.' She realized she was begging, hated herself for it.

'I've been doing some serious thinking while you've been off on your travels, Kitty.' He was lacing up the other shoe now. 'And I've decided that I don't think I love you any more. In fact – ' he stood up, towering over her, a formidable figure in his cashmere polo neck, impeccably pressed jeans and handmade shoes. She felt scruffy, insignificant and plain, in the hodge podge of garments she had thrown on.

'We've reached the end of the road, Katherine.'

'No. Jean-Claude – you can't mean it, you simply *can't.*'

'Oh but I can.' He shrugged on the tweed jacket she had given him for his birthday, frowning at himself in the mirror as he adjusted the shoulders. 'I've been putting up with your tantrums, and your insecurities, and your self-obsession for far too long. You don't want to commit to me. You don't want to get married to me. You won't come to Vegas with me. You don't want this, and you don't want that. Well let me tell you something, *chérie*. I've got to get on with my life, and I'm going to do it without you. It's high time sweetheart. *C'est la fin de l'histoire*.'

'But you told me I was your life... You told me you couldn't live without me – oh God, God, what's come over you, Jean-Claude?'

'Reality, *chérie*, reality,' he said, and reaching casually into his pocket, he retrieved the silver heart-shaped key ring, complete with house key, that she had given him two months ago, and threw it calmly on to the coffee table.

'Look at me hard, Katherine, because you're never going to see me again. *Au'voir*, *chérie*,' he said as he sauntered out of the front door. 'But don't think it hasn't been fun.'

CHAPTER TEN

After Jean-Claude left, Katherine sobbed for so long that her eyes swelled to slits. It was incomprehensible that he had walked out on her. In two months they had never even had an argument. Whatever could have happened, during her two weeks away, to turn him into such a totally different, cold-hearted creature?

'Is *señora* all right?' There was a tentative tap on the door; Maria sounded genuinely concerned. Katherine stifled her sobs.

'Yes – thank you. I'll be fine,' she whispered croakily. 'Er – Maria – please call the studio – say – say that I've had an little accident – er – I slipped in the bath. Nothing serious. That I'll be there as soon as I can – and please, bring me some coffee and an icepack right away.'

'Yes, *señora*.'

Katherine examined the ravages of a face that, within a couple of hours, would be photographed for millions to see.

'Oh – *shit*,' she hissed to her bloated tearstained reflection. 'Shit-shit-shit...pull yourself together, you idiot, otherwise your ship will really start to sink. He'll come back, he has to...he loves ya, baby.'

Once Maria had put icepacks on Katherine's swollen eyes and face, she managed to get to the studio and struggle through the day, but only by a supreme effort of will. She had to stop thinking about Jean-Claude. Her agent arrived, while she was finishing what could be her penultimate scene in *The Skeffingtons*. He was to take her to the all-important meeting with Gabe. She was dreading it.

They strode across the hot and sticky tarmac to the great man's office where Gabe sat behind his desk, alone. Today he was wearing a black baseball cap and a T-shirt with 'Welcome to LA – Adjust your attitude!' printed on it. Katherine felt simultaneously light-headed and heavy with dread. This was make it or break it time. Now, finally, she would discover her fate.

An hour later a subdued, but happy, actress and her agent returned to her dressing room.

'You should be thrilled, Kitty,' Hal gloated. 'You've gotten 'em by the balls, sweetheart. You play it cool now, don't make too many waves and we'll go for the big raise before the season ends.'

'Good – that's great Hal.' Katherine's voice sounded flat to her own ears.

Sure, she'd won. Viewers all over America had flooded the network with complaints after *Who Dunnit?* aired. Katherine was the woman they loved to hate. No way could the network kill her off now. Whatever the tabloids said – the public had the final say, and they simply adored her.

'You're invincible, kid,' crowed Hal. 'It's fan-fuckin'-tastic.'

Katherine nodded, her thoughts only of Jean-Claude. It was a victory, and yet it felt hollow, for she had no one, other than Tommy and Brenda, with whom really to share it.

'If only I were invulnerable,' she muttered, as she closed her dressing room door. 'If only I didn't care about the bastard so much.'

* * *

The inevitable call came from her mother. Katherine could hear Oprah Winfrey in the background, berating some unhappy dysfunctional family.

'I told you to be careful, Kit-Kat. You just have no idea how to handle men. I suppose you were bossing him about. You've got to make your man feel like a man, honey.'

Katherine sighed. Vera seemed increasingly to confuse her with Georgia Skeffington.

'It said in *The Tattler* that he's been having a bit of a fling with that Eleonor. Is it true, Kit-Kat, is that why he's dumped you?'

'No it isn't.' Katherine felt a flash of anger. 'Don't worry, Mama,' she said through gritted teeth. 'I'll get him back.'

At this point Brenda arrived in the dressing room.

'Are you sure you really want him?' she asked, as Kitty put down the receiver.

'Goddammit,' Katherine exploded. 'I wish everyone would just butt out of my life, and let me sort this out myself.'

The following days drifted by in a meaningless blur of fittings, fourteen-hour bouts of work, publicity lunches and dinners. Suddenly Katherine was the golden girl again, and everyone wanted her. Everyone except the one person she wanted. Katherine willed herself to become numb to Jean-Claude's absence. He, who had controlled almost all her waking thoughts, whose opinion she had sought about the most trivial of matters, would not be allowed to dominate the major place in her head, even though he still ruled her heart.

Meanwhile Brenda attempted to find out where Quentin was. The old man had, to all intents and purposes, disappeared. His voice on the answering machine was all Katherine heard when she rang his number – sometimes as often as five times a day. What is more, he seemed to be Jean-

Claude's only friend in LA; the only person who could possibly shed light on his whereabouts.

Every morning Katherine awoke before dawn, staring wide-eyed into the blackness of her bedroom, willing her subconscious to stop thinking about Jean-Claude. Her feelings veered wildly between fury and despair. Sometimes she was reduced to floods of tears; sometimes she felt an overpowering rage, which made her scream until her throat ached, or beat her knuckles raw against the mirrored walls. But on the fourth day after Jean-Claude's disappearance, she awoke clear-headed and decisive.

'Fuck Jean-Claude, fuck the bastard and all the men in the world. First they suck you in and then they suck you dry,' Katherine muttered to herself as she drove towards the studio, through the shabby streets of Santa Monica. She had given Sam the morning off. Sinatra was crooning *My Way* on the stereo, the sun was shining, and the world was starting to look rosy again. 'He belongs in the pen with the rest of the pigs. If you think you can get away with doing this to me, Monsieur Jean-Claude Valmer, you better think again. Bastard!' She braked sharply, almost knocking over an extra as she went in through the studio gates. She tried to compose herself and smiled at the cop who waved her in.

'Hi Kitty – you're looking swell today. Gotta long day ahead, huh?'

'Sure have, Sandy. Thanks for asking.' The grizzled ex-cop touched his cap. Katherine Bennet was a real lady, always treated everyone nice. Never snooty or hoity-toity, like that fake British bitch, Eleonor Norman.

Katherine parked outside the faded pink stucco building that housed the wardrobe, hair and make-up departments. As usual, it was a hive of activity. Five television shows were shooting on the lot. Each show employed seven or eight resident actors, plus weekly guest stars, and they all seemed to be on call today. The air was thick with cigarette smoke, with the smell of coffee and doughnuts, and with the animated gossip of actors.

Katherine poked her head around the door of her hairdresser.

'Hi, Mona. Ready for me?'

'Gimme another twenty minutes hon, *please*.' The harried hairdresser was using toupee tape to attach a thick thatch of burnished auburn hair on to Albert Amory's bald head. 'Go grab a coffee, hon, then I'll be ready for you.'

Katherine nodded to Eleonor in the corridor, just before her rival sauntered into Albert's make-up room.

'Morning, Albert darling.' Eleonor pecked his orange-coated cheek, whilst checking herself in the mirror.

'Good morning, my dear.' He looked appreciatively at her bottom, in its tight white shorts.

The word on the street was that she was sensational in *Emma Hamilton*, and if so, he hoped Katherine Bennet, that second-rate Broadway actress, would soon be consigned to the TV has-been bin.

Meanwhile Katherine reclined in the red leather make-up chair and let Blackie do his best with her face. She ignored the concerned clucking as he applied soothing gel under her puffy eyes, moisturizer to her chapped cheeks, and concealer to the red blotches on her face. She was vaguely conscious of whispers and raised eyebrows from the other two make-up artists, but she paid no attention, consumed as she was by her new-found anger with Jean-Claude. She had to stop thinking about him, exorcise him from her consciousness. He was just a man. There were many more out there for her, weren't there?

'No,' whispered her inner voice. 'Jean-Claude *was* special, and that's why you loved him so much.' A sudden memory of Jean-Claude's eyes, looking deep into hers as they made love, made her want to cry.

'Morning daahlings!' Katherine's reverie was interrupted by the stomp of stilettos, and a waft of inappropriate morning scent, as Eleonor clattered in, air-kissed everyone in the room and plopped herself into a make-up chair with a theatrical sigh.

'Oh God, I look like *shit* today.'

You can say that again, thought Katherine, with a sidelong glance at Eleonor.

'Work your magic, Nina,' commanded Eleonor. 'Make me *gorgeous*, sweetie.'

The make-up girl raised her eyebrows infinitesimally, then whipped a white cotton sheet over Eleonor's pink sequinned T-shirt, and went to work.

'What a night!' exclaimed Eleonor to nobody in particular, as Optrex-soaked pads were applied to her eyes. 'The Johnsons' party was *fab*. Why weren't you there, Kitty dahling? With your *divine* new man?'

'I was exhausted,' Katherine answered truthfully. 'Besides, those parties are all the same.'

'Ah yes they are indeed, but dahling, you should've seen the frocks last night! The absolute *dernier-cri* of the frocky horror show.'

She laughed, her tinkling drama-school laugh, and, despite the prominent No Smoking signs everywhere, lit a cigarette.

'So, what's going on, dahling?' she asked.

'So what's going on with what?' Katherine replied coldly.

'Well where *is* Mr Mahvellous, the answer to every maiden's prayer? Rumour hath it, *dahling*, that the Froggie's done a bunk on you.'

Eleonor removed the Optrex pads, and fastened curious red-rimmed eyes on Katherine, who kept hers firmly closed. The make-up artists glanced knowingly at each other. The gossip was that Katherine's misery was caused by man trouble. Now maybe they'd find out.

So this bitch suspected did she? thought Katherine. This meant the wrecking crews had been talking. What else did they have to do, after their early morning cosmetic attacks, except gossip? None of them was exactly stupid. Jean-Claude usually called the set at least twice a day. If the crew knew that he wasn't calling any more, and Eleonor suspected as much, how long before the gossip columnists found out?

But Katherine wasn't about to give Eleonor the satisfaction of an answer. She opened her eyes and stared disdainfully at the black roots beginning to show in Eleonor's blonde hair.

'I had always thought, Eleonor my dear, that the English were the most civilized people on earth. That is, until I met you.'

'Bingo!' Eleonor grinned. 'I got it in one, didn't I, dahling? Jean-Claude's chucked you, hasn't he?'

Kitty's mind flashed back to Jake Moffatt's party. Two heads together, laughing intimately; Jean-Claude and Eleonor. Had something gone on with them?

'Well, sweetie?' Eleonor's triumphant voice demanded an answer. When none came, she crowed. 'I always thought he was gay, anyway. Blond, forty, and never been married. Sounds like a faggot to me.'

The make-up people held their breath, and applied themselves even more diligently to patting foundation on to the increasingly flushed cheeks of their respective actresses. The hidden enmity, so potent on camera, was bursting out of the closet now, and no one wanted to miss a minute of it.

'What you lack in talent, dear, you more than make up for in vitriol,' Katherine said icily.

'Ha!' Eleonor smirked. 'You think you're so friggin' talented, dearie? And I *did* hit a nerve, didn't I? Why don't you ask our producer just who is featured more in the new scripts? And while you're at it, call the fan mail department and see *who* gets the bulk of the letters these days.'

'You, I suppose.' Katherine was weary of the venom, but Blackie had her trapped in the make-up chair.

'You bet your lace knickers it's me,' Eleonor crowed. 'The fans may've liked you better at first, luvvie, because you're oh so *fabulous* at being bitchy and hard and aggressive – but the worm has finally turned, *dahling*. Take a look at *this*.'

Triumphantly she whipped something from her enormous Gucci hold-all. It was a copy of *The TV Quotient*, a top-secret guide for producers and studio executives. This was a small, highly confidential manual, published by the company who computed the TV Neilson Ratings. It supposedly didn't exist, and certainly had never been seen by any actor. It listed shows and performers in order of popularity, credibility and recognizability with the American public. How Eleonor had come to get hold of a copy was a mystery.

'Page seventeen,' Eleonor gloated. 'Read it and weep, Kitty dahling. Your days of wine and roses, Krug and cover-stories, are numbered, I think.'

Blackie passed the thin dog-eared magazine to Katherine. The list of actors ran to three or four hundred names. At the top (as he had been for the past three years) was Bill Cosby, then came Johnny Carson, Angela Lansbury and Larry Hagman. At number five, where – according to unofficial reports – Katherine's name had been a fixture for three years, was Eleonor Norman.

Katherine's eyes rapidly scanned the list, looking for her own name. Then there it was: number twenty-three, sandwiched between a game-show bimbo and an aging cowboy star. Twenty-three – Katherine Bennet! It was more shocking than she could have imagined – and yet – even on the national publicity tour, with screaming fans constantly surrounding her, Katherine had sometimes been afraid that her reception wasn't as enthusiastic as it had been two years ago. That was the trouble with not only playing a bitch, but being painted as one in every newspaper column in the world.

'What goes up must come down, sweetie.' Eleonor relished her moment of victory.

'And vice versa,' said Katherine quietly.

Blackie finished his work and passed her a mirror, but she didn't bother to check it. She walked to the door and turned with dignity:

'For your information, Eleonor *dahling*, that book is now yesterday's news. Gabe has told me that as of next week, the scripts will be more concentrated on Georgia Skeffington's character than on any of the others. So put that in your Dunhill and smoke it, duckie.'

Then she popped her head back around the door with a wicked grin, and said, 'See you on the set, *dahling*, and *do* try not to blow your lines for a change.'

In spite of feeling temporarily buoyed up by her anger, Katherine's heart still ached for Jean-Claude. She continued to call Quentin at least once a day, and poured out her feelings to Brenda and Steven. They were the only people she felt she could really trust. She couldn't talk to Tommy; he was frankly jubilant at Jean-Claude's disappearance.

Then, one lunchtime, while trussed into a thick Irish tweed suit which was hotter than a sauna, Katherine heard a new message on Quentin's machine. It told her that the old man was staying at Caesar's Palace Hotel in Las Vegas.

Katherine called him that night.

'Quentin, where is Jean-Claude? Have you heard from him?'

There was a long pause.

'Sure I've heard from him.' From across the wire, Katherine could hear, in the background, the clatter of dice on green baize tables.

'Where is he? Please tell me.'

'Listen, kiddo, you know I can't tell you that. He doesn't want anyone to know where he is.'

'Not even me?'

Another pause.

'Especially you, kiddo.'

Katherine felt gooseflesh rise on her arms and she shivered.

'Quentin, listen, you must tell me, please. I've got to sort this out. Jean-Claude *couldn't* have meant to end it, Quentin, it was just some kind of – I don't know – aberration. I'd never seen him like that. It just wasn't like him.'

'Yeah – well – you know guys, Kitty.'

'I *thought* I knew this guy. Look, Quentin you've seen us together, you know how much we meant to each other, how much he loved me.'

'Kitty, it's between you two. What can I tell you? Jean-Claude's – well – he's Jean-Claude. And Kitty he told me I'm not to reveal to anyone where he is, or what he's up to.'

She became even icier. 'I don't understand. But I'm determined to find out, and to find him. He's always been his own man, and I guess maybe I haven't been quite fair with him lately. He thinks I've been consumed with my career, and never concerned about his work, but frankly he never seemed to want to talk about himself. I asked him *many* times about it, but he always changed the subject.'

'He's half French, Kitty.'

'Yes I know. The other half's Irish. What's that got to do with it?'

'It's a potent combination, fiery, stubborn and opinionated.'

'I know that. But has he told you what happened to us? At least tell me that.'

'Yeah, sure he has. But don't ask me any more. I don't want to be disloyal. He's like a son to me.'

'Is there someone else?' she pressed. 'Another woman? Oh God – another man? At least answer that question, please.'

'How can you ask me that, Kitty?'

'Is there?'

'Jean-Claude'll kill me if he knows I spoke to you.' Quentin sounded wary.

'Tell me, *please*. If he's been off with someone while I was on the road I've got to know. Look, I can take another woman – really I can – I just can't take not knowing *why* this has happened.'

Here it comes, thought Katherine. He's been balling some bimbo while I was on tour.

'Dames!' Quentin said dryly. 'Never trust dames. Dames and dice'll cut a guy's balls off quicker than anything else.'

'Look it's Thursday now – ' Katherine quickly mustered her considerable charm. 'I must see Jean-Claude once more, just to find out if it's really over. So, darling Quentin, *please* – if you know where he is, please tell me.'

There was a long pause, then he answered slowly. 'Because you're a real nice dame, Kitty, I'll tell you. But if you ever tell Jean-Claude – that's it, kiddo – finito to our friendship.'

'Yes, of course, I promise I won't breathe a word ever.' Katherine felt the blood rushing back to her cheeks, and her adrenalin start pumping as she grabbed pen and paper from her bedside table.

'He's right here in Vegas, stayin' at Caesar's. And if you find him, don't tell him I told you.'

'Thank you, Quentin – thank you,' she said – but he had hung up.

Katherine lay back on her white silk bedcover with a smile of satisfaction on her face. Caesar's Palace, Vegas. She knew it well. She was going to find her long-lost lover, and she was going to get him back.

CHAPTER ELEVEN

Katherine thought carefully about how she could conduct her Vegas search for Jean-Claude without being recognized. She decided to tell Brenda but not Tommy, and to take Blackie partly into her confidence. She told him that she had set her heart on a hassle-free weekend in Las Vegas. After a couple of practice runs, they finally settled on the Tootsie look, complete with padded body-suit, tight, grey, permed wig, and large pale plastic glasses.

Blackie assured Katherine that this disguise was virtually foolproof.

'It's also easy as pie for you to do yourself, honey.'

The moment shooting finished on Friday evening, Katherine rushed into her dressing room and changed into the disguise. The body-suit, borrowed from wardrobe, was a lightweight all-in-one garment that zipped up the back. It covered Katherine from ankle to wrist to neck and, after a few tentative trips down the make-up department corridors, she found that it was relatively easy to move in. She even managed to adopt a waddling, plump woman's walk. Then came the clothes. A shell suit of purple and cerise polyester, with horizontal stripes on the thighs and across the chest, accentuated her size, bulky, stained white trainers, with thick purple sports socks, disguised the thinness of her ankles, and across her midriff she slung a rhinestone-studded body bag for money and keys.

'Now all we do to your face, is this.' Blackie showed her a rubber nose, painstakingly cast from her own.

'Just put the surgical adhesive inside, press down for a minute, and presto. Now we blend foundation all over.' He dabbed reddish brown pancake liberally over her face, neck and nose, to make a mottled effect. 'And – instant middle America – a gal who's spent much too much time on the range.'

He placed a wig of tight grey curls on her head; she put on the pink plastic glasses, and they both surveyed the effect.

'Hello, Grandma.' Blackie laughed triumphantly.

'It's amazing!' Katherine stared at herself in the mirror. She looked like an elderly, weathered woman.

'I'd never recognize myself in a million years!'

'Neither will anyone else.' Blackie started stowing his equipment. 'Have fun, honey. And put five bucks on number thirteen for me – will ya?'

'You bet I will, Blackie – and a million thanks.'

She kissed him, and furtively tiptoed down the back stairs to where Brenda's Honda was waiting. No one noticed as Katherine Bennet sped off into the night towards LAX Airport.

Vegas was even more frenetic than usual. Even the airport lounge was dominated by the shattering clunk of the one-armed bandits, reminding Katherine of why people became addicted to this glittering city. She hailed a cab to Caesar's Palace.

She was given a tiny room, which was an ill-matched mishmash of gold and lime rococo wallpaper, peeling at the edges, imitation Louis XIV furniture, and fake Tiffany lamps nailed, against theft, to the bedside tables. As soon as she had closed the door, she rang the hotel operator.

'Mr Jean-Claude Valmer please.'

'Sorry. We have no one registered by that name,' intoned the nasal voice flatly. Since Katherine hadn't expected Jean-Claude to be under his own name anyway, she asked for Quentin Rogers, but got the same answer.

'Oh well, it's finally into that damned breach, I guess,' she muttered, and with a last critical look at the frump in the mirror, sallied forth into the sparkling Las Vegas night.

The main floor of Caesar's Palace consisted of six or seven enormous gambling rooms, a corridor of shops selling everything from toothpaste to emerald and diamond necklaces, and several restaurants, nightclubs and cocktail lounges. There were crowds everywhere – hordes of weekend visitors, gambling, gazing, grazing. Those who weren't at the tables or slots seemed to be generally milling about in an aimless fashion.

Katherine cased all the main casinos, well aware that she was being scrutinized all the time by security guards. She knew that a team of vigilantes kept constant watch on the floor from their vantage points in the ceiling above the tables. It took her the better part of two hours to meander casually through the whole place. She wandered through all the casinos three times, sometimes playing the slots for ten minutes, occasionally throwing a few chips on to the roulette tables, whilst her eyes searched the crowd. No one took any notice of her. She was just one of the fat, faceless, optimistic thousands who trekked to 'Lost Wages' for a fun weekend, and the chance of an easy buck.

Steve Lawrence and Edie Gorme were playing to capacity at the Bacchanale Room, where long lines of punters waited to catch their favourite saloon duo. Katherine thought she caught a glimpse of Jean-Claude several times, but it was always a look-alike. By midnight, exhausted and frustrated, she muttered, 'What the hell am I doing here?' gloomily watching her last quarter disappear into the bowels of a particularly vicious coin-eating slot machine. 'I must be insane. What a wild goose chase.'

She was starving, and, realizing that she'd eaten nothing since lunch, waddled across the casino to the delicatessen. There she ordered a cheeseburger and a chocolate shake, not her usual fare, but appropriate for a size eighteen. Then she froze. The delicatessen was three-walled. The fourth wall looked out on to the crowded hall and there Katherine saw the unmistakable shape of Jean-Claude. He was walking slowly across the room, deep in conversation with a small, bald man.

Almost choking, Katherine slammed a ten dollar bill on to the table, and with her mouth still full of cheeseburger, she rushed from the restaurant after them.

'Who is it?' Jean-Claude awoke from a deep sleep, to an insistent knocking on the door.

'I have a message for you, sir,' said the voice. 'Very important, sir. From Mr Rogers.'

'Shit. Why would Quentin be sending him messages in the middle of the night?' Jean-Claude threw on a robe and, bleary-eyed, flung open the door.

Katherine stood there, poised, cool, and exquisitely dressed in an ice-white pant suit, with her hair a dark aureola around her face, and the pallor of her skin accentuated by ruby lips and smoky Cleopatra eyes.

'Hello Jean-Claude,' she said with a smile. 'How are you, darling?'

'*Mon Dieu* – Katherine – what the hell are you doing here? How did you find me?'

'Elementary, my dear Watson.' Katherine was determined to keep it light, although she could hardly hear her words for the thumping of her heart. 'You'll never get away from me.' It was an Ethel Merman imitation, but she knew it had fallen flat. She inwardly cursed herself for acting like a buffoon.

Jean-Claude's pale eyes were enigmatic, but there was a hint of amusement in them.

'Well, aren't you going to ask me in? Baby it's cold outside.'

Oh God, what if he said no? What if he told her to fuck off, get the hell out of his life? What would she do? She was crazy about him. She was deeply in love with him; she knew that more than ever now. She put a hand on her heart as if to stop it pounding, and after staring at her for about a year, Jean-Claude nodded.

'OK, come on in.'

She entered a bedroom which was almost identical to hers.

'They told me you weren't registered,' she said.

He snorted with laughter. 'In this hotel all you need to do is tell the operator you're not here, and for enough bucks they'll lie their asses off.'

Throwing her pride to the wind, Katherine said, 'Look, Jean-Claude, I had to see you, just one more time – to know for sure that you really meant what you said. That you really do *want* to end our relationship.'

He lit a cigarette, staring at her with unreadable eyes. 'Sit down, Kitty,' he said softly.

She perched on the edge of a slime-green velveteen sofa, with plastic anti-macassars on the arms, aware that he could probably hear her heart pounding. He'd thrown on a pale blue terrycloth robe, and looked more devastating than ever.

'You want a drink?' She shook her head. This was no time to drink. This was sink or swim time for Kitty Bennet. This was her life.

'I'm sorry I hurt you, Kitty; you know I am.'

'How was I supposed to know that? I haven't heard a word from you since you walked out a week ago – I didn't know what to think, what to do. I've been completely miserable. It's been hell.'

Her voice sounded nagging, whining, complaining. This was no good – she had to be cool – cool and in charge, just like her television character. But unfortunately she wasn't Georgia Poison-Peach Skeffington, she was Katherine Bennet, and she was fighting to hold on to the man she loved.

'Yes – well it's been tough for me too.' He frowned. 'But, *mon Dieu*, Kitty, you must understand my side of things – I have to have some self-respect. I can't go on any more with the whole world thinking I'm your kept man, just a gigolo.'

'Oh my God, they *don't*, Jean-Claude. Don't be ridiculous. Nobody thinks that. It's just that no one is really sure what you do. You never talk about yourself.'

'Can you imagine what it's like, being called Katherine Bennet's stud all the time?' he asked sarcastically. 'Can you, Kitty?'

'No one who knows us calls you that. Anyone who's seen us together knows how deep our relationship is. Who'd be so insensitive?'

'Your world is full of insensitive pricks, Kitty you must know that.' The ash from his cigarette fell on to the carpet. 'What am I? Who am I? What was I to you, Kitty – really...?'

'The man I loved – the man I still love,' she whispered.

'No, that's not true. I'm just a man you met, fancied, and shacked up with. Some guy you keep on a leash, like a pet dog.'

'That is ridiculous, Jean-Claude. I've *never* thought of you like that. You were always your own man, with your own identity – always.'

'Yeah – sure.' He dragged heavily on his cigarette and blew two perfect streams of smoke from his nostrils. 'How come, Kitty, that I always had to fall in with *your* plans, never you with mine?'

'Like what? We always discussed what we would do together.'

'Like – oh – like taking a weekend in Vegas for example. Or Reno. You always said you hated it here – that you couldn't go anywhere crowded, because you couldn't stand being stared at. That you always got mobbed, and couldn't have any privacy. Fuss, fuss, fuss. Yet here you are Kitty, larger than life. Why?'

'I came to find you. Because I still love you, and I don't want us to end.'

'Love!' – with a snort of contempt he stood up and poured himself some vodka from the half-empty bottle on the dresser.

'Love is a two-way street, Kitty, and I finally realized that for months we'd only been going down it your way.'

She was silent, knowing it was almost true. They had usually done things her way. She had manipulated him, without meaning to. He handed her a vodka.

'Everything had to be the way it was, because of *your* career Kitty, or because of Tommy, or because of any number of reasons that kept me from being a full partner in your life, sharing it with you properly. I did some serious, serious thinking while you were off on tour, entrancing America, and I decided that what I want is what you have always said you *don't* want.'

'Which is what?' She already knew his answer.

'Marriage,' he said. 'I wanted to be married to you, Kitty. I wanted to share your life, to be your man, and you to be my woman.'

'But – but I told you before, I'm just not ready for marriage so soon Jean-Claude, and since I probably can't have any more children, what's the rush? Look darling, if two people really love each other, marriage shouldn't be an issue.'

'Bullshit,' he snapped. 'It is the fucking issue, Kitty. It is the only issue. Children or not, I refuse to be just another part of your household menagerie. Kitty's Man of the

Month, or the year, or whatever. It's a question of pride. My self-respect, my machismo or whatever you want to call it, won't allow me to...' he shrugged. 'But we've had this conversation too many times before, *chérie*, and I've finally seen the light.'

'What light?'

'The light at the end of the tunnel. The light that says, "get out of there, Jean-Claude, and get a life. Get *your* life back onto the right track and stop living in Katherine Bennet's shadow". I'm a man, Kitty. I won't live like a kept dog.'

Seeing him so strong – so assertive and positive – Katherine longed to have his arms around her, her head on his shoulder. She longed to have him at the helm of her life.

'So are you saying that, after all this, you still want to marry me?'

'Kitty – *Christ*. I adore you. And yes – I still want to marry you – I want to be with you forever. I want to be with you when you're old, and to look after you when you're sick.'

He sat down next to her. A dart of pleasure made her shiver, as his hand gently stroked her bare shoulder. She inhaled his scent – warm, spicy, remembered. He bent his head, and gently kissed her shoulder. She felt herself beginning to float down a blissfully familiar lake. His hands, their touch like a mantra, were caressing her body more intimately now. Teasing, fondling, stoking the fire that could only be extinguished by the movement of his body inside hers.

'Marry me, Kitty, marry me now,' he breathed into her hair. 'I'll make you happy, I promise I will.'

'Oh, but I...' Then his mouth crushed hers, and her protestations were blown away like a leaf in the wind.

Light-headed, she heard her voice as if from far away.

'What if I can't – won't marry you? What then?'

The magic fingers, hands and lips stopped their tender explorations, and he leaned back against the sofa, surveying her with sad green eyes.

'Then we part. Forever. We end it. *Zut.*' He made a cutting motion across his throat. 'Just like this. Sharp finish – no lingering death like the death of a thousand cuts. The Chinese know how to torture. They carve tiny little slices from a man's body, until he's nothing but a raw open wound, begging for death, craving it more than anything he's ever wanted before. It's an unspeakable way to die.'

Katherine shuddered, already missing the closeness of his body. So what could she lose by marrying him? He had always been honourable towards her. He was a perfect gentleman – gallant – tender, funny – with a superb sense of the ridiculous. He adored her and she adored him. They made love together as no one ever had before in the whole history of lovers. What was she so scared of?

Do it – said Katherine's inner voice. Do it, you *fool*. You've tracked him down all the way to Vegas – what the hell do you want? Have you made a fool of yourself just for a *schtupp*? If the tabloids get hold of this disguise scam, you'll be even more of a laughing stock in Tinsel Town than you are already.

'Relationships have to go forward, not backwards,' Jean-Claude said firmly. 'So if I'm not going to be with you, Kitty, then I must get back to my life here in Vegas – without you.'

His hands were on her again, the promise of all the delights he could offer making her body want to surrender.

'All right,' she whispered, 'if that's what you really want – I'll marry you.'

He pulled away, and looked searchingly into her eyes.

'Ah no, Kitty. That's not good enough. It isn't enough for me to want this marriage. *You* must want it too.'

'I do,' she whispered fervently, feeling the warmth of his hand on her thigh – wanting him to move it to the place where she ached for him. 'Oh yes I *do*, Jean-Claude – I want to be your wife, truly I do.'

They made love all through the night. Katherine, who had barely thought about sex for weeks, was carried away on a wave of such overwhelming passion that her mind became a blank. The only reality was her body melding with Jean-Claude's. By the time the grey morning light filtered through the cheap blackout curtains, she was weak from lovemaking, but at that point he became more insatiable. Now that she had agreed to be his wife, it was as if he had to prove he was the greatest lover she had ever had. And he certainly was. By far far and away he was.

They ordered room service at noon. Champagne and orange juice, bacon, and eggs and croissants, devouring them as rapidly as possible, so that they could make love again – and again – and again. Finally they slept in each other's arms, and when they awoke it was dark once more.

He kissed her sleeping eyes awake. 'Wake up wife,' he whispered. 'Time to get ready. Today is your wedding day.'

They were married by a crumpled Justice of the Peace, in a shabby little pink rococo chapel on the Strip. It was next door to a cheap casino and they could hear the shouts of punters, and the whirring of the slot machines as they made their vows. Jean-Claude had bought her a simple gold wedding band from the Caesar's Palace jewellers, and Quentin miraculously appeared to make all the other arrangements.

By the time they flew back to Los Angeles by private jet on Sunday, after yet another night of ecstatic lovemaking, Katherine thought she was the luckiest woman in the world.

CHAPTER TWELVE

As Madame Jean-Claude Valmer, Katherine thought she had never been happier. Jean-Claude was everything she had ever wanted in a man, but had not believed existed. Their love was pure and real; their sex life bold, carnal and unbelievably erotic. Every day and every night he wanted her, and every day and every night she wanted him. Often during the afternoon, or at weekends when she was studying lines, or lying by the pool, he would take her hand, pull her to her feet, and lead her into the bedroom. She had never known a man who loved loving so much. He made each time a glorious act of commitment and passion. Each morning, when she left for work in the cold Los Angeles dawn, he would touch her and whisper, '*Je t'embrasse, chérie* '. He was teaching her French; he planned that one day they would buy a little house in the Loire valley.

'You must learn my language, *chérie*,' he insisted. 'French is the most beautiful language – difficult, of course, which is why so few Americans ever master it. Americans like things made easy for them.' Twice a week at dinner he insisted that she and Tommy conversed only in French with him. During these times Tommy would usually be quite silent.

There was no doubt that her son didn't like his new stepfather. Katherine remonstrated in vain that she, too, was entitled to happiness, and that Jean-Claude made her happier than she'd been in years. Even Brenda, who did not greatly care for Jean-Claude, tried to explain that Katherine's state of mind was the most important thing in the equation.

The fact was that Tommy didn't want to listen; after one typical argument, he stalked out of the house, slamming the door behind him, and announced that from now on he was going to stay with his father. The next morning – rather sheepishly – he came back, and Katherine didn't utter a word of reproach. She knew perfectly well that life in Johnny Bennet's squalid apartment would have been even less bearable for Tommy, than rubbing along with Jean-Claude.

Vera was probably the only one of Kitty's close circle to be truly overjoyed by the wedding – especially when she saw the pictures on the front page of all the tabloids. Quentin had managed to take a few snaps in the Las Vegas chapel, and Jean-Claude had negotiated an astronomical sum of money for their use.

'You looked beautiful in that white suit, though you shouldn't have worn white for your second marriage,' said Kitty's mother. 'And you'd better put some collagen on that neck of yours. It's looking a bit scrawny. Men don't like women to be too skinny, Kit-Kat; they like a bit of meat on the bones.'

Katherine laughed. Nothing her mother, or anyone else said could affect her mood these days. She was in love, and more and more obsessed by her husband; he dominated every waking thought. All the clichés of every love song she'd ever listened to became reality, from 'A trip to the moon on gossamer wings', to 'All the things you are', and 'Oh no, they can't take this away from me'. Only when she was on the set, as Georgia Skeffington, could she forget him.

Jean-Claude seemed to want nothing from Katherine except to be with her.

'Your happiness is all that matters to me, *chérie*,' he said, proving it over and over again.

He would often shake his head sadly when he saw her arguing on the telephone with her business manager or her agent. Although she had proved beyond a shadow of doubt that the American public loved her, Hal didn't seem to be able to find work for her on any of the other networks. Now that she was back on *The Skeffingtons*, she was unable to star in the promised series for Lew Lupino.

'I can't get a project for you for the next hiatus,' admitted Hal.

'If I'm so popular with the public – why not?'

'The problem is that you play that goddamned part too well. The other networks have done surveys with the public. You, Katherine Bennet, are one hundred per cent identified with the Georgia Poison-Peach character. No two ways about it. That's the way the cookie crumble. I'm sorry.'

Jean-Claude listened to this conversation, and saw Kitty's disappointed face. 'Why don't you let me help you, *chérie*?' he asked. 'First of all I think your business is being handled atrociously. Brett is not only a crook, but worse than that, he's a moron. A crook might be skimming off the top, but at least he would be giving you some of the benefits. A moron isn't worth the time of day. Look – ' Jean-Claude was sitting in his new office, at his laptop computer. He had converted a room next to the kitchen. 'I'm going to show you a few sums.' Expertly he tapped out some figures. She stood behind him, watching.

'If you do this,' he said, 'there's no reason why you shouldn't be able to save at *least* twenty per cent of your salary. At the moment you're spending more than you're making. You know the old Chinese proverb?'

'Another one?' She laughed, and stroked the back of his neck.

'Man who make hundred dollars a week, and spend ninety-nine dollars and ninety-nine cents is happy man. Man who make hundred dollars a week, and spend hundred and one dollars is miserable man.'

'Damn right,' said Katherine ruefully.

'Show business is littered with stars, executives and producers who were once rich, but are now living in poverty.' His voice had the ring of authority. 'Most actors and performers are *notoriously* bad at business. Lawyers, accountants, agents, business managers, all the sharks and piranhas in Hollywood know this, and they prey on them, *chérie.*'

'How do you know?'

'I know,' he said enigmatically. 'My father was an accountant. Small potatoes, I know, but I learned a lot from him. Then Quentin handled all my money when I was a pop star. He didn't teach me how to make it, but he sure taught me how to save and invest it.'

'And did you?'

'Sure, I did. I don't want to brag, Madame Valmer, but look at this.' He kissed her hand then continued to type rapidly more figures on to the computer.

'*Voilà*! This is the empire of Jean-Claude Valmer. And it is growing. You won't have to work your pretty little *derrière* off, all your life, *chérie*, because you have a husband who, one day soon, will be able to take care of you.'

Katherine stared at the figures.

'However,' said Jean-Claude, frowning as he tapped away, 'at this precise moment most of my assets are tied up in my new Vegas venture. Temporarily, of course.'

'Of course.' Katherine watched his agile fingers. She was glad he was beginning to share something of his life with her.

'Now, *chérie*, it's important for you to have your own money, *n'est-ce pas*?'

She nodded.

'And *malheureusement*, mine is completely tied up in the hotels. So, *chérie*, although I can contribute a little bit to my share of the household expenses, you must realize that I am not yet financially equipped to be able to pay for all of your outgoings, even though, as your husband, I would like to.'

'I'm a liberated woman; I would never expect you to pay for Tommy and his school, or this house, or all of the people and things that I need.'

'But nevertheless, *chérie* –' he typed out a few more figures, which immediately showed up on the screen, 'you must do two things which are *essential* for your future.'

'These are?'

'Number one, you need to make more money.'

'Ha! Easier said than done. I mean, forty thousand dollars an episode is not chopped liver, but do you know how much I actually get to *keep*?'

'Not a lot, I should think.' He frowned again.

'Damned right, not a lot. In fact, I'm in debt up to my eyebrows. I dread to think how much Brett has mortgaged this house for.'

'We'll work on that,' he said. 'The second thing is, you need to *conserve* the money that you make, and both of these things I think I can do for you.'

'That's a tall order, darling.'

'You know what I think about Brett, and the same goes for Hal. They're useless. You remember it was *I* who got you a possible series with the other network, when you were about to be dropped from *The Skeffingtons*?'

'Of course I remember, darling.'

'It was a little psychological game I played with Carolyn Lupino. Not too difficult, if you know the rules of business, and the way people work. OK. So, let me show you my ideas for your financial future. Then I'll tell you what I think you should do for your career, and how I can help you.'

They spent the rest of the evening poring over account books, cheque book stubs, tax returns, receipts, bills. It was all the mundane and boring administration that Katherine never had the time or energy to deal with, and, at the end of the evening, she was convinced of two things. Not only was Jean-Claude a genius with money, but she was going to fire Brett, and let her husband take over her financial affairs.

'You won't be sorry, *chérie*,' he kissed her forehead, and looked deep into her eyes. 'I promise I will make this work for you.'

'Are you out of your Chinese mind?' Brenda's voice reached an unexpected crescendo. 'You *can't* let him handle all your financial stuff, you simply *can't*!'

'Why not?' asked Katherine. 'He can't possibly do a worse job than my accountants and advisors have done in the past. Jean-Claude has proved to me that Brett's completely hopeless. My affairs are in a worse state now than when he took over. What've I got to lose?'

'I don't know. It just doesn't feel right to me.' Brenda was sitting on the sofa in Katherine's dressing room, going through a pile of fan mail. 'I mean, you don't really know that much about this guy. You meet him in France – he calls you – comes out and *schtupps* you a few times, you marry him, and now you're handing him your life on a plate. Why?'

'Instinct,' said Katherine. 'We've both been through the mill and back. He understands this shitty business as well as I do. We've got so much in common, and I trust him.'

'Trust him! – Oh my God!' said Brenda. 'It's too soon – you've only just got married – you've only known him for three months, for Chrissake.'

'Three months is long enough to believe in someone,' said Katherine firmly. 'Look, Brenda, I know Jean-Claude's an exceedingly persuasive man, but he's so utterly honest that I'd be mad to doubt him for a second.'

'Oh God,' moaned Brenda.

'Look, he said I must check up on him, that I'd be foolish to trust him completely. So I did, and everything he said adds up. It's done, Brenda, so please don't say another word.'

Brenda didn't. Not to Katherine, but she rang Steven to tell him the news.

'You won't believe what he's made her do, Steve. I can only see trouble ahead.'

'She's a big girl and a smart woman,' said Steven. 'She knows what she's doing.'

'I just hope you're right,' said Brenda, but she felt certain that he was not.

Two or three times each month, Jean-Claude travelled to Las Vegas, to oversee the building of his new hotel, and once or twice Katherine went with him. She was concerned that the hotel was so far off the beaten track, nearly eight miles away from the mainstream Strip, from Caesar's, MGM Grand, Harrahs and the rest of the Vegas fleshpots. When she told Jean-Claude that she was afraid the average Vegas punter wanted action, crowds, and to be in the centre of things, he laughed.

'*Chérie*, this is not going to be a cheap honky tonk casino saloon, like the rest of them. This is going to be more like a French inn, such as you would find in Provence, or in the Loire Valley. Yes, we are going to have blackjack, crap tables and slot machines, but we are catering to a completely different clientele. Much more select and European.'

'Don't you think that a select European clientele would prefer to gamble in Monaco, or Atlantic City? Why would they come to Vegas, if they wanted a classy atmosphere?' But Jean-Claude was too full of enthusiasm to listen. Katherine shrugged. It was his business, she thought, and she'd better keep her nose out of it.

Quentin was Jean-Claude's full-time partner and they were backed by a syndicate of French financiers.

'The same group who backed my hotel in France,' Jean-Claude told Katherine. 'Isn't it beautiful?' He showed her a brochure with pictures of an enchanting, medieval-style inn. 'It's right in the Loire Valley,' he said. 'I'd love you to visit it one day.'

They were sitting by the fire after dinner.

'I want to, Jean-Claude. When shall we go?'

'Sooner than you think. I've been working on a deal for you.'

'What kind of a deal?'

'In four months *The Skeffingtons* starts hiatus. *Non*?'

She nodded. 'Yes, and as usual Hal, and the rest of the suits at the agency have said there's nothing on the horizon for me.'

'Bullshit, *chérie*. You're much too talented to play a bitch goddess all your life. I took it upon myself to talk to a couple of friends.'

'You did?' She looked at him, smiling.

'Of course, some of them are your friends too, *chérie*, but unfortunately you have never known how to use contacts to your best advantage.'

'I have a few friends in LA,' she said, 'but I've always thought that friendships in Hollywood were generally based on how successful you were in the business. I know I'm pretty successful at the moment, but I must admit I don't really trust anybody in this town.'

'It's OK to be cynical, *chérie*,' he stroked her bare leg, sending familiar shivers up her spine. 'Do you realize what that show would be without you?'

'Still pretty entertaining, I guess.'

'No. You are the spice in the mixture. They need you desperately, and without you, I think it wouldn't be high in the ratings much longer.'

'I don't think it's going to be around for much longer, as it is,' said Kitty. 'The ratings are so-so, and slipping again. Several of the new shows are overtaking us this season.'

'*Exactement.*' He nodded. 'So, speaking as a husband who loves you madly, do you not think we should exploit your worth?'

'How?'

'By maximizing your potential. By making you much more of a force in the television industry.' He started pacing the room, tall, lean and elegant, in his black jeans and black polo neck.

'It's extraordinary to me, Kitty, that you aren't starring in a mini-series, or even a movie of the week during your hiatus. Quentin and I were talking about it only the other day. He thinks it's criminal, particularly when that no-talent British woman got such a wonderful role in *Emma Hamilton*. You would have been sensational in that, Kitty.'

'That's show biz. You have to understand I've been an actress for twenty-four years. I know this business inside out. I don't care about this stardom crap. It's all a joke to me. The fans, the autograph hunters, the fawning maître d's in restaurants, the good things and the bad things that are written in the magazines. It doesn't mean *anything* to me, because I know it's all ephemeral.'

'*Exactement.* Ephemeral is right. But while you are on the crest of this wave, Kitty, you must try and make more of a killing.'

'I call Hal all the time. He says there's nothing happening out there.'

'Hal. *Merde.*' He lit a cigarette. 'Hal and his agency aren't worth a bean. I think you should get rid of him, Kitty.'

'Get rid of him?' Her voice rose, 'This will be the fourth agent I've fired in four years. It's almost a record.'

'You must stop caring so much about what other people think, *chérie.*' He sat next to her in front of the fire; she took his cigarette from him, and puffed at it, staring into the flickering flames.

'You're right,' she murmured.

'I'm always right,' he said firmly. 'When I married you, Kitty, it wasn't just because I was crazily in love with you, and still am. It was because I wanted to be totally committed to you. Not only to you as a woman, but to you as an actress, and to your whole life. I've been watching these idiots ruin your career, and the even more moronic jerk-offs running your business, and I think it's about time you let me help you.'

'Well, why not?' said Katherine blithely.

Although, like most women of her generation, she considered herself a feminist, she had a grudging admiration for the dominant male. Jean-Claude was strong, but not pushily aggressive like so many men in Hollywood. Gallic charm and subtlety tempered everything that he did.

'I've talked to Lew Lupino again. He's a big supporter of yours. There's a project he could put you into right away. He would produce, I would be associate producer, and you would be executive producer. It would take care of the hiatus.'

'Are you crazy?' Katherine laughed. 'When I approached my agents about having more control over what I did, and maybe becoming a producer, they laughed in my face. They said that the networks would *never* consider an actress becoming a producer. "What about Goldie Hawn and Barbra Streisand," I asked. "Movies," they said. "Those dames are real movie stars, you're just a TV actress, and lucky to be working".'

'What do they know? Those people are nothing, Kitty. If only you realized how ignorant and uncultured most people running studios, and networks, or producing television shows and movies are. It's a joke. I used to see them in Cannes, during the festival. I used to sit near them in restaurants, hearing their loud, dumb talk, and letting my dinner be ruined by the smell of their cheap cigars. Most of them are morons, Kitty, and the sooner you realize that, the better off you'll be.'

'Mm, I guess you're right,' Kitty stared into the fire, watching the way it made dancing pictures.

'I think you should give me authority to negotiate a mini-series deal with Lupino. And I should do it alone. Because of my relationship with Lew, we don't need an agent. When did an agent last actually get you a job?'

'A couple of years ago, I was in a movie of the week.'

'Okay. So what have you possibly got to lose?'

'Nothing, I guess. Let's go for it, darling,' laughed Katherine. And so the die was cast.

Within two weeks, not only had Jean-Claude negotiated an incredibly lucrative deal for Katherine to star in her own mini-series during the hiatus, but he had also opened avenues for other things. A Katherine Bennet clothes label was under discussion, as well as a cosmetics line.

'None of these has even been *touched* by your so-called advisers,' said Jean-Claude. 'They've just ignored exciting ways to make more money, Kitty.'

Even Brenda was impressed. 'He certainly has your best interests at heart, honey. I take back everything I ever said about him. You are one lucky woman.'

'Don't I know it. Sometimes it all seems too good to be true,' Kitty said.

After so many years of trauma, drama and financial despair, things were going smoothly, and Katherine threw herself into preparations for her new mini-series, *All That Glitters*, with enthusiasm. What with *The Skeffingtons*, her cosmetics and clothes lines, and being wildly in love with her husband, Katherine didn't notice that her son was gradually slipping away from her.

CHAPTER THIRTEEN

Tommy watched as the crack dealer dexterously played with his paraphernalia. Nag was cooking crack, and he was the expert.

'This'll be the best damned fix you ever had, man! This shit's so pure it'll blow your mind to kingdom come, and this candy man never lies!' Nag unscrewed the top of a small plastic Evian bottle, poured three-quarters of the water on to the floor, burned a little hole in the plastic with his cigarette, just above the waterline, then inserted an empty ballpoint pen tube halfway inside the bottle.

Tommy looked at Todd, his heart pounding with anticipation. It was only his second trip to the Green House, but he had already experienced the immediate, addictive rush any user got from crack-cocaine. He wasn't bothered. The last trip had been the biggest turn on he'd ever experienced.

Nag put a strip of tinfoil over the top of the bottle, then, with a rusty safety pin, pricked several holes in the foil, before sealing that and the ballpoint hole tightly with blu-tac. Then he carefully tapped a little pile of cigarette ash on to the foil.

'Mus' be fresh ash,' he said, 'to make a real good bed for the crack.'

Nag put a white crystal on top of the ash, with the delicacy of a jeweller placing a diamond in a platinum setting. Then, flicking his lighter over the crystal, he quickly handed the bottle to Tommy and whispered urgently: 'Draw man, draw!'

Tommy inhaled fast, and immediately felt the electrifying effect of the drug tearing into his brain.

'Jeez that looks fan-fuckin'-tastic.' It was Todd's third trip to this shooting gallery, and he was trembling with anticipation. 'I can hardly wait.'

The Rastafarian, who, although not yet thirty, only had two or three teeth left, gave a gappy grin.

'OK, my men,' he said, handing the plastic bottle to Todd. 'Here's Johnny! Here comes the boy.'

As soon as the drug hit, both boys immediately felt an euphoric buzz, and they started to pretend-punch each other, jumping around the room, yelling happily.

'OK, OK, OK, my men, *out* now, you hear.' The Rastafarian had no time for high-spirited teenagers, once they'd paid.

Stoned and satisfied, the boys swaggered out on to a dingy street. Todd and Tommy were the only white kids around. Although only a few blocks past Fairfax and Vine, the tall skyscrapers of downtown LA were barely visible through the acrid yellow smog. Weeds sprouted from cracks in the pitted pavement, and broken-down hulks of burnt-out cars lined the rutted road. The crack house was next to a grocery store, so encrusted with graffiti, that it was practically impossible to read any of the scribbled Spanish signs announcing the bargains of the day. There were few shoppers inside, but a couple of young Hispanics leaned against the wall outside. They stared contemptuously at the two honkies.

'Hey, dudes,' the taller one flipped his cigarette in Tommy's direction. 'Whatcha'll doin' down here?'

The cigarette landed on Tommy's unlaced sneaker; he flicked it off, and glared at the youth.

'Ah said, what you doing heah, man? This is our territory. Ya'all know that.'

'So what?' Tommy tried to walk on, but the Mexican barred his path. As if from nowhere, three other Hispanics appeared at his side.

A girl, no more than fourteen, ran past with a squalling baby under one arm and a bag of groceries on the other. Todd, who hadn't smoked as much crack as Tommy, still had a bit of sense left. He nudged Tommy urgently: 'Let's split *now*. This ain't our neighbourhood.' But Tommy, cocky with drug-induced bravado, wasn't ready to leave.

'You fucker,' he growled. 'You Spic fucker.'

'You talkin' to *me*, man? You talkin' to me?' The big youth stepped forward, swinging a baseball bat, which one of his companions had given him.

'You better get off my pitch, man. You better get the fuck outta here right now, man, or you in a lot of trouble, you hear?'

Tommy took another step forward. 'Yeah, yeah, yeah? So what you gonna do about it, you big ugly mother-fucking bastard? What does a pig-ugly Spic like you know about anything – huh?'

Todd stared at Tommy in horror. It was absolute suicide to insult a Hispanic gang, on their own pitch, in downtown LA.

'I'm outta here, man,' he hissed. '*Now*. You better come too, 'cos there's no one around to help us.'

'Fuckin' go then, you coward.' Tommy didn't take his eyes off the Hispanic kid. 'I can handle it on my own.'

Todd was neither a coward nor an idiot, and he made one last attempt to grab his friend's arm. Tommy shook him off.

'Fuck off, Todd,' he shouted. 'Get out of here.'

Todd turned on his heel and ran for it. As he revved the engine of his car, he heard the crunch of bat on bone and a scream. It was a terrible sound; a pack of ghetto kids attacking their prey. In the seconds it took Todd to accelerate around the corner into the main street, he heard coarse, jeering laughter and the receding slap of trainers on asphalt.

Once in the Street he saw Tommy, lying where they had left him, crumpled on the pavement. 'Jesus Christ,' said Todd, as he slammed on the brakes.

Katherine was in the middle of a love scene when Brenda snatched her away from the set.

'Tommy's been hurt.' Brenda tried to sound calm. 'He's in the hospital,' then she burst into tears.

Katherine felt her knees start to shake.

'We've got to go to him.' Katherine was light-headed with fear. 'Get the car – I don't care what Gabe or anyone says – I've got to see him.'

As they sped towards the hospital, Brenda filled Katherine in with what little the police had told her.

'Is he badly hurt? You must tell me the truth, Bren.'

'I just don't know that much. All they said is that he's been beat up pretty bad, and he's in intensive care at Cedars.'

'Intensive care,' croaked Katherine. 'Oh my God.'

A grave Dr Lindsey greeted them. 'You've got to be very brave, Kitty. It's not good news I'm afraid.'

'Is Tommy all right? Is he going to live?'

'He's been hurt badly. He has multiple concussion, a fractured collarbone, two broken kneecaps and – '

Dr Lindsey exchanged glances with Brenda.

'And? And what?'

'And, I'm afraid he's in a coma.'

Kitty went even whiter, and Brenda gripped her hand so hard that her fingernails cut into her palm.

'A coma? What does that mean exactly, doctor?'

'It means the brain has suffered so much trauma that it's shut itself off.'

'How long will it last?' Kitty's only experience of a coma was of her own in *The Skeffingtons*. She had lain in hospital with her head swathed in bandages, her face plastered in full make-up, and her nails painted scarlet. The coma had lasted for about a week.

'We can't ever tell,' he said. 'Every case is different, and *everything* depends on the next twenty-four hours. If Tommy regains consciousness within that time, his chances are good.'

'Chances of what?' A claw of fear raked her.

'His chances of survival.'

'What do you rate those at now, doctor?' Brenda asked quietly, tears running down her face unchecked.

'About fifty-fifty. Everything depends on tonight. But you must go and see him, Kitty. The best thing you can do for him is to sit there and talk to him.'

Kitty was still white-faced with shock, and when they reached the intensive care ward, she couldn't prevent a cry of despair escaping. Tommy had tubes and drips attached to every part of his body. His head was shaved, and his closed eyes were swollen black and blue. His legs were heavily bandaged, and raised on pulleys.

'Both his knees are broken, I'm afraid,' said Dr Lindsey. 'They smashed his legs with a baseball bat.'

'Bastards!' Tears were still rolling down Brenda's cheeks. But Katherine could only stare, dry-eyed, at the broken body of her son.

'Oh God! Oh my God, Tommy, what have they done to you?'

Throughout the night, Katherine sat next to her son, talking, holding his hand, begging him to hear her prayers. She neither ate, slept, nor changed out of her black satin television outfit. The press had heard the news, and gathered outside the hospital, clamouring for a photograph of her at Tommy's bedside. PR officers, Kingsley and Raquel, came to fend off unwelcome visitors, but they could not reach Johnny, and there was no word from Jean-Claude, who was in Nevada inspecting the site for his new hotel. He had only planned to be away for two nights so had left no telephone numbers, and he never listened to the news, therefore wouldn't know what had happened.

The following morning Katherine told Brenda that she thought she'd seen Tommy's eyelids flicker.

Brenda said: 'You're right, Kitty, you're right. There *is* a flicker in his eyes – there is. Look.'

The women watched intently, to see if Tommy's lids moved again, but all the rest of that day he lay as still as a stone.

That afternoon Dr Lindsey arrived for an examination and shook his head.

'It's been twenty hours since he was brought in, and there's been no change, so we're going to take him for another brain scan. Usually with youngsters, a head trauma will show definite signs of improvement within twenty-four hours. If it doesn't, that means it could be – ' His voice trailed off.

'What?' Katherine's voice was sharp. 'What are you saying? Permanent? He could be in a permanent coma?'

'Something like that, I'm afraid.' The doctor seemed uncomfortable.

'You mean he could be permanently brain-damaged or even handicapped?'

Dr Lindsey stared at Katherine.

'We live in a terrible world, Kitty. Do you know how many injuries like this I see every year?'

Numbly Katherine shook her head.

'Hundreds,' he said bitterly. 'Maybe thousands. Young people, mostly male, beaten, cut down in their prime, turned into vegetables. And you know who does it?'

Again she shook her head.

'Other young people. They're all killing each other. What a world,' he said. 'What a terrible world we live in.'

At that moment they heard a faint sound, and turning towards the bed, saw that this time there was no doubt.

Tommy's eyelids were beginning to flicker, and while they watched, his mouth started to move.

'Tommy, Tommy, it's me, Mom,' said Katherine. 'Can you hear me? If you can hear me, squeeze my hand, darling, squeeze it now – please.'

There was complete silence in the ward, broken only by the ticking of machines which hooked other patients to their life support systems. Then Kitty felt a pressure on her fingers, a tiny squeeze.

Throughout that night Katherine sat beside her son, gripping his hand tightly, and speaking to him in a low soft voice. Interns and nurses paused by the bed to stare surreptitiously at the famous star, now scruffy and without make-up. Patients who had heard that a celebrity was in their midst, jostled each other outside the semi-glassed doors of intensive care, to catch a glimpse of their heroine. The press also descended en masse, to keep vigil at the end of the corridor. One of the more inventive of the paparazzi borrowed a doctor's uniform, and sneaked several photographs through the window in the door.

Katherine talked to Tommy about everything under the sun. She remembered stories from his childhood. She recalled journeys to Fire Island and Montauk, when he was two or three years old, adventures at Disneyland, fishing trips with his father, when Johnny had been a caring, giving father. When she ran out of memories, Katherine recited poetry: poems from her childhood, long hidden in the recesses of her mind.

Every now and again Tommy's eyes moved, and once or twice Katherine thought he was making an attempt to speak, but it wasn't until dawn crept into the antiseptic room, that his eyes finally opened properly, and focussed on her.

'Hi Mom,' he whispered. 'What are you doing here?'

* * *

'It's a miracle.' Dr Lindsey smiled. 'I don't usually believe in miracles but you must have done something amazing, Kitty.'

They sat on either side of a bruised, but remarkably normal, Tommy. He had apparently come out of the coma unscathed. Dr Lindsey was astounded.

'Tomorrow we can move him out of intensive care, but he's going to be wheelchair-bound for some time. His left knee, in particular, is pretty badly smashed.'

'Will he be able to walk properly?' asked Kitty. 'Play baseball? He's crazy for baseball.'

The doctor shrugged. 'He's lucky to be alive, Kitty. Forget about ball games for a while, physical scars take a while to heal. We'll know more about that in a few months, after his bones have healed. The main thing is that you've got your son back mentally. Now, let me ask you something. What in the hell was Tommy doing downtown, stoned and fighting with an Hispanic gang?'

Kitty looked at her son's face. 'I don't know, doctor, but I'm damn well going to find out.'

That evening they moved Tommy into a private room. He announced that he was ravenous, and wanted a cheeseburger, fries and a chocolate malt. Katherine decided that now was as good a time as any to find out what she needed to know.

'OK darling, shoot. What happened?'

'I don't want to talk about it, Mom.'

'You've got to. Why were you stoned that afternoon?'

He stared sulkily ahead at the plain cream wall. 'Dunno.'

'Come on, Tommy, you almost *died*. You owe me an explanation.'

'Owe *you*?' He stared at her, green eyes blazing. 'Are you kidding? I don't owe *nothing* to you, Mom, nothing at all.'

'I'm not asking for gratitude, Tommy. Heaven knows I get none from your father, but what you're doing to yourself with these drugs is absolutely suicidal.'

'Don't you *dare* bring Dad into this,' Tommy blazed. 'He's sick, much sicker than you know, Mom.'

'I'm sorry.' She stroked Tommy's forehead gently. 'I'm sorry, darling. Tommy, please, tell me about it. What happened? We've got to get things straight. I need to know what's bugging you, so I can help – or at least I can try.'

'Him.' Tommy's bitter eyes stared up at the ceiling. 'That frog you married, Mom, that fucking French *creep*. If you love him I guess that's OK for you, but...'

'But it's *not* OK, Tommy, it's not OK at all. It means a lot to me that we're a family, a threesome. We used to do things together, and I want to do things together again.'

'Ha.' Tommy snorted. 'If you think I want to do things with him, you're wrong. He's a liar and a cheat, and he's no damn good.'

'That's not true, Tommy.'

'It is *true*. Look, don't be dumb. I know everybody thinks he's the greatest thing since sliced bread, and I know he's been doing ace things for your career, but he's been a shit to me, right from the start. I think he's bad news, Mom. The only person that I've talked to about it, is Dad. He agrees with me.'

'How could Johnny agree with you? That's the most ridiculous thing I've ever heard. He doesn't even know Jean-Claude.'

'But he knows you. He knows what turns you on, and he knows what it takes to press your buttons. I guess –' He shrugged. 'I guess he sees that this Frog's gotten in on the ground floor. Anyway, it's not important. I guess that's why I've been hanging out with Todd, and we've been hitting the dope. A lot of the kids do it.'

'A lot of the kids do it,' she mimicked. 'All you kids had better *stop* doing it, Tommy, before you destroy yourselves. You've almost got killed this time. Do you have any idea how close you came to that?'

Suddenly, all the fight went out of him. 'Yeah, Mom, I know.' His eyelids were getting heavy. 'You're right. You always are Mom. Hey, I gotta go to sleep, I'm feeling weird.'

His eyes closed, and he murmured, 'Night, Mom, and I'm sorry – real sorry. I won't be doing crack again, that's for sure.'

Jean-Claude had said not to wait up for him, but Katherine was so overwrought that she couldn't sleep, and at midnight she was still wide-eyed, staring at the clock's fluorescent light. She had to get up in four hours. Why the hell wasn't he back yet? Eventually, just as she'd dropped off, Jean-Claude came in.

'*Chérie*, I'm so sorry.' She put her arms around him and inhaled his familiar scent.

'If I'd only known, I'd have been here with you. I can't believe you had to go through all of that alone.'

'Oh God, darling, darling, I've missed you so much. It's been hell.'

'I know, *chérie*. Can you believe I only just heard about it? I saw yesterday's newspaper on the plane. I tried to call you as soon as we landed, but none of the damned airport phones were working. Oh Kitty, Kitty, I've missed you – so much.'

He nuzzled her shoulder, and his hands started their familiar explorations of her body.

Kitty's eyes flicked to her clock. Three a.m. In the back of her mind a tiny voice asked some questions. What flights arrive at LAX from Nevada after midnight? Why hadn't he taken his mobile phone? Why didn't Jean-Claude ask more questions about Tommy? Where had he been? But she pushed the nagging thoughts away; in two hours' time she would be getting up. Then she'd have fourteen gruelling hours on the set. After all, her son *was* going to recover, and making love with her husband was the most important thing now.

Afterwards, as they lay entwined, he stroked her hair, and said casually, '*Chérie*, I've been thinking about your character in *All That Glitters*.'

'What about her?' Katherine mumbled sleepily.

'Well, Paulette de Waldner is a feisty, sensual, wildly attractive woman.' Jean-Claude paused significantly.

'So, don't you think I'm those things?' she joked.

'Yes, yes, of course, *chérie*. You are all of those and much more, but...' He paused again.

'But what, darling?' She snuggled in closer.

'Those eighteenth-century costumes that you'll be wearing – I've seen the sketches and – you'll look wonderful in them, *chérie*. Especially after you lose a little weight.'

Kitty, always defensive about her weight, opened her eyes. 'We don't start shooting for another ten weeks. I intend to lose at least six or seven pounds by then. There's no point in doing it now.'

'Well I think there is,' Jean–Claude said softly. '*Chérie*, don't take this the wrong way please, but we've always been honest with each other, and I think I have to be honest with you now.'

Now Katherine was wide awake. At a quarter to four there was hardly any point in trying to sleep. Better to coast through the day on caffeine, than just have one hour's sleep.

'What are you getting at?'

'There's a wonderful doctor I know in Las Vegas, who specializes in breast implants.'

Katherine sat up, eyes wide and shocked. She switched on the light. 'Are you suggesting that I need to have plastic surgery on my breasts? Are you crazy, Jean-Claude?'

'Calm down, calm down, Kitty.' He patted her as if she were a small, angry dog. '*Chérie*, you must be practical. You're forty-three. We're going to have a lot of very beautiful, very young girls in this movie with you. You don't want to look – ' He paused, searching for the word.

'Look what?' Angrily she grabbed a cigarette and lit up, ignoring his annoyed sigh. Jean-Claude hated smoking in bed. Well, too bad. She hated the idea that he thought she needed to improve her bosom.

'You won't have anything to worry about, *chérie*, it's quite safe. He's a world-renowned plastic surgeon whose specialty is breasts. He's brilliant. He's done practically everybody. Cher – Dolly – Jane. You name them, he's done them.'

'How do you know? Have you actually had a close-up view of them?' She puffed away, heedless of the ash falling on to the embroidered white linen coverlet.

He laughed, and tried to grab her, but she moved away from him. 'I can't believe what you're saying,' she snapped.

'*Chérie*, I never pretended that I was a saint before I met you, did I?'

Katherine didn't answer. No longer tired, she felt flinty and cold. She almost wished the alarm would ring, so that she could get up and go to work.

'Look, Kitty darling, you've got to face the fact. No one can look as good in their forties as they did in their twenties.'

'Quite,' she said icily, 'and there is nothing more pathetic, particularly in this town, than forty-five or fifty-year-old women *trying* to look twenty-five. I've never been one of those, and I'm not going to start now.'

'But it's for the sake of your *career*, *chérie*. Surely that means something to you?'

'I don't see how a tit implant is going to affect my damned career.' Katherine stubbed out the cigarette, then immediately lit another.

'Suit yourself.' Jean-Claude shrugged, and the icy tone that she dreaded came into his voice. 'But don't blame me, when you see the dailies, and you find that your breasts look saggy and raddled in those low-cut gowns.'

'Saggy! Raddled? Well, you certainly know how to stab me in the back. I don't see what's wrong with them.' She ran her hand over her breasts, as though to confirm that they still existed. 'They were good enough for Georgia, and they'll certainly be good enough for Paulette.'

'OK, I don't want to discuss it any more, Kitty. It's your problem. It's your life, so you do what you want. You always do anyway. However as the producer of the picture, I'm only telling you what I think would be best, not only for you, but for Paulette, and for the movie.'

'Thanks. I'll bear it in mind.'

But Jean-Claude had not finished. His cold voice said: 'He's bad news your son – just like his father. He's probably going to end up like him too – a hopeless junkie.'

Katherine stubbed out her cigarette, so hard that sparks burned her fingernails, then she switched off the light and lay wide awake, seething into the darkness. She had always despised the silicon-breasted, stretched and tweaked females of Beverly Hills, and she was determined that she would never be, or look anything like them. Yet, as she examined her bleary-eyed countenance in the harsh make-up lights the next morning, she began to have some doubt.

She looked tired and middle-aged. 'Of course you do, dear,' said the voice in her head. 'You've only had one hour's sleep. Not even Molly Ringwald could get by on *that.*' At lunchtime Steven and Brenda joined her for a sandwich in her dressing room, and she called Dr Lindsey.

'Your boy's a miracle,' he said. 'He's improving by leaps and bounds, and when the X-rays came back, we found out that his knees are going to heal perfectly well. I'm extremely optimistic.'

'Thank God,' said Katherine.

'His collarbone's no big deal; It just needs time and rest; so I think we can probably send him home within a week.'

Kitty hung up, and turned to Brenda and Steven. 'Tommy's going to be all right.' She smiled brilliantly.

'Hey, Kitty,' said Steve, 'you're one lucky Mama, you know that?'

'Do I ever,' she said fervently.

At the end of the day, Katherine dashed to Cedars Sinai, to find Tommy sitting up in bed, surrounded by music videos, sports magazines, candy, boxes of doughnuts, and in the chair beside him, a smiling Jean-Claude.

Katherine knew better than to show surprise. 'Hi, boys,' she said breezily. 'You look happy.'

'Hi Mom,' Tommy smiled. 'We are – we're going to play backgammon.'

Jean-Claude got up and kissed Katherine, squeezing her arm intimately.

'Had a good day?' Tommy asked.

'Yes darling, it went well. Did you?'

'Yup, sure did. Doc says I can go home on Friday, and on Sunday Jean-Claude says he'll take me to the Lakers game.' He grinned, 'I'm gonna be in a wheelchair, but only for a few weeks. It's sorta fun don't you think?'

'Yes, darling. It's going to be an adventure.'

Katherine flopped into the armchair and heaved a sigh of exhaustion. Whatever problems there had been between her son and her husband, seemed to have blown away like a summer breeze. Tommy's tirade of the previous night appeared like a figment of her imagination now. Too tired to think, she closed her eyes and drifted off to sleep, with the click-clack of backgammon in the background.

Within weeks Tommy was out of his wheelchair and negotiating the house on crutches. Steven often came over to shoot pool, and Tommy loved to play with him.

One night after dinner, Steven, Brenda and Katherine were relaxing in the den by the fire. Tommy had gone to bed, and Jean-Claude was with his computer.

Katherine said, 'Tommy seems in really good shape.' Brenda and Steven exchanged significant glances.

'What do those meaningful looks mean, may I ask?'

There was an uncomfortable silence.

'Come on guys, out with it,' said Katherine impatiently.

'OK I guess you have to know.' Steven sighed. 'Tell her, Brenda.'

'I've found pot in Tommy's bedside drawer. I confronted him, and he admitted it.'

'Did he say why he's doing it?'

'He said he'd *quit* crack, and pot was just like smoking a normal cigarette to kids today – he said it's no big deal and all the kids...'

'...Do it,' sighed Katherine. 'That's his cop-out.'

'But guess where he got it,' said Brenda. 'His father gave it to him.'

'Johnny? – That's unbelievable; he's always complaining he doesn't have enough money for groceries, and he's buying marijuana?'

'Yes,' said Brenda.

'Well I'm going to talk to him about it right *now*.' Katherine angrily started dialling, and as soon as Johnny answered, she lashed into him.

'How dare you give Tommy dope – what in the *hell* has happened to you? Are you crazy?'

'Ahh shit, a coupla joints for Christ's sake,' her ex-husband whined. 'Stop being so square, Kitty.'

'Square? Square? Giving a sixteen-year-old kid dope is supposed to be *cool*? You are an absolute fool, Johnny, and if you give him any more, ever, you'll find your allowance has been cut.'

'You can't do that. I need that money.'

'Oh yes I can, and I will,' she slammed down the phone, and lit a cigarette with shaky hands.

'What was all that about?'

The three of them turned to see Jean-Claude, framed in the doorway.

'Oh – nothing, darling,' said Katherine.

Jean-Claude looked coldly at Steven and Brenda. 'Why do you confide in other people, *chérie*? I'm your husband – it's me you should share your problems with.'

'Yes but – '

'Not another word, *chérie*.' He stopped her with a kiss on the forehead.

Steven was infuriated. He got up and finished off his drink.

'Well I'm off. I'll leave you two lovebirds to it.' The sarcasm in his tone was thinly disguised.

'Yes, do.' Jean-Claude's eyes never left Kitty's face. 'Get back and sort out your own problems.'

'I'm sorry about all this, Steve,' said Katherine.

'Not another word, *chérie*.' Jean-Claude flashed a warning look at his wife. 'It's time you went to bed, you look exhausted.'

Brenda started to say something, but Jean-Claude turned on her, flinty-eyed.

'Listen, fatso – if my wife has any problems, she shares them with *me*, you understand? Not you, and not *him*.' He looked disparagingly at Steven. 'I'm her husband.'

'And I'm outta here.'

Jean-Claude called after him: 'I haven't finished yet.'

'Well I have, thanks,' Steven replied sarcastically, and slammed the front door.

'Jean-Claude, what are you trying to do? These people are my friends; they're just helping me solve a problem with Tommy.'

'If you have any problems with Tommy, you discuss them with me, OK?'

Brenda sighed, rolled her eyes heavenwards, and mumbled, 'Night, you guys.'

'Kitty, Kitty, *why* do you go behind my back?' Jean-Claude started massaging her neck. He looked sorrowful. 'We are a team. It's me you should trust, not them.'

Katherine's eyes flicked to the clock. Midnight. She had to be up in five hours. There was only one thing for it, if she didn't want to be kept awake all night by a blazing row.

'I'm sorry, darling. I will talk to you about it next time, I promise.' The actress in her rose to the fore. 'It won't happen again, I assure you.'

CHAPTER FOURTEEN

From the moment he took over her affairs, Jean-Claude insisted that Katherine witness all the decisions he was making on her behalf. He made her sit with him at his desk at least once a week, and watch the magic dollar signs flash up on his computer screen.

'I want you to check up on me,' he said. 'The trouble is that you've always been too trusting and naive. That's why you've been ripped off by that bunch of morons you thought were taking care of you.'

Katherine had to admit that Jean-Claude's figures were impressive. He had managed to get an excellent advance for the clothes line that she was plugging on the Home Shopping Channel, as well as eight per cent of retail sales. The cosmetics were well into the planning stage; a selection of skincare and body products called *Peach*, and a scent of the same name were to be launched in the autumn to coincide with the first episode of *All That Glitters*.

Once he had fired most of Katherine's staff, Jean-Claude took on a part-time secretary to help him organize the big grey filing cabinet which held Katherine's business papers and contracts. She was a twenty-year-old economics major, fresh out of UCLA, a pert redhead called Ali, and she was to dedicate herself entirely to Jean-Claude's work.

He had also found Kitty a new lawyer, called Kenneth Stringer, who confided to her: 'Jean-Claude really has your best interests at heart. I've never seen anyone fight so hard at the table. You should see him negotiate your deals. He's like a tiger. He doesn't give an inch, and you know what? He usually wins – it's amazing.'

'He's certainly got me a great mini-series. *And* we get to produce it too.'

'He's very talented – a powerhouse. You're a lucky woman, Kitty.'

'I know,' said Katherine. 'You don't have to tell me.'

Over the months, Jean-Claude had cleared the dead wood out of Katherine's life. Half the household staff had been fired, and the ones who were left, faithful Maria, Won, Esperanza the new maid, and the gardener, had been told to pull their socks up, otherwise they, too, would go. Barry Lefkowitz was advised that, unless he stopped sending bills for endless 'incidentals', he would never be used again. Kingsley Warwick was put on a retainer.

Jean-Claude said, 'You've got to get more important publicity for Kitty. It isn't enough just having fashion snaps in the style section of *The Enquirer*, and those puff pieces in the local columns. If you don't do better for her, you'll be out.' The last people to be axed were Sam, the chauffeur, and the accountant.

'I'll do the accounts for you,' Jean-Claude said. 'I've done my own since I was a pop star. As for the chauffeur, you don't need one. I always drive at night, and Brenda can take you around during the day.'

Brenda was warned to stop spending on Kitty's credit cards.

'I've never seen so much money spent on stationery,' Jean-Claude barked. 'One hundred and fifteen dollars last month just for writing paper, notebooks and pencils! What are we running here, Merrill Lynch?'

He analysed three months' food and housekeeping bills, and stripped the budget to the bone.

'The larder isn't even half full, yet you spend over seven hundred bucks a week at Gelson's! They must be feeding half their families on you,' Jean-Claude snapped.

Kitty protested, not liking the implicit accusation against loyal Maria, but Jean-Claude stared at his computer, and tapped in more facts and figures. 'Never trust anybody. Priorities, *chérie*! Priorities! You've got to save money, otherwise you'll be broke.'

Katherine had to admit that her bank balance was improving under his care. She was indeed beginning to save money for the first time.

Sometimes when she came home, Jean-Claude was so involved with his computer that he only gave her a perfunctory kiss before joining her for dinner, but more often than not he dropped everything and devoted his evening to her.

'Did anyone ever tell you that you're the most beautiful and elegant woman in the world?' he murmured, as they sat in front of the fire, entwined in each other's arms.

'All the time,' joked Kitty. 'I tell myself that *every* morning, darling, whenever I see a mirror.'

'Well it's true, *chérie* – you are the fairest of them all, and I'm a lucky man.'

With barely six weeks left of the *Skeffington* season, Kitty was deep in preparation for the new mini-series. Many lunch breaks were taken up with fittings for the elaborate, eighteenth-century costumes and wigs, and at home she was often so dog-tired, that she was relieved when Jean-Claude returned to his computer instead of coming to bed.

Every two weeks Jean-Claude visited the building site in Nevada, to check up on his new hotel, but no longer asked Kitty to accompany him. She was glad of the break, for although she adored him, at those times she could sleep for hours, or be with Tommy.

On the Saturday before they were leaving for France, Kitty and Jean-Claude threw a big celebration at the house. It was partly a wedding reception, partly a farewell to LA, and the first big party they had ever given. In a town blasé with entertainments, Kitty wanted it to be an event to remember. She had planned everything in the most minute detail with Brenda, but to her dismay, on the morning itself, it started to pour with rain. Brenda frantically called the rental company, to ask them for a tent with plastic sides.

'July isn't usually rainy in Los Angeles,' Kitty looked sadly at the sodden grounds.

'There ain't nothin' you can take for granted in LaLa land,' replied Brenda, bitterly. 'All we need now is an earthquake, then probably half our guests'll decide not to come.'

In the garden, a team of workmen attempted to erect scaffolding and the tent, but the wind and rain were so forceful, that it blew down as fast as they put it up.

'I hope it's not a bad omen.' Kitty was eternally superstitious.

'Don't be silly. The party'll be a smash. Everything's coming up roses for you, hon. About time too.'

At that moment they heard screaming from the house. As they ran towards the sound, they saw that Jean-Claude seemed to be throwing Esperanza bodily out of the door.

'What the hell is going on here?' Kitty cried.

'Mind your own fucking business.' He turned his back on her, and began to walk away, back towards his office. Kitty followed him, almost bursting with rage.

'Jean-Claude, will you *kindly* tell me what you're doing? This is my house; how dare you throw my maid out of it? What on earth could she possibly have done?'

Jean-Claude ignored her, and went on walking. Kitty felt black fury erupt in her.

'Will you answer me, you bastard?' She yelled so loudly that the construction workmen looked up, then nodded knowingly to each other.

'Yeah, Georgia really is a bitch'.

But Katherine did not care who heard her.

'You'd better tell me what's going on, Jean-Claude,' she hissed breathlessly. 'Right *now*.'

His green eyes glittered, and his mouth was set in a thin, dangerous line.

'And you'd better mind your own business, Miss Katherine Bennet, and get out of my way – otherwise I'm walking out of here, right now.'

Katherine stood open-mouthed. Jean-Claude was in almost as foul a mood as he'd been after her publicity tour.

'All I want to know, is what Esperanza did to deserve what you did to her.' Katherine forced herself to be calm, although her face was scarlet with anger.

Then Jean-Claude grabbed her arm, and pulled her roughly out of earshot of the staff.

'OK, I'll tell you what that stupid bitch of a maid did. She picked up my private phone line.'

'So what's so terrible about that?'

'It's *my* line,' he hissed. 'My private line, for me only. Nobody picks it up, you understand? Nobody, not even you.'

'Well anyone can make a mistake.'

'Oh no, Kitty, you're wrong. *Nobody* makes mistakes around me. They make a mistake once and that's it. Finito. So – get rid of that fucking maid, or I'm out of here – I mean it, Katherine. I'm going.'

He slammed his office door, leaving Kitty quivering outside. After a few minutes she heard the familiar, irritating tap of the computer again. She had to compose herself. She couldn't afford a major row. In seven hours the house would be filled with friends, acquaintances, business associates, and the usual wallpaper rent-a-crowd which attended every Hollywood party.

Brenda put her arm around Kitty. 'I heard it honey. Ignore him; try to ignore him. Men are mostly shits y'know? When Frank got in a mood, life would be hell for all of us. It didn't happen very often, but when it did, I paid no attention, let him get it out of his system. For God's sake, Kitty, don't let that bastard affect the party. It's costing you twenty grand as it is, so you better enjoy yourself.'

'But how can I ignore him? He's flung my maid out of my own house – how dare he?'

'Just keep Esperanza out of Jean-Claude's way for a few days, and he'll forget about it. I'll take care of her, she can stay in Warwick's guesthouse.'

'OK, Bren,' Kitty sighed. 'I guess you're right. Best not rock the boat, but goddamn it, what the hell is wrong with him?'

'He's a man,' said Brenda pragmatically. 'Flawed, like all the rest of the sons-of-bitches.'

'I thought Jean-Claude was different.'

'Most guys are no damn good. You know what they say – can't live with 'em – can't kill 'em.'

'I know, I know. Well, like Scarlett O'Hara, I'll think about that tomorrow.'

Jean-Claude remained locked in his office until an hour before the party, then he stalked into Katherine's dressing room, and coldly announced:

'My telephone is sacrosanct, do you understand?'

Katherine was still so furious that she wanted to scream at him, but this was a battle of wills, and she knew if she said or did anything negative he wouldn't stay for the party, and by walking out on her, he would establish that he was boss. Who was really the boss in this relationship? She was undoubtedly the breadwinner, for although Jean-Claude paid for his clothes, travel, and occasional dinners, the bulk of the expenses and the staff's salaries came from Kitty's pocket. Tonight she couldn't face two hundred people asking where her new husband was, particularly since the guests included Eleonor and Albert. Summoning up all her acting skills, she smiled angelically at Jean-Claude.

'Of course not, darling, I wouldn't *dream* of answering your telephone – I hate the damn things anyway.'

'Good.' He gave a thin smile. 'By the way, I'm in charge of security arrangements tonight.'

'I've already given the guards explicit instructions about how I want the security handled,' she said.

'That won't be necessary, I have told them how I want it handled. I'm not your lapdog any more Katherine Bennet, so don't think you can boss me around like you do everyone else.'

He strode into his dressing room, slammed the door, and turned on the shower full blast. Katherine stared into the mirror.

'What is going on around here,' she whispered to her reflection. 'Who the hell is this man?'

But despite Jean-Claude, the party went off brilliantly. The food was delicious, the fashionable New York orchestra played a mixture of hits from the sixties and seventies, and most people stayed until well past midnight, unusual in Hollywood.

Most of the evening Jean-Claude was Mr Wonderful, oozing charm, doting on Kitty, encouraging the photographers to snap them both with every one of their celebrity guests.

'You're so damned lucky, Kitty,' gushed Carolyn Lupino. 'Jean-Claude is the most wonderful, adorable man I've ever met in this screwed-up town – other than *my* husband, of course.'

'Of course.' Across the room, Kitty saw Jean-Claude holding court. Candlelight burnished his tanned skin, and his hair seemed even more golden than usual. He looked incredibly handsome in his impeccable evening clothes. Almost too handsome.

Sharon Lasker joined them. 'You sure got the gold ring there, honey. What wouldn't all of us girls give to have Jean-Claude in our beds! You're one lucky dame, Kitty.'

'Hang on to him,' sighed Carolyn Lupino. 'Don't let him get away.'

Just before dinner was served, Jean-Claude became twitchy, stalking nervously between the various entrances to the house, checking with the security men that there had been no gatecrashers. On one of these prowls, he caught sight of Brenda, photographing a group of guests with her instamatic.

'What the fuck are you doing, Brenda?' he shouted, and grabbed her camera.

Brenda was never one to be pushed around; she snatched the camera back, and drawing herself up to her full five feet two, said frostily, 'I'm taking photographs for Kitty's private album. How dare you manhandle me. Who the hell do you think you are?'

'I don't *think*. I know who I am. I'm Katherine Bennet's husband.' He loomed over Brenda, his tall frame dwarfing her, and with a black scowl, said, 'We have our own photographer here tonight, as you know, Brenda, and we've made an extremely lucrative deal to sell the party pictures to several important magazines. I don't want this fucked up, OK?'

Then his face changed again, and he gave Brenda a dazzling smile. She was so stunned by the transformation, that she allowed him to take her camera again, and remove the film; then he presented it back, with a formal bow.

'Please understand, Brenda, it is for Kitty's sake I do this. I have my wife's best interests at heart, and I don't want her to forfeit the money we're receiving from these exclusive pictures, because some amateur's snaps appear somewhere. *Comprenez?*'

Brenda nodded grimly. It was difficult to reconcile this charmer with the growling creature of a minute ago.

'Sure, Jean-Claude, I *comprend*. Can I go now?'

He smiled, 'Of course, my dear. But please, Brenda, no more photographs.'

'No sir.' Brenda flounced out, mumbling, 'That guy changes personalities more often than a three-dollar hooker changes clothes.'

The guests sat at twenty dinner tables of ten. Each table had a silver lame cover, overlaid with white lace. The centrepieces were eighteenth-century silver bowls, full of lilies, cream roses, and trailing white ostrich feathers, entwined with honeysuckle. Pale beeswax candles cast a flattering light from four-branched sconces, and gleamed on the sterling-silver place settings.

Katherine's bubbly mood returned; she put her darker thoughts to the back of her mind, and set out to charm Gabe Heller and Lew Lupino, who were seated on either side of her. Her efforts paid instant dividends: to Eleonor Norman's fury, and Katherine's delight, Gabe made an extremely complimentary speech about her after dinner.

As soon as the dancing started, Katherine and Jean-Claude took to the floor alone. He bent his head and whispered, 'You look gorgeous tonight, my wife.'

'Thank you, darling.'

'Think about how much more gorgeous you'd look with a wonderful new cleavage.'

'You sure know how to ruin our evening.' Katherine pulled away, but he held her closer and laughed.

'I was only joking, *chérie*, can't you take a joke?'

'I don't think it's very funny, actually.'

He'd burst her bubble of excitement; there was a cold void inside her now, and a warning voice which she refused to listen to.

'Kitty, Kitty, *chérie*,' he laughed, ebullient again. 'Don't be cross, little wifie. Where's that famous sense of humour?'

'Hibernating, I guess.'

'Well, I didn't mean it.' His breath warmed her ear. 'You are so beautiful and you have a *belle poitrine*; later I'll show you how much I love all of it.'

'What a gorgeous couple,' Carolyn Lupino sighed to Steven.

'*She* certainly is,' he said. 'In fact she's so gorgeous, it's time I asked her for a dance – after you, of course, Carolyn.'

Jean-Claude bent his head, whispering into Katherine's ear, while the band played *Lady in Red*, the song she always thought of as theirs.

Later, when the beat turned jazzier, Steven cut in; saying, 'You look good enough to eat.'

'Do I?' Her eyes looked sad.

'Hey, Kitty, of course you do. And by the way, you don't have to save face for me. Any time you want to talk, I'm here. Don't let yourself become a victim.'

'I promise you, I'm not,' said Katherine.

'Then dry those eyes, sugar. No guy is worth it.'

'And the same goes for you, Steve. Any sign of Mandy coming back?'

'Nope – I guess that's it. She and the Schwarzenegger lookalike are playing happy families together.'

He noticed that Katherine was still looking sad, and that she was staring at Jean-Claude, who was dancing with Eleonor.

'She gives new meaning to the word predator,' Steve said. 'The only things that interest that woman are cocktails, coke and cock. In no particular order.'

Kitty looked at Eleonor, who was trying to twine her sinewy lycra-clad arms around Jean-Claude, and wondered, yet again, if her rival was behind the vicious whispering campaign against her.

'How's the script coming, by the way?' asked Steven.

'Fine, I think it's good, but I haven't seen the latest rewrites. Lew says we'll need a final polish, but they won't know for sure until next week, when the final draft is delivered.'

'Well, if you need a script doctor, this hack's for hire during this hiatus.' He gazed into her face, and asked, 'Are you sure you're OK?'

'Sure I'm sure,' she quipped. 'Everything's fine, honestly, Steve.'

Later when Steven danced with Brenda, they watched Katherine and Jean-Claude together.

'She looks gorgeous,' he said, 'but I'm worried about her, Brenda.'

'You and me both. That guy's a snake in a tuxedo, if you ask me. Hey, get a load of the secretary.' She glanced over to where Ali, Jean-Claude's PA, was dancing with Tommy.

'He can't take his eyes off her cleavage.' Steven laughed.

'Yeah, and *she* can't take her eyes off her boss – see?'

It was true. Even though Ali was with Tommy she constantly darted little looks in Jean-Claude's direction, and manoeuvred the boy closer to him.

'Watch this space,' said Brenda darkly. 'There's another one that's after him.'

'Do you think we should tell Kitty?' asked Steven.

'No – not yet. But I'm going to be keeping my eyes out on stalks from now on.'

As soon as the guests had departed, Jean-Claude started caressing Katherine in the living room, and trying to make love. She had drunk more than her fair share of champagne, and soon his sensuality melted her. 'Pretend it didn't happen,' said her inner voice. 'Don't you want a peaceful life?'

The next morning they awoke late, stretching luxuriously in linen sheets which were crumpled from last night's lovemaking. She smiled with satisfaction. Jean-Claude's passion seemed to be limitless, and he pleased her more in bed than any man had the right to. Last night had been more rapturous than ever. He took her throughout the night, with a ferocious intensity that left her fulfilled, and more in love than ever – despite remembered anger and pain. Now he was determined she should have their baby. She protested in vain that she was too old; that night he was so tender, and so ardent that Katherine felt she might almost be able conceive, after all.

A cloud crossed her mind as she remembered Esperanza, but Jean-Claude had persuaded her that the maid couldn't be trusted.

'I've caught her too many times, snooping around my private papers when she was supposed to be dusting. You're better off without her, *chérie*.'

She put her hands on her breasts. Was it her imagination or were they, as Jean-Claude had pointed out when they were dancing, becoming smaller? Shrinking in fact? She was dieting for the mini-series, but she wanted to lose weight from her waist and stomach, not her bosom.

Leaving Jean-Claude asleep, she tiptoed into her bathroom and stood on the scales. Yes, she had lost three pounds since last week. She looked in the full-length mirror. Those three pounds did seem to have evaporated mostly from her breasts. She was looking, she admitted, rather scrawny. That would never do for lusty Paulette, who was a buxom eighteenth-century wench. She wondered if she should finally submit to a breast implant, then shuddered. The thought of having a knife anywhere near her body made her feel ill. Besides, there wasn't enough time. They were leaving for Paris the following week.

There was a knock on the back door of her dressing room, and Tommy bounded in, with only a trace of a limp.

'Hey, Mom, can I borrow the keys to the Merc?'

'Darling, why can't you drive your Volvo?' She had bought him the small stick-shift car for his sixteenth birthday, and it was his pride and joy.

'Oh Mom, I'm sorry. I had to put it in the shop, I – er – had a little accident.'

'How little?' She quickly scanned Tommy for signs of drug-taking, but he looked particularly adorable today, scrubbed and innocent.

'It was nothin' – some stupid guy rear-ended my tail-lights. It wasn't my fault – Brenda spoke to the insurers. She didn't want to bother you about it.'

'OK, darling.' She sighed. 'Jean-Claude has the keys. I'll go get them.'

She picked the keys up from Jean-Claude's bedside table silently, so as not to disturb him, but he awoke instantly, his eyes snapping open. He grabbed her wrist with the speed of a jungle cat.

'What are you doing, *chérie*?'

'I'm taking the Mercedes keys for Tommy.'

'Why are you giving him my car?'

'Darling it's not your car, it's my car. I've had it for four years.'

'Ah yes, of course it is. Well you shouldn't give an irresponsible sixteen-year-old kid, who goes around getting himself stoned and beat up by gang thugs, a thirty-thousand-dollar Mercedes to fool around in. Let him drive the maid's car.'

Katherine could see signs of another row beginning, despite the evidence of their passionate lovemaking in the crumpled sheets. She threw the keys on the bed. She couldn't face more fights today.

'I'm not going to argue about this. You're tired, and obviously have a hangover. Just don't forget that Tommy is my son, and if I want to let him drive my car, I damn well will.'

'You spoil him rotten.'

'I don't need you to tell me how to raise Tommy, and I certainly don't need you to force me into a bad mood again. If you want to behave like this, I suggest we spend the rest of the day apart.'

'Fine with me, *chérie*,' he shrugged, burrowing back under the bedclothes. 'If that's what you want.'

Kitty slammed the door. She told Tommy that he could use Maria's battered old Ford, since Jean-Claude needed the Mercedes, and carefully ignored Tommy's sulky reply.

Kitty had planned to be with her husband all day, her hopes raised by their passionate night together. She decided to forget her unhappiness and take a swim, but she'd forgotten about the dozens of workmen dismantling the tent, and removing last night's refuse. The place was bedlam; crates, trucks, spilled food and upturned trestle tables were everywhere. Maria was busily scrubbing the white carpet, trying to remove the stains of dropped food, wine and cigarette ash. Kitty was astonished at how slovenly some of her guests had been, even grinding cigarettes out on the carpet. She shrugged. What the hell? What difference did it make if this house was falling to pieces? In some horrible way, so was her life.

She returned to her bedroom, the only sanctuary left. Jean-Claude was still asleep there; Katherine figured he would be out of it until early afternoon. The day was hers. She could concentrate on the heavy beauty maintenance which was becoming more necessary to her face and body. She would also work on the script, and start preparing for Paris.

Paris! Her favourite city in the world. A brand new movie, a brand new adventure. She couldn't wait to start. She refused to worry about the discord in her brand new marriage. It was both her strength and her weakness that she could close her eyes to problems and now she chose not to see.

'I'll think about that tomorrow,' she whispered to herself.

CHAPTER FIFTEEN

Before *All That Glitters* began shooting, they stopped off in Palm Beach. Katherine was to be honoured as Humanitarian of the Year at a charity for heart disease, and as a tribute to her career. Her father had died from a stroke, so it was a cause she cared deeply about. They were staying at the Breakers, a classically elegant hotel, in the most desirable area of Palm Beach.

'The evening's a sell-out.' Brenda was helping Katherine into a black and silver bugle-beaded gown, while a local hairdresser fluffed her hair. Harry Winston had sent over two security guards, bearing a tray of blazing diamonds for Katherine to borrow.

'They love you honey-chile! All that old money – those doddery dowagers, ancient widowers, and every facelift in Palm Beach is going to be there tonight,' crowed Brenda. 'They'll be giving you heavy scrutiny, so you better look fantastic.'

'I'm trying.' Kitty winced as Brenda tried to zip her up. 'Bloody hell, this dress is so tight it's agony.'

'You've got to suffer to be – '

'Beautiful, yeah – I *know*,' mocked Kitty. 'But this dress is Spanish Inquisition time.'

'You've certainly lost the weight you needed, and some. You look fabuloso.'

'Don't you think I'm too flat-chested though? Should I stick in a couple of enhancers to give me the big boobs look?'

'Don't be stupid. This dress gives you elegance, you don't need boobs for that. Dolly Parton you ain't.' But as Katherine still fiddled with her cleavage, Brenda expostulated:

'Kitty, don't let Jean-Claude give you a complex about your body. You're a beautiful woman. For God's sake, stop feeling insecure because some Frog says you're flat-chested.'

'I know I shouldn't, but you know Jean-Claude's a perfectionist, particularly about this role. He wants me to be one hundred per cent.'

'Pity he ain't a hundred per cent himself. Hey honey, let's get this show on the road. Stop torturing yourself with your tits. I can't wait to see those old broads in their fancy finery checking you out! You look good enough to eat.'

In the lobby, waiting photographers were rudely repulsed by Jean-Claude.

'Sorry boys, no pictures.'

'Hey c'mon, Jean-Claude, please. Give us a break. You're almost newlyweds. We want a picture of the two of you. No one's seen any pics of you together recently. Hey you've gotta give the public what they want.'

Jean-Claude gave them his cold smile.

'Miss Bennet is the star, ladies and gentlemen. She is the prima donna tonight. I'm just an arm-piece.'

'Oh darling, don't be ridiculous.' Kitty heard her voice, pleading and unfamiliar, but Jean-Claude ignored it, as he strode towards the limousine. The photographers swivelled their cameras on to Kitty.

Brenda whispered, 'Smile now. *Don't* let him get to you.'

'I won't. It's water off a duck's back these days.' Kitty's lips felt like granite, as she forced her most dazzling smile. At last Brenda called a halt.

'Okay everybody, hey boys, *enough*. Let Miss Bennet get to the main event, please, gentlemen.'

In the front seat of the limousine, Jean-Claude ignored the women, and talked politics with the chauffeur all the way.

'Take no notice of him,' said Brenda. 'This is *your* night. Enjoy it, girl.'

'Sure.' Kitty smiled, but there was a nasty feeling in the pit of her stomach. 'It's going to be a blast.'

Outside the theatre, it seemed as though the entire population of Palm Beach had come to stare and cheer. Kitty needed all of the ten guards for protection, as the crowds pressed in on her.

A woman who must have been eighty if she was a day, grabbed Kitty's arm with a wizened crimson-tipped claw.

'I love ya, Georgia,' she rasped, through carmine-painted lips. 'I identify with your character *so* much, sweetie. You're just like me, you little witch. Half devil, half angel!'

Another woman elbowed her out of the way.

'My daughter looks just like you,' she gushed, 'but younger, of course. She wants to *be* you when she grows up. A great *actress*. She's hoping to study at the Actors' Stu...'

The bodyguard dragged Katherine away through the cheering, whistling crowd, up red-carpeted stairs, through a forest of waving, be-ringed hands. To many middle-aged women, Katherine Bennet was a heroine: a success story for the over-forties. In some way they all identified with her, and now they applauded, laughed, and cheered the film clips in all the right places. When she made her speech, she was greeted with a standing ovation. Afterwards, as guest of honour at three parties, she was jostled by an eager crush of admirers, desperate to meet her and shake her hand. Katherine smiled and posed for photographs, accepting the adulation. This was one of the times she really felt like a star, and appreciated what it really meant.

A man with a face like a robber's dog, and with a thick ginger toupee, like a dead cat, perched on his head, squeezed her hand so hard that she winced. Pushing his face so close to hers that she almost fainted, he yelped:

'I've written a script – especially for you, dear. It'll make the world see you as the wonderful woman *we* all know you really are, sweetie.'

'Great.' Katherine was being dragged off again by the guards.

'Dontcha wanna know what it's called?' the toupee wheezed.

She nodded and smiled over her shoulder, the breath almost pressed out of her body by the crowd.

'My Yiddisher Momma!' he yelled triumphantly. 'You'll be *fabulous* in it, sweetie. You are Jewish, aren't you?'

Katherine shook her head apologetically, but he was not about to give up.

'Never mind, sweetie. We all think of you as one of us, anyway. Heart, that's what you've got, girl lots and lotsa *heart*.'

But the adulation was starting to cloy.

'Let's hit the ladies room,' she mouthed to Brenda, separating herself from the clawing hands, the fawning faces. 'I need an adulation break – it's getting to be overkill time.'

The ladies room was a monument to nouveau riche bad taste. It was lined with peach-coloured mirrors, embellished so heavily with art-deco naked women, that there was scarcely room for Brenda and Kitty to see their faces. As Katherine powdered, painted, and fluffed her hair, two guests with almost identical black beehives, and wearing a ton and a half of make-up, stared at her in the mirror, and whispered to each other.

Brenda glared, but Katherine ignored them. She was all too used to conversations stopping dead when she entered a room, or worse still, being talked about as if she weren't there.

'Her skin's not great,' hissed Bouffant One to Bouffant Two.

'All those hot lights, I guess.' Bouffant Two was making a clumsy attempt to get closer to Katherine.

'What didja say?' Brenda was in combative mood. She put hands on ample gold-beaded hips, ready for battle, and stepped between Katherine and the two beehives.

'We are *great* admirers of Miss Bennet,' gushed Beehive One.

'We're her biggest fans, and we love her dearly,' trilled Beehive Two.

Katherine smiled faintly at them, which unfortunately, the women immediately took as encouragement. But Brenda wasn't having it. Katherine needed these few minutes of privacy, and to be stared at and whispered about was an intrusion.

'Come on, ladies, time to get back to the party,' she said heartily, trying to edge them out of the room.

'We wanna talk to the Peach,' said Beehive One. 'It's us, her fans, that made her, we gotta right.'

'Without us she'd be nowhere,' agreed Beehive Two. 'We're always loyal, in spite of the papers.'

'Well, be that as it may,' said Brenda, 'we'd like to be alone now, so goodbye, ladies.'

'We only want to see how she does her make-up,' wheedled Bouffant One. 'Why are you stopping us from looking at her?'

'Because this is not a zoo,' stormed Brenda. 'If you want to stare, do it at the party, but for God's sake, let her have a bit of peace in here, can't you?'

'Well, I guess what the tabloids say is all true then.' Beehive One snapped shut her diamanté *minaudière*, which was shaped like a poodle. Tossing her heavily lacquered hair, she said, 'C'mon Doris, we're wasting our time trying to be friendly. Her career's not going to last long, if she's rude to the fans like this.'

As they huffed out, Brenda heard them mutter, 'Yeah, she really is a bitch, and she don't look so good close up, either.'

Kitty laughed. 'They make Eleonor seem sweeter than Mother Teresa.'

'Trouble is, Kitty, that you're too damn famous, and everyone wants a piece of you. C'mon, now, let's git over to the next fun-fest.'

At the final party so many fawning fans crowded around Katherine, that when they left, the guards had to clear a path for her. As usual, Kitty got into the limousine first, followed by Jean-Claude and then Brenda. Katherine dipped into the back seat, bottom first, legs following gracefully. As soon as Jean-Claude scrambled in, Katherine sensed his fury. He turned to her, his face livid, and spat:

'You bloody diva, you big headed prima donna. Who the hell do you think you are?'

'Are you drunk?' she asked coldly.

'No, I'm not drunk – not yet – but I should be, married to you. You'd turn anyone to drink. Just because every gawping idiot's wanting to grab a piece of you, you act like you're the fucking Queen of England.'

Kitty detested public squabbling, and the chauffeur's and bodyguards' ears were wagging. Any of them could call the gossip rags tomorrow. She bit her tongue, and lit a cigarette:

'Calm down, Jean-Claude, and stop acting like a child.'

This enraged him even more.

'I've been a celebrity too, you know,' he hissed. 'When I was a pop star I was much bigger than you are now, Katherine Bennet, and I had a lot more people screaming at me than you had tonight.'

'You've told me that many times, Jean-Claude; why don't you make another record of it?' Kitty pressed a button, so that the window went up to shield them from the chauffeur and bodyguards.

Brenda stared at Jean-Claude contemptuously.

'Why don't you lay off Kitty, for Christ's sake? Just cool it.'

Jean-Claude turned to her, his face contorted with bad temper.

'If you don't shut the hell up, and mind your own business, *Miss Fifties Flavour of the Month*, I'll throw you out of the car on to your fat ass – OK?'

Brenda's face flamed. How dared he behave like this to her? More than that, why did Katherine take it?

'Jean-Claude, this is *not* a competition to decide who's the best.' Katherine tried to stay calm, although the hand holding her cigarette was trembling. 'This is supposed to be a night of tribute to me – so please do tell me, husband *dearest*, why you're behaving like a jealous idiot?'

'Don't you dare call me an idiot. You'll be sorry for this, Katherine. You jump in the car first, you don't even leave room on the seat for me when you get in. You sit all puffed up with that stupid smile on your face, as if you owned the world, you selfish bitch.'

'That's how we've *always* done it. We never tumble into the limo all together. It's planned like a military operation, otherwise it'd be chaos. Don't you see that? Oh for God's sake, let's not argue, Jean-Claude. Let's just enjoy the rest of the evening. We're leaving tomorrow.'

'OK, OK, Miss Queen Bee, have it your own way. You always do, anyway.' With a theatrical sigh, Jean-Claude turned to stare at the shimmering lights on the water. Leaden silence fell, until they reached the Breakers, when Jean-Claude sloped off sullenly to bed. Kitty and Brenda stayed in the suite for a nightcap.

'What the hell's come over him?' Katherine poured herself a stiff cognac. 'He's becoming Jekyll and Hyde. I *don't* understand why.'

'I don't know, honey. I really wish I understood his problem; and it's getting worse. My Frank would have a crisis sometimes, but then he'd be fine for months. It *is* as though Jean-Claude has two different personalities.'

'I feel like I don't even know him any more. Since we've been married, he seems to have turned into another person. He was never like this before.'

'What about that time he disappeared to Vegas?'

'Well yes – stupid of me – I forgot about that. Maybe I should've realized then, how cruel he could be. But I thought that incident was just a one-off, because he loved me and wanted to marry me – ha!' She drained her cognac.

'Dump him,' Brenda said unceremoniously.

'*Dump* him? How can I? We've only been married three months. I haven't given it a proper try. Maybe it's my fault – maybe I'm too bossy. Maybe, after all, marriage isn't for me,' she mused.

'It's not marriage that isn't for you, it's this guy who isn't,' said Brenda. 'Give him his walking papers, Kitty – so what if it's a mistake? He who is afraid to make mistakes is afraid to live. I learned that at my mom's knee.'

'But my mother taught me that, if at first you don't succeed, try, try and try again,' said Katherine. 'I'm not going to give up yet, Brenda. At least not until the movie's over.'

She lit another cigarette. 'And then, I swear to you, that if Jean-Claude doesn't stop behaving like a schizophrenic monster, I'll get the marriage annulled.' She poured them both more cognac. '*After* I finish the picture.'

'I'll hold you to it.' Brenda raised her glass in a toast and sipped reflectively. 'And I'll drink to it.'

But the following day, on the plane, Jean-Claude went on berating Kitty about her diva-like behaviour. 'Your stardom's gone to your head,' he said. 'You care about nothing but yourself. Not me, not your son, nothing except your career.'

On and on he went, in a sanctimonious whisper, listing Kitty's 'sins'. Selfishness, self–obsession, narcissism, hypocrisy, egoism. At last Katherine could bear it no longer, and she shouted:

'Listen, you crazy bastard, we've only been married three months, but if this is how you are, I want out as soon as we get to France. You understand! *C'est la fin de l'histoire*, as you would say, and I mean it, we'll finish this farce of a marriage as soon as possible.'

He didn't answer, but stared sullenly out of the window at the dense, Transatlantic blackness. Kitty went back into Business Class, and spent the rest of the long night over water, getting drunk with Brenda.

The manager of the Ritz smilingly bowed himself out of the Duke of Windsor suite. Another perk of stardom was always being able to get the best rooms, or the best restaurant table at the last minute. Jean-Claude turned towards his icy-faced wife as soon as the door closed, and in a voice cracking with emotion, said:

'Can you ever forgive me, *chérie*? I'm sorry, so terribly sorry for what I've said and done. I behaved like an *imbecile*, I know I did.'

Kitty was picking the cards out of all the exquisite arrangements of flowers she'd been sent. Most of them came from the best florist on the Place Vendôme. They swamped the marquetry and gilt tables, and the Louis XIV commodes; their scent was overpoweringly sensual. She stared at her husband coldly.

'I don't know why you've behaved like a pig towards me since the night of our party. You've embarrassed me publicly, not to mention privately. You've insulted me, humiliated me, and now you just smile sadly, turn on your little boy charm, and say you're *sorry*. Do you really expect me to forget everything?'

'But I *am* sorry,' his brilliant green eyes glistened. 'Truly sorry. I can't help what comes over me sometimes. You must forgive me. Please, Kitty, don't make me beg; I'm a proud man. You, more than anyone, know that sometimes my pride gets in the way of my intelligence.'

'You're certainly right about that.' Kitty sank on to a damask sofa, shot through with silver thread and embroidered with cornflowers, and inspected her fingernails. 'But I don't understand your terrible moods any more. I love you – or did – I'm married to you, but I simply *do not* understand you.'

'Neither do I, sometimes. Neither, my darling Kitty, do I.'

He removed a miniature brandy from the well-stocked mini-bar and offered her one.

She shook her head. 'I want to know what's wrong with you, Jean-Claude. These last three days have been absolute hell, not only for me, but for Brenda too. She's almost more concerned about everything than I am.'

'Yes, of course she is; I understand.' He drank the brandy, slumped into an armchair, lowered his blond head into his hands, and sighed heavily. He looked so unutterably miserable that Kitty had to fight the urge to comfort him. She knew that would be a major mistake. Whatever devils lurked in Jean-Claude's psyche, she knew she had to help him conquer them, or end her marriage.

'I simply can't go on being married to you, if you behave like this.' Katherine stared out of the window at the perfect Parisian blue sky. 'I can't think... I can't concentrate on the movie... I can't focus on anything.'

'No one understands that more than I, *chérie*, and I'm mortified. Really, truly ashamed. I simply don't understand what comes over me.' He stalked across the thick Aubusson carpet to gaze blankly down at the tourists in Place Vendome. 'Except that I do,' he added darkly.

'Have you thought about seeing a shrink? You need help, Jean-Claude, and I'm *prepared* to help you. I have to, because otherwise this marriage is finished.'

He retrieved another brandy from the bar and went back to stare out of the window. Then, he started speaking in a soft, slow voice.

'I don't need a shrink, *chérie*. I know what I need, and I thought I'd found it in you. I need a woman who loves me enough to understand my pain, and to accept me as I am. Unconditionally. To realize that sometimes I go through these torments which I can't help. It's like...' He paused, his face suddenly pale. 'It's like – it's not happening to me but to someone else.'

'Go on,' she said, but not altogether sympathetically.

'It all started a long time ago. I don't know if you believe all this psychiatric and psychological bullshit, but if you do, I suppose you could say that my childhood has made me what I am.'

'What do you mean?' said Katherine, still angry enough to suspect that he might be shooting a line.

'My mother was an exceptionally strange woman. As was my father.' He ran his fingers through his hair, shifting restlessly, still staring outside. The sky was deepening now, and a few summer clouds began to darken the room.

'Please go on,' Kitty said, more gently. This was the first time that Jean-Claude had ever told her anything about his childhood. Certainly he had talked to her about his brief stint as a pop idol, but he had never spoken much about his family, and she hadn't liked to press him.

'My brother, Didier, was always the family favourite,' Jean-Claude said bitterly. 'Always. From the time he came into my life, nothing I did was ever right. I was older by two years, but I was criticised and humiliated by both my father and my mother.'

'You weren't...abused?'

'If abuse means making a child's life a living hell, then certainly I *was* abused, *chérie*. But I think the kind of abuse you mean is sexual, so the answer is no. Thirty years ago in the Loire Valley, child abuse wasn't a popular recreation.' He paused to light another Gauloise from the stub of his last.

'Didier was younger than me, but by the time he was three, he was bigger. I was, I suppose, the runt of the litter. So I always wore *his* cast-off clothes. Our family was quite poor, you see – we could only afford one pair of shoes each school year and Didier always got those. At school I was a mediocre student. No question about it; reading, writing and particularly arithmetic were almost beyond me, so by the time I was seven, I was still almost illiterate. Do you know what that means for a French schoolchild?'

'I don't really, but pretty embarrassing, I guess.'

'Damn right. But of course Didier was the golden boy. His hair was even blonder than mine if you can imagine, his eyes were very blue, and he was tall, husky and extremely clever. My parents worshipped him, and hated me.'

'*Hated* you? Surely they couldn't have hated their own son. What exactly did they do?'

'Hit me, all the time.' His voice was harsh. 'I was the family punchbag. They didn't hit Didier of course.'

'Couldn't you say anything to anyone – an aunt or a grandparent?'

'How can you say something to someone when you're only seven years old? What do you say? "Hey *Maman's* playing favourites. She likes my brother better than me". I always believed that if Didier disappeared, my life would be bearable again.' His face darkened. 'But in the end, you see, I killed him.'

'*Killed* him?' Katherine was aghast.

'Yes.' Jean-Claude looked at her, the agony visible on his face. 'It's time I told you everything. Then you can decide if you still want me.'

'Oh God,' said Katherine, lighting a cigarette.

'It was the night before his fifth birthday. We had one of those summer storms that we get in the Loire. They come very suddenly and the clouds seem to fight with each other. Then the lightning comes, zig-zagging in great bursts. The thunder was extremely loud, and frightening, and Didier started to cry,' Jean-Claude said softly. 'I told him to shut up, but he started screaming – he wanted his mother.'

'Where was she?'

'Where she always was. In the kitchen, not cooking or baking, but trimming a hat or making herself another silly blouse. We might have been poor, but *Maman* had a wardrobe to rival Christian Dior. I told Didier to stop screaming, but he got out of bed and stood at the top of the stairs, howling his head off. I shook him hard, yelled at him to stop bawling, and grow up. Then I started shouting for *Maman* as well.'

'And then?'

'And then...' Jean-Claude shrugged. 'Didier slipped and fell down the stairs, which our mother, the good French bourgeoise, always kept polished like a skating rink.'

Kitty dreaded the answer, but she had to ask: 'What then?'

'He broke his neck,' Jean-Claude whispered. 'The angel-child's neck snapped like a stick. *Maman* and *Papa* certainly believed that I did it, that I pushed him, but I didn't – I swear to God I didn't. I've wondered a million times if I could have saved him as he fell over the top step.'

Kitty had moved over to join him by the window. Now she tentatively stroked his hand. 'I can see exactly how it happened. You couldn't have helped him. But what happened then?'

'Then we went through a period of crying, hysterics from *Maman*, and misery for everyone. My parents treated me as though I didn't exist. They blocked me out – hardly spoke to me and when they did, it was always in anger. My mother died of cancer four years ago, and I didn't even go to the funeral. My father died a year later.'

'Didn't you have anybody else to talk to?'

'Eventually, Quentin. He saw me singing. I was a choirboy in the church in Nîmes where we went to live after Didier's death. I was fifteen then. He convinced me that with my looks and voice I could be the next Johnny Halliday. I left Nîmes without a word to my parents, packed a rucksack, went to Paris. Quentin became my manager. I never told my parents where I was, and I don't think they ever even looked for me.'

'I wish you'd told me this before, Jean-Claude.' Katherine put her arms tightly around him. 'Now I understand everything.'

Together they stared out at the sky. Rain had started pelting down, the tourists had gone, and there was the rumble of thunder in the distance. She glanced at Jean-Claude to see if he was affected by the storm, but he smiled, hugging her tightly.

'Don't worry, *chérie*. Since that day, thunder and lightning have never bothered me.'

Then, looking deep into her eyes, he said: 'Kitty, you are the *only* woman I have ever truly loved. You're the only person I have even been able to love. If I sometimes seem to be difficult...' He stopped. 'I suppose difficult is too light a word. Impossible would be more like it. Will you please try to forgive me at those times, Kitty darling? Please, my love?'

She nodded, her heart filled with hope.

'Yes my darling, I forgive you. And I promise I'll try to understand.'

CHAPTER SIXTEEN

Kitty threw herself enthusiastically into pre-production on *All That Glitters*. Her days filled with fittings for the gorgeous costumes and elaborate wigs, auditioning French and English actors, and rehearsing with the director, Joe Havana.

Joe had been a hotshot with various gritty, true life miniseries, but the networks had recently cooled on him. He was a short, stocky, Italian–American, with unruly grey hair, and a cigar clamped almost permanently between his teeth. It had been Quentin's idea to use him, even though he had been out of favour in Hollywood ever since his last TV movie had bombed. Kitty also liked Joe. She wasn't certain his bombastic, tough guy approach was quite right for a period film, but since her nights were once again filled with Jean-Claude's astonishing passion and protestations of love, she refused to worry about it.

She spoke every day to Tommy, who was having such a great time with Todd in the Hamptons, that he didn't want to leave for Paris yet. Katherine was glad. That was one less thing to worry about. Although Tommy had sworn to her he was off drugs, she knew there could be temptations in Paris. The outdoor lifestyle in the Hamptons was healthier for him, and she knew Todd's father was a tough disciplinarian with the children. Paris was a magical place in the early summer and since his confession, Jean-Claude was a changed man, more loving and more in love with Katherine than ever.

After shooting started, each evening before dinner they congregated, with some of the cast and executives, in the Ritz Bar to gossip about the day's events. One evening Joe arrived, with his normally untidy hair almost standing on end. Throwing himself down, he slapped his dog-eared script on the table, and barked at a hovering waiter, 'Bring me a Bud right away.' Then he said, 'This script stinks.'

'A bit late to decide that, isn't it?' Jean-Claude said sarcastically. 'We've been shooting for six days already. How bad can it be?'

Joe swigged his beer from the bottle. 'The network says it needs a ton of work, and, in their eyes, that makes it bad. It wouldn't matter if a goddamned Pulitzer prize winner had written it.'

'But we don't have time to work on it any more,' said Kitty. 'I have to start *The Skeffingtons* again in the middle of September.'

'I know, I know, but the network are threatening to pull the plug unless we get a script doctor, pronto,' said Joe. 'A good one. And we need him *today*.'

'That's impossible,' snapped Jean-Claude. 'First, any writer worth his salt won't be available at short notice, and secondly the logistics of putting the cast and crew on hold, are out of the question. Why can't we make this script work?'

'Because we can't,' Joe snapped. 'The network says it's crap, and if we go on shooting this draft, they think it'll be a fucking disaster.'

'But it *isn't*,' said Katherine. 'It's a terrific script – we all know that.'

'Sure we do,' said Joe. 'But unfortunately, kids, the joker who gave us the green light on the network has just been fired, and the new joker who's in charge of mini-series, wants to put us in turnaround, unless we modernize the dialogue for the under twenty-fives. Can you *fucking* believe it?'

'Bullshit,' Jean-Claude said. 'You Americans. How can you modernize the French eighteenth century?'

'Yeah, I admit it's a challenge,' said Joe. 'But a decent script doctor could do it, and do it fast. If we want this to work, kids, we've got to go along with it.'

'What about Steve?' Kitty suggested. 'Steven Leigh? He's brilliant at changing dialogue, and I think he's available. He can whip a script into shape overnight. He does it all the time on the series, and the network loves him. What do you say?'

'Call him.' Joe lit up one of the dozen cigars he got through each day. 'And tell him to get on the next fuckin' plane.'

Steven took the next plane to Paris, and was relieved to do so. He'd not been working for two months and was going stir crazy at his house. It was lonely without Mandy and the kids, but more than that, he missed Katherine – their jokes, their companionable friendship, her beauty. He knew in his heart of hearts that he loved her, perhaps always had, always would.

He met her now in one of the Paris production offices. He thought that she had never looked more beautiful. The strain, which he had detected in her face and in her eyes at the party, seemed to have gone. Perhaps, he thought, this marriage of hers was going to work out after all. God, he hoped so – at least, he *thought* he hoped so.

For a week they worked closely together on the new dialogue, and within ten days, Steven had hammered something out that was modern enough for the network to green-light again. Principal photography began again in Paris on 30 July.

Steven put his head round the door of Katherine's portable dressing room.

'Come on in. I'm just finishing up,' she said.

She was sitting in front of her dressing table, exquisite in an eighteenth century white satin dress, a glittering, authentic diamond parure, and a massively built-up white wig, which tumbled around her shoulders in waves and curls. Steven felt the breath catch in his throat.

'The ice-maiden cometh. Do you look good, or what?' Then, softly, 'OK?'

'Yes thanks, it all seems to be under control now. I understand what makes Jean-Claude the way he is sometimes.'

'And what, for God's sake, is that?'

'I can't tell you, Steve. Some other time. We've worked things out, though. I don't ask for your pity, but just for your understanding.' She looked at him questioningly.

'You got me.' He frowned. 'What's that from?'

'*Sweet Bird of Youth.*' They smiled at each other.

'Good one. You're getting better.' There was a rap at the door, and the assistant director called:

'Let's get your nose back to the grindstone Kitty. We're ready for you!'

Steven squeezed her arm.

'Good luck, kid – you're going to be great in this, I know you are.'

Instead of setting up his office at the studio where the other producers were, Jean-Claude had taken a small room down the corridor from the Duke of Windsor suite. There he installed his usual state-of-the-art technological paraphernalia, and when not meeting with Joe Havana, or telephoning the network and Lew Lupino, the bulk of his day was spent at his computers. Kitty hardly saw him, except when they dined at one or other of Paris's romantic bistros. There was always plenty to discuss, since the movie had attracted a distinguished group of the finest French and

English actors and actresses. Sir John Gielgud, Nigel Hawthorne and Jeanne Moreau were all playing key roles, and Louis XV was being played by Gerard le Blanche, a Frenchman of such devastating charm that he had remained a star in France for over thirty years. Now he was in his early fifties, with greying hair discreetly dyed brown, but time had not dimmed his sex appeal one jot. After four years of acting opposite irascible Albert Amory it was a relief for Katherine to have such a charmer as her leading man.

Three weeks into shooting, Brenda stormed into Katherine's mobile dressing room.

'Maria's just called. She's hysterical, because the electricity company are threatening to cut the power off at the house.'

'You're kidding.' Kitty was preparing to shoot with Sir John Gielgud and slightly nervous about it. She was having her considerable cleavage powdered white, and trying to study some new dialogue at the same time. Underneath her bodice were large pads which pushed her breasts up high. Her waist was laced to an agonizing twenty-three inches, and her two-foot-tall wig was a complicated construction of ropes of pearls, satin ribbons, and swathes of chiffon tulle. Balancing the contraption on her head was a major achievement, and to say that she was uncomfortable was an understatement.

'I kid you not. Here, read it.' Brenda handed Kitty a scrap of paper. 'She's real upset, Kitty. We've got to do something. If they turn off the power, Maria said she's going to quit, and we *need* someone at the house. She's all you've got left, staffwise.'

'Cut to the chase will you,' said Katherine. 'I've got to get on the set; Sir John's waiting and I'm late.'

'OK. Bottom line. As you know, the bills for everything are sent to your loving husband.'

'Yes, then I sign the cheques after he's printed them, and you mail them. So what's the problem?'

'Have you signed any cheques recently?' asked Brenda.

Kitty looked surprised. 'Well as a matter of fact, I don't remember signing any since before the party. I guess that's over a month ago.'

'Right. And it's right that you shouldn't be bothered with all this, but Maria told me that not only has there been a final demand from the electricity company, but that none of the people connected with the party have been paid either. Creditors have been knocking at the door for weeks, every one of 'em, from the band to the caterers. Maria's going crazy.'

'But where are all the bills? Why hasn't Jean-Claude given them to me for signing?'

'Don't ask me. Ask 'im in his lair.'

Brenda had the kind of memory that made an elephant look thick, and the incident with her camera was fresh in her mind. She hadn't trusted Jean-Claude since then, but as long as things seemed to have settled down, she had been prepared to keep her own counsel.

Kitty had given no thought to whether bills were paid or not; like most actors, she was not knowledgeable about finance. When Jean-Claude took over her affairs she had done as he suggested, called the banks and stockbrokers to check out his computer figures. But very soon she felt so secure that everything was in order, that she stopped.

'I'll discuss it with him tonight, Bren, I promise, but I can't do it now. Sir John awaits – and I'm a quivering wreck about that.'

Because of night shooting, Katherine had the following morning off, and she intended to go shopping with Brenda on the Left Bank. Before she went, she knocked on Jean-Claude's office door.

'What do you want?' He seemed reluctant to let her in.

'To talk to you, darling. It's important.'

'OK, let's go to our suite.' He started to close the door, but she pushed past into his sanctum. He had made it into a replica of his LA office. Filing cabinets were perched on top of Louis XIV furniture, and the beautiful antique marquetry desk had three different types of computers on it.

Ali, with her red hair tumbling around her shoulders, and dressed in the shortest mini-skirt Katherine had ever seen, was taking notes. Jean-Claude waved a dismissive hand at her, and she got to her feet and scuttled out.

'I thought you were going shopping?' He looked peeved.

'I am, but there's a little matter to be discussed first.'

'You must learn to use your spare time for more than just shopping and getting your hair done.'

Kitty didn't bother to answer. It was useless explaining that she spent very little time shopping, and that doing her hair was usually for work. Glancing around, she spotted a pile of bills in the in-tray. She flicked through them.

'God Almighty, Jean-Claude, look at these! There are at least *fifty* unpaid bills here. Why haven't you made out cheques for them?'

'There's plenty of time, *chérie*.' He reclined in the black leather chair which he had ordered from the most expensive shop on rue Madeleine, and stared at the painted ceiling, excavating his teeth with a gold pick as he did so.

'But there are bills here from all the credit card companies, Jean-Claude. Look! Visa, Diners, American Express. We owe *thousands* on them. Why haven't you printed out cheques?'

His face settled in the old obstinate expression which she dreaded, and he continued staring blankly into space.

'I'm going shopping today. If the bills haven't been paid, and if I use any of these cards, they won't be accepted.'

'Forget it, *chérie*, I've taken care of it. I sent every one of them a bank draft. Don't fuss. It'll be OK.' His drawling tone of voice meant 'shut up, otherwise there's going to be trouble'.

Pushing papers and paraphernalia on the desk aside, Katherine leaned angrily towards him.

'You better print those cheques out now, Jean-Claude. Do you understand? *Not* this afternoon *not* tomorrow – now.'

He looked appraisingly at her body. She was wearing beige pants and a silk shirt. Her ass looks as if it's been cut off with a bacon-slicer, he thought dispassionately. He'd told her to diet, but now she looked scrawny. It was a good thing those costumes pushed and pulled her up in all the right places.

'Maybe I will, and maybe I won't.'

'You make these cheques out, Jean-Claude,' Kitty said ominously. 'Otherwise I'll send everything to Ken, and tell him to take care of them.'

He fixed her with an icy stare. 'You'd better not do any such thing, *chérie*. I told you I'm taking care of it. I'm in charge of this end of things, so mind your own business, get on with your acting and don't interfere.'

Katherine, determined not to let him get away with anything this time, waved a bunch of cheques in his face.

'Jean-Claude, this is my business. Don't you dare tell me not to interfere with what is mine.'

'You had nothing when you met me, Katherine Bennet, and you'll have nothing without me, mark my words.' His furious face was red. 'You're useless in business, and you'll lose everything, without me to guide you.'

Katherine was outraged that he actually believed that, but she refused to argue any more. He might have possession of the master cheque book, but she had her own.

'Right,' she snapped. 'If you really believe that, then you're going totally insane.'

With that she slammed the door, returned to their suite and scribbled a cheque to the electricity company on her personal account.

'Here, Brenda, FedEx this to Maria, right away. And for God's sake let's go shopping.'

'Yeah, when the going gets tough, that's where the tough should go,' Brenda smiled with relief. 'You deserve a treat.'

But to Kitty's embarrassment, none of her credit cards was accepted in any of the boutiques. Her face flamed, as purchase after purchase was refused, and she became increasingly furious with Jean-Claude. She returned to the hotel determined to have a showdown, only to find a stack of printed cheques piled neatly on her desk, ready for signature. Even more surprisingly, Jean-Claude was all charm, sweetness and affection once more.

But Katherine wasn't about to buy it.

'Did you know that my credit rating has now been ruined?' she snapped. 'I went through a nightmare like this once before in New York, when the IRS "removed" all monies from my bank account, for so-called unpaid taxes. I vowed I'd never be humiliated like that again, and I *won't*, Jean-Claude – I absolutely will *not*.'

A heart-melting smile lit up his handsome face, and he tried to caress her, but she moved away angrily.

'Calm down, *chérie*, calm down, for goodness sake. You're over-excited, you look all hot, like an angry puppy. You're working too hard,' he soothed.

'You bet your ass I'm working too hard,' she stormed. 'I have new dialogue to learn every day, I'm in agony with those damned corsets and wigs, and to know that my business world is falling apart, too, makes me feel like a complete fool. Goddamn it, Jean-Claude, are you trying to drive me crazy?'

'It's all fine now, *chérie*.' He smoothed her hair softly. 'Everything's going to be all right now, Kitten. You know I always make everything all right don't I?'

She looked at his calm face. He had locked his arms around her reassuringly, trying to make her feel safe and loved.

'For God's sake, stop these insane games,' she whispered. 'You must, I can't take it any more. Honestly I can't.'

'You imagine things, Kitty. I only do what's best for you. I only want for you what I want for myself, because I love you more than I love myself.' He stroked her shoulders and she sighed, feeling her body melt into his against her will. He held her tighter, murmuring, 'Don't ever leave me, Kitten, and don't threaten me. If you ever leave me I'll – '

'You'll what?'

He didn't answer, gently unbuttoning her silk blouse, brushing her neck with tender lips.

'What will you do, Jean-Claude?'

'I'll kill you.' He smiled angelically, kissed her yielding mouth and picked her up in his arms. Then he carried her through to the connecting bedroom.

As she put on her flimsy lace peignoir for the fight-rape scene, Katherine was unaccountably nervous. The costume looked as frail and delicate as she felt. In fact it was extremely durable. Each time Gerard le Blanche ripped it off her, the wardrobe mistress would sew it together again for the next take. It was a complicated arrangement of chiffon, silk ribbons and velcro, cleverly constructed to give the illusion of nudity, without being revealing enough to offend the ever-vigilant television censors. Joe wanted to do the master in one take, and adrenalin was high as shooting began.

It was a scene in which the king enters, drunk, to find Paulette de Waldner (played by Kitty) rummaging through his trunk. He starts to insult her and their exchanges become more and more heated, until the king says, 'Come to think of it, Paulette, my dear, maybe you are exactly the kind of woman I've been waiting for,' and moves menacingly towards her. Paulette smashes a bottle and holds the broken end threateningly towards him, but the king laughs and grabs her.

As they acted, Kitty saw Louis XV in Gerard's eyes. Sensual, violent, terrifying. Mesmerized by the actor's passion, she felt blind to everything except this moment. This was no longer acting; it was reality. It was a humid night in Versailles in 1776. She was feisty Paulette de Waldner, a woman fascinated yet repelled by the King of France.

The fight scene which followed had been choreographed in infinitesimal detail, but up until this take, the actors had only marked and rehearsed it at half speed. Gerard threw her on to the sofa; Katherine twisted her head away from his demanding hands and mouth. Bounding from the couch, she almost managed to escape, but he caught her by the hem of the peignoir, and ripped it off her. When she collapsed on to the floor, the struggle began in earnest, until finally Gerard caught Kitty, picked her up, and carried her over to the bed. Then he started forcing her to make love, until Joe called: 'OK. Cut – beautiful, kids – just great.'

The crew applauded, but as Gerard hugged Katherine, she suddenly felt a stabbing pain in her stomach and bent over with a cry of distress. Steven rushed to her side, but Kitty couldn't speak, managing only to shake her head, before she collapsed on to the sofa.

'Hurts,' she indicated her heart and upper stomach. 'Real bad.'

'Call an ambulance!' Steven took command, his face white with dread.

'Jesus H Christ, three weeks into shooting and the leading lady gets a friggin' heart attack,' Joe whispered. 'Just my fuckin' luck.'

'Is that all you care about?' Steven glared at him. 'The picture?'

Joe glared back. 'No it ain't, but I'm calling the network ASAP to see if Donna Mills is available – OK? We've had enough problems on this epic. If Katherine Bennet snuffs it, we better have a stand-by ready to go or we're in deep, deep shit.'

Steve joined the shocked cast and crew, who had gathered around Katherine as she lay on the couch, wincing with pain. Each wince made Joe grumble more.

'Shit, shit, *shit*, why the fuck didn't we cast Donna in the first place?'

The screaming ambulance took Kitty, Brenda and Steve to the emergency room at the local hospital. Kitty was put on to a gurney and left alone in a corridor. Steven held her hand, and a sister took Katherine's medical and credit card details from Brenda. A heavily pregnant gypsy woman, with a toddler clutching the hem of her dress, and a crying baby in her arms, sat on a bench, sobbing a stream of unintelligible laments.

Kitty mouthed through a gap in her pain. 'Sounds like World War Three's just broken out.'

'Just another day in Emergency. It's all happy, bereaved families here.' Steven tried to joke, as another agonizing wave of pain engulfed Kitty.

'For God's sake,' Steven grabbed a passing intern. 'Can't you help her! She's having a heart attack, she needs a doctor.'

The intern shrugged Steven away. 'All in good time, *m'sieur*, all in good time. This lady isn't the only one hurt around here.'

'Hurt! She's not *hurt*,' said Steven. 'She's having a stroke, a heart attack. Can't you see she's probably dying – for God's sake – do something please.'

Brenda hurried back with two interns and a nurse, bristling with efficiency.

'I had to tell them who she was, Steve. It's the only way to get some attention around here.'

They wheeled Kitty away; Brenda and Steve tried to follow, but the nurse waved them back. 'You cannot come in here, *m'sieur*. Stay away, *s'il vous plait*.'

In the ward, shielded from the other patients by a flimsy screen, Katherine was unceremoniously stripped to the waist, and a selection of rubber-faced electrodes were attached to her upper body. A nurse monitored her heart, gave her a shot, and Kitty felt herself drifting off to sleep – until a loud shout, and flashing strobe lights forced her back into consciousness.

'It *is* her! It's Katherine Bennet. Hello Madame Katherine! Poison Peach. How are you? Hey look over here please – *mon dieu*, the poor woman looks terrible! *S'il vous plait, oui*, look here. That's right. *Merci beaucoup! Merci*, Madame Katherine.'

The face leering at her over the camera had the rat-like features of a paparazzo on the make. Where in *hell* had he come from? How had he known she was here? But just as she began to puzzle over these questions, the pain receded, and the drug took her into no-man's land.

Ali let herself into Jean-Claude's office suite at the hotel. It was, as usual, immaculately tidy, all the files locked, and the various computers were neatly covered in their grey plastic covers. A tiny thrill went through her as she wondered if he were asleep on the small bed in the connecting room. Now that she was newly arrived in Paris, she hoped he would sleep with her more often. She wanted him to. She was crazy about Jean-Claude, totally, madly in love with him.

She tiptoed into the other room, careful not to wake him. She knew how angry he became if his sleep was disturbed. She'd never known a man who liked to sleep so much. She'd never known a man who liked to make love so much either. Ali shivered with anticipation. Usually he would make love to her as soon as she arrived in the morning. She would wake him gently, slipping between the sheets and stroking his body. It excited her that he was always ready. She only had to brush him with her fingertips.

At lunchtime they'd usually stop work for a sandwich and a glass of wine, and he would take her again with such force that he would often have to put his hand over her mouth to silence her cries of pleasure. In the evening, before he left to meet Kitty, they would have another quickie, and it would be as good, if not better than before. Although Ali, at twenty, had been with a few boys, she had never had one as virile and passionate as Jean-Claude.

She poked her head around the door, and gasped with secret pleasure. There he was, sleeping like a baby, his golden hair spread out on the pillow, one muscular arm flung across his tanned chest. She shivered again with anticipation, stripped off her leggings and shirt, and decided she would surprise him. She would put on one of the special outfits that he kept locked in one of the file cabinets. Only she had the key. She wouldn't wake him up; that would annoy him. She would just be stretched out in the armchair, in his favourite position, when he woke.

The collection of buckled rubber straps that criss-crossed her body left her most erogenous zones bare. She gave a little giggle. What would that old bitch of a wife of his think, if she knew what really went on in her husband's office? Then she shrugged. What did she care? The world revolved around Jean-Claude as far as Ali was concerned, and that was the way it was going to stay.

'Where the *hell* is Jean-Claude?' growled Steve.

'I don't know,' said Brenda grimly. 'When I called the hotel, they said he's out, and they don't know where he is. He's going to get a piece of my mind when he shows up.'

'He should be with her, for Christ's sake. What a hopeless schmuck he is.'

'We both know what Mr Jean-Claude Frog-Face is, Steve. But he does his own thing, I'm afraid. Whenever he feels like it, the freaky bastard.'

Late in the afternoon, Jean-Claude's secretary finally rang.

'We got your message,' Ali said breathlessly. 'Is Madame Valmer OK?'

'We don't know yet, they're still doing tests,' snapped Brenda. 'Where's her husband?'

'Oh, he's in the office. He's – uh – still asleep.'

'Asleep! It's nearly four o'clock, for God's sake.'

'Gee, I know,' Ali's voice was apologetic. 'It's just awful. I tried to wake him up, but he won't budge,' she giggled. 'You know what he's like.'

'Yeah, I know what he's like, but I sure as hell wish I didn't.' Brenda was disgusted. 'You've got to wake him, Ali. Tell him Kitty's really sick. She may have had a stroke.'

'Oh, I told him that when Mr Havana called.' Ali sounded brave. 'But Mr Valmer just rolled over and went back to sleep. I know he was up real late, because when I came to work this morning, he was just arriving.'

'What a charmer. OK, Ali, tell the sleeping beauty we're still at the hospital, and we'll be staying with Kitty as long as she needs us.'

'Have you told Tommy yet?'

'We decided it was better not to. It might upset him,' Brenda said grimly. 'Though he'll be considerably more upset if his mother dies.'

CHAPTER SEVENTEEN

Even in the darkened hotel room, Brenda could tell that Katherine was awake.

'Hi,' she whispered, tiptoeing into the room with a tray. 'How are you feeling?'

Kitty struggled to sit up. 'Much better, darling. God I'm sorry about all this. I guess the tabloids are right, Kitty Bennet'll do anything for attention.' She attempted a wan grin.

Brenda put the tray on the cluttered bedside table. 'You've been overdoing things, Kitty.'

'We all have, Bren.' Kitty munched a croissant hungrily. 'The main thing is, I'm fine. Oh God, you've no *idea* how scared I was when I felt that pain in my chest. I was sure I was a goner. I've never been in such agony.'

'The doctor said gastroenteritis does that,' Brenda plumped the pillows behind Kitty's head. 'Hurts so much, you feel like you're going to die.'

'Gastroenteritis? Is that all it was? How embarrassing!' Katherine giggled, and began tucking into the scrambled eggs. 'Now there's a tabloid headline for you. Glamorous Paulette de Waldner gets a bellyache from fighting off King Louis. It's too embarrassing – the crew must think I'm a real idiot.'

'The doctor said you were obviously nervous about the fight scene, so your stomach went into spasms. He said these kind of contractions are usually brought on by severe stress.'

'Stress? – Me?' Katherine sipped her tea. 'Don't know the meaning of the word.'

'Well, the doctor says it's a one-off – won't happen again – but you've got to try and stay away from stress, Kitty.' And stay away from that husband too, she wanted to add.

'Does Tommy know what happened?'

'I called him at Todd's, but I played it down. They're going to the movies today, there's a Schwarzenegger playing.'

'Good. I don't want to give him any more to worry about – not with the news about Johnny.'

'Listen, Johnny brought that on himself. Everyone knows that if you smoke sixty cigarettes a day, you're asking for trouble.'

'It's going to be terrible for Tommy when his father dies.' Katherine's eyes glistened. 'Tommy really cares about him.'

'It's *not* your problem,' said Brenda. 'You've got enough on your plate already. Don't take on any more.'

Kitty finished the eggs then asked, 'Any other news?'

'I guess I better show you this.' Brenda handed Kitty a copy of *Le Figaro*. 'I know it's a bummer, but you have to see it. The phones have been ringing off the hook all morning. Every hack in the world wants an exclusive about your "near death" experience.'

'That bastard paparazzo!' Kitty stared at the photograph bitterly. 'How the hell did he get into the hospital?'

'Slime always manages to ooze in somewhere.' Brenda shrugged. 'At least you've got a sheet over you. Five minutes earlier, and the scum would've caught you with your tiny tits hanging out.'

'Thank God for small mercies.' Katherine glanced at the photograph again. 'God, I look like hell. What a vile shot.'

'You sure do.'

'*And* they've got my age wrong,' Kitty sat up indignantly. 'Forty-four! I won't be forty-four for months!'

'Typical sleaze-rag – even the Froggies have 'em. Now don't let 'em get to you, sweetie.'

'Oh I won't.' Katherine snuggled under the covers. She looked so vulnerable that Brenda's heart went out to her.

'Oh by the way, Jean-Claude came to visit you last night, but you were flat out. He's on his way over now, roses and tender loving care at the ready.' Brenda fussed around the bed covers.

'Good.' Katherine closed her eyes and sighed, 'I miss him.'

'I know you do, hon.' Brenda didn't meet Katherine's eyes, remembering the tableau she had interrupted last night in Jean-Claude's office. Ali was perched on his bed, running her hands through his hair, and murmuring endearments to her sleepy boss. That was not the sort of thing Brenda wanted Katherine to know. Not yet, anyhow.

One week after Katherine's recovery, Jean-Claude strode into her portable dressing room and plonked another pile of cheques on to her dressing table. 'Sign,' he commanded.

Kitty was being laced into a corset that seemed tighter than usual, and trying to hold her breath for Mona, Brenda, and Blackie who were all hands on deck for this hateful, twice daily event.

They pulled the corset so tightly that she felt faint. They were all worried about her today, she was looking pale and distinctly fragile. 'Not at this moment, darling. Can't you see I'm busy?'

Jean-Claude raised disdainful eyebrows. 'Suit yourself, Katherine. But make sure Brenda sends them off Federal Express asap.'

Brenda didn't look at him. 'Yes, sir. Anythin' you say, boss.'

Jean-Claude stared at her with open hostility. There was little pretence of civility between them now. Brenda was determined to tell Katherine about Ali, but she dared not throw a spanner in the works at this point. When the movie was finished, she intended to tell Katherine everything she knew.

They laced Katherine in tighter. 'You don't want to hold things up on your own production, do you?' Katherine said breathlessly, while Jean-Claude stood in the doorway staring at her.

'Of course not. Do I ever?' he said, and left, slamming the door so hard that the trailer shook, and a bottle of make-up clattered to the floor.

'What a charmer,' said Brenda, exchanging looks with the wrecking crew. 'Gives new meaning to the word gallant.'

That night Katherine signed cheques totalling ninety-five thousand dollars. Brenda FedExed them to Los Angeles, but one week later, when they were shooting in Chartres, a fax arrived from the bank.

'Regret to inform you that there are insufficient funds in Katherine Bennet's accounts to cover latest cheques. Have had to stop payment on $47,000. Please advise. Cordially, Henry S Belver. Manager, Bank of America.'

Brenda was horrified; she remembered Kitty assuring her that Jean-Claude had saved her money, and that she had almost $750,000 in her accounts. Now they were almost empty? What had happened? It was time to beard the lion in his den, Brenda decided. Jean-Claude had taken a room at the country inn, and transformed it into his usual high-tech office. Brenda stormed in unannounced, and confronted him.

Jean-Claude wadded the fax into a ball, and threw it into the corner.

'It's bullshit, Brenda. You know what banks are like; they've just moved the funds from one of Kitty's accounts to another. Obviously they've made a mistake.'

'I know this bank, Jean-Claude. We've been with them for five years. They don't make mistakes.'

'So, call them. Ask them what they've done with Kitty's money.'

'It's *you* I should be asking. You're the money genius, the financial whizz kid. You're the person who controls the funds, the person Kitty has put all her faith in.'

'Yeah, so maybe she made a mistake with me.' His eyes had a dangerous gleam. 'Maybe she should have stuck with her own kind. Actors. Showbiz types – Johnny Bennet – low-life junkies and drunks.'

His scorn infuriated Brenda even more. 'Johnny may be a drunk, but he's more of a man than you'll ever be. Now listen to me, Jean-Claude Valmer, or whatever the hell your name is, I'm not going to tell Kitty about all this money disappearing. The strain of shooting in this humid weather, in unbelievably uncomfortable costumes, is taking its toll. She's been to hospital, she's fainted twice this week, and she's worried about Tommy's knee still not healing. She's concerned about Johnny. And she's worried about the way she looks. Thanks to you telling her she's too fat, she's losing too much weight. Damn it, Jean-Claude, I am not going to lay this pile of crap on her plate, and you'd better do something about this money pronto – or else.'

'Or else what?' he said in a bored voice, staring up at the ceiling.

'I'll tell her all the things I know.'

'Like what?' he raised his eyebrows.

'Like you know what. Put that money back, Jean-Claude, I *know* you took it. If you return it to the account, I won't tell Kitty, or anything else I know about you and that redhead, I promise.'

She crossed her fingers behind her back. She certainly would tell Kitty, but not until this picture was over.

Jean-Claude leaned back, laced his fingers together, and glared insolently at Brenda for a long moment. Then he said, 'OK, Brenda, leave it to me. I'll talk to the bank. There's obviously been some sort of computer error. I expect some of the money was accidentally moved from one of her accounts to mine. Yes, I'm sure that's what probably happened.'

'Yeah, that must be it, I guess.' Brenda kept most of the sarcasm from her voice, and screwed her homely features into a reluctant smile. 'Well, I'll be off back to the set, then. Are you gracing us with your presence today?'

'No, I've got too much to do,' he twirled around in his leather chair, until his back was to her. 'I'll catch up with Kitty tonight.' And started tapping dismissively on the computer.

Tommy arrived, looking tanned and happy, from the Hamptons, to spend the last two weeks of filming with Katherine. He was still limping slightly, but his cast was due to come off soon. Although it was still cool inside the ancient villas and country chateaux where they were shooting, the weather was semi-tropical now. Tommy hung around the sets, and explored the museums, but after a couple of days it was clear that he was getting bored. Brenda asked Katherine if she could take him on a gastronomic tour.

'We'll gorge ourselves on French food, and I'll probably come back twice the size,' said Brenda.

'But what a way to go!' said Katherine. 'I'm jealous.'

The following day, Jean-Claude told Katherine that he suddenly had some important business to deal with in Nevada. That night Katherine dined with Steven at an old, dimly lit restaurant in Chartres where the food was exquisite: a place strictly for the French, where no tourists were allowed. He was still fine-tuning the script, and it was turning out better than anyone had anticipated.

'So, how's golden boy?' The candlelight reflected in Steven's brown eyes. Unusually, he wasn't wearing glasses and Katherine noticed how thick and dark his eyelashes were, how candid his gaze. His light brown hair, which usually hung untidily over his forehead, was brushed back, and he looked clean-cut and boyish.

Mellow after several glasses of Chateau Lafitte, Katherine felt like confiding a bit.

'Sometimes I think it's the worst marriage in the world. The trouble is that Jean-Claude has suddenly become so secretive. He was never especially open, but now he never wants to tell me about anything. It's as though he has another life that he wants to keep completely separate from mine.'

She didn't want to tell him about the most recent confrontation. It was about her money again. No, she couldn't tell Steve that; it was her burden and she had to bear it alone. She pushed away her orugala salad with truffles, and lit a cigarette, frowning.

'He doesn't even seem to be interested in the movie any more.'

'He's never on the set, that's for sure.' Steve marvelled at how beautiful Katherine looked tonight, but how sad.

'I know. Sometimes I wonder if it's only the money he's interested in, and not the producing side at all. God I'm lousy at marriage, aren't I?'

'Just because one marriage failed, and another is tricky, doesn't mean you're hopeless. Back out if you want to, Kitty. Everyone's allowed mistakes. Don't be a martyr.'

'I'm not,' she said, 'I don't have the martyr mentality.'

'Maybe you should dump him. Give him a one-way ticket to Palookaville.'

'Palookaville? Where's that from?'

'*On the Waterfront*, remember?'

'Sure – how could I forget.'

He refilled her glass and said: 'Get rid of him, Kitty. Cut your losses, and start all over again; he's no good for you, believe me.'

'Trouble is, in spite of his moods and faults, I think I still love him, and I understand his problems. They're – complicated.' She sipped her wine pensively.

'Well, please keep your eyes and ears open, and for God's sake, try to keep one step ahead of him.'

'I do, all the time. Don't worry so much about me, Steve.'

Oh Lord, why is love so blind? thought Steve, then raising his glass:

'My God, but you're lovely!'

'Here's looking at you, kid.' And they both started laughing.

Brenda needed to confide her suspicions about Jean-Claude to someone, so finally she told Steven everything she knew, and some things she suspected.

He was not surprised. 'I've always thought the no-good son-of-bitch was a real bastard, and Kitty's a city girl – she's never seen a pig up close.'

'Are you ever serious, Steve? What's that one from?'

'*Young Lions*. Good line – underrated movie. And yes – I'm very serious, especially about Katherine.'

'So what are we going to do about him?'

'Nothing, right now,' said Steve. 'He's got the hook in Kitty too deep. She's got to finish this picture, so we watch and we wait, and we're there for her when she needs us.'

Katherine was becoming tedious and haggard; Jean-Claude was getting bored with her. Bored with her in bed, bored with her all-consuming interest in her brat of a son – fed up with her insecurities, her narcissism, and her actress's neuroses, and irritated by the dreadful Brenda, who walked in her shadow. He knew she disliked him as much as he loathed her. He was actually getting bored with Ali too, but she gave him the kinky sex he craved. Kitty had never liked it. He knew from what Kitty had told him about her marriage to Johnny, that she would never appreciate the joys of sadomasochism, bondage and voyeurism. She was a white bread, conventional all-American girl sexually, and he was frustrated by it. Fortunately she was so exhausted these days, that she was half asleep as her head hit the pillow, so their sex life had become desultory and occasional.

Jean-Claude needed sex like most men needed food and drink, and he was single-minded in his quest for it. It didn't particularly matter who it was with; practically any reasonable looking female would do, even the occasional beautiful boy, but he was shrewd enough to know that when he snared a superior catch like Katherine Bennet, he had to play by her rules. He thoroughly understood the games that would appeal to her. Protestations of eternal, unconditional love, romantic passion, intense lust. He knew that women were easily hooked by these things because so many men were uninspired and lazy about lovemaking. But not Jean-Claude.

He had studied the Marquis de Sade and Henry Miller when he was barely out of his teens. He'd researched books about sexual obsession and fetishism, not to mention Freud, Jung, Masters and Johnson, and even Shere Hite. He found it ridiculously easy to make the younger boys at school fall in love with him, and when he left school and became a pop star women flocked around him. He had perfected the art of the mind-blowing fuck, and those feverish erotic games which fascinated so many women. He knew which buttons to press in any woman, but for his part it was merely the slaking of an appetite which needed to be satisfied three, four, even five times a day. Sex meant nothing more to him. It was the same as eating, or drinking. However, he knew its power over women, and he knew how to wield that power to devastating effect.

He looked at himself dispassionately in the bathroom mirror. Time to slap some more peroxide on those dark roots. He was glad he didn't have to dye his pubic hair too; luckily it was a light enough brown already. He looked at his watch. Just enough time before he caught the plane, to do what he had the itch for. He opened the door to the connecting room where Ali was sitting expectantly on the bed. Waiting for love, he thought contemptuously. He despised her, even while he felt the uncontrollable yearning that drove him.

'Take your clothes off,' he commanded. 'Slowly.'

Ali obeyed, cheeks pink, eyes shining with anticipation. Aflame with desire for him she stripped off slowly, sensuously, like he had taught her to.

He strode to the bed, lifted her up by her long red hair and crushed his mouth to hers in a kiss which was as brutal as it was passionate. Ali's knees started to buckle. They always went weak at the knees, thought Jean-Claude, as his tongue tenderly explored her lips. He kissed well, he knew that. Katherine often joked that he must have majored in kissing. Then, tearing off his clothes, Jean-Claude made love to his secretary with such passionate intensity that she begged for more. But Jean-Claude didn't have time for more. This moment of love was brief. The feeling of power over any female who serviced him was over almost immediately. Tonight he had other things on his mind.

As Jean-Claude showered, thoughts of Eleonor Norman crossed his mind for a moment. Now there was a woman who shared his fantasies. A woman who would do anything for sexual satisfaction. Break boundaries – go to the limit of the most bizarre desires. Eleonor had confided that she had been forced to have sex with an old movie producer when she was seven years old. He had found these stories unbelievably exciting, more tantalizing, even, than making love. He would lie naked beside Eleonor after lovemaking, listening as she described what the dirty old man had done to the sweet little girl, idly running his hands over her huge, siliconed breasts until she began to groan with need of him. Then he would make her beg for him, and she would. Oh yes, how she would. She would do anything he wanted her to. Yes, Eleonor Norman was almost his equal there.

He had spent many a satisfactory morning and afternoon making love to her in her bed, on her floor, in her swimming pool, while Kitty worked. Eleonor's pleasure at fucking her rival's husband was only matched by her fear of what Jean-Claude would do if she ever revealed their secret. For Eleonor had the measure of this man. She had delved into the darkest side of his sexuality, but, like every other woman he had ever made love to, she craved him. Jean-Claude's power over women was almost supernatural.

As soon as Jean-Claude returned from his trip, he announced he was sending Tommy back to LA. Katherine was devoting too much time to him. 'You should be studying lines, and getting some beauty sleep.'

Katherine stared at him flinty-eyed. This was almost the last straw.

'You are joking, I hope,' she said.

'You need rest,' he calmly studied his perfect reflection in the mirror. 'You look like hell.'

'Thanks,' Katherine said bitterly. 'But I'm not sending Tommy anywhere. He's coming to Antibes and to Venice, so don't try to manipulate me, Jean-Claude. I'm not playing your game this time.'

She had just been playing Scrabble with Tommy, and wanted to go to bed – alone.

'You stay up with that spoiled brat all night – no wonder the network says you're looking tired and used-up in the dailies.' Jean-Claude cupped her chin in his hands, and inspected her face. She pushed his hand away.

Katherine had seen the dailies. With Lazlo's special lighting she was looking radiant, not a day over thirty, but she was too weary to argue any more. Too weary and, she hated to admit it, too frightened. Jean-Claude's recent behaviour was so bizarre that she could no longer judge how he would act in any given set of circumstances. She had broached the idea of separation.

'If you divorce me I'll sell the story of our marriage to the tabloids. I'll tell them you're a sexually insatiable slut, and that you treat your staff, and the actors on the set like shit; that you're really a bitch.'

'You wouldn't do that – you couldn't.'

'Ah but I would. You cross *me*, Katherine Bennet, and you open a Pandora's box you never thought existed.'

Katherine stood up, eyes blazing, hands on hips.

'I'm fed up to the teeth with your insults and abuse and threats. If you don't change your attitude, and curb your vile temper, Jean-Claude, I will get an annulment.'

'You'll look like the biggest idiot in the world,' he sneered. 'Typical actress, spoiled megastar – can't stay married for more than three months. The public will think you really are a joke, *chérie*.'

'I don't give a damn any more what the public thinks. This is my life. This ain't a rehearsal. This is opening night every night. If I'm going to be as miserable with you as I've been the past weeks, I want *out*.'

'You do that, and I'll make your ex-husband look like a pussycat. I'll get half of everything you've made. You've made big bucks because of me, Katherine, so don't cross me. I'm warning you, I've taken steps. I'm ahead of you. That agreement is worthless. Don't attempt to get rid of me, because you can't, and if you won't send that spoiled brat of yours home, I don't want him around me.'

'Well to hell with you, too, Jean-Claude. My son stays here with me – where he belongs.'

Katherine whirled round, to find Brenda standing in the doorway.

'You fat bitch. What the hell are you spying on us for?' said Jean-Claude.

'Stop it, stop it,' screamed Katherine.

'Shove off, fat lady. And don't you *ever* interfere between my wife and me again, do you hear?'

'Brenda, you better go.' Kitty saw the hurt in Brenda's eyes, but there was nothing she could do. Jean-Claude was so full of rage that his face was purple. There was no telling what he might do next.

'Please, Brenda, please – leave us alone.'

'Sure, I'll go,' she said. 'And if I never see you again, Jean-Claude, it won't be soon enough for me.'

Jean-Claude shoved Brenda out of the door, slammed it shut, and turned to Katherine triumphantly.

'Now you know who's boss around here, Miss Diva Queen. I don't give a damn about your son – although I know you think the sun shines out of his ass. Just don't make any more waves with me, I'm warning you.'

He stalked out, and Katherine heard the locks turn in his office next door.

Try it, just try it. Katherine knew she should but she was afraid. And she wasn't feeling at all well. She hadn't told anyone, but the effort involved in making this film was exhausting her more and more. Sometimes the simple effort of getting out of bed in the morning made her feel so dizzy that she had to sit on a chair with her head in her hands. It took her a long time each day to shower and get ready, partly because she was feeling so sick all the time; occasionally she even threw up. She carried a tiny bottle of smelling salts with her when she was on the set, and this stopped her feeling faint. Although it scarcely seemed possible, she was beginning to think she might be pregnant.

She dared not confide in anyone; they would insist on bringing a doctor on to the set to watch over her. She couldn't stand the idea of everyone fussing over her all the time. They fussed around her enough already. She felt that her life was being lived in slow motion; she knew that the only way she could get through the final weeks of shooting was to be acquiescent until the film ended: go along with Jean-Claude, however vile he seemed.

She was frightened of him now. She felt that he had the power to destroy her, and she had no time to think, no peace; she was always being called; it was always time to go to work, it seemed.

Katherine sighed heavily and inhaled the smelling salts, then walked slowly out to the humid set.

At the end of September, principal photography finished in Chartres. The company still had two days' night shooting in Antibes, then off to Venice for the ending. On the second afternoon, Jean-Claude insisted on taking Tommy, Brenda and Kitty out on the water. Kitty was desperate to relax in the sun, but it was forbidden, because Paulette had to have an eighteenth-century milk-white complexion. Even so, it was luxury to lie in the bows of the boat, with her face and body covered. Katherine dozed as the sleek Riva Aqua Rama zoomed across the Mediterranean. Jean-Claude was exceptionally charming today, the captivating man who had swept Katherine away, but she wasn't rising to the bait. All she wanted was for him to leave her alone. There were the merest embers left of her passion for him. She just hoped that her suspicions weren't correct. She prayed that she wasn't pregnant. Kitty sighed. She was so tired. She just wanted to finish this movie, and then this marriage.

They found a beach and picnicked under an umbrella on country pâtes, Provencal cheeses, and fresh baguettes, washed down with a deliciously light but potent Pétale de

Roses. The boat rocked gently, and after lunch Katherine lay dozing again, while Jean-Claude decided to water-ski. He did this, like everything else, exceedingly well, and as he monoskiied across the wake, back to the hotel, Tommy said:

'I'm pissed, Mom, that I can't ski too. I'm fed up with this cast, it's makin' me crazy.'

'Only two more days, darling,' Kitty said. 'Right before we leave for Venice, off it comes.'

Tommy looked uneasy, then blurted out: 'Mom – hey I don't want to worry you 'cos I know you've got enough on your plate, but it's about Dad. He's in a bit of trouble. He called me this morning, but I didn't want to tell you before we sailed...' He paused and Katherine asked: 'Tell me what, darling?'

'Well – Dad told me that when he came back from his hospital treatment last week, he found a guy standin' on his doorstep with a writ for back taxes.'

'Everybody gets those. It's no big deal.'

'I dunno about everybody, Mom, all I know is that this guy with this subpoena thing, said that if Dad didn't pay ten thousand dollars by the end of September, they were going to sling him in jail.' Tommy looked at his mother appealingly. 'Dad's real upset, 'cos it's a last demand or something. What can we do? Can't we help him?'

Not another problem, thought Kitty. But putting her arms around Tommy, she said comfortingly, 'We'll do what we can, darling, I'll do everything I can to help him, I promise you.'

That evening, as Blackie and Mona fussed around her in the trailer, Katherine thought about the most diplomatic way to inform Jean-Claude that she wanted to give more money to her ex-husband.

'That creep's bled you dry,' he had stormed before. 'You've got to stop feeding him cash. He blows it all on dope, anyhow.'

Katherine hated these arguments, so she usually gave in, but this time it was different. Prison? She'd never forgive herself, and Tommy would never forgive her if his father were jailed.

There was a knock on the door. Jean-Claude – the last person she expected – holding a red leather gift box.

'These are for you, *chérie*.' He exuded ebullient charm as he presented the box to her. 'Happy birthday.'

Kitty was amazed when she opened the box and saw the beautiful earrings nestling in red velvet. Perfectly matched black pearls in a setting of baguettes and rose-cut diamonds. She wondered how Jean-Claude could afford them. They were from the most expensive jeweller in Nice, and had to be worth at least twenty or thirty thousand dollars. Was that twenty or thirty thousand of *her* money?

'They're lovely, Jean-Claude,' she said warily. 'But it's not my birthday for eight more months. Why the gift?'

'For me every day's a birthday with you, *chérie*.' He kissed the back of her neck; Blackie and Mona exchanged meaningful glances. Katherine moved her head away and lit a cigarette.

'They're lovely. Thank you.'

'Not as lovely as you.' He kissed her fingers, and she realized this was the time to talk...

'Would you take five, kids? I need to have a word with Jean-Claude for a minute,' she said to her wrecking crew.

Once Mona and Blackie had gone, Katherine told Jean-Claude about Johnny.

'You must be joking,' Jean-Claude's eyebrows curved over flinty eyes. 'Give that drunk ten thousand dollars? No way, *chérie*, not in a million years. Let him go to his other friends: let him go to jail. It serves him right.'

'No, I'm sorry, Jean-Claude, but you can't do that. I won't *allow* it.'

Jean-Claude's face metamorphosed in the way that she detested.

'I'm not giving that bastard one penny, do you understand, Katherine, not a fucking penny.'

'No, *you're* not giving it, Jean-Claude. It's my money. Are you so blind that you can't see what this means to me? Not to mention to Tommy. Johnny's his father, I won't see him go to jail.'

Jean-Claude was looming over her now, and his voice carried to the chateau, where the crew were kicking their heels. Time was of the essence. They had three more days of night shooting, and the schedule was extremely tight. But Jean-Claude was oblivious as he yelled at Katherine, heedless of the listening crew, and of the time running out.

'Listen, you bastard,' Kitty finally exploded. 'I don't know who you think you are, or why you think you can push me around like this, but I'm sending that money to Johnny tomorrow, and *nothing's* going to stop me, do you understand?'

'Then we're finished,' he roared. 'This marriage is over, and I'm finished with you.'

'Yes, we are finished, Jean-Claude, finally – and about time too.' She put out her cigarette and picked up the smelling salts. She felt completely faint, and drained of all emotion.

'You devious bitch.' He stood behind her chair, staring at their reflections in the mirror. 'You're exactly how the newspapers paint you.'

'If that's what you think, then it's best you get the hell out of my life.' Kitty's heart thumped, and she thought she might be having another gastroenteritis attack.

'Please get out of here, and leave me alone. For God's sake, let me get on with my life and with this movie.'

'Is that what you want? Is that what you want?' His eyes were almost mad, his voice shrill.

'Yes,' she said faintly, leaning back on the chair 'That's what I want – this marriage is over. I want you out of my life forever – out of here now.'

There was a knock at the door, and the assistant director's voice called out nervously, 'We need you Katherine now, please, everyone's been waiting.'

'I don't give a shit,' Jean-Claude barked, 'Get away from here. Get the hell out. I'm talking to my wife.'

'Jean-Claude, you simply *cannot* hold up production any more.' Kitty's make-up was smudged and her face scarlet.

'Do you think I give a damn?' he bellowed. 'Do you think I really give a toss about any of this stupid movie shit? It's all a bunch of narcissistic crap. Look at this, look at it.'

Disdainfully he jabbed at Katherine's delicate, enormous wig. It was a masterpiece, with tiny stuffed birds in cages perched among the high curls, and trailing roses and pearls interwoven across the crown. He grabbed her shoulders and shook her ferociously, until birds, pearls and flowers started falling on to the floor.

'Stop it, Jean-Claude, for God's sake, stop,' Katherine screamed.

He leaned closer; her adrenelin started pumping, and she felt a stab of genuine fear.

'You bitch. You stupid bitch. This is your loss. You'll never find anyone like me again. Never.'

Then he grabbed her by the neck, and shook her so violently that the flimsy walls of the trailer trembled, and the lights started flickering.

'You stupid moron, I'm your husband. Your husband *forever*! Don't you dare threaten to leave me again, ever, d'you hear me? I'll kill you if you do.'

Unable to breathe, let alone speak, Katherine clawed at Jean-Claude's hands, feeling herself beginning to faint. A red mist seemed to float in front of her eyes, and her heart was hammering so hard she thought it would explode. Then the trailer door flew open, and Blackie and Steven burst in.

'What the hell's going on?' Steven demanded.

Jean-Claude, whose back was to them, froze. Then he released Kitty, and turned to face the two men, with a charming smile.

'Good evening, gentlemen, I was helping my wife to adjust her coiffure.' He took Kitty's hand, and kissed the back of it, whispering:

'I will send the cheque to John, *immediatement*, *chérie*. Do not worry, it is as good as done. *Au'voir ma belle. A tout a l'heure.*'

At the doorway he turned, still with a smile on his face:

'I'll be off to Venice early tomorrow morning, *chérie*. I need a couple of days to get the office properly organized and everything in place before you all arrive.'

Katherine could only nod; her throat was constricted by unshed tears, and she was unable to speak. Jean-Claude stared at everyone for a second sardonically, then, with a loud slamming of the flimsy trailer door, he was gone.

An almost palpable feeling of relief swept over the room. Katherine sprawled in the make-up chair, and let Blackie's witch hazel pads soothe her scarlet face. She couldn't afford self-pity now. She couldn't afford to be exhausted, to be sick or to faint. She had to pull herself together, get reconstructed for this scene which they *must* finish tonight. There was a stabbing pain in her gut. Oh God please don't let it be true, she thought. I *can't* be pregnant with his child.

With less than seven hours before dawn, they were now way behind schedule.

Brenda came in and started picking up the detritus that littered the floor. She silently handed the bits to Mona who had removed Katherine's ruined coiffure and was re-dressing it on the wig stand. Whenever they were on location, she looked after both Katherine's hair and clothes. Katherine stared at her bedraggled face, hair and at her bruised neck. She looked as if she'd been dragged through a hedge.

'What the hell's happened?' asked Brenda.

'Nothing,' said Katherine, then looked appealingly at Mona and Blackie. 'Would you mind re-dressing it in the hairdresser's, honey? I just need five minutes with Brenda and Steven – OK?'

Blackie and Mona left, and Katherine started repairing her make-up.

'That man's a psycho, sweetheart, I know he is,' said Steven, 'A sadistic sociopath. I've seen a couple before, but he's an expert. These people have no sense of morality whatsoever, but unfortunately they can charm the birds from the trees when they want to.'

'How could I be such a complete fool as to be taken in by him?' Katherine whispered. 'How did he manage to do it?'

'My God, Kitty, it's not your fault,' said Steve. 'Jean-Claude's a *classic* sociopath. He's handsome, worldly, charming, affectionate, but he's unable to feel, or consider anybody else's feelings or emotions except his own.'

'Is it true that sociopaths are completely split personalities, that they can even fool their closest friends and family, for years sometimes, without showing their true colours?' asked Katherine.

'Right; they're unable to understand their own sociopathic tendencies. If they're confronted with them, they'll deny everything. They're totally manipulative, brilliant liars; they always think they're in the right, and they'll step on anyone to get what they want.'

'Which is what?' Katherine was feeling sicker than ever.

'Which is usually money, or power, and total control over everyone and everything close to them. I'm sorry sweetheart.'

'I've only got myself to blame, for allowing him to get such a hold on my life,' she whispered.

'That's not strictly true, hon. Don't be so hard on yourself. You were needy, and he filled all those needs – brilliantly. He's a clever son of a bitch, I'll give him that,' said Brenda.

'But what the hell do I do now?' Katherine paced across the tiny floor of her trailer. 'He's got control of everything. Everything to do with my finances, contracts, business and banking life is in his office, under his jurisdiction. Hundreds of files, computer read-outs, all my tax returns. He refuses to give anything to my lawyer. He's prevented me having access to my files, and they're all locked in cabinets to which only he's got the key.'

'You mean he's schlepped the whole lot from LA?' Steven blew a long low whistle. 'First to Paris, then Nice, now it's been shipped to Venice?'

'Yes – air freight no less.'

'That's damned weird.'

'And I've been missing money from my accounts. Brenda tried to keep it from me, but I found out.'

'I'm sorry now I didn't tell you,' murmured Brenda, 'I was just thinking of the movie.'

'Hell!' said Steve. 'I don't believe this. How much money?'

'Well he lied about a big chunk from Home Shopping going in – said it hadn't arrived, but I checked with them, and it was definitely sent to the bank. They say it went out again almost the next day.'

'Where to?'

'How do I know? When I bring it up, Jean-Claude scoffs – says I don't know what I'm talking about, that I'm stupid. Then he drags me over to the computer and runs all those phoney figures by on it and says, "Look at this Kitty. *This* is the truth – you're worth more than a million dollars cash, so stop whining." '

Steve shook his head. 'I'd like to kill the son-of-a-bitch.'

'It's like being on a see-saw. A few days ago, he threatened to destroy my bank statements and tax records, so that I would be in trouble with the IRS. After that I found out that, besides my producer's fee, I seem to be missing hundreds of thousands of dollars out of my account as well. I've got to get every bit of information vital to my financial life, and it's all in those damned files. I'm worried now that he'll use the shredder to cover his tracks.'

'Damn,' said Steven, 'This gets worse and worse.'

'Can you believe I even had to ask his permission to look at my contracts for the various deals? Often he wouldn't let me see them. God, was I stupid. Everyone's going to say I deserved what I got, but I've been working so hard, it just seemed easier to let things slide.'

'How can you still *care* about this guy? He's an unspeakable bastard.'

'I don't care about him any more, Steve – but just as it takes time to fall in love with someone, I guess it takes time to fall out of love, too.'

There was a sharp rap at the door. 'Miss Bennet, we've got to shoot this scene.' The assistant director sounded anxious.

'And so it goes.' Katherine wriggled to adjust her bodice more comfortably, and Mona finished her wig.

'Onward, kiddo,' said Steve. 'You go to work. I've gotta get back to LA tomorrow, and I'm going to put my thinking cap on, to see if I can help you out of this mess.'

'Thanks Steve, darling – you're the best.'

She brushed his cheek with her lips before she left the trailer, and Steve stared after her, then turned to Brenda.

'Dammit, someone's got to do something about that pyscho-freak, and I guess it's going to be me.'

CHAPTER EIGHTEEN

The realization that she was probably carrying Jean-Claude's child filled Katherine with dread. There was less than a week's shooting left. She had to continue her ghastly charade of a marriage until she returned to LA, and could start divorce proceedings. She no longer cared what the world, or anyone else, for that matter, thought. She wanted out, whatever the cost.

But first she had to discover what he had done with her money. She must unlock his filing cabinets, find the computer software, and retrieve all the files and documents which Ken Stringer needed before he could file her tax returns. Jean-Claude had insisted that he didn't have any back-ups, which everyone knew to be a lie. He had everything, and they had to get hold of it. Kitty needed to confide in the one person she could totally trust. Brenda was Kitty's only rock in this churning sea of turmoil. That was more than she could say for her mother.

Vera had called from New York, ostensibly to talk about Kitty's appearance in the latest tabloids but really to chide her for the chinks appearing in her marriage.

'It said in Liz Smith's column this morning that Jean-Claude's been spending more time away from you, and that you're not as lovey-dovey as you were. Is that true, Kit-Kat?'

'No it's not, Mama,' she said. 'Are you really only calling me about that?'

'Jean-Claude's a good guy – you better hang on to him, dear.'

'Yes, Mama.' Katherine wondered wearily how Vera could possibly know anything about Jean-Claude, other than from the columns. The last person she could discuss her marriage problems with was her mother.

But she did need to talk, and so she asked Brenda to have dinner with her the night before leaving for Venice. But no sooner had they settled down in her bedroom after dinner, than Jean-Claude arrived, unannounced and unexpected. Brenda got up at once, with a mumbled, 'Goodnight. And good riddance.'

Kitty tried to make her stay, but Brenda shook her head and left.

Jean-Claude stood frowning in front of the mirror, and examined his hairline. He was wearing his newly acquired casual look: an expensive leather bomber jacket with wide padded shoulders in a particularly sickly shade of peacock blue, and matching gabardine trousers and socks. It contrasted oddly with his usual elegantly tailored look, and made him appear obvious and flashy.

'I thought you were going to Venice today?' Kitty went to sit at her dressing table, and started brushing her hair.

'Trying to get rid of me too?' He moved behind her and Kitty watched him apprehensively. She recognized the familiar gleam in his eyes, the predatory look she'd once loved, but now loathed. His hands started untying the satin ribbons on the shoulders of her nightgown.

'What are you doing?'

'What do you think I'm doing?' He pulled at one of the ribbons, until her gown fell open to the waist. 'I'm cooling you off.' He laughed unpleasantly.

'Please don't, Jean-Claude.'

Kitty pulled up the gown to cover her breasts, but he grabbed her shoulders, and, pulling her to her feet, spun her around to face him.

'Please don't, Jean-Claude?' he mocked. 'You're my wife, Katherine. Or have you forgotten?'

'How could I?' She moved away, shivering. Why hadn't she worn an old terrycloth robe? Why had she stupidly put on this provocative negligee? Because it's too damned hot, that's why, she answered herself.

'I'm exhausted, and the heat's really getting to me. I've got an early call and I've got to get some sleep.'

'Oh have you really?' His tone became even more sarcastic. 'Well, it's only ten o'clock, *chérie* and I'm not tired at all.' He grabbed her, pushed her on to the bed, and started kissing her mouth lasciviously.

Katherine felt almost physically sick as his mouth and tongue crudely explored hers. His hands were digging into her throat. She couldn't bear what was coming next.

'Jean-Claude, please stop. Not now.'

'Not now? Stop? Pray why not now, my diva queen?' His hands tightened around her neck then he moved his fully clothed body on top of her. His leatherjacket smelled like the interior of a cheap new car, and there was another smell lingering on him – a cut-price shop girl scent which she thought she recognized.

'For God's sake!' She wrenched her face away from his probing mouth, and tried to move her body, but he was much too strong and too fast, and tightened his hands on her neck.

'Shut up, bitch, or I'll give you a bruise no amount of paint will cover.' Then he slapped her face. She gasped with shock. Jean-Claude had never hit her before, he had never even threatened to.

She started to scream, but he slammed one hand over her mouth, and with the other, unzipped his trousers. He was as hard as he'd ever been, and he forced himself into her so ferociously that she prayed he would destroy the thing growing inside her. As he pounded into her, with one hand gripping her neck so tightly that she could barely breathe or speak, he hissed: 'What about all those lovers of yours, Kitty? I've heard all about them. All those other men you've fucked – all those grips and electricians and camera-men – you liked it rough with them didn't you, my sweet? You like rough trade, admit it. So why not with me?'

She wondered where he'd got that preposterous idea. She longed for the horror to end, but he wanted to prolong it, and continued pounding into her, whispering obscenities until he climaxed with a triumphant cry. He got off her immediately without a word, and sauntered into the bathroom.

He had thrown his jacket on to the bed; she angrily kicked it off to the floor and heard a metallic clank. She looked and saw a bunch of keys sticking out of the pocket. Keys! A dozen of them. Which could be the keys to her files, the files that held her past and her future? Jean-Claude's shower was running at full blast, and she heard him singing his hateful rabbit-versus-fox song. She picked up the keys and examined them. Some were for Yale or Banham locks, some were Vuitton keys, for the new luggage he'd recently purchased. Jean-Claude hadn't stinted himself in the shopping department since they'd been in Europe.

Then she saw two tiny file keys: unmistakable, small, thin and identical. She couldn't afford to take both, but one of them must open at least some of her files. She unclipped one from the keyring, and stuffed it into the zippered compartment of her handbag. Then lay back on the bed, looking drained and exhausted, while her heart thumped excitedly. A few minutes later, he came out, calmly towelling his hair.

'I have to go to Venice tonight, *chérie*,' he announced. 'Get everything prepared for you.'

She didn't answer, massaged her aching neck.

'Haven't you got anything to say?' He picked up her hand mirror, and inspected his faint five o'clock shadow. For a blond he had extremely dark facial hair.

'What do you expect me to say – thanks for a great fuck? Why don't you go? It's better you do.'

'Well then, aren't you going to say you'll miss me? I'm going to miss you.'

Silently she put on her robe.

'For God's sake, you just raped me. I'm not going to lie any more. Are you crazy enough to think I'm going to miss you, when you behave like an unspeakable animal?'

'You know you loved it.' He chuckled and checked his stubble again. 'All women do. Oh, by the way, I wouldn't keep bothering the bank manager about your accounts, if I were you. I've told you a million times about the state of your finances.'

Kitty stared at her husband, unable to disguise her disgust, then she went to the dressing table to brush her hair again. Only another week and she would be done with Jean-Claude. But she couldn't let him know that she had definitely made up her mind. She needed to be cleverer than he was. At least she had the key to her files – oh God let it be the right one.

'Answer me Kitty – answer me.'

She didn't want to meet his eyes, which lately had seemed to read her mind. There was an agonizing pain deep inside her, which she hoped was the beginnings of a miscarriage.

'I guess – I'm just imagining things about the money.' How she hated herself for lying. 'It's the strain of the movie. I'm not myself these days, and I don't feel so great – maybe I'm getting sick.'

'I'm sorry you don't feel well. I love you *chérie*, you know how much. When this is all over, we'll go away together somewhere wonderful.'

His voice softened, and she tensed, praying he wasn't going to try to make love again. The frenzied features of minutes ago had transformed themselves into a tender expression. Stroking her cheek, he crooned: 'You know I only have your best interests at heart, don't you? And you know how much I love you?'

Katherine gritted her teeth. She felt physically ill. How many times had she heard him say those cloying, insincere words? *How* had she ever been such a fool as to believe in them? She dragged her eyes back to him, and for a second they stared at each other. She saw that guileless tenderness and compassion which had hoodwinked her for so long. But she knew better now. He was not normal. A sociopath, if not a psychopath, and she had to play him at his own game, if she were to escape from this hideous marriage. Katherine felt unutterably weary. Her body ached, and her heart was heavy with the miserable knowledge that her husband was a brutal, lying sadist and worse, that she had become his victim. She had never been a victim before; she had always been a survivor. But now, at least, she had the key. The tide was definitely going to turn. It had to.

On the way back to LA, Steven decided to stop over in Paris to find out a few home truths about Jean-Claude. The first thing he discovered during his research for information on Jean-Claude in Paris, was that there was no such person as Jean-Claude Valmer, born 22nd November, 1947. Steven searched the department of births and deaths records under Valmer for 1945, 1946, and for several years before and after, but came to a dead end. He paced the streets, his mind racing, then remembered that Kitty had said Jean-Claude had been a pop star in the sixties.

Contacting Felix Lafitte, an old friend, and a journalist on *Le Figaro*, Steven obtained permission, on the pretext of researching a script, to visit the newspaper's 'morgue'. There, until his eyes could barely focus, he delved into decades-worth of old newspapers, bound into huge monthly books. He then went through individual files named Valmer, but again came up with nothing. Whatever Jean-Claude Valmer called himself as a pop star, it wasn't the name he went by now.

Steven met Felix in a cafe later that day, and they sipped absinthe, watching Parisian street life jostle by.

'This is the guy I'm looking for.' Steve handed him a recent photograph. 'Do you recognize him?'

Felix studied it. 'A pop star, you say. When?'

'Oh I guess mid-sixties, somewhere around then.'

'Hmm. This guy certainly looks familiar.' Felix held the photograph away from him, and squinted at it. 'Are you sure he's really a blond?'

'Well, I haven't seen him *au naturel*, but Kitty's never hinted otherwise.'

'Katherine Bennet. Of course. This is that man she married, isn't it. We sent one of our journalists to do a story on her a few weeks ago in Versailles. We wanted pictures of her with her new husband, but he wasn't around.'

'There must be some photos of him in Kitty's file,' said Steven. 'They've been married for five months. The wedding pictures, for example.'

'What wedding pictures?' said Felix. 'Weren't they married privately in Las Vegas?'

'Yes, they were, but they had a big party a few months later. A photographer took lots of pictures for *Hola*, *Paris Match* and all those gossip magazines. Don't you remember seeing them?'

'*Non*,' said Felix. 'But I don't read that sort of trash. Come on. Let's go through Kitty's file.'

They scanned Katherine's four-inch-thick file carefully, but the only pictures they found of her with Jean-Claude, showed him either in profile, or with his head down. Very few caught him face on, except for some early photographs at a London theatre.

'Wait a minute.' Felix suddenly pulled out a fuzzy paparazzi photograph of the two of them leaving Le Dome restaurant. 'This guy *does* look familiar. Let's consult our expert in the pop scene, maybe he can tell us who this Dr Jekyll really is.'

As the popular music critic for *Le Figaro*, Laurence Delanger's memory was encylopaedic. He sat behind a desk piled high with CDs and records, studying Jean-Claude's picture, the ash from a Gauloise falling unheeded on to his frayed, grey sweater.

'Yes, of course I know who he is. His name is, or was, Jean-Jacques Costello, but that is not his real name, either. He had a couple of hits in the late sixties; I can't remember their names now, but I seem to remember there was some scandal attached to *him* later on.'

'What sort of scandal?' Steven said eagerly. 'How can I find out about it?'

'Look in the files.' Laurence blew smoke rings to the ceiling, 'It's all in the files. If you dig long enough you'll find out everything you want to know about *anyone*.'

'Thanks, Laurence,' Steven said. 'I really appreciate this.'

He returned to the morgue, looked up Jean-Jacques Costello, and almost immediately found what he was looking for.

Jean-Jacques Costello most definitely had been a famous pop singer in France for a short time in 1967. In the photograph he was nineteen, with thick dark, wavy hair. But there was no mistaking that face. Twenty-two years younger, but unmistakably Jean-Claude Valmer. He hadn't changed that much. Here he was a little fuller in the face, which had none of the shadows and grooves of a forty-one-year old, and his hair was a little shorter.

Steven studied Jean-Jacques Costello's file in the fading afternoon light. It was thin, most of the clippings compacted into the one-year period around 1967. Jean-Jacques Costello's singing career had had a short shelf-life but Steven read every story carefully. The adulatory ones, the press handouts, the critiques and the puff pieces, until he found a long article called 'Whatever happened to Jean-Jacques Costello?' in the conservative French newspaper, *Le Monde*. The story had been written eighteen years after Jean-Claude's pop career had ended, written, in fact, in 1984. The writer revealed that Jean-Jacques Costello had changed his name to Pierre Rondeau. In 1983 Pierre had been released from prison where he had spent the past seven years incarcerated for bigamy and embezzlement.

CHAPTER NINETEEN

Katherine and Tommy were quickly whisked through the crowds at Leonardo da Vinci airport by their mustachioed Venetian bodyguard, Fabrizio. He carried a portophone, and a clipboard on which her name was written, displaying it prominently while Katherine, sunglasses on, head down, tried to avoid eye-contact with the swarms of tourists. Fabrizio then escorted them into a water taxi, while Brenda stayed behind to organize the luggage.

The fading sun was a huge orange ball, sinking in to the west, as they sped down the waterway. Seagulls were perched on the tall mast-like structures which divided the water road, and the taxi speeded until it arrived at the mouth of a small canal, when it slowed to a crawl, and heavy silence enveloped them like fog. Katherine could hear nothing but the sound of the boat's engine, and she noticed that the temperature had dropped several degrees. The buildings on either side of the canal were darkly derelict, and looked as though they had been there for thousands of years. The water was black and slimy, and occasionally Kitty saw rats slithering in and out. There was an eerie stillness in the air, even though it was the tourist season, a heavy oppressiveness. Kitty rubbed her bruised neck. It was the first time that Jean-Claude had been physically violent towards her, but she was determined that it would be the last. He would never come near her again. Her mouth set in a bitter line. It was over. Short, sharp and swift, not like the Chinese death.

She had attempted to call Steven several times in LA, to tell him about the key to the filing cabinet, but he was never at home, and her mobile phone was notoriously unpredictable. She waved at Tommy, who was sitting up front with the taxi driver, chattering away in broken Italian. Yesterday the French doctor had removed his cast, and announced that he was as fit as any other sixteen-year-old, and could now live a normal life.

The taxi ended its serpentine journey through the backwaters, and entered the bustling Grand Canal. Enormous *vaporetti*, water buses crammed with sightseers, cruised up and down the wide waterway. On either side of the canal were crumbling palazzos and bus stops, small wooden platforms jutting over the water.

As they headed towards the centre of Venice, the buildings became smarter and less gloomy. Spruce blue and white awnings contrasted sharply with the decaying stonework, and the medieval baroque carving on front doors. Some of the balconies contained bright flowering shrubs. Each building had its own distinctive character, yet all possessed the same majestic grandeur.

In open-air restaurants, bedecked with hanging vines, late afternoon diners sipped drinks, and stared out at the choppy grey waves. Small arched bridges crossed the canals, and at various intersections, gondoliers, wearing their traditional blue and white striped T-shirts, became embroiled in traffic jams with motor taxis and buses. Occasionally Kitty thought she glimpsed women from another era drifting by, elegantly dressed and coiffed, holding parasols. She wondered if these old-fashioned visions were the ghosts for which Venice was famous, or was she imagining things? They passed the house where Byron had lived. He would swim every morning from there to breakfast at Harry's Bar. This still had the reputation of serving the best breakfast in Italy, but no one could swim today in the polluted water of the Grand Canal.

The taxi finally halted at a tiny narrow entrance; they could see the dome of Santa Maria della Salute in the distance, looking like an enormous iced cake.

'I thought we were going straight to the Palazzo Albrizzi,' Kitty said to Fabrizio.

'Ah *si! si! signora* – we are. There are two entrances, but the congestion to the main one is terrible at this time of day. The back way to the palazzo is down this Street. It's just a little walk, *signora* – not too long. *Scusi.*'

The production company thought that Katherine wouldn't want to be bothered by tourists, so had given her the choice of staying either at an hotel, or at the palazzo. They would be shooting there some of the time, and the production manager thought it would be easier for her at the latter.

Fabrizio walked swiftly through the Campo della Pescaria, the bustling fruit and fish market next to the quay, occasionally whispering hoarsely into his portophone. Artists seated on camp stools captured a scene which was a painter's dream. The buildings were a riot of typically Venetian colours; yellow ochre, amber, burnt sienna. A neon-lit butcher's shop sold every possible cut of meat. In the grocers, giant mushrooms, porcini, were displayed next to bright green basil; huge pumpkins were stacked beside crates of ripe, purple figs, and bright shiny yellow peppers, and everywhere the rich scent of ripe peaches, fresh fish, and garlic filled the air.

The fruit market opened into a warren of alleys and high-domed buildings and shops, where inexpensive clothes were displayed next to glass jewellery, tiny gondolas made of painted tin, leather bags, and photograph frames and exquisite Venetian mirrors of all sizes. In the windows of the mask shop were jesters, jokers, Bacchanalian satyrs, masks with huge Pinnochio noses, evil masks, angelic masks,

Punchinello masks of comedy and tragedy, and elaborate gold and silver masks with ostrich feathers.

'Hey, Mom – I got to get one of those for the masked ball,' Tommy grinned.

Fabrizio picked up speed down an alley so narrow that people in opposite windows could quite easily have shaken hands. Although it was only six o'clock, it was becoming dark and astonishingly quiet, and their footsteps echoed eerily on the cobblestones. Fabrizio turned left, right, then seemed to lose his way at a junction of three alleys branching off in different directions. He stood scratching his head.

'A *sinistra*? – A *destra*? Ah, no – sorry, *signora*, it is to the left here, I think. *Si*, *si*, that is it. Follow me please, *signora.* The palazzo is a little difficult to find sometimes. Follow me please.'

In a small cobbled piazza, where the trees grew even taller than the narrow houses, stood the decaying Palazzo Albrizzi. Its massive mahogany front door was as dark as ebony, and carved on it in bas relief, were the faces of grinning blackamoors. Fabrizio rang the bell, which echoed loudly through the square.

The piazza was empty, save for a small boy in shorts chasing a ball, who soon disappeared behind one of the narrow alleys that snaked away into the unknown depths of Venice.

The door creaked open, and an ancient butler demanded: 'What do you want?'

'*Ciao,*' Fabrizio greeted the old man. '*Ciao, Alessandro. Ecco la Signora Bennet e suofiglio. Signora* – here is Alessandro, the butler. And now I go.' With a bow and a flash of gold tooth, Fabrizio took his leave. 'Goodbye, dear *signora.*'

'But aren't you supposed to be staying here with me?' Katherine asked.

'*Ah no, signora. Scusi.* Fabrizio will be with the *signora* only when she works. When the *signora* is staying in the palazzo, Fabrizio will not be with the *signora*.'

'But didn't the production company ask you to guard me *all* the time?'

'Ah no, *signora*, they did not. If they had, *signora* – of course I would stay. *Scusi signora*.' Fabrizio glanced at his watch. 'I must leave now. I have another job with the Ministry in half an hour. *Scusi. Arrivederci, signora*.' He tipped an imaginary hat, barked a few words in Italian into his portophone, and evaporated into the still, strange dusk.

'Oh well,' Katherine shrugged. 'Adventure time.'

'It'll be OK,' said Tommy. 'Hey, Mom, this place is spooky but neat. I wish me and Brenda were staying here too.'

The butler mumbled something unintelligible, beckoned to them to follow, and they entered a wide, dark hallway, where the paint and plaster had almost completely worn off the walls, leaving only rough brick underneath. Their footsteps echoed eerily on the marble floor and the only illumination came from one tiny flickering bulb, in an enormous black iron lantern. The hall became progressively darker, and Katherine felt a strange sensation, almost as if death was in the air. She'd heard the rumours that the palazzo was haunted by a beautiful contessa, decapitated by her husband in a fit of jealous rage, four hundred years earlier. Katherine tried not to let that bother her as they walked down the dark passageway.

Urns full of dried flowers stood in shadowed corners, and marble busts of frowning aristocrats glowered from tables and sideboards.

'Hey what's that?' Tommy pointed to a coat-of-arms, featuring on one side a fifteenth century knight with golden plumes in his helmet, on the other a gloved hand holding aloft a sword.

The old man answered in broken English, 'That is the coat-of-arms of the ancient Albrizzi family, who lived in the palazzo for five hundred years.'

'What happened to their descendants?' asked Katherine.

'Unfortunately, *signora*, the last Count Albrizzi suffered a sad accident, twenty years ago – he had no children – so – Alessandro shrugged. 'The Albrizzi family line was finished – *che peccatto – fu una tragedia enorme.*'

'It's real creepy here. How old do you think this place is, Mom? I bet it's at least a thousand years old.'

'Maybe a bit less,' said Katherine. 'It was probably renovated in the nineteenth century.'

They followed Alessandro up wide, crumbling stone stairs, covered in threadbare red carpet. On the first landing, lead-paned windows faced a darkened courtyard, in which twisted branches of trees and plants vied for the sun. At the top of the stairs was an enormously wide, long room with a black and white marble checked floor, and a ceiling completely carved out of stone blackamoors and *putti*. Branching off it were several more carved wooden doors.

'This was the ballroom,' Alessandro said proudly. 'Every year the Albrizzi family would give a masked ball here. And this is where we will make the masked ball for your film, *signora*, just like the family used to do.'

Katherine nodded, admiring the baroque splendour of the room, and the paintings which lined the walls. Alessandro ushered them up another, smaller winding staircase, until they arrived at her bedroom. The connecting rooms were already occupied by Blackie and Mona, busily preparing for the following day's shooting.

The rooms all had a curiously dank smell, and they looked out on to a tiny, dark courtyard. Red silk curtains hung at the windows of Katherine's room, and a faint light from the street lamp filtered through them. The high ceiling was painted with nymphs, shepherds, and a strange looking devil who peered down at them with a quizzical expression.

'Gee, Mom, this is like a horror movie. D'you really have to stay here?'

'Lots of luck sleeping in here, honey.' Mona hung Katherine's lavish eighteenth-century ballgown on a rail. 'This place gives me the creeps.'

'And I've heard it's haunted.' Blackie raised a laconic eyebrow. 'Not that I believe in things like that, of course. I'm from LA after all. The only thing we worry about is earthquakes. But you're really staying here alone?'

'Yes, I am, but maybe it isn't such a great idea.' Katherine stared at the blood-coloured curtains. 'Funny coloured drapes for a bedroom.'

'Funny place, if you ask me,' said Blackie. 'I spoke to the wrinkled retainer, and he says that this place has been haunted for over four hundred years.'

'Oh stop it Blackie,' snapped Mona. 'You'll scare her to death.'

'We know it's all bullshit.' Blackie was placing pencils and brushes in military order out on the portable dressing table, 'But I've seen the picture of the woman who was killed here, and she's no oil painting I can tell you.'

'Where is she?' asked Kitty eagerly. 'I'd like to see her.'

'In the dining room,' said Mona. 'And although you'll think I'm being stupid, I definitely *don't* think you should stay here, Kitty. It doesn't seem safe.'

Katherine glanced at the ancient four poster bed, hung with musty crimson drapes. 'I don't believe in spirits and all that stuff, Blackie.'

'Don't say that,' said Mona. 'It's bad luck to tempt them. C'mon let's try this new gown on, see how it fits.'

As the shadows started deepening in the bedroom, and the dim electric lights began to flicker, Katherine felt an unmistakable chill.

'Even though I don't believe in ghosts, I don't like to think of you here alone, Kitty,' said Blackie.

'I feel someone here, with us in this room – don't you?' Mona added with a superstitious shiver. 'All the hairs on my arms are standing on end.'

'OK, OK, knock it off, you two. I guess you're right. You win. I'll have to pull rank, make the company find a hotel room for me. You know that means one of you will have to stay here, don't you.' Kitty grinned mischievously, green eyes dancing.

'No way.' Mona shuddered, 'I'd rather sleep in St Mark's Square.'

Franco, the Italian production manager, found Katherine a room at the Cipriani, where Brenda and Tommy were staying. He apologized that he couldn't get her into the hotel where Jean-Claude had already set up his offices.

'Signor Valmer *assured* us that the *signora* wanted to stay at the Palazzo Albrizzi,' said Franco. 'He said you needed privacy, and wanted to be alone. I'm sorry.'

'Don't worry, Franco. I'm relieved that I don't have to sleep in there. Tell me, do you believe it's haunted by the ghost of a murdered contessa?'

'I don't believe in ghosts; on the other hand I don't *not* believe in them, either. But I did wonder why Jean-Claude insisted that you stay at the palazzo.'

Katherine shrugged. Her husband's behaviour had become too bizarre to contemplate, but now she had to prevent him from getting on to the set. She didn't care what mood he was in, she didn't want to see him, and whatever the consequences, she wasn't going to. She told Franco the problem.

'But Kitty, Jean-Claude is the executive producer – how can I prevent him from coming on to the set? In thirty years in the business, I've never heard of a producer being barred.'

'Franco do you want me to finish this film in one piece, or not? Look at this!' Katherine pulled off her chiffon scarf, to reveal a mass of black and blue bruises on her neck.

'Jean-Claude did this to you?'

She nodded. 'If you want me to tell Joe Havana about it, I will, but you know how crazy and temperamental he is. If Joe sees these bruises, he'll probably try to beat the hell out of Jean-Claude, and with only two days of shooting left, we can't have that, can we?'

'We definitely *cannot.*' Franco was already concerned about the schedule, about the weather and about his job with the American company which was coming next to shoot in Venice. They were way over budget, and couldn't afford a single setback in the last two days.

'I'd rather you just posted guards at every entrance to the palazzo, to prevent him getting in. I want you to call him, and tell him I don't want to see him, and that he's barred from the set.'

'Oh my God, that's a tall order.' Franco was dismayed.

'OK then. On second thoughts – I'd better do it myself,' Katherine said firmly.

Jean-Claude wasn't at the hotel when Katherine called, but Ali was. Not wanting to reveal anything to his gopher, Katherine told the girl to have Jean-Claude telephone her when he returned from Rome. Ali said he had suddenly gone there on urgent business. What urgent business? Katherine wished she could talk to Steven in LA, but he was never at his house. She had to make a plan; she was going to tell Brenda to get Ali out of the office on some pretext, and get into the files herself. Brenda would do it. She was always game for anything.

Katherine stared at the dazzling lagoon outside the Cipriani, admiring the sun's reflection on the sparkling blue water. It was a hot, beautiful morning and she was glad she was here, instead of at that dank palazzo. They had shot the exteriors there last night, and tonight would be the final one. It was to be the all-important masked ball scene, the climax of the movie. But now it was only ten o'clock on a glorious Venetian morning, time to join Brenda and Tommy at the beach.

She put on sunglasses, a black swimsuit under a short terrycloth robe, and grabbed a straw hat and her canvas bag. Outside, breathing in the clear, sunlit air, she felt the cobwebs in her brain clearing away. It was going to be all right. She would get through this obstacle in her life in the same way that she had survived so many others.

She had just stepped on to the beach, when she saw that there was a commotion near the shoreline: a crowd, people crying, and in the distance the faint sound of ambulance sirens. Dimly she saw that something or someone was lying on the ground, and as she drew nearer, a beach attendant pushed through the onlookers, and began to run towards her. As if at some secret signal, the crowd turned to stare at Katherine, their curious eyes shocked, filled with pity. The beach attendant reached her, and put an arm around her shoulder.

'I'm sorry, *signora*. I have very bad news; you must prepare yourself for a shock.'

'Oh God...Tommy...?'

The attendant was still talking, but she wasn't listening, and she set off at a run towards the crowd, pushing through them until she reached what was indeed a body on the ground. Not Tommy, though, but Brenda. Brenda apparently unconscious, with a weeping Tommy cradling her head.

'She's dead, Mom, she's dead. Brenda drowned and it was all my fault!'

Kitty felt two contradictory emotions overwhelm her almost simultaneously; first relief that Tommy was safe, then enormous guilt: guilt that her best and most trusted friend was dead, and that for one ghastly moment she had actually been glad that it was her and not Tommy.

Later they told her what had happened. Brenda was never a great swimmer, but she loved the sea, and Tommy, now liberated from crutches, and in high spirits, had challenged her to a race to the floating raft half a mile from the beach. She made it to the raft all right, but the swim back proved too much for her, and less than halfway to the shore, she suffered a massive heart attack. By the time the beach attendant saw what was happening, it was too late.

'Oh my God.' Katherine poured out a brandy. She couldn't believe that Brenda, her feisty, fun-loving confidante, and Tommy's best friend, was gone. Tommy was now weeping almost incoherently, and for his sake, Katherine was trying to be brave, but a lump in her throat, the size of a melon, felt as if it was choking her.

'You need friends to be with you,' said the sympathetic hotel manager. 'And a doctor for some sedation, I think.'

'I'm going to call some friends to come over to us,' said Katherine

'I'll call them for you, *signora*,' said the manager. 'You must try to be calm now.'

The sky had gradually been darkening, and thunder rumbled in the distance. Thunder reminded Katherine of Jean-Claude, and of his brother's accident. She shuddered, and took another sip of brandy. Blackie and Mona, recovering from the rigours of the night shooting, were still at their hotel, and immediately rushed with Franco to the Cipriani. Tommy, who was crushed with guilt, was given a sedative, and the doctor suggested Katherine should take a light tranquillizer. Katherine wasn't used to taking pills, and was in a daze when the telephone rang. Mona answered.

'It's Jean-Claude for you.'

Katherine took it without thinking, then went cold when she heard his voice.

'Kitty – I'm sorry you haven't heard from me but I had to go to Rome suddenly. Are you all right, *chérie*?' His honeyed voice was compassionate, caring.

'No, I'm *not* all right.' Katherine told him without emotion, about the tragedy.

'Oh *chérie*, I'm so sorry. I'm coming right over.'

'No Jean-Claude. Don't come. I don't want to see you. Not tonight – or any night.' Trying to be as detached as possible, Katherine gritted her teeth.

'What are you saying.' His voice became hard. 'You don't mean that, *chérie*. You can't.'

'Oh, but I do.' Her heart was hammering, but she felt a hazy calmness from the pill. 'Speak to Franco about it. I'm too exhausted to talk any more. Here.' She handed the phone to Franco, and collapsed on to the sofa.

Tommy was sleeping in the bedroom next door, and Blackie tried to soothe Kitty, who was shivering, but struggling to pull herself together. Only one more day. She had to finish this film. She'd grieve for Brenda tomorrow, cry for her lost loveless marriage, but right now she couldn't afford these luxuries.

'Katherine, you can't possibly work tonight,' said Blackie, feeling her thin shoulders shaking. 'It's impossible!'

'How can you say that?' Franco's voice rose. 'We must shoot this scene tonight. I've already talked to the insurance company. They absolutely *will not pay* compensation for Katherine not working because she's upset. I know it's terrible; I know it's tough, but we have four hundred extras on call, some of whom are already in make-up. We must shoot this scene tonight.'

'It's inhumane,' barked Blackie.

'It's television,' said Franco.

'Franco's right, Blackie.' Katherine intervened. 'We've got to shoot, I want to, and Brenda would want me to. We'll shoot this last scene, then we fly back to the States the next day. I want to get out of here, we all do.'

'OK. What about Tommy? He's in pretty bad shape. Do you think he'll be able to fly?'

'The doctor's given him sedatives. If he rests, and Mona stays with him tonight – he'll be OK. He's got youth on his side. But I've got to talk to Steven. I got a fax from him. Very strange; he's in Paris. Do you know where he's staying?'

Franco shook his head. 'There are ten thousand hotels in Paris; we couldn't possibly call them all. I'm sure he'll turn up, as soon as he hears the news about Brenda. The wire services have already contacted us.'

'They would,' said Katherine grimly. 'Is it OK for Mona to stay with Tommy tonight?'

'Sure,' said Blackie. 'I can handle your hair. But, are you certain you're up to it?'

'I have to be.' She looked at Franco. 'As long as you promise to do what we discussed, Franco?'

'Yes,' said Franco. 'I'll double the guards at all the doors, I promise.'

Steven banged the receiver down in frustration. First there were no international phone lines available, and hours later, when he finally got through to the hotel, neither Kitty, Brenda, nor any of the unit, were there. He dialled the number of the portophone that Kitty sometimes carried, but thanks to Brenda's forgetfulness at recharging the battery, it usually wasn't functioning This phone was also attached to an answering machine, which Brenda had connected to her hotel or office. It wasn't one hundred per cent reliable, but Steven figured that if Brenda was around, she would get his message.

He had to warn Kitty; he had a strong feeling she was in trouble. He checked his watch. Three thirty. Everyone must have left for the location, but what the hell was the name of that damned palazzo where they were shooting? He couldn't remember.

Steven had read all Jean-Claude's files, and what he had discovered was deeply disturbing. Jean-Claude had been arrested twice. Once for bigamy and embezzlement of a rich widow's money, for which he had served seven years, the second time for blackmail. Again a woman had been involved, a woman with whom Jean-Claude had been living at the time but that case had been dropped. The last mention of Jean-Claude in the newspapers was in 1985, when he married an Italian heiress at the Mamounia Hotel in Marrakesh. Jean-Claude was thirty-eight, the heiress eighteen, and he had called himself Pierre Rondeau. There were no reports after that. Did that mean Jean-Claude was still married to the girl? If so, he was once again a bigamist, and Katherine's marriage null and void.

Kitty knew nothing about Jean-Claude's past, but she had told Steven about his increasingly violent outbursts of temper, and he was extremely worried. He called the concierge to find out when the next plane to Venice was due to leave.

'The last direct flight to Venice will depart at seventeen hundred hours, but I'm sorry, *monsieur*, I am afraid you are too late to catch it.'

'Goddamn it, what other way can I get there?'

'Well you can fly from Charles de Gaulle airport, to Rome Ciamino Airport, then change planes for a flight to Venice at twenty hundred. That arrives at twenty-one fifteen. And then – ' There was a rustle of papers as he checked his guides, 'There is also a direct flight from Rome to Venice at twenty-two twenty arriving at approximately twenty-three thirty hours. I say approximately, sir, because it is a prop plane, and this airline sometimes cancels flights at the last minute if there aren't enough passengers travelling from Rome to Venice.'

'How the hell can they cancel flights just like that? What do they expect people to do, if they've got to get there?' Steven was frantic, but he realized that if he didn't get moving now, he'd miss any of the other flights to Rome.

'I'm sorry, *m'sieur*, I do not run the airlines.' The concierge's tone was frosty. 'I just give you the information.'

'OK, OK. I'm sorry,' said Steven. 'Get me bookings on both of those flights, will you? I've got to get to Venice tonight. It's urgent.'

CHAPTER TWENTY

Jean-Claude sat in his office at the Danielli, fiddling with the dials of the latest Japanese listening device, a complicated state-of-the-art machine which allowed him to tap into any conversations or messages left on Kitty's expensive new answering machine. He had convinced Brenda that they couldn't live without it, and he thanked his stars for that, as he listened to Steven's message.

'Kitty darling, I'm in Paris, but I'm catching the next plane to Venice. I've got some disturbing news about Jean-Claude. It's pretty bad I'm afraid. He's not who you think he is; he's an ex-con with a record as long as my arm. An embezzler and – get this – a bigamist. So you're not even married to him, Kitty. Try not to be alone with him, or have any contact with him. I'll tell you everything when I get there. I've gotta catch that plane.'

Jean-Claude's face set itself into a mask of fury. So the gig was up, was it?

'Not by a long chalk, my friend,' he muttered. 'I've been one step ahead of all of you, and I'll still be one jump ahead of you from now on.'

He thought about the Palazzo Albrizzi, which he had convinced the company to use for the ballroom scene. He was well aware of its dark past. During his time in prison he had studied the occult, and read about dozens of supernatural incidents which had occurred in old mansions and palaces around the world. Since the murder of the Contessa Albrizzi, four hundred years ago, many people had died at the palazzo in unexpected and sometimes violent circumstances. Bizarre places like the Palazzo Albrizzi appealed to Jean-Claude's humour. Not that he himself believed for one second in ghosts, demons and all the rest of that superstitious claptrap, but he knew that many people did, and he knew how strong the power of suggestion could be.

The phone rang; he waited until he heard who was on the answering machine, before picking it up and barking a bad tempered, 'Yes?'

'Jean-Claude? Franco Fabbri here.' The voice was wary. Franco knew all about Jean-Claude's temper, and there was no love lost between them. Jean-Claude had only visited the set twice during the nine week shoot; the film crew thought he was a talentless gigolo, riding on Katherine's coat-tails.

'What is it?'

'I've got some bad news, and I'm not going to beat around the bush.'

'Spit it out then, man. Get to the point.'

Franco told Jean-Claude that, on Katherine's instructions, he wouldn't be allowed on the set any more. Jean-Claude greeted the news first with silence, then with a furious stream of obscenities. Franco said firmly 'That's the way Katherine wants it, I'm afraid, and that's the way it's going to be. I'm warning you, stay away.' Then he hung up.

Jean-Claude stared at the phone. Barred from his own set? He was the producer, he had been instrumental in getting this film made! This film that he had set up for that stupid, ungrateful bitch, his wife.

'We'll see about *that*. We'll just see about that Miss Diva Queen.'

* * *

Blackie escorted Kitty into her dressing room at four o'clock; the butler had given her an urgent phone message to call Steven in Paris. She tried to call him back, but Venice was in the middle of a blackout, because of the thunder storms, so it was impossible to call in or out.

Joe Havana wasn't at all happy with the weather. 'Goddammit,' he growled to the skies, while they growled back at him. 'How we gonna get this scene in the can with this crap goin' on?'

The crew were outside the canal entrance of the Palazzo Albrizzi. They were filming one last long shot of the exquisitely costumed guests, as they arrived by gondola for the Venetian ball given by Paulette de Waldner in honour of King Louis. All of them, with the exception of Kitty and Gerard, were extras or featured players, and the scene was incredibly difficult to organize. Busloads of camera-toting tourists kept getting into every shot, and the distant lightning, which made the dome of St Mark's Cathedral look like a fiery wedding cake, caused the lights to flicker constantly. Background thunder wasn't helping the sound, so Franco suggested to a grumbling Joe that they had enough exteriors, and they should start shooting the interior of the ballroom.

'This is the last day of shooting,' he said. 'We've got a ton of stuff to get done.'

Blackie had put on Katherine's wig, and made her up in her upstairs bedroom. She was pale and shivery.

'I hate it here, Blackie. I know this place is haunted; don't you sense something?'

'Look, I know you're upset, but even if it is haunted, ghosts can't hurt you. Read Shirley MacLaine's book – they're just tormented spirits that can't rest.'

'Like me,' said Katherine wryly.

'Hey, that valium's making you over-react. Don't start seeing things. Come on, I'll take care of you. Let's get down to the set. We don't want to hold 'em up.'

Kitty sat in a director's chair, in a corner of the great marble ballroom, chain-smoking. The valium had dulled her senses and she felt curiously light-headed and carefree. Whenever thoughts of Brenda came into her fuzzy mind, she pushed them away and tried to think about nothing. She had to work. They must finish these scenes tonight, and then she would be able to grieve for her lost friend, and for her lost marriage. For lost it now was – irretrievably. She had checked with Franco, who had assured her that the palazzo was safe from all intruders – particularly Jean-Claude.

The heavy silver lâmé costume, and the powdered white wig with long ringlets hanging over one shoulder, were extremely uncomfortable. A frivolous silver tricorne hat with a silver birdcage filled with stuffed white doves, sat on top, and weighed a ton. Thick strands of pearls and diamonds cascaded around her neck and ears, and because of the tightness of the silver satin sleeves which ended in wrist ruffles of silver lace, it was hell moving her arms. The corset of her ballgown was cinched tightly. She knew she had put on weight, and her heart ached with the reason for it. What perverse fate had made her conceive, when, for sixteen years, she had believed she couldn't? The ramifications were too miserable to dwell upon. She took another pill. Unable to eat since breakfast in the turgid, pre-storm heat, now she was feeling faint. She took a sniff of her smelling salts, and fanned herself with an oversized, silver lace fan.

'Are you OK?' Franco asked.

'Sure, I'm fine, Franco, thanks.' She managed a wan smile. 'Any calls from Steven?'

'No,' said Franco. 'But the phones are still out because of the storms. Venice goes back to the dark ages when thunder hits.'

'I guess he's still in Paris.'

'Well at least Jean-Claude hasn't tried to get in,' said Franco.

'That's a blessing.' Katherine puffed at her cigarette with a trembling hand.

'OK. Relax, we'll be ready for you in ten minutes. Anything you need?'

'Thanks. If I need anything, Fabrizio'll get it. He's never out of my eyeline.'

Suddenly Katherine felt eyes upon her. A tall man, one of the extras, was standing staring in a shadowy corner of the ballroom, wearing a long, curly Charles the Second wig, a broad-brimmed black hat with high floating ostrich plumes, and an ebony mask, with an expression of such evil painted on it, that it made Katherine feel nervously uncomfortable.

'Who's that?' Katherine asked Fabrizio.

'That's Olivio, the local chemist. The company hired all the locals to play the extras. You want to meet him, *signora*?'

Katherine shivered. 'No thanks.'

She leaned back to look up at the impressive, almost three dimensional painted ceiling, decorated with angels, and cherubs blowing trumpets or playing harps. An ornate gold fleur de lys pattern picked out the detailed mouldings in bas relief. Behind Kitty was an enormous painting of a laughing satyr, amidst dark skies rent by thunder and lightning. She stared at the picture, hypnotized by the demon face, then there was an enormous burst of thunder, and the ballroom shook. This was followed by lightning which illuminated the room as if it were midday.

'What the hell is that?' Joe Havana's mood was lousier than usual, and the assistant director hastened to placate him.

'It's just a storm, Signor Havana, Venice has many storms this time of year.'

'Well, if Venice has many storms this time of year,' Joe mimicked Pablo's Italian accent, 'why the hell didn't the fucking studio tell me?' He glared accusingly at Franco. 'Why didn't *you* tell me, for Christ's sake?'

Franco, whose job was on the line if tonight's shoot didn't end on schedule, apologized. 'I didn't know about them, Joe. The report we received was that Venice weather was always fine in September. I've made three movies here over the past four years, it's always been good weather.'

Pablo gave Franco a pitying look. 'Venice is never fine at any time of the year. Venice has a life, feelings, and a mind of her own.' Pablo didn't want to add that maybe Venice, and the Palazzo Albrizzi, weren't too thrilled about their tranquillity being interrupted by a boisterously disruptive film crew.

'Right, well the friggin' storm's quietened down, so let's get this crap in the can *now*,' yelled Joe. 'We've only got six hours to get the mother-fucker, so let's get rolling, for Christ's sake.'

During the following five hours only distant rumblings of thunder disturbed their shots until they came to the scene in the dining room. Kitty was immediately conscious of a strange sensation, something like a powerful envy, which emanated from the portrait of the Contessa. But with her mind numbed by tranquillizers, Kitty was becoming too disorientated to focus properly. The painting seemed to glower at her. Katherine turned away. She must be imagining things.

A gust of wind blew some of the flowers from the table centrepiece, and a cascade of red and white petals fell on to the red carpet. They formed the shape of a scimitar.

'A scimitar. just like the one that killed the Contessa.' Alessandro crossed himself, whispering to some of the extras, who were part-time servants. When they saw the petals on the ground, they, too, crossed themselves.

'It's a bad omen, *signora*,' Alessandro whispered to Kitty.

The enormous chandelier swayed, casting long, weird shadows of the extras on to the walls. Once more Kitty found her eyes directed towards the man in the black mask. Why should he fill her with fear? He was just a chemist after all, even though he wore such a frightening mask. Many of the others were far more grotesque. She turned away to stare again at the Contessa Albrizzi's portrait. In the flickering light the eyes of the haughty old aristocrat seemed to hypnotize Kitty. Alessandro crept up silently and whispered something in Italian. Only the words *mala donna* made sense. Katherine felt gooseflesh on her arms; she wasn't going to spend any more time in that room than she had to.

She couldn't reach Tommy because of the telephone breakdown, and heartbroken about the death of Brenda, Katherine felt leaden and hollow. Tears came to her eyes, tears that she'd been shedding all afternoon. But she mustn't weep now, not in the middle of shooting. She was an actress and the show had got to go on. She took another small pink tranquillizer, how many had she taken now? She couldn't remember; she only knew that they blessedly numbed her misery. She lay back in her chair, pushed at her bulky wig, and closed her eyes, until Franco announced that most of the extras were dismissed.

'We're now just going to be shooting on close-ups of the principals,' he said.

The crew moved to the far end of the ballroom for the last few set-ups involving Kitty and Gerard. But the thunder was becoming much louder now, and the storm caused the lights to flicker constantly. Suddenly there was a clap so deafening that it sounded like two 707S colliding over the roof; lightning brilliantly lit up the hall. When it stopped, all the lights went out, leaving the flickering candles in the wall sconces as the only source of illumination. Then suddenly, they too, were extinguished by a savage blast of wind, that filled out the blood-red silk curtains like the sails of a ship.

'Fuck, fuck, *fuck*!!' Joe Havana almost pulled out what remained of his hair. 'Where's the friggin' *generator*, for God's sake?'

Sandy, the chief grip, scratched his head. 'Sorry, Joe, but the genny's on the blink. I guess that lady doesn't want us to shoot here any more *tonight*.' He glanced over at the portrait, with a nervous laugh.

'Well fix it, for Christ's sake,' roared Joe. 'We've gotta get these four more shots in the can tonight.'

'No can do,' said Sandy. 'The lightning's struck a conduit, which has fused the main genny. It's completely out of action and imposs...'

'I don't give a flying fuck,' Joe interrupted. 'You're just gotta *fix* it.'

'Can you make it work?' asked Franco.

'Sure, if we work on it for three or four hours with flashlights, maybe we can fix it,' said Sandy.

'By then it'll be daylight – oh double shit. 'Joe put his head in his hands and sighed. 'I'll never work again after this mother-fuckin' fiasco.' Then he went into a huddle with Franco and Pablo. A few minutes later Franco clapped his hands for attention.

'OK everyone, we'll continue this scene tomorrow. I'm sorry this is going to interfere with some of your travel plans, but it's an Act of God – and thank heavens we're insured for it.' There was a ragged cheer from the crew. 'The call is four pm for crew and extras, five o'clock for Miss Bennet and Mr Le Blanche. Have a good evening, folks – what's left of it.'

There was a rush to leave, and the crew packed their equipment swiftly, leaving boxes, arc lamps, and scrims stacked in corners.

Blackie handed Kitty a tiny flashlight. 'What a bummer,' he said. 'Listen, I'm sorry, but I had to send your dresser home. She said she was having bad cramps, but I think she got the wind up about this ghost business. I'll send up one of the local girls to help you undress.'

'No, don't bother,' said Kitty, who preferred to undress herself, rather than face the curiosity of strangers. 'I can manage, if you help unlace the corset.'

Kitty and Blackie wearily climbed the winding stone stairs to her dressing room, holding the flashlight. There was another burst of thunder, and she hung back nervously. Was it her imagination, or had she glimpsed the man in black lurking in one corner, after the other extras had gone? She shook her head. She was seeing things. She was too tired and spaced out to think properly.

'Where's Fabrizio?' asked Blackie, loosening the laces in her corset.

'That's strange, he's been hanging round me all day; I saw him a few minutes ago.'

'He's not supposed to let you out of his sight,' said Blackie.

'I guess he's in the john,' said Katherine.

Blackie removed Katherine's hat by the flickering candlelight, then he took out the birds and pearls, and was running an acetone Q-tip along the lace edge of her wig, when there was another horrifically loud thunderclap, and a bright zigzag blast of lightning.

'This is a nightmare.' Katherine tried to laugh, then there was a shout from one of the crew.

'Hey Blackie, are ya comin'? The last launch is leaving for the hotel.'

'Are you sure you'll be OK doing this by yourself?' Blackie asked.

'Sure – don't worry – Fabrizio'll be waiting for me in my gondola. Go on – go – don't miss the launch, Blackie. I want out of here, too, so I'll take all this stuff off back at the hotel.'

'C'mon, Blackie,' called Franco irritably. 'Last call for the crew's launch.

'Let's go.' Blackie gathered up his bag, and together they left the dark room. 'You keep the flashlight, Kitty.'

He went down the front steps and as she ran down the hall, Katherine thought she heard Jean-Claude's voice calling her. She stopped to listen, but there was only silence. Katherine felt completely light-headed, almost as if she were floating. Again, she heard a voice calling her, but almost biblical crashes of thunder were drowning it. She ran through the marble ballroom, then felt strangely drawn towards the dining room, and the portrait of the Contessa. She resisted the impulse and hurried down the hall, holding up her heavy skirt. Then she heard footsteps behind her, and Jean-Claude's voice again. She threw open the back entrance and burst into the small, cobbled square, which was lit only by one flickering street light. It was empty. Where was Fabrizio and her gondola?

The black water of the canal glittered in the flashes of lightning, but she could see neither her gondola, nor the gondolier with his familiar yellow straw hat. She stood, undecided where to go, or what to do. Then lightning lit up the piazza and she distinctly heard her name called. She looked back at the palazzo and saw a face staring out of a ground floor window. It was the man in the black mask, and above the sound of the storm, she heard his dreaded voice calling:

'Kitty – Kitty, *chérie*, it's me, your husband – Darling I have to see you – please wait – let me talk to you.'

With a start of fear, she sped into the nearest alley. It was so narrow that the delicate material of her skirt caught on the rough walls, and trying to pull it, she knocked her flashlight from her hand. No time to find it. She had to get away. The cobblestones were slick with rain; she ran through a maze of unlit, winding alleyways, praying for more lightning to give her some sense of direction. She stopped to catch her breath;

then in the distance she heard the sound she feared. Running feet. Jean-Claude's feet, and his pleading voice:

'If you save a life, Kitty it belongs to you. I saved yours *chérie* – now you are mine.'

He hadn't saved her life. What did he mean? Was he totally crazy? In her befuddled state Katherine couldn't think straight. She slipped, then scrambled to her feet, and started running again. She had no idea where she was going; she only knew she had to get away from Jean-Claude. He had become her enemy. The thought of him coming near her again, maybe trying to rape her, gave Katherine unexpected energy.

In the distance a cathedral clock struck four. At four o'clock, Venice was a town fast asleep and Katherine realized that calling for help wouldn't wake anyone. Even if she did manage to rouse someone, Jean-Claude was so persuasive that he would convince them they were a married couple having a little spat.

She fled down another narrow alley, hampered by her enormous hooped skirt, and with agility born of terror, grabbed at the crumbling, pitted walls for balance. She smelled the stench of rotting fish and realized that she must be near the Pescaria. She prayed that some fishermen would be bringing in their catch, but she knew it was still too early. She bolted through the fish market, where the stalls were empty, and the cobbled ground slimy with fish scales. Jean-Claude's thudding footsteps were still behind her, his voice calling, pleading for her to stop.

She raised her skirt, skimming along the fetid ground as rapidly as she could, but the sound of his footsteps told her that he was gaining. There was no point in screaming, she might as well save what was left of her breath. The square was dark and silent, and the iron barred windows surrounding it, showed no signs of life.

Katherine vaguely realized that the Pescaria widened out on to the Rialto, near St Mark's Square. Surely there would be somebody there?

Another bolt of lightning illuminated the tiny terraced Street full of shops. During the day thousands of tourists passed through here; now there was not even a seagull or a pigeon, just decay and the stench of death. Her heel caught in a cobblestone and she almost fell, but she kicked off her shoes, and raised her sodden skirt waist-high, thankful that she hadn't worn stockings. She found she could grip the ground more easily with bare feet.

Jean-Claude's footsteps were coming closer, his voice cajoling:

'Kitty? Here, Kitty, Kitty, Kitty! Don't run away from me. I'm your destiny. I'm your forever man, the man you've been waiting for all your life. The man you love. You told me that, Kitty – didn't you? You told me you'd love me forever, just as I love you.'

He stopped running, and she bent over to catch her breath. There was an agonizing cramp in her stomach, a wrenching, uprooting, familiar throb. She'd felt it once before, two years before Tommy was born. It was the pain of an incipient miscarriage, and she prayed to bring it on. But not now, please God, not at this moment. The rain stopped momentarily and there was deadly silence in the alley. Nothing moved in the gloom-infested labyrinth. All she could hear was the dripping sound of water. Then:

'Here, Kitty, Kitty, Kitty. Come to your husband please Kitty, please, darling Kitty.' Jean-Claude's voice was beguiling, seductive. He sounded as though he was calling for a pet cat. She had to escape from him. There was no knowing what he could do if he found her. He was totally mad.

At Rome airport, Steven was informed that the plane to Venice was unable to take off because of severe weather.

'Dammit, let me *hire* a plane, a helicopter, whatever,' he fumed, 'I've got to get to Venice. It's a matter of life or death.'

'Sorry, *signor*,' said the Alitalia clerk, composed and elegant in her pale grey uniform. 'Nothing is flying in or out tonight. We have very bad weather problems. However, we have been told that, by two o'clock this morning, perhaps the plane may be able to take off. That's if it clears. Meanwhile you must wait *signor*, like everyone else. Take a cappucino. There is a very nice cafe in the terminal.'

Steven strode to the telephone kiosk. It was one-thirty, so maybe Brenda and Tommy were back at the hotel by now. He tried again, and was told that no one was answering in the suite. He called Brenda's answering machine, and left another urgent message.

With the advantage of being barefooted, Katherine tiptoed along the passage, keeping close to the shopfronts. As she neared the canal, the sound seemed to change. The walls gave off a hollow echo, but she could barely hear it for the hammering of her heart. She went up some shallow steps, covered in ancient green moss, so narrow that it seemed only a child could manage them, then through another maze of twisted alleys. She paused under a stone bridge which dripped water. As she listened, something slithered over her foot, and she knew it must have been a rat. She screamed so loudly that Jean-Claude must surely have heard her, and she started to run again.

His footsteps were getting closer; she could hear him laughing and he seemed to be running faster. Katherine was aware of how fit Jean-Claude was. Thrice weekly sessions at the gym, tennis, jogging, squash, and fanatically healthy eating. Then with incredible suddenness, the street down which she ran came to a dead end. There was an alley to the left and an alley to the right. She decided to take the left.

She heard his footsteps stopping at the junction for a few seconds. Then he took off. With a sob of relief, Katherine realized he had gone in the opposite direction. She bolted down the dark, twisting passageway, which was so narrow that again her enormous skirt became caught on a piece of crumbling stone wall. She pulled it desperately, the sound of tearing fabric so loud that she felt sure Jean-Claude could hear it. Suddenly there was another enormous clap of thunder, rain started pelting down again, and the cobblestones became as slippery as an ice rink.

There were no street lights, and the black windows of the surrounding houses were like shuttered eyes. Something flapped in her face and she gasped, but it was just washing on a line. Then the tiny winding passageway opened out on to what Katherine saw, with a sob of relief, was a main waterway. Surely there would be somebody there now? A *vaporetto* taking early workers, a taxi driver, a gondolier. Somebody, someone.

'Help,' she screamed. 'Please help me.' Katherine didn't care now if Jean-Claude heard her. Help must be near; it had to be. But the waterway was completely deserted, the empty gondolas, moored next to the quay, were covered in dark tarpaulin, rocking dangerously. In the distance she could see the dome of St Mark's Cathedral, and ran towards it.

Then she heard the footsteps again, and his ghostly voice, bleating: 'Here, Kitty, Kitty, Kitty. Here, Kitty. Be a good girl Kitty, darling, come to your husband.'

Katherine found herself at another intersection where three tiny streets branched off in different directions. Another flash of lightning illuminated the canal, from which a yellow mist rose, and she saw a small bridge in the distance. Kitty's heavy dress was so drenched with rain that it was hampering her badly; each step was torture but a surge of adrenalin propelled her towards the bridge. The shallow steps were slick, and the sharp edges of the rough stone cut into her bare feet. Over the bridge she raced, gasping for breath, praying that it would lead to the Rialto, where there should be some activity.

Katherine glanced back, and saw her black-garbed pursuer behind her. Then, miraculously, she was on the Rialto, the Grand Canal. She had hoped for people, but it was empty. Not even a water taxi cruised in the storm, and every building was firmly shuttered. She was on her last legs – the pain in her stomach was agonizing, and she was gasping for breath. To her right she saw the open gates of a church. Edging inside, the remnants of her skirt became caught on the sharp wrought-iron gate; she feverishly pulled it until it almost ripped off.

The church smelled of incense and musk; it was a sanctuary, the only light came from one or two candles flickering on the votive table. Katherine tiptoed along the stone floor. If she could hide here for an hour or two, surely Jean-Claude wouldn't find her? By five-thirty the *vaporetti* would be running, and fishermen would be congregating in the Pescaria. She bent over with a cry, as another stab of pain hit her, then she noticed a niche in which a headless marble statue of a robed woman reposed. With trembling fingers Katherine tore off the rest of her sodden ballgown. The laces of the corset were stiff with rain and cut into her fingers, but she had to remove it. Underneath she wore a tank-top and cotton leggings; a tiny bodybag, containing money and cigarettes, was slung around her hips. She had to hide the dress.

She padded down to the font, and, wadding it into an unwieldy ball, jammed it beneath the front pew. More lightning flashed through the stained glass window arches, illuminating the altar at which the Christ figure stood, arms outstretched, blood streaming from his wounds. Katherine tried to pull off her wig but it was still stuck with so many pins and adhesives to her hairline, that it was impossible. She felt dizzy, dehydrated, and shaking with shock. She wanted to lie down, to sleep, for all this to be over. She wanted to be back in LA, safely with Brenda and Tommy, she wished Jean-Claude had never existed.

But he did exist, and in her mind he had become a demonic figure. She was convinced he was trying to kill her. His words rang in her head.

'If you ever leave me, *chérie*, I'll kill you, I swear I will. I love you too much to let you go.'

In the deathly silence of the church, there was no sound except the rumblings of distant thunder. Katherine's eyes had adjusted to the gloom, and when the next lightning blast came, she saw a narrow corridor half hidden behind the altar. The steep stone steps crumbled like old cheese as she scrambled up them. It was black as pitch on the stairwell, and Katherine had no idea what was up there, or where she was going. She only knew that she had to hide. Summoning her last ounce of strength, almost sobbing with effort, she crawled to the top.

Jean-Claude stood indecisively on the Rialto. He'd lost his prey. Dammit. He had done so well until now – wangling himself on to the set as an extra, knocking Fabrizio out. Where had the woman gone? He had to find her, he must get her back. Now, because of the boyfriend Steven, she knew his secrets. More to the point, if Katherine knew that he was still married to that stupid Italian bitch, he could be back in the slammer again, and that made him go cold inside.

Jean-Claude had always been too handsome for his own good, and in jail he'd realized just how dangerous that was. Nightly rapes by fellow inmates had only ceased when he found himself a protector, in the shape of a six feet six inch Haitian – it would have been hard to say which was worse. No, he couldn't ever go back. He had to persuade Kitty of his devotion, make her love him again, and go on trying to get his marriage to the Italian girl dissolved. Jean-Claude's Italian lawyer had promised to sort out the endless legalities, but it was taking too long – far, far too long.

Jean-Claude threw off his hampering cloak, and flung it into the canal. He turned back to the Rialto, and in a sudden burst of lightning, glimpsed a scrap of silver lace caught on the church gates.

So there she was! She'd taken sanctuary in the church, and he'd found her. At last. He pushed open the gates, which closed silently behind him. There was no need to hurry now – she couldn't escape. Dust from the stone floor swirled up in a grey mist before him, as he walked slowly into the church.

'Kitty?' he whispered. 'Here Kitty, Kitty, Kitty, I know where you are, *chérie*. Come on out, Kitty. Come on out, and see your husband.'

The pilot of the two-engined prop plane stared at the ominous sky, then looked at his watch again in frustration.

Mama mia, this was to be a night he was going to remember, the night planned for months when he was finally going to meet his Venetian girlfriend. Her husband was away for two days and she was waiting for him, perfumed and ready. Damn it. Damn this thunder and lightning. When would it stop? He stormed into Air Traffic Control again, and consulted with the meteorologist.

'What are the chances of the Venice storm ending soon?'

'Not before four or five o'clock, so we've been told. But it's not really that bad now. In fact, it's clearing. If you don't mind taking an extra shift, we've had information from the control tower that your plane could take off within forty minutes.'

'*Grazie, grazie, cara.*' The pilot kissed the middle-aged meteorologist on both cheeks, and gave a little whoop. It was going to be all right, he would see her tonight. Even if he didn't get to her apartment until five o'clock, what did it matter? They would spend all day making love.

Shortly before four am the Iberia plane took off in the pale dawn light towards Venice. Steven sat in an aisle seat. There were only eight other passengers, all looking out nervously at the lightning which was still flashing faintly in the distance. Steven didn't care about the lightning, he only cared about getting to Venice, and to Kitty, before Jean-Claude did.

Kitty had reached the top of the crumbling steps. It was pitch dark and she couldn't see a thing. She heard something scurrying across the stone floor, and stifled a desire to scream. She felt her way gingerly around the walls. She appeared to be in a round stone room of some kind, without windows. She could still hear thunder, but there was no lightning. Katherine fumbled in her body belt and found her lighter. She flicked it on, and saw that she was in a disused belfry, dominated by an enormous iron bell, covered in spiders' webs and rust. It had obviously not been used for years. Against one wall, a piece of ragged sacking covered what looked like a statue. This room was where she would have to hide. There was nowhere else to go. She extinguished the lighter, and edged her way around the rough walls. Then she felt something attach itself to her tall wig. She put her hand up and felt the mass of hair impaled on an iron spike sticking out from the wall. Unable to move, she tugged frantically to release herself, feeling agonizing pain as some of her hair was torn out by the roots. Katherine didn't care if the spike ripped away half her scalp. Her wig had to come off. With a desperate sob of pain, Katherine wrenched the wig from her head.

Like a predator stalking his prey, Jean-Claude followed Kitty's scent. He could smell the spicy perfume of her new signature scent, Peach. It lingered in the church, so he knew that she wasn't far away. He removed his boots, and crept silently in stockinged feet up the crumbling stone steps which she had only recently climbed. He paused. The storm seemed to have abated slightly; in the silence he thought he heard Katherine's breathing. A dog barked in the distance, and he heard a cock crowing. Then a church bell struck five. It would soon be light. He had to find her.

Jean-Claude reached the belfry.

'Kitty? I know you're here Kitty.' He could definitely hear her breathing now. 'I know you're here, *chérie*, so please come out. Come on, Kitty, I need you, I can't live without you, please, *chérie*, we have to talk.' His voice was at its most seductive, as he felt his way around the walls. Then he found her. He smiled to himself. Clever little thing, she'd covered herself up in a piece of sacking. His hands moved up her body and he felt the curls of her thick wig.

Dawn had faintly started to illuminate the belfry from a skylight. 'I found you, my little Kitty,' Jean-Claude whispered and ripped off the sacking.

He came face to face with the grinning, naked statue of an old man, his head was thrown back in a soundless cackle; his tongue lolled out and perched on the statue's head was Kitty's white wig.

'Damn you, bitch!' muttered Jean-Claude, then he heard a sound, and whirling around, glimpsed Katherine edging towards the stairs. He walked slowly towards her, smiling enchantingly.

'Kitty, *chérie* – please don't try to run away from me. I'm your husband, and I adore you, you know how much. Let's put all our little misunderstandings behind us. Surely you must see how much I care.'

'Don't come near me.' Katherine edged back towards the steps, as Jean-Claude took another step. 'You're not my husband, I hate you – '

'Please let's forget the last month, *chérie*, I beg you. Let's start all over again.'

In the dim light, and in Katherine's dazed state, Jean-Claude's smile made him look like a madman. Black paint from the mask was smeared all over his face, and his matted hair was pressed flat to his head. He looked like a grotesque grinning skull.

'Don't – don't come any closer Jean-Claude,' Katherine whispered. 'I'm warning you – our marriage is over.'

'But *chérie* – I love you. You're my life – please Kitty, we *have* to talk!' He was close enough to touch her, but she cringed away from him. Was this the man she'd been so crazy about that she couldn't think straight? This man was a maniac, an insane sociopath, and Steven's prophetic words returned to her:

'There are two kinds of people in this world Kitty, and Jean-Claude's *not* one of them. He's in a class of his own. He's a sociopathic psychopath, and you never know when a psycho's going to show his blackest side.'

Jean-Claude's clammy hand touched her neck; she gave a cry of fear and started scrabbling down the steps. His hand was outstretched; he tried to follow, but she pressed herself closely against the wall. Suddenly Jean-Claude found himself grabbing at air, he lost his balance, and started falling down the steps, down, down, down. His screams echoed through the church; the pigeons which had been nesting on the top of the belfry rose into the air in alarm. The storm, which had slightly abated, started again. Thunder crashed, and vast bolts of lightning lit up the gloomy, pitted walls of the stairwell, as Jean-Claude hit the marble floor, and his screams turned to silence.

Very slowly, Kitty tiptoed down the winding stairs, and stared at the ground, where the crumpled body of her husband lay sprawled on the marble floor.

'Oh my God,' she whispered. 'Oh my God, Jean-Claude, what have I done?' then her stomach wrenched with another agonizing spasm, and she fell to the ground beside him.

EPILOGUE

One year later

The handsome raven-haired man sat on an over-upholstered chaise-longue, watching television. One hand caressed the bony shoulder of the red-headed woman sitting next to him; the other lifted his fifth Jack Daniels of the evening to his lips. But his eyes were fixed on the screen. Any moment now the names of the Academy of Television Arts and Sciences nominees, for best actress in a TV movie or series, would be announced. His companion turned to him:

'Who d'you think's going to win the Emmy, honey?'

He shook his head, knocking back the last of his drink. There would be another dozen or so before the evening ended, and the night began, for this woman, his wife, was insatiable. Mamie de Montpelier was elderly and rich, and knew exactly what she wanted from her new husband – sex, and plenty of it – in return for the use of her glittering Palm Beach mansion and all the other accessories. The shiny black BMW she had bought him, the even shinier pale silk suits from Bijan of Beverly Hills, the diamond-encrusted solid gold Rolex, and the diamond and gold identity bracelet which she liked him to wear. It matched her own, on which the initials, MDM, were picked out in fifteen carat diamonds. His initials were LDM: Louis de Montpelier, once known as Jean-Claude Valmer.

Jean-Claude owed his new wife a great deal. Sentenced to three years for fraud and misappropriation of Kitty's funds, and two years for bigamy, he had faced a bleak future as a forty-year-old cripple. He had received hundreds of fan letters from lovesick women, along with photographs, flowers and presents. But it was only Mamie – contacting him via her lawyer – who had the power to free him.

Thanks to her vast fortune, to an enormous amount of influence in many of the right and wrong places, and a voracious appetite for gorgeous men, she had been able to ensure that he served only two months of his five-year prison sentence. But she had extracted him from jail at a price, and Jean-Claude was well aware that if he put one foot wrong, Mamie would not hesitate to dump him. Her lawyers would ensure that if they divorced, he would be left with nothing but the Rolex, his identity bracelet, and his pastel silk suits.

Jean-Claude's fury at Steven Leigh, for discovering his past and destroying his future, still burned inside him – almost as strongly as the torch he still carried for Katherine. During those soul-destroying weeks in jail he'd realized how much he had really cared for Kitty. Although he had plotted and used her, just as he'd used women all his life, in his way he had loved her. Now he was waiting for her to appear on the screen; it would be the first time he had seen her for nearly a year.

Mamie gripped her husband's arm tightly with jewel-encrusted, liver-spotted hands.

'D'ya think she'll win?' she hissed excitedly.

While Kitty waited for the five Emmy nominees to be declared, her mind wandered back to that horrendous morning in the Venetian church.

Both she and Jean-Claude had been unconscious when the priest discovered them at dawn, at the bottom of the stone steps. Kitty had haemorrhaged after a miscarriage, and Jean-

Claude had head injuries, multiple fractures to his arms and legs, and a shattered kneecap. It was a miracle that he hadn't died – although Kitty sometimes thought it might have been better for him if he had.

The subsequent bigamy case was shocking even by Hollywood standards, but Kitty survived it with Steven, Tommy and Vera to lean on. She had grown increasingly to rely on their support, especially on the comforting strength of Steven's friendship. Now that his divorce from Mandy had come through, they were together more and more. Kitty was beginning to suspect that their shared humour, warmth and compatibility was turning into love. Not that she felt under any pressure from Steven. He was far too wise, and had loved her secretly for too long to push her into something she wasn't ready for. Her mother however had no such inhibitions.

'Marry him,' she said firmly. Her asthma had miraculously disappeared soon after she settled in Los Angeles to look after her daughter and grandson, and she was feistier than ever.

'You'll not find a better man, nor one that cares for you as much as Steven does.'

'Give me time, Mama,' Katherine insisted.

'Don't make him wait too long – he's a catch, Kit-Kat, and at your age they're getting harder and harder to find.'

Katherine turned to smile at Steven's intense, bespectacled face, his gaze riveted now to the stage, where Bill Cosby was announcing the names of the nominees.

Steven squeezed her hand, and whispered, 'You're going to get it, babe, I know you are.'

Kitty laughed. It would be fun to win, but she didn't really care, for she knew she'd found in him something more precious than fame, more lasting than stardom.

Cosby was tearing open the envelope which contained the winner's name: 'And the Emmy for the best actress in a television movie or mini-series goes to –' he boomed the words, then paused theatrically – 'to Katherine Bennet, for *All That Glitters*!'

The auditorium erupted. Tommy whooped and hugged her.

'Well done, Mom.' He grinned. 'I knew you'd win.'

Steven kissed her and said, 'Did anyone ever tell you that you're the most ravishingly talented woman in the whole western hemisphere?'

'Yes, I'm afraid someone did once tell me that.' She put her face close to his, mischievously. 'But enough of this flattery. There's an award to be picked up.'

She walked gracefully down the aisle to ringing cheers and clapping. Everywhere she saw excited faces and outstretched hands: the adulation not of fans, but of her peers, of producers, directors, agents, actors, people who seemed genuinely thrilled that she had won the coveted prize.

No one, of course, was more thrilled than Vera, who had managed to wheedle a front-row aisle seat for herself out of the Academy. As her daughter passed, she grabbed her arm.

'I'm proud of you, Kit-Kat, real proud, and you look beautiful tonight.'

Kitty blew her mother a kiss of thanks, and glided up the stairs to the stage. There, with the golden trophy in her hands, overwhelmed still by the tumult of applause, she looked down at the packed auditorium, and the sea of smiling faces. As the audience rose to give her a standing ovation, she thought of Brenda, and of how much she would have adored this moment. And as she paid silent tribute to her friend, she remembered something Brenda had once said. Something about being too damn famous.

Well Bren, wherever you are, thought Kitty, I guess tonight even you would agree that it was worth the effort after all.

Joan Collins

Love & Desire & Hate

Acapulco, 1955 – the cream of Hollywood comes together to make an extravagant epic about the Spanish conquest of Mexico. As temperatures rise and dark secrets bubble to the surface, the lives of an English matinee idol, a French starlet and her eccentric chaperone, an eager, young director and a tyrannical producer are irrevocably changed by the loathing inspired by one man. But the saga begins in wartime Paris, when a brutal Italian officer savagely abuses a beautiful young woman...

'Packed full of intrigue, sex, sadism and murder, against the backdrop of luscious film locations and glamorous characters' – *Daily Express*

JOAN COLLINS

PRIME TIME

Actress and singer Chloe Carriere has been up and down the celebrity ladder for more than twenty-five years, but when a prime opportunity for superstardom arises she finds herself taking part in the most breathtaking casting battle since the search for Scarlet O'Hara. Meanwhile, a more personal conflict takes place as Chloe wonders whether her on-off partner, an erratic and devastatingly good-looking musician, will ever stop playing away from home. Bitter rivalry, sexual infidelity and a smouldering casting couch are the compelling ingredients of this sizzling tale.

'In her long reign as America's Queen of Soap, Joan Collins has kept her eyes wide open and her notebook at the ready. The result is a first novel of gloriously enthusiastic revenge...juicy, irresistible and a lot of fun' *Today*

'It's lavish, it's tense – it's pure Joan Collins' *New Woman*

Joan Collins

Second Act

Second Act is the most candid and revealing of memoirs, composed by a superstar. Joan Collins shares remarkable anecdotes about her personal and professional life with the kind of insight and humour that only a woman of her calibre and experience could possess. The result is a captivating book that draws you into her spectacular world.

'Joan Collins is splendid and her autobiography *Second Act* is a hoot. Springing from a family with generations in vaudeville, she was a star at seventeen. Affairs with Warren Beatty, bitchy battles with Madonna, Dynasty, marriages quite as bad as anything Liz Taylor can muster, that spat with Random House about whether she could write – it's all there' – *The Independent*

'Joan Collins is many things: actress, vamp, soap star, icon. But none of the above does her justice. Mere words cannot explain her charisma' – *Evening Standard*

Joan Collins

Star Quality

From a legendary woman with stardom in her genes comes a breathtaking story that spans a century of showbiz.

When gutsy redhead Millie McLancey defies her humble beginnings to pursue a life on the stage, she becomes the first of four generations of inspiring women who take us on a thrilling ride from the West End to Broadway to Hollywood, and to a breathtaking finale in New York, in a stirring tale of ambition, betrayal, romance, scandal, sex and survival.

PAYMENT

Please tick currency you wish to use:

☐ £ (Sterling) ☐ $ (US) ☐ $ (CAN) ☐ € (Euros)

Allow for shipping costs charged per order plus an amount per book as set out in the tables below:

CURRENCY/DESTINATION

	£(Sterling)	$(US)	$(CAN)	€(Euros)
Cost per order				
UK	1.50	2.25	3.50	2.50
Europe	3.00	4.50	6.75	5.00
North America	3.00	3.50	5.25	5.00
Rest of World	3.00	4.50	6.75	5.00
Additional cost per book				
UK	0.50	0.75	1.15	0.85
Europe	1.00	1.50	2.25	1.70
North America	1.00	1.00	1.50	1.70
Rest of World	1.50	2.25	3.50	3.00

PLEASE SEND CHEQUE OR INTERNATIONAL MONEY ORDER.
payable to: STRATUS HOLDINGS plc or HOUSE OF STRATUS INC. or card payment as indicated

STERLING EXAMPLE

Cost of book(s): .... Example: 3 x books at £6.99 each: £20.97
Cost of order: .... Example: £1.50 (Delivery to UK address)
Additional cost per book: .... Example: 3 x £0.50: £1.50
Order total including shipping: .... Example: £23.97

VISA, MASTERCARD, SWITCH, AMEX:

☐☐☐☐☐☐☐☐☐☐☐☐☐☐☐☐☐☐☐☐

Issue number (Switch only):

☐☐☐

Start Date: ☐☐/☐☐ **Expiry Date:** ☐☐/☐☐

Signature: ______________________

NAME: ______________________

ADDRESS: ______________________

COUNTRY: ______________________

ZIP/POSTCODE: ______________________

Please allow 28 days for delivery. Despatch normally within 48 hours.

Prices subject to change without notice.
Please tick box if you do not wish to receive any additional information. ☐

House of Stratus publishes many other titles in this genre; please check our website (**www.houseofstratus.com**) for more details.